POKÉMON®
ADVENTURES

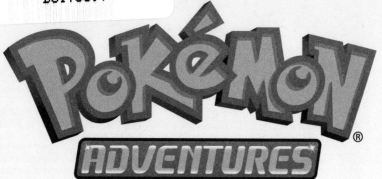

Pokémon ADVENTURES
Volume 2
VIZ Kids Edition

Story by HIDENORI KUSAKA
Art by MATO

© 2009 Pokémon.
© 1995–2009 Nintendo/Creatures Inc./GAME FREAK inc.
TM and ® and character names are trademarks of Nintendo.
© 1997 Hidenori KUSAKA and MATO/Shogakukan
All rights reserved.
Original Japanese edition "POCKET MONSTER SPECIAL"
published by SHOGAKUKAN Inc.

English Adaptation/Gerard Jones
Translation/Kaori Inoue
Miscellaneous Text Adaptation/Ben Costa
Touch-up & Lettering/Wayne Truman
Design/Sean D. Williams
Editor, 1st Edition/William Flanagan
Editor, VIZ Kids Edition/Annette Roman

Printed in the U.S.A.

Published by VIZ Media, LLC
P.O. Box 77010
San Francisco, CA 94107

10 9 8 7
First printing, August 2009
Seventh printing, February 2013

www.vizkids.com

www.viz.com

Pokémon® Adventures

2
Volume Two

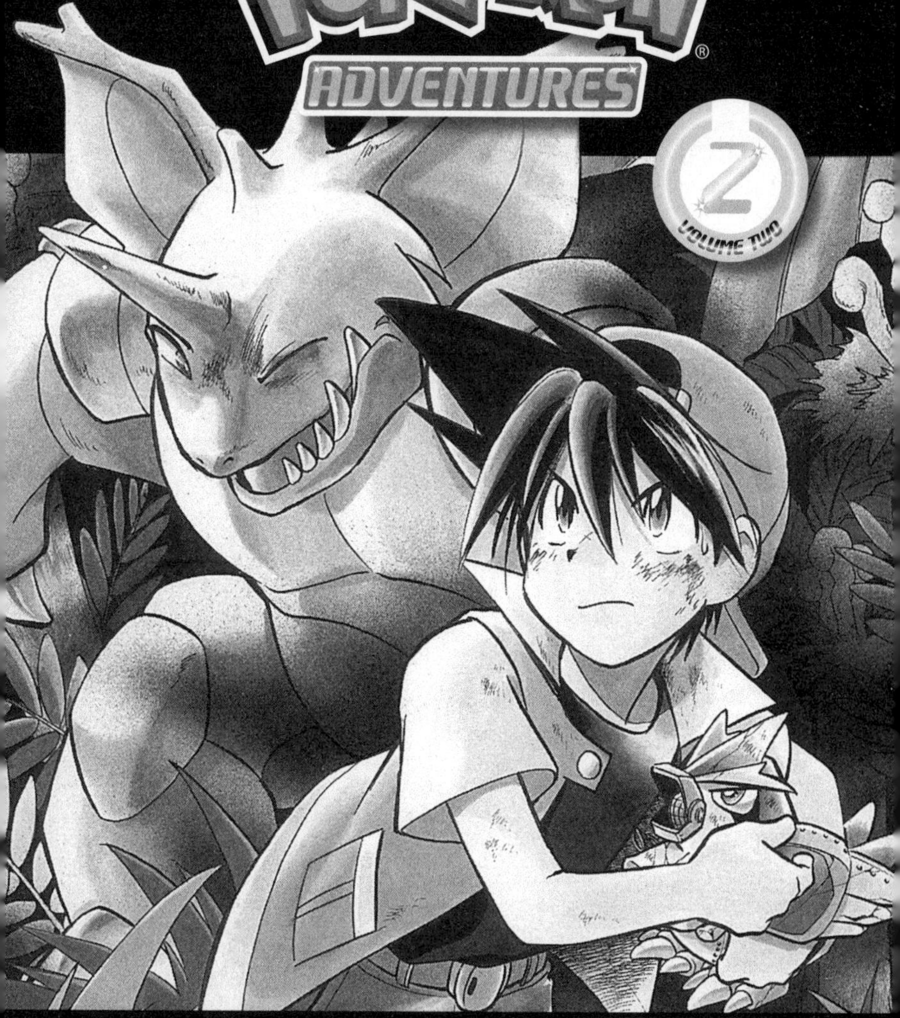

Story by Hidenori Kusaka

Art by Mato

CHARACTERS

THUS FAR...

POLIWRATH

PIKACHU

BULBASAUR

RED

Red leaves his home in Pallet Town, Pokédex in hand, to embark on a quest to become the greatest Pokémon trainer ever. Along the way, he meets and makes friends with fellow trainers Misty, Bill, and Blue—who becomes his greatest rival.

A determined boy on a journey to become the ultimate Pokémon trainer!

CITY GYM LEADERS

CINNABAR TOWN GYM LEADER	CELADON CITY GYM LEADER	CERULEAN CITY GYM LEADER	PEWTER CITY GYM LEADER
?	?	MISTY	BROCK

MAIN

JOURNEY

PROFESSOR OAK

World renowned Pokémon expert and Blue's grandfather.

BILL

A Pokémon researcher who lives in the Sea Cottage. Inventor of the Pokémon transport system.

CHARMELEON

BLUE

Red's rival, who likes to use Charmeleon in battle. Lacks humility, but is actually quite a skilled trainer.

As Red and Blue follow a similar path, challenging the gym leaders of each city, Red has to either compete against Blue or join forces with him to defeat those who would stand in their way. At the top of their list of enemies is the evil organization Team Rocket, a group that secretly harbors gym leaders in its ranks!

VIRIDIAN CITY GYM LEADER	SAFFRON CITY GYM LEADER	FUCHSIA CITY GYM LEADER	VERMILION CITY GYM LEADER
● ? ●	● ? ●	● KOGA ●	● LT.SURGE ●

CONTENTS

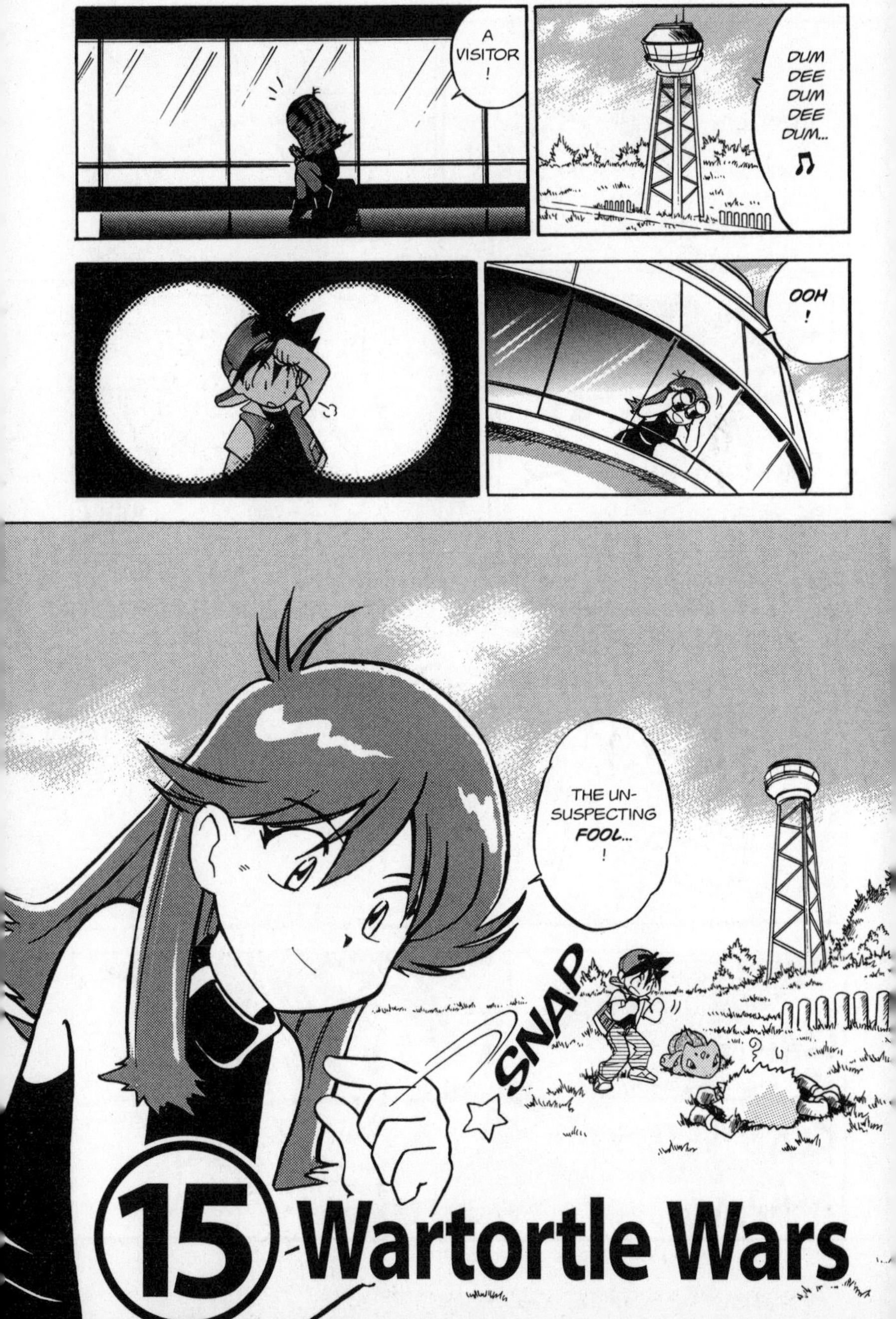
DUM DEE DUM DEE DUM... ♫
A VISITOR !
OOH !
THE UN-SUSPECTING FOOL... !
SNAP
15 Wartortle Wars

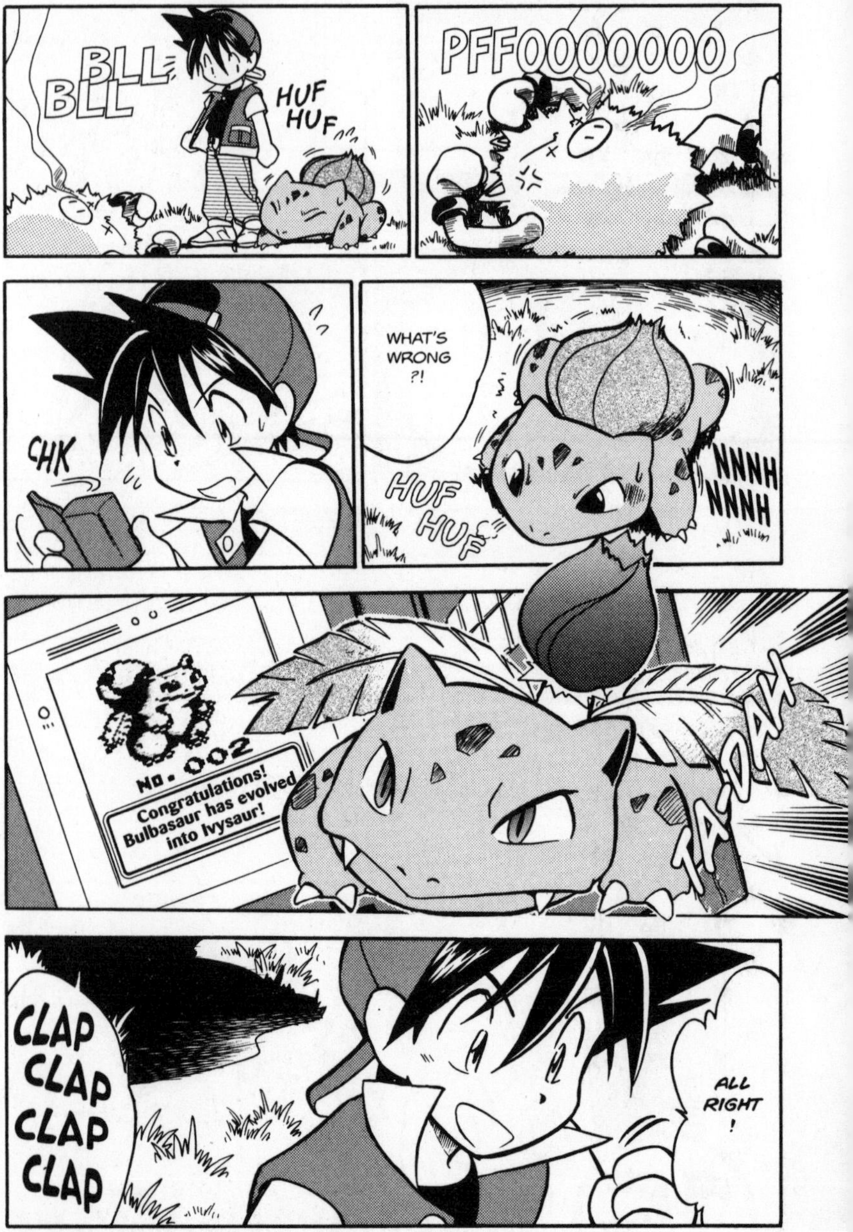
PFFOOOOOOO
BLL BLL
HUF HUF
WHAT'S WRONG ?!
NNNH NNNH
HUF HUF
CHK
TA-DAH
NO. 002
Congratulations! Bulbasaur has evolved into Ivysaur!
ALL RIGHT !
CLAP CLAP CLAP CLAP

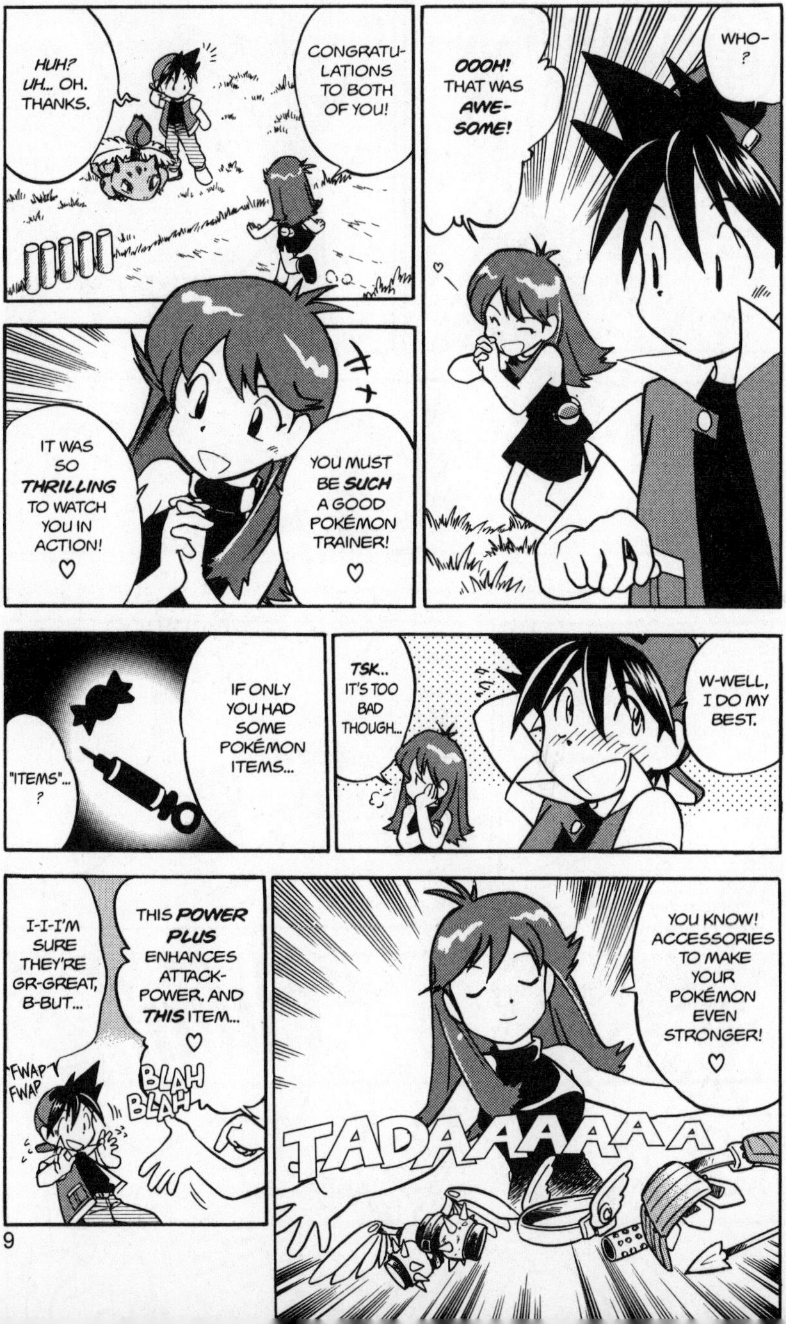
WHO-?
OOOH! THAT WAS AWESOME!
CONGRATULATIONS TO BOTH OF YOU!
HUH? UH... OH. THANKS.
YOU MUST BE SUCH A GOOD POKÉMON TRAINER! ♡
IT WAS SO THRILLING TO WATCH YOU IN ACTION! ♡
W-WELL, I DO MY BEST.
TSK.. IT'S TOO BAD THOUGH...
IF ONLY YOU HAD SOME POKÉMON ITEMS...
"ITEMS"... ?
YOU KNOW! ACCESSORIES TO MAKE YOUR POKÉMON EVEN STRONGER! ♡
TADAAAAAAA
THIS POWER PLUS ENHANCES ATTACK-POWER. AND THIS ITEM... ♡
I-I-I'M SURE THEY'RE GR-GREAT, B-BUT...
BLAH BLAH
FWAP FWAP

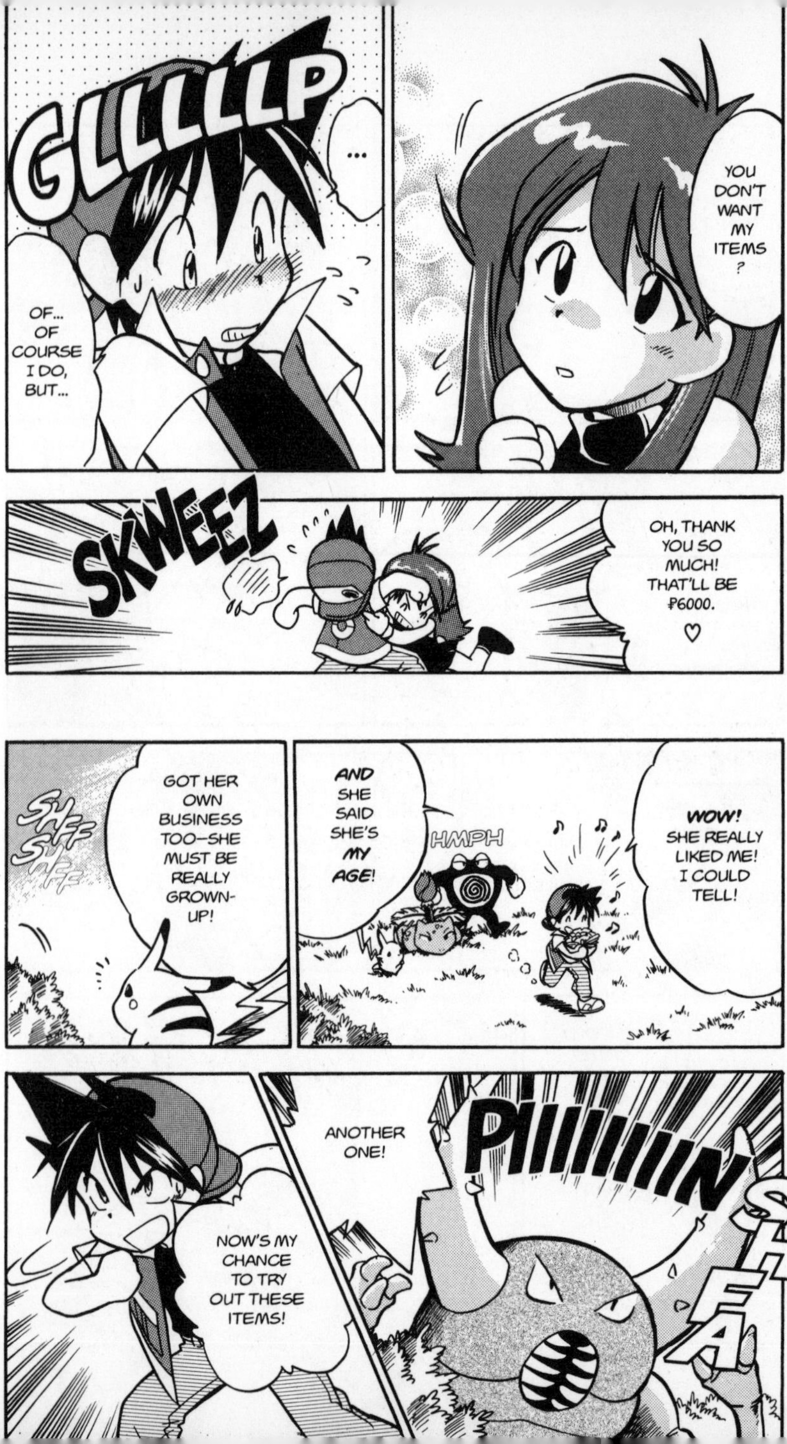
YOU DON'T WANT MY ITEMS?
GLLLLLP
...
OF... OF COURSE I DO, BUT...
OH, THANK YOU SO MUCH! THAT'LL BE ₽6000. ♡
SKWEEZ
WOW! SHE REALLY LIKED ME! I COULD TELL!
HMPH
AND SHE SAID SHE'S MY AGE!
GOT HER OWN BUSINESS TOO—SHE MUST BE REALLY GROWN-UP!
SHFF SHFF
PIIIIIIN
SHFA
ANOTHER ONE!
NOW'S MY CHANCE TO TRY OUT THESE ITEMS!

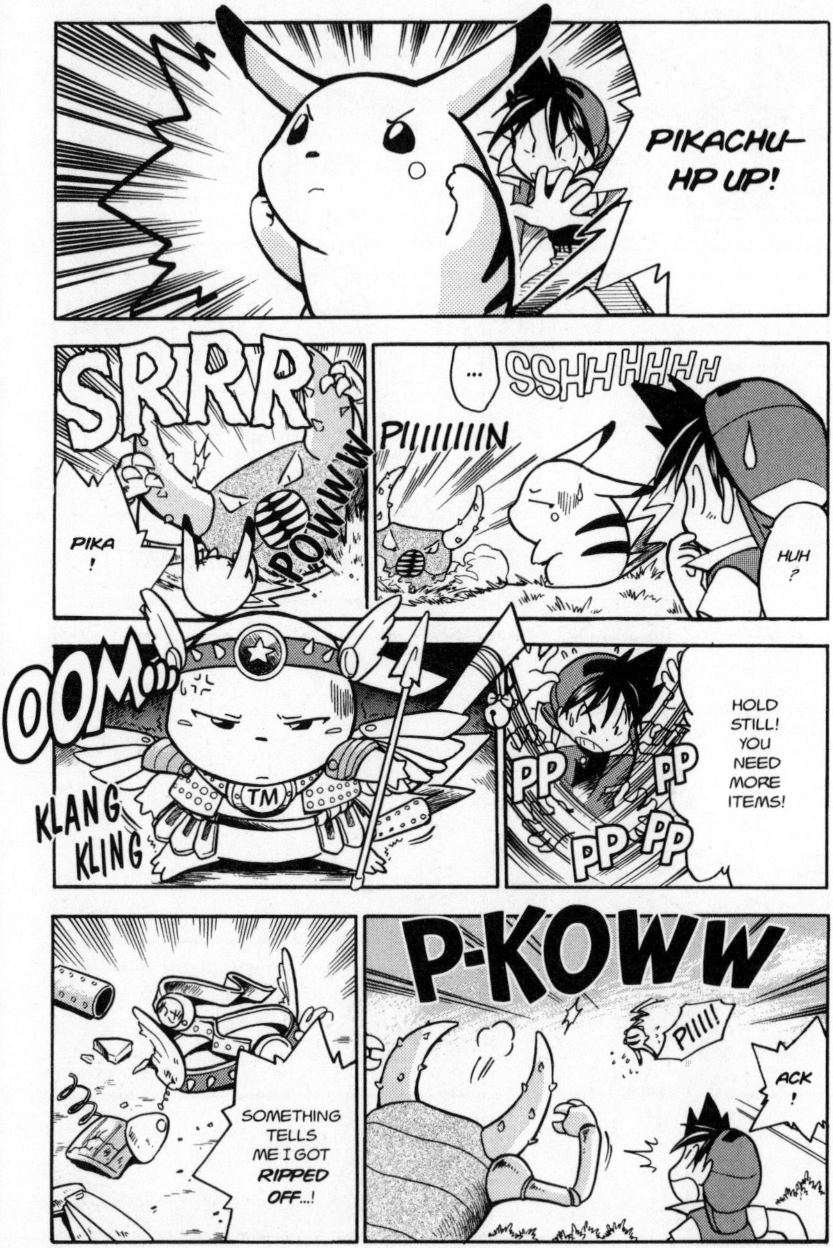
PIKACHU—
HP UP!
...
SSHHHHHH
PIIIIIIIN
HUH?
SRRR
POWWW
PIKA!
HOLD STILL! YOU NEED MORE ITEMS!
PP PP
PP PP
OOM...
TM
KLANG KLING
P-KOWW
PIIII!
ACK!
SOMETHING TELLS ME I GOT ***RIPPED OFF***...!

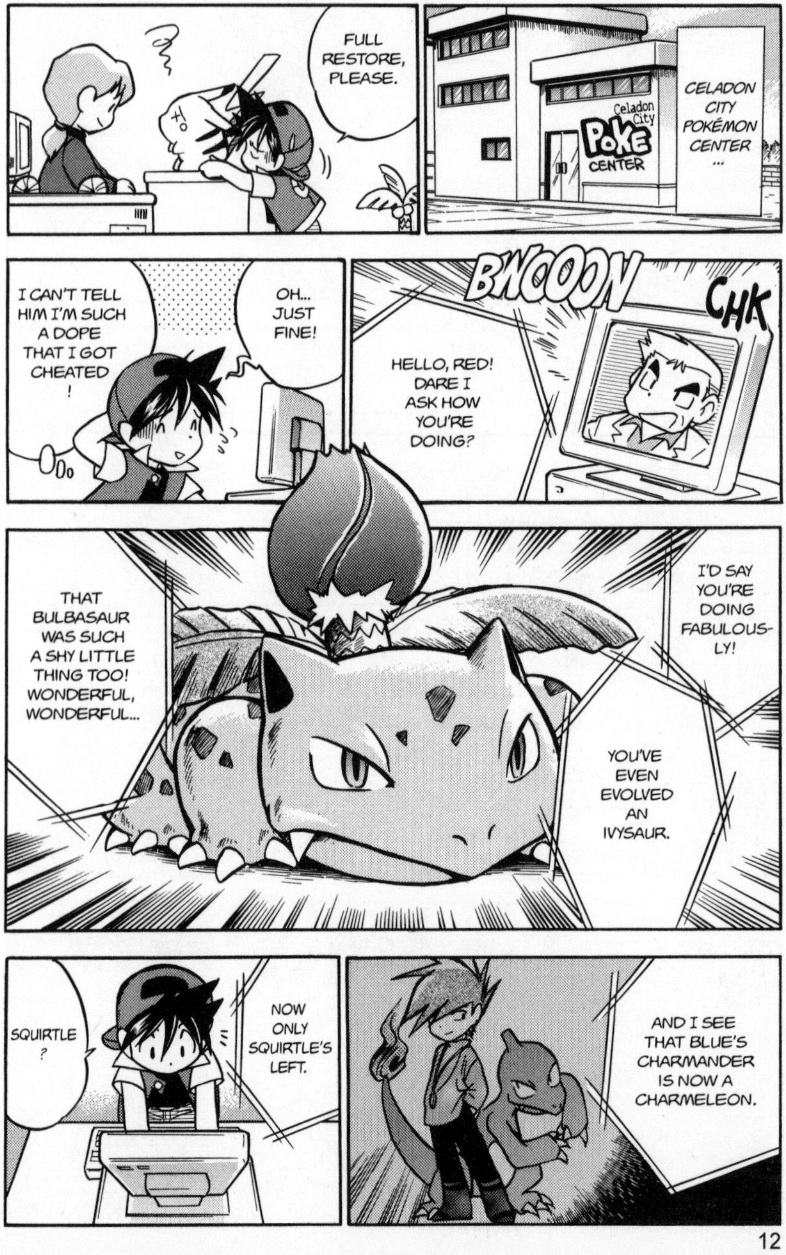

CELADON CITY POKÉMON CENTER ...
Celadon City
POKé CENTER
FULL RESTORE, PLEASE.
CHK
BWOOON
HELLO, RED! DARE I ASK HOW YOU'RE DOING?
OH... JUST FINE!
I CAN'T TELL HIM I'M SUCH A DOPE THAT I GOT CHEATED!
I'D SAY YOU'RE DOING FABULOUS-LY!
YOU'VE EVEN EVOLVED AN IVYSAUR.
THAT BULBASAUR WAS SUCH A SHY LITTLE THING TOO! WONDERFUL, WONDERFUL...
AND I SEE THAT BLUE'S CHARMANDER IS NOW A CHARMELEON.
NOW ONLY SQUIRTLE'S LEFT.
SQUIRTLE?

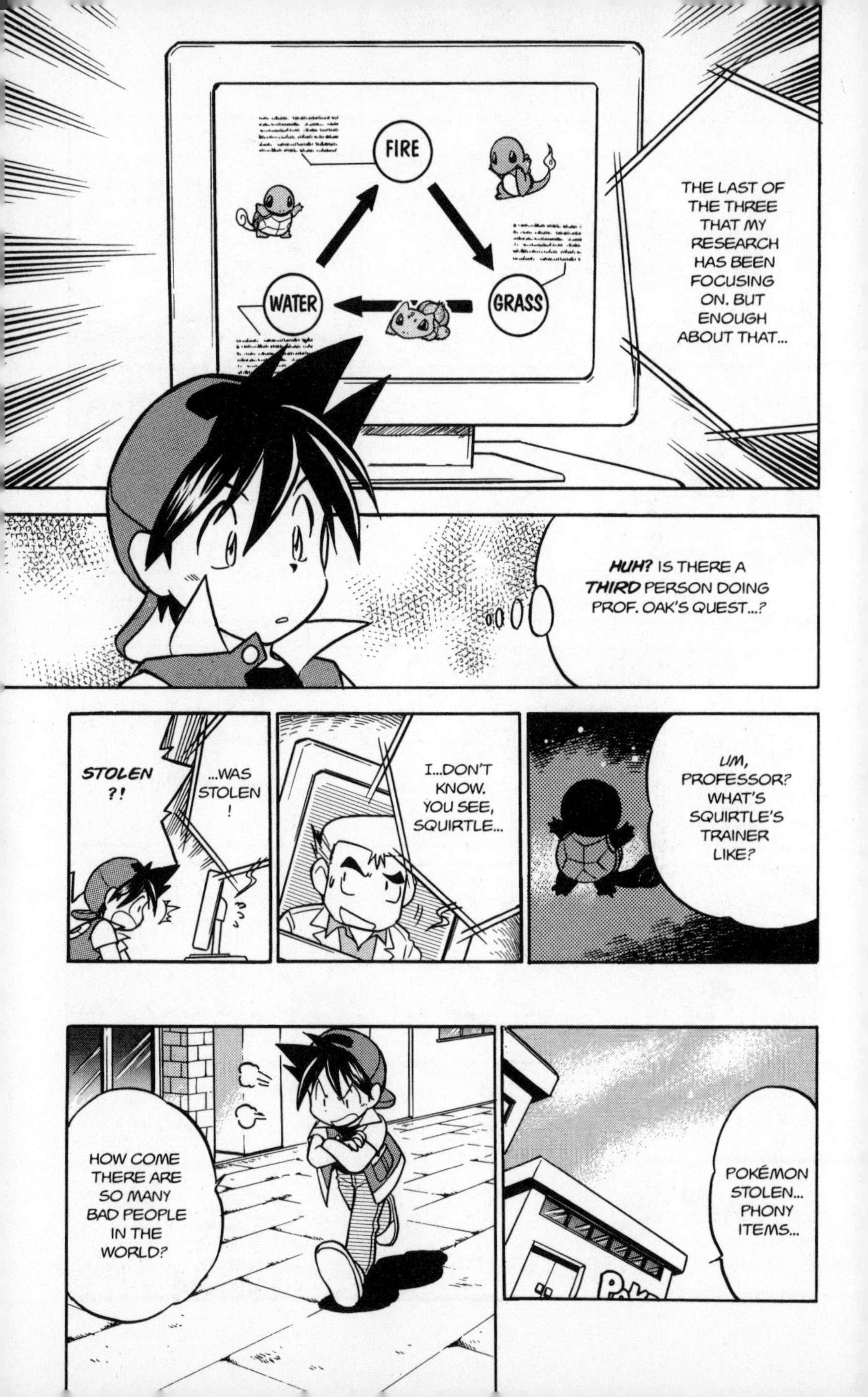
THE LAST OF THE THREE THAT MY RESEARCH HAS BEEN FOCUSING ON. BUT ENOUGH ABOUT THAT...
FIRE
GRASS
WATER
HUH? IS THERE A THIRD PERSON DOING PROF. OAK'S QUEST...?
UM, PROFESSOR? WHAT'S SQUIRTLE'S TRAINER LIKE?
I...DON'T KNOW. YOU SEE, SQUIRTLE...
...WAS STOLEN!
STOLEN?!
POKÉMON STOLEN... PHONY ITEMS...
HOW COME THERE ARE SO MANY BAD PEOPLE IN THE WORLD?

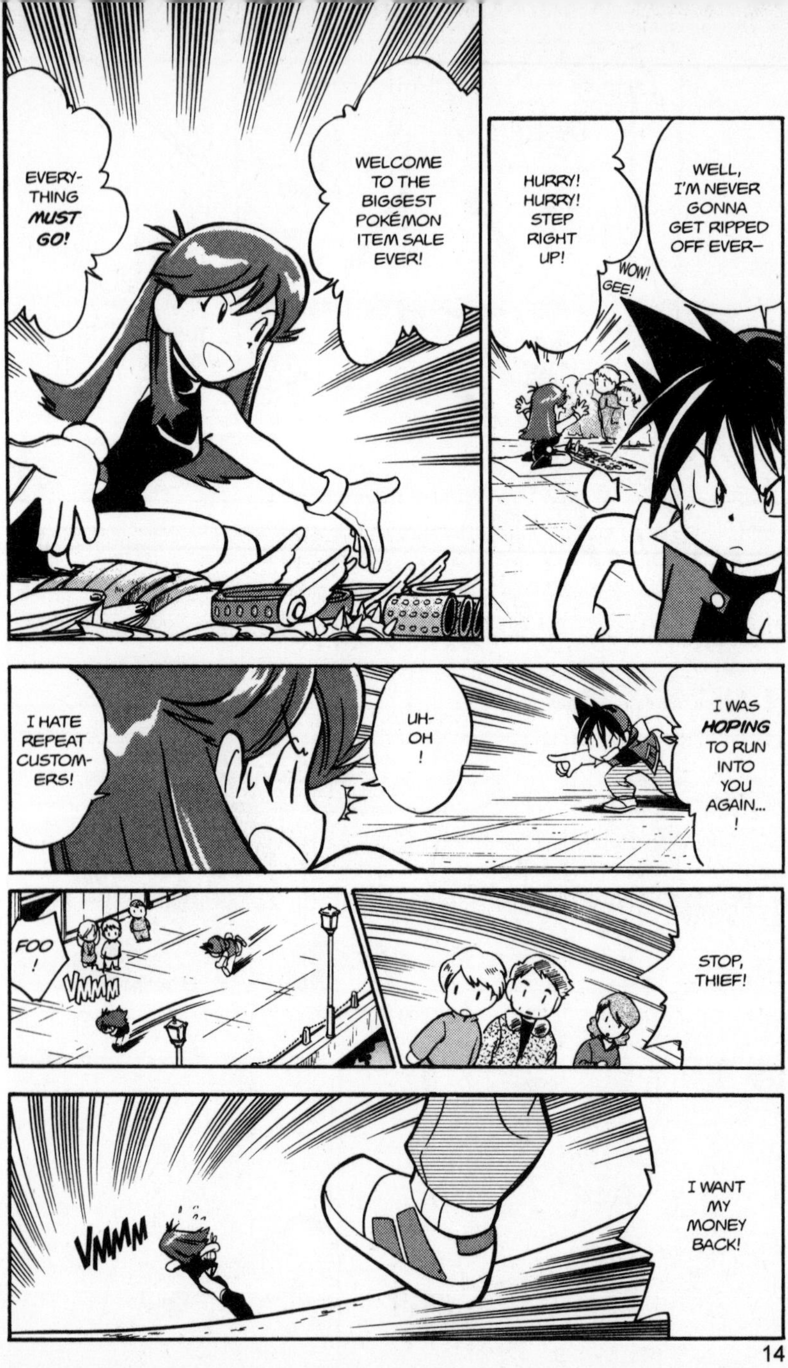
WELL, I'M NEVER GONNA GET RIPPED OFF EVER—
HURRY! HURRY! STEP RIGHT UP!
WOW!
GEE!
WELCOME TO THE BIGGEST POKÉMON ITEM SALE EVER!
EVERY-THING MUST GO!
I WAS HOPING TO RUN INTO YOU AGAIN...!
UH-OH!
I HATE REPEAT CUSTOM-ERS!
STOP, THIEF!
FOO!
VMMM
I WANT MY MONEY BACK!
VMMM

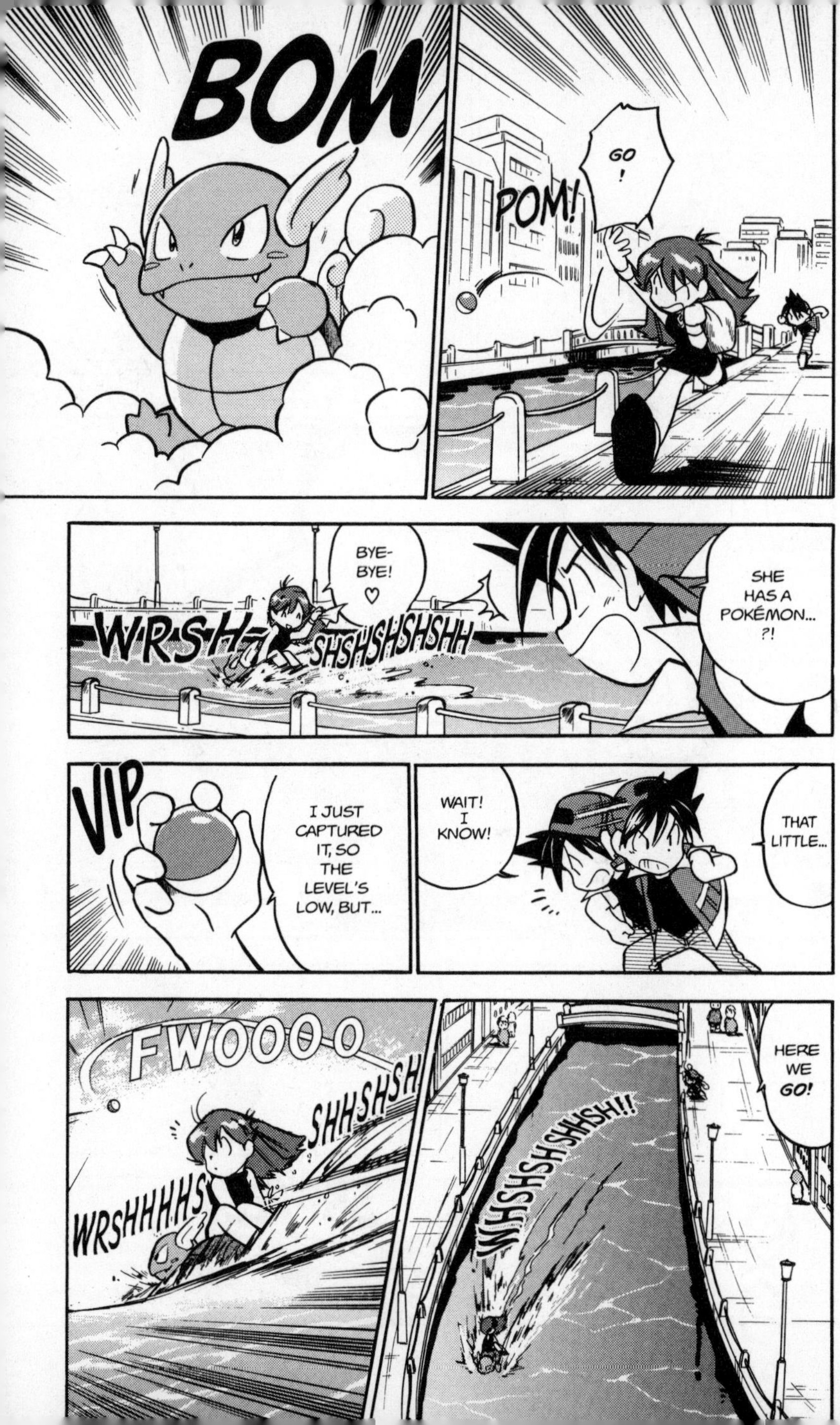
GO!
POM!
BOM
SHE HAS A POKÉMON...?!
BYE-BYE! ♡
WRSH
SHSHSHSHSHH
THAT LITTLE...
WAIT! I KNOW!
I JUST CAPTURED IT, SO THE LEVEL'S LOW, BUT...
VIP
HERE WE GO!
WHSHSHSHSHSH!!
FWOOOO
SHHSHSH
WRSHHHHS

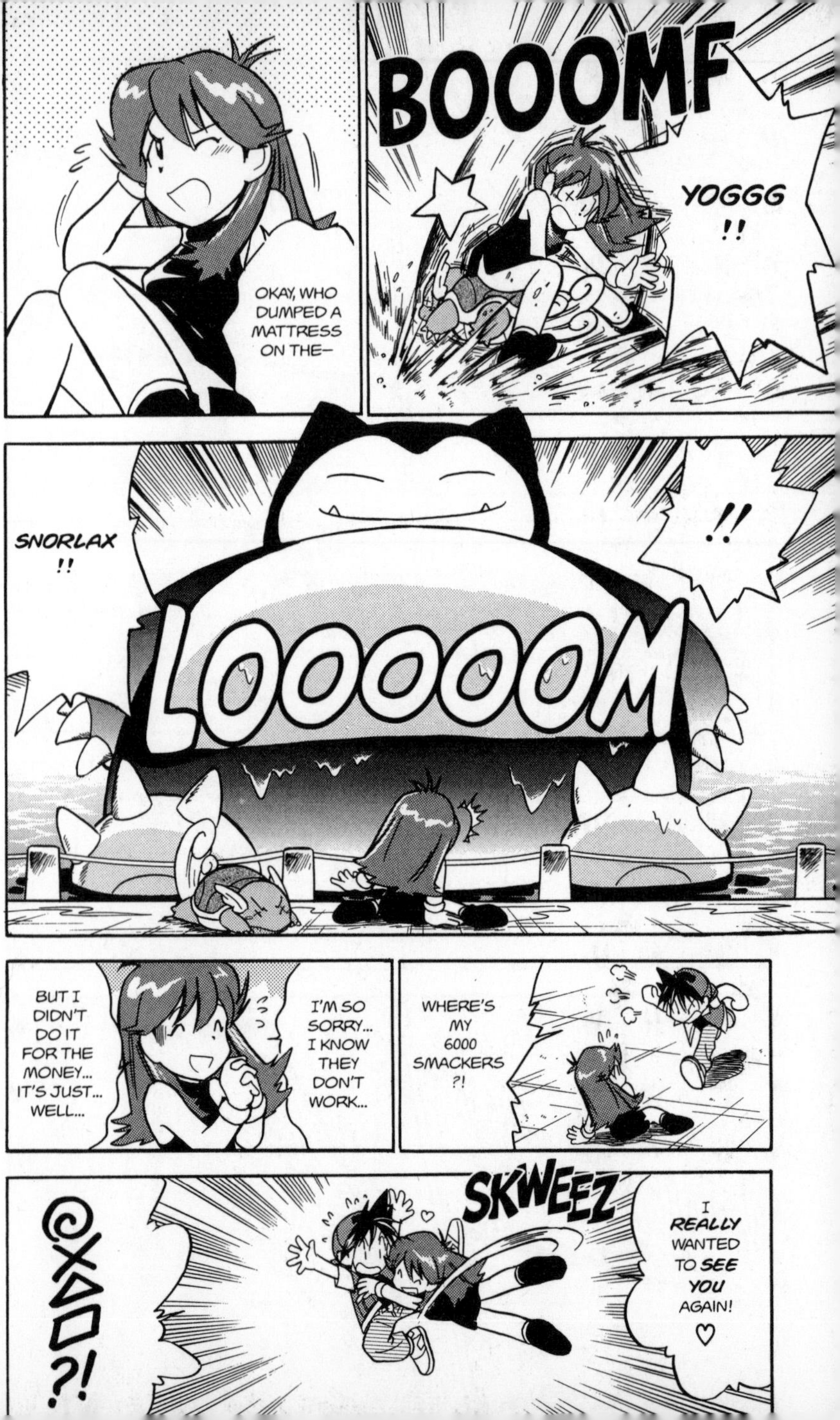
BOOOMF
YOGGG !!
OKAY, WHO DUMPED A MATTRESS ON THE—
!!
SNORLAX !!
LOOOOOM
WHERE'S MY 6000 SMACKERS ?!
I'M SO SORRY... I KNOW THEY DON'T WORK...
BUT I DIDN'T DO IT FOR THE MONEY... IT'S JUST... WELL...
I REALLY WANTED TO SEE YOU AGAIN! ♡
SKWEEZ
@×△□?!

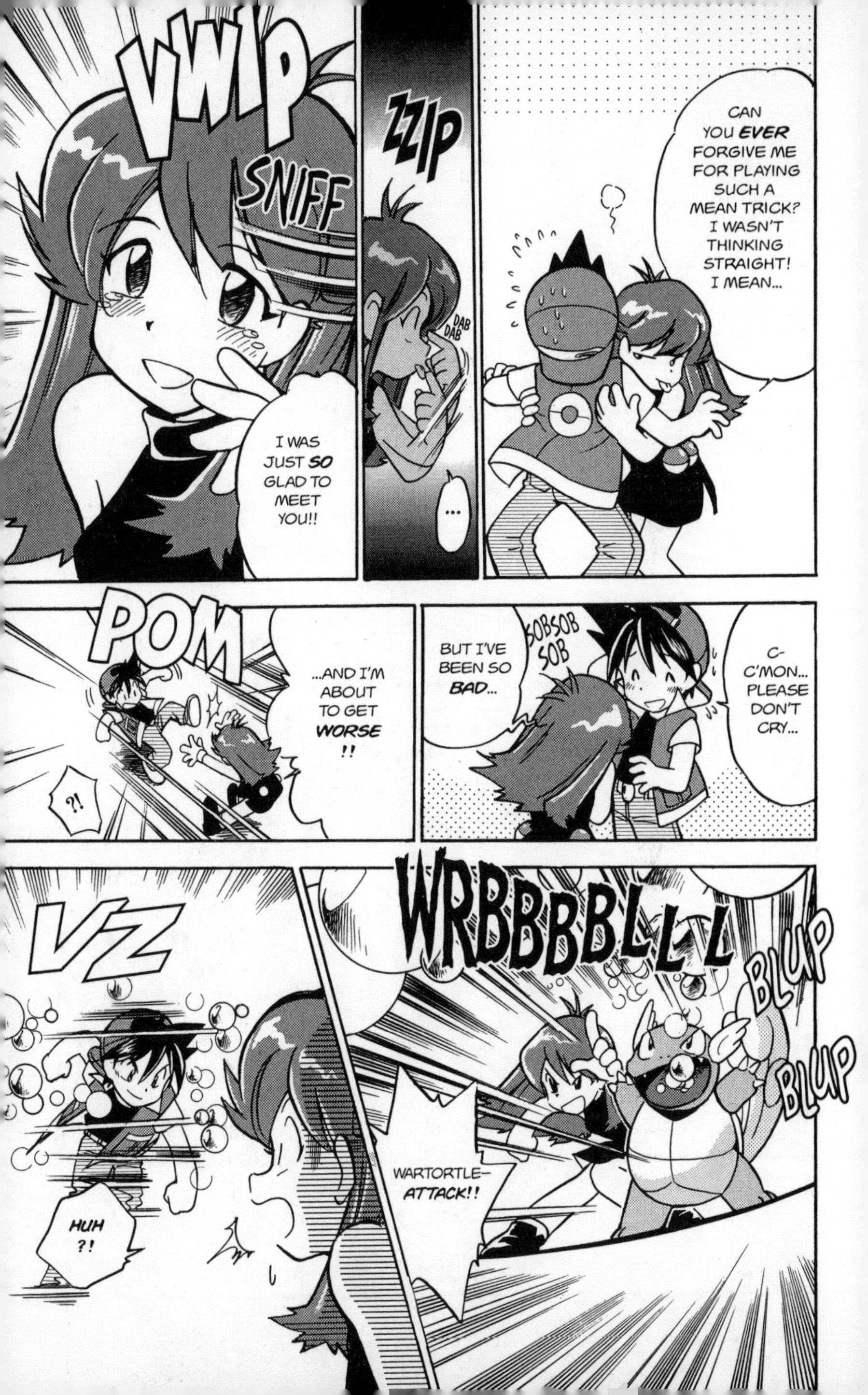
CAN YOU EVER FORGIVE ME FOR PLAYING SUCH A MEAN TRICK? I WASN'T THINKING STRAIGHT! I MEAN...
ZZIP
DAB DAB
...
VWIP
SNIFF
I WAS JUST SO GLAD TO MEET YOU!!
C-C'MON... PLEASE DON'T CRY...
SOBSOB SOB
BUT I'VE BEEN SO BAD...
POM
...AND I'M ABOUT TO GET WORSE!!
?!
WRBBBBLLL
BLUP
BLUP
WARTORTLE—ATTACK!!
VZ
HUH?!

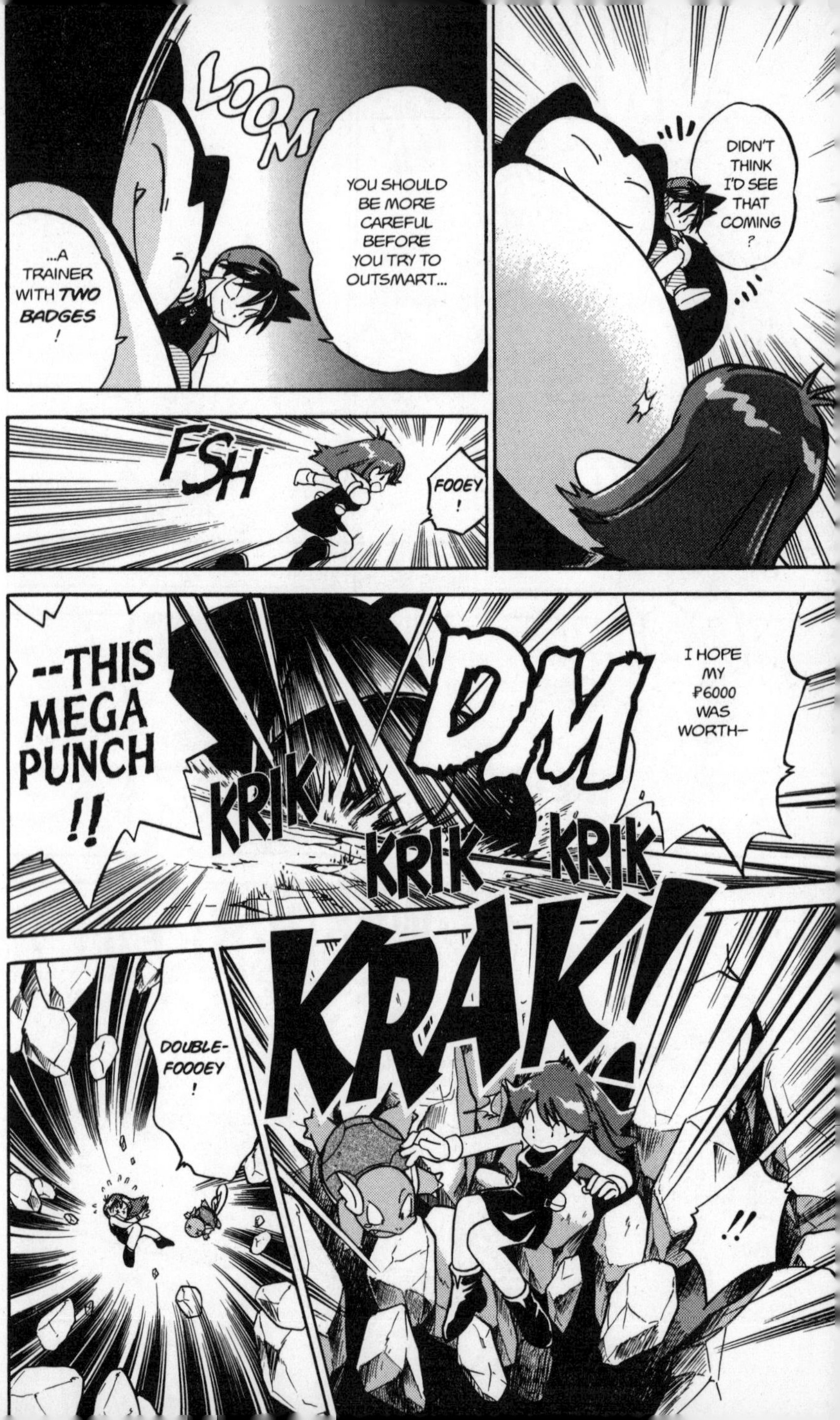

DIDN'T THINK I'D SEE THAT COMING?
VOOM
YOU SHOULD BE MORE CAREFUL BEFORE YOU TRY TO OUTSMART...
...A TRAINER WITH TWO BADGES!
FSH
FOOEY!
I HOPE MY ₽6000 WAS WORTH—
DM
KRIK
KRIK
KRIK
--THIS MEGA PUNCH!!
KRAK!
!!
DOUBLE-FOOOEY!

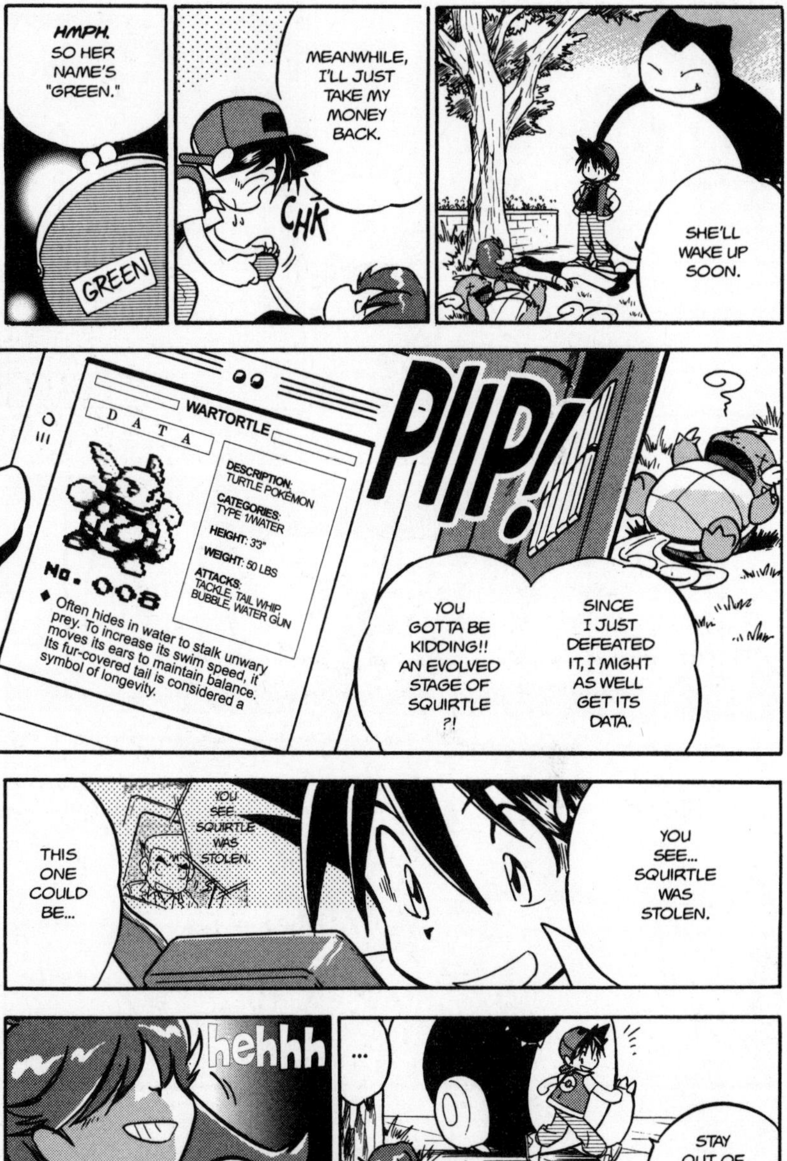
SHE'LL WAKE UP SOON.
MEANWHILE, I'LL JUST TAKE MY MONEY BACK.
CHK
HMPH. SO HER NAME'S "GREEN."
GREEN
?
PIIP!
SINCE I JUST DEFEATED IT, I MIGHT AS WELL GET ITS DATA.
YOU GOTTA BE KIDDING!! AN EVOLVED STAGE OF SQUIRTLE ?!
WARTORTLE
DATA
DESCRIPTION: TURTLE POKÉMON
CATEGORIES: TYPE 1/WATER
HEIGHT: 3'3"
WEIGHT: 50 LBS
ATTACKS: TACKLE, TAIL WHIP BUBBLE, WATER GUN
No. 008
◆ Often hides in water to stalk unwary prey. To increase its swim speed, it moves its ears to maintain balance. Its fur-covered tail is considered a symbol of longevity.
YOU SEE... SQUIRTLE WAS STOLEN.
YOU SEE. SQUIRTLE WAS STOLEN.
THIS ONE COULD BE...
STAY OUT OF TROUBLE NOW!
...
hehhh

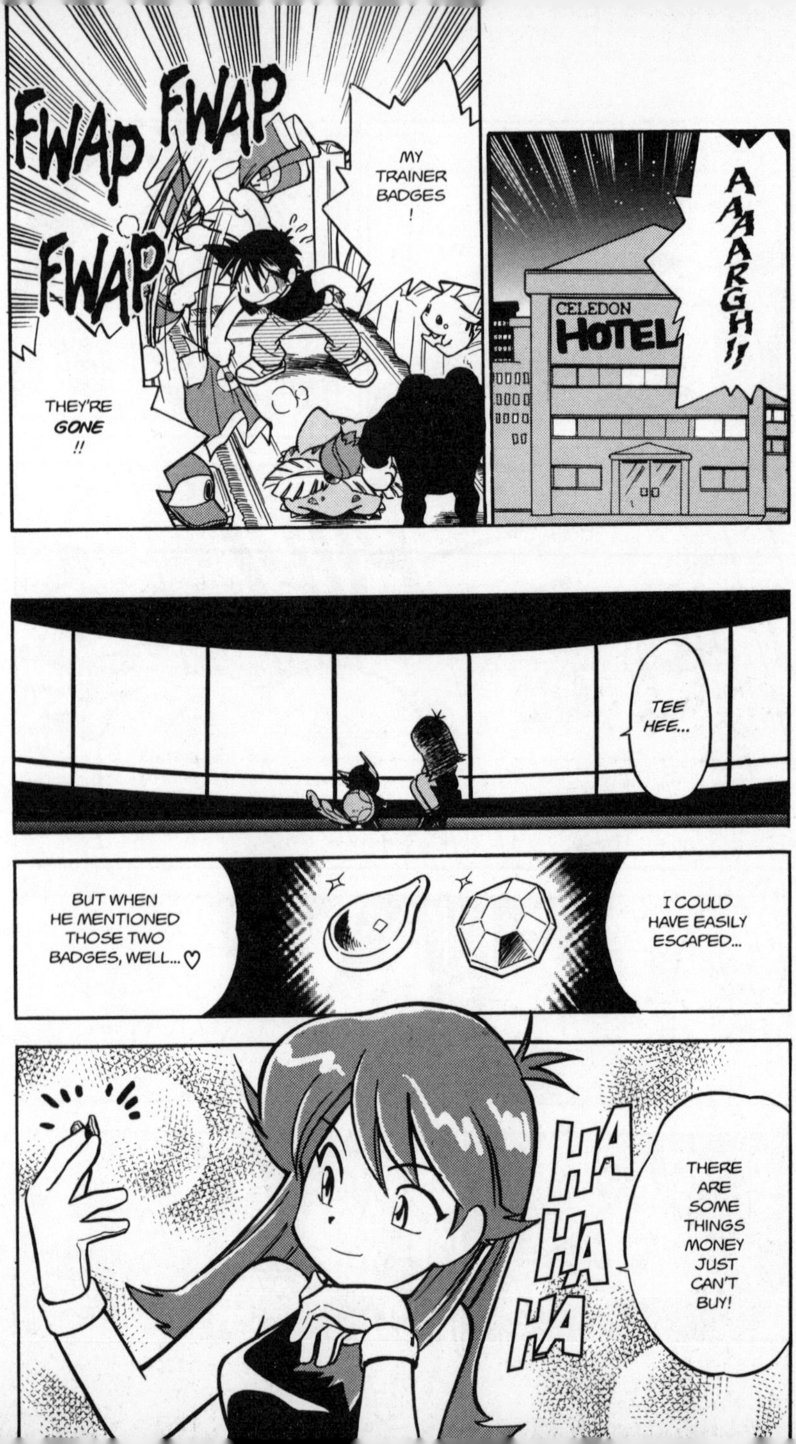
AAAARGH!!
CELEDON HOTEL
FWAP FWAP
MY TRAINER BADGES!
FWAP
THEY'RE GONE!!
TEE HEE...
I COULD HAVE EASILY ESCAPED...
BUT WHEN HE MENTIONED THOSE TWO BADGES, WELL...♡
THERE ARE SOME THINGS MONEY JUST CAN'T BUY!
HA HA HA HA

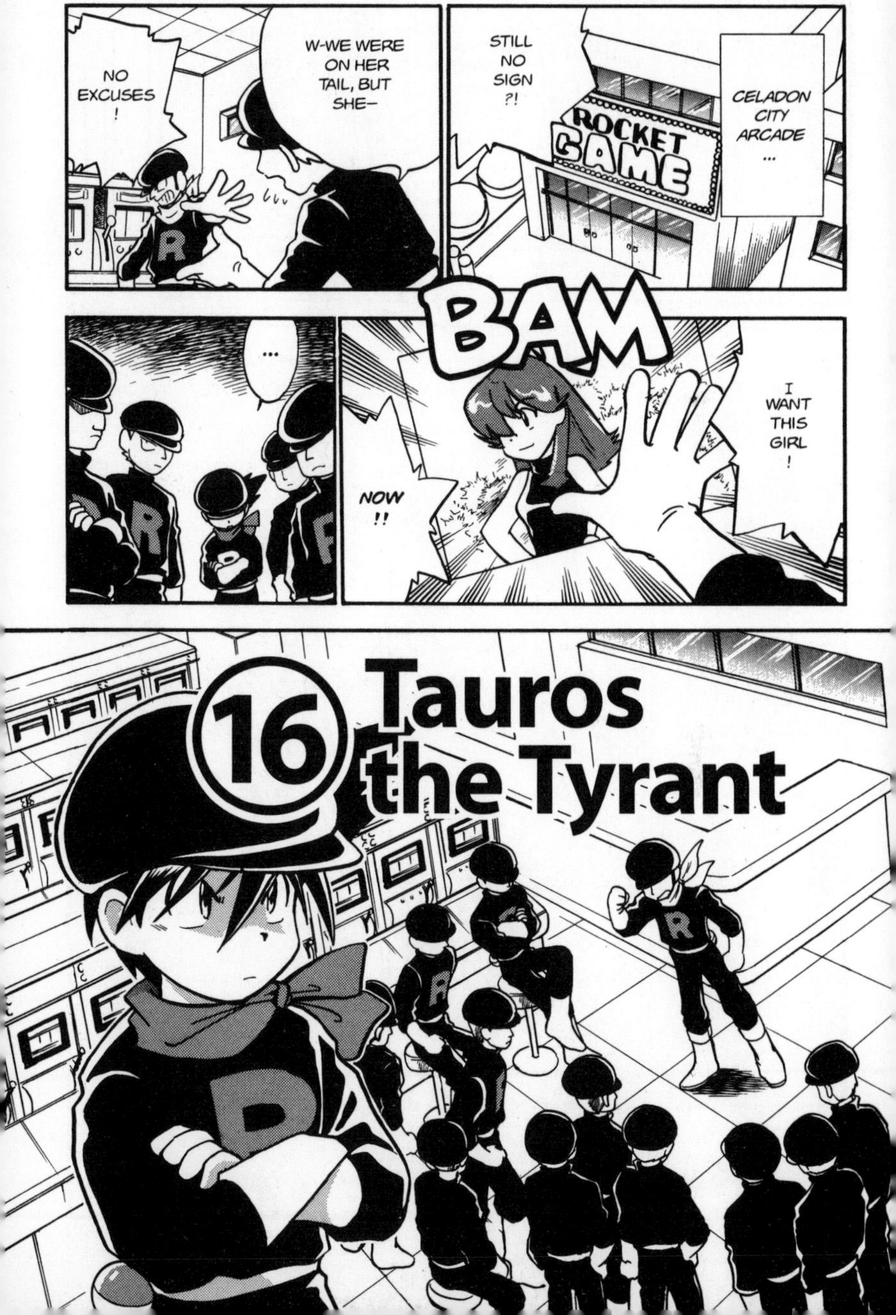
CELADON CITY ARCADE ...
STILL NO SIGN ?!
ROCKET GAME
W-WE WERE ON HER TAIL, BUT SHE—
NO EXCUSES !
BAM
I WANT THIS GIRL !
NOW !!
...
16 Tauros the Tyrant

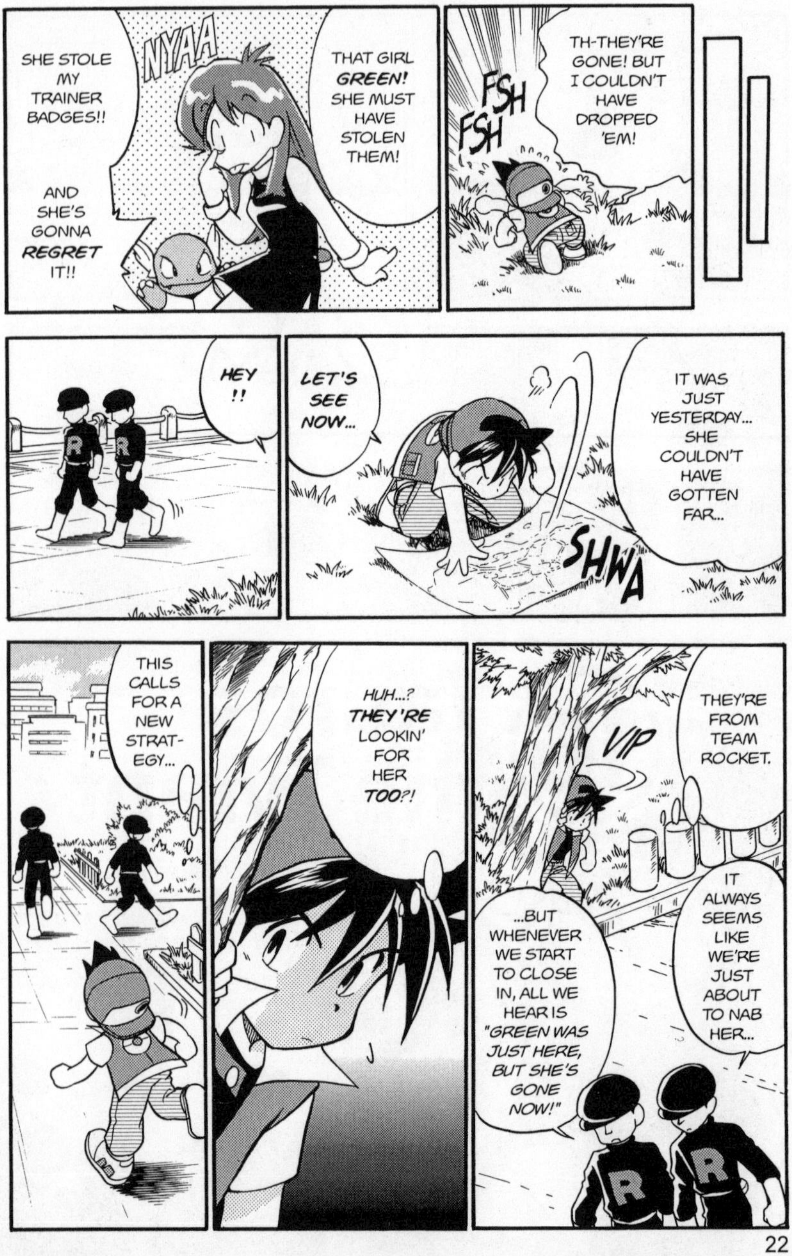
FSH
FSH
TH-THEY'RE GONE! BUT I COULDN'T HAVE DROPPED 'EM!
THAT GIRL GREEN! SHE MUST HAVE STOLEN THEM!
NYAA
SHE STOLE MY TRAINER BADGES!!
AND SHE'S GONNA REGRET IT!!
IT WAS JUST YESTERDAY... SHE COULDN'T HAVE GOTTEN FAR...
SHWA
LET'S SEE NOW...
HEY!!
THEY'RE FROM TEAM ROCKET.
VIP
IT ALWAYS SEEMS LIKE WE'RE JUST ABOUT TO NAB HER...
...BUT WHENEVER WE START TO CLOSE IN, ALL WE HEAR IS "GREEN WAS JUST HERE, BUT SHE'S GONE NOW!"
HUH...? THEY'RE LOOKIN' FOR HER TOO?!
THIS CALLS FOR A NEW STRAT-EGY...

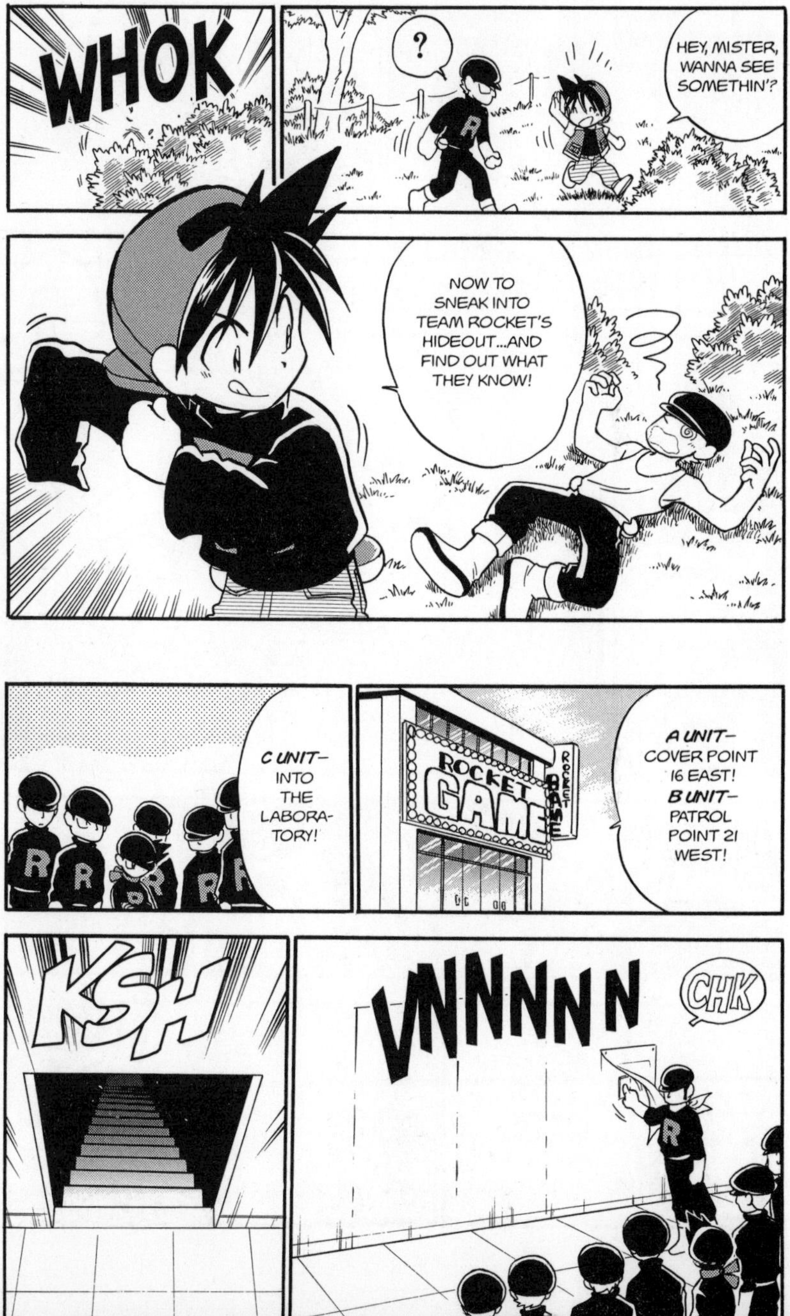
HEY, MISTER, WANNA SEE SOMETHIN'?
?
WHOK
NOW TO SNEAK INTO TEAM ROCKET'S HIDEOUT...AND FIND OUT WHAT THEY KNOW!
ROCKET GAME
A UNIT—COVER POINT 16 EAST! *B UNIT*—PATROL POINT 21 WEST!
C UNIT—INTO THE LABORA-TORY!
CHK
VNNNNN
KSH

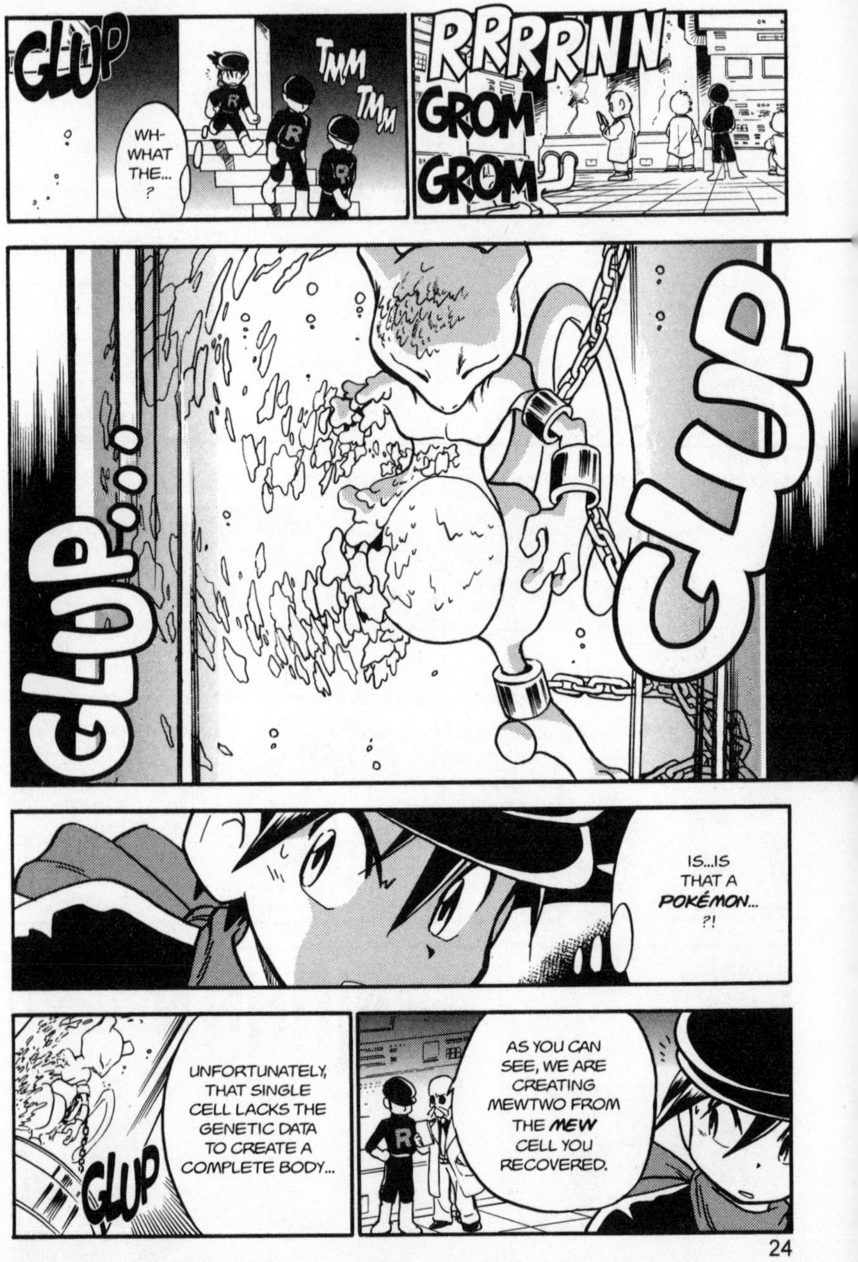
RRRRNN
GROM
GROM
TMM
TMM
GLUP
WH-WHAT THE...?
GLUP
GLUP...
IS...IS THAT A POKÉMON...?!
AS YOU CAN SEE, WE ARE CREATING MEWTWO FROM THE MEW CELL YOU RECOVERED.
UNFORTUNATELY, THAT SINGLE CELL LACKS THE GENETIC DATA TO CREATE A COMPLETE BODY...
GLUP

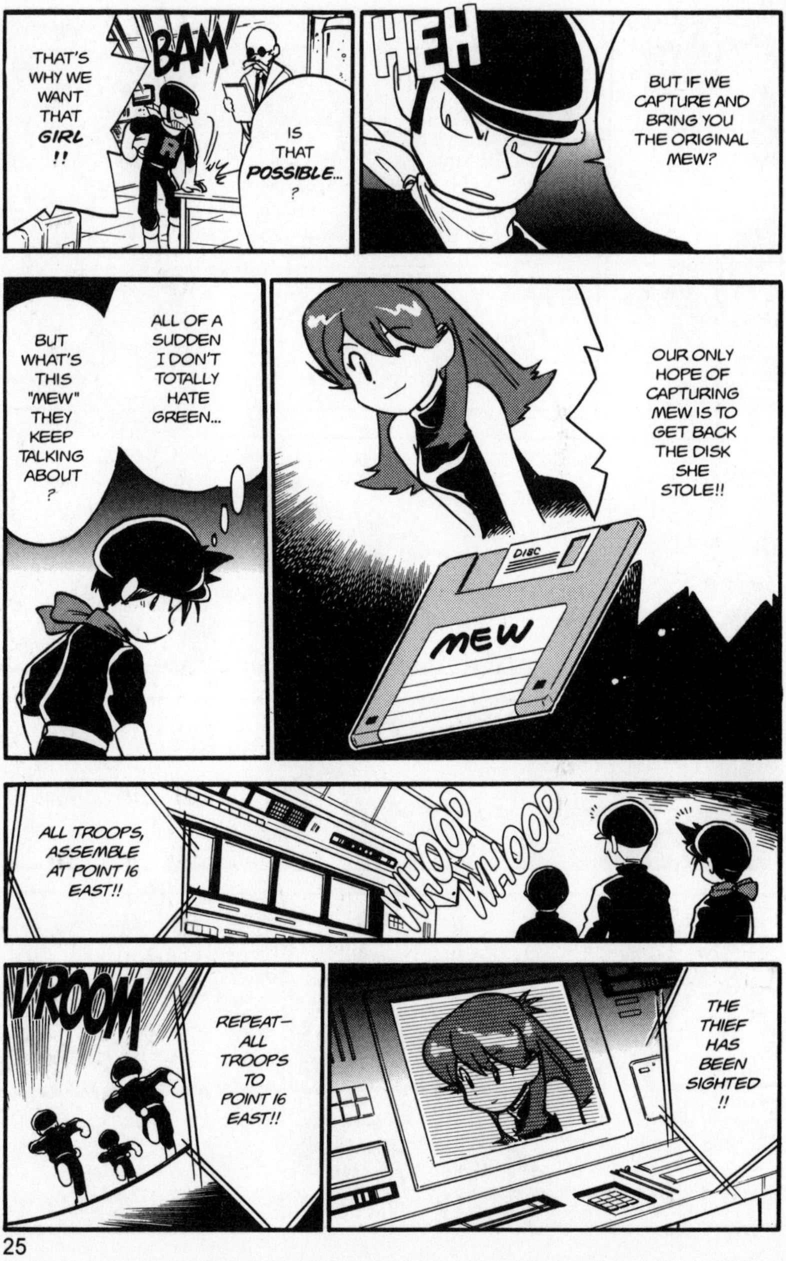

HEH
BUT IF WE CAPTURE AND BRING YOU THE ORIGINAL MEW?
BAM
IS THAT POSSIBLE...?
THAT'S WHY WE WANT THAT GIRL!!
OUR ONLY HOPE OF CAPTURING MEW IS TO GET BACK THE DISK SHE STOLE!!
DISC
MEW
ALL OF A SUDDEN I DON'T TOTALLY HATE GREEN...
BUT WHAT'S THIS "MEW" THEY KEEP TALKING ABOUT?
WHOOP WHOOP
ALL TROOPS, ASSEMBLE AT POINT 16 EAST!!
THE THIEF HAS BEEN SIGHTED!!
VROOM
REPEAT— ALL TROOPS TO POINT 16 EAST!!

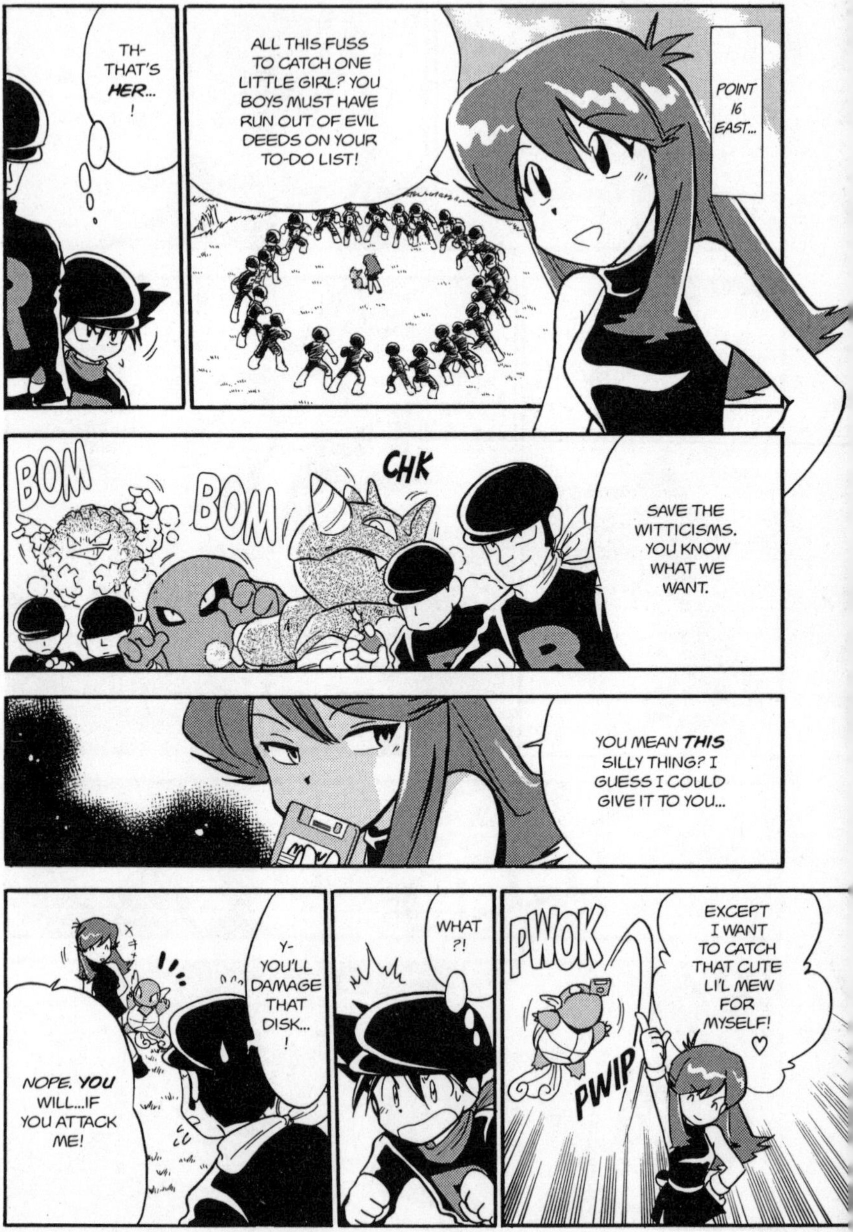
POINT 16 EAST...
ALL THIS FUSS TO CATCH ONE LITTLE GIRL? YOU BOYS MUST HAVE RUN OUT OF EVIL DEEDS ON YOUR TO-DO LIST!
TH-THAT'S *HER*...!
SAVE THE WITTICISMS. YOU KNOW WHAT WE WANT.
CHK
BOM
BOM
YOU MEAN *THIS* SILLY THING? I GUESS I COULD GIVE IT TO YOU...
EXCEPT I WANT TO CATCH THAT CUTE LI'L MEW FOR MYSELF! ♡
PWOK
PWIP
WHAT?!
Y-YOU'LL DAMAGE THAT DISK...!
NOPE. *YOU* WILL...IF YOU ATTACK ME!

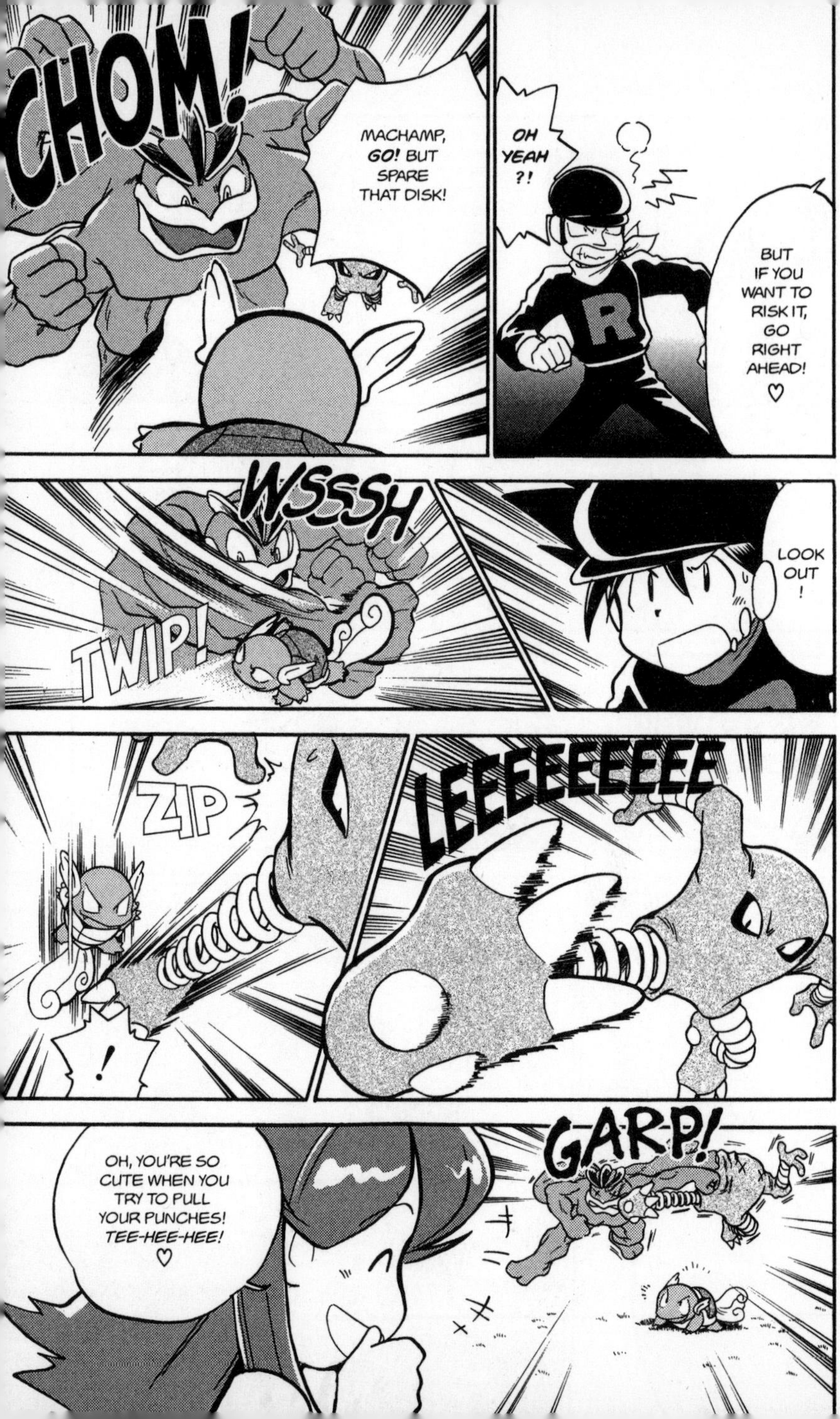
OH YEAH?!
BUT IF YOU WANT TO RISK IT, GO RIGHT AHEAD! ♡
CHOM!
MACHAMP, GO! BUT SPARE THAT DISK!
LOOK OUT!
WSSSH
TWIP!
LEEEEEEEEEE
ZIP
!
GARP!
OH, YOU'RE SO CUTE WHEN YOU TRY TO PULL YOUR PUNCHES! TEE-HEE-HEE! ♡

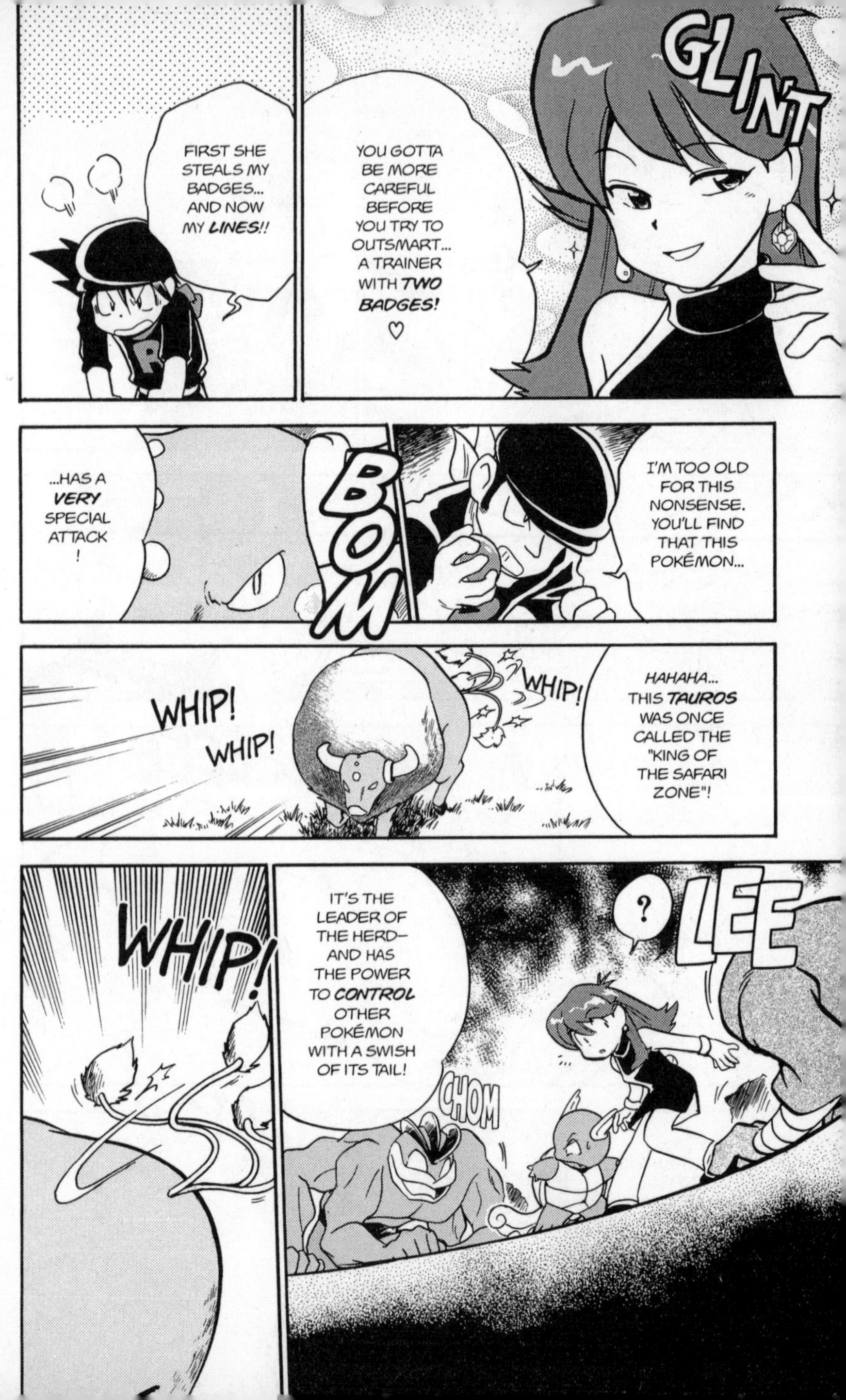
GLINT
YOU GOTTA BE MORE CAREFUL BEFORE YOU TRY TO OUTSMART... A TRAINER WITH TWO BADGES! ♡
FIRST SHE STEALS MY BADGES... AND NOW MY LINES!!
I'M TOO OLD FOR THIS NONSENSE. YOU'LL FIND THAT THIS POKÉMON...
BOM
...HAS A VERY SPECIAL ATTACK !
HAHAHA... THIS TAUROS WAS ONCE CALLED THE "KING OF THE SAFARI ZONE"!
WHIP!
WHIP!
WHIP!
LEE
?
IT'S THE LEADER OF THE HERD—AND HAS THE POWER TO CONTROL OTHER POKÉMON WITH A SWISH OF ITS TAIL!
CHOM
WHIP!

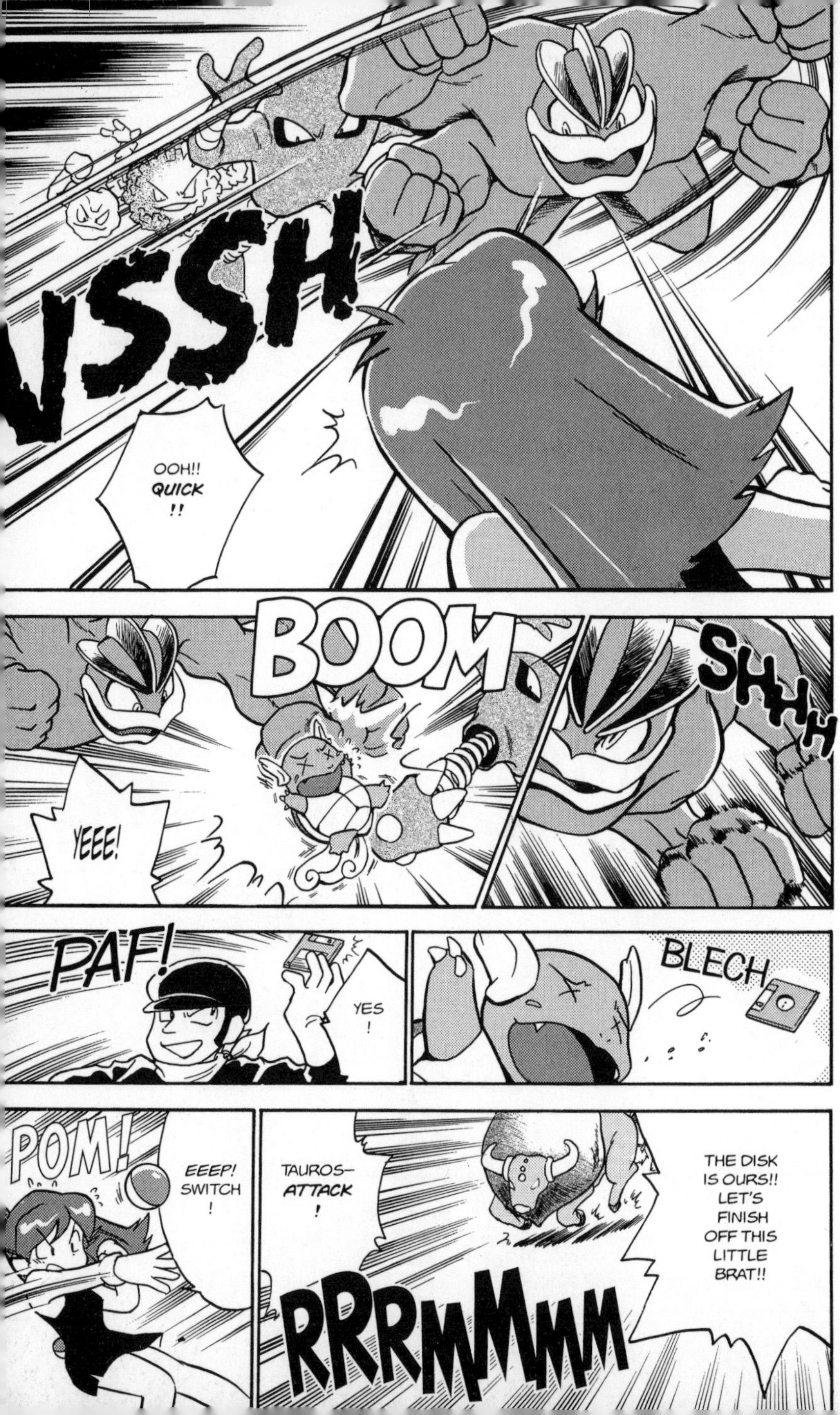
VSSH
OOH!! QUICK !!
SHHH
BOOM
YEEE!
BLECH
PAF!
YES !
THE DISK IS OURS!! LET'S FINISH OFF THIS LITTLE BRAT!!
TAUROS— ATTACK !
RRRMMMMM
POM!
EEEP! SWITCH !

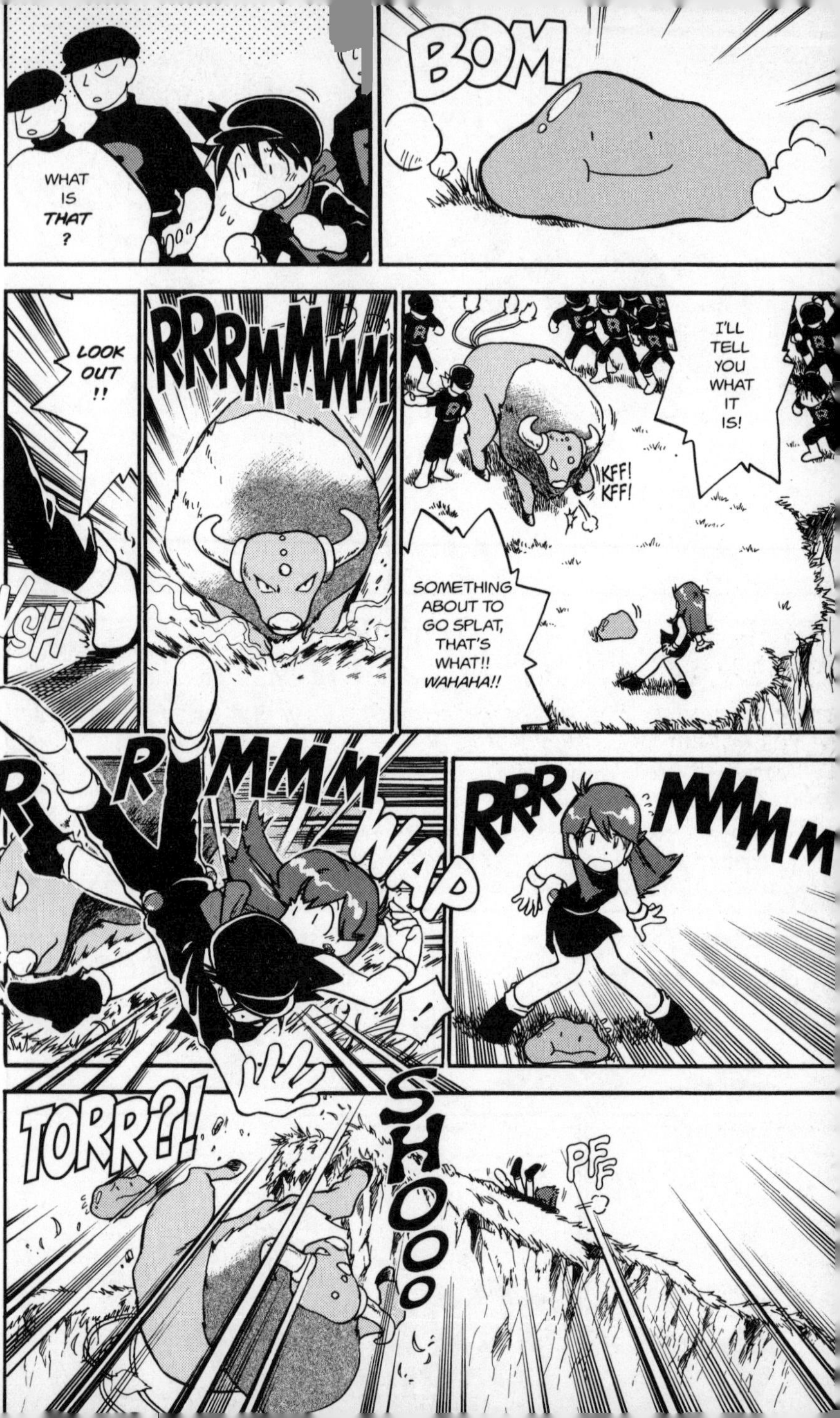
BOM
WHAT IS *THAT* ?
I'LL TELL YOU WHAT IT IS!
KFF! KFF!
SOMETHING ABOUT TO GO SPLAT, THAT'S WHAT!! *WAHAHA!!*
RRRMMMMM
LOOK OUT !!
VSH
RRRMMMMM
RRMMMM
WAP
!
TORR?!
SHOOO
PFF

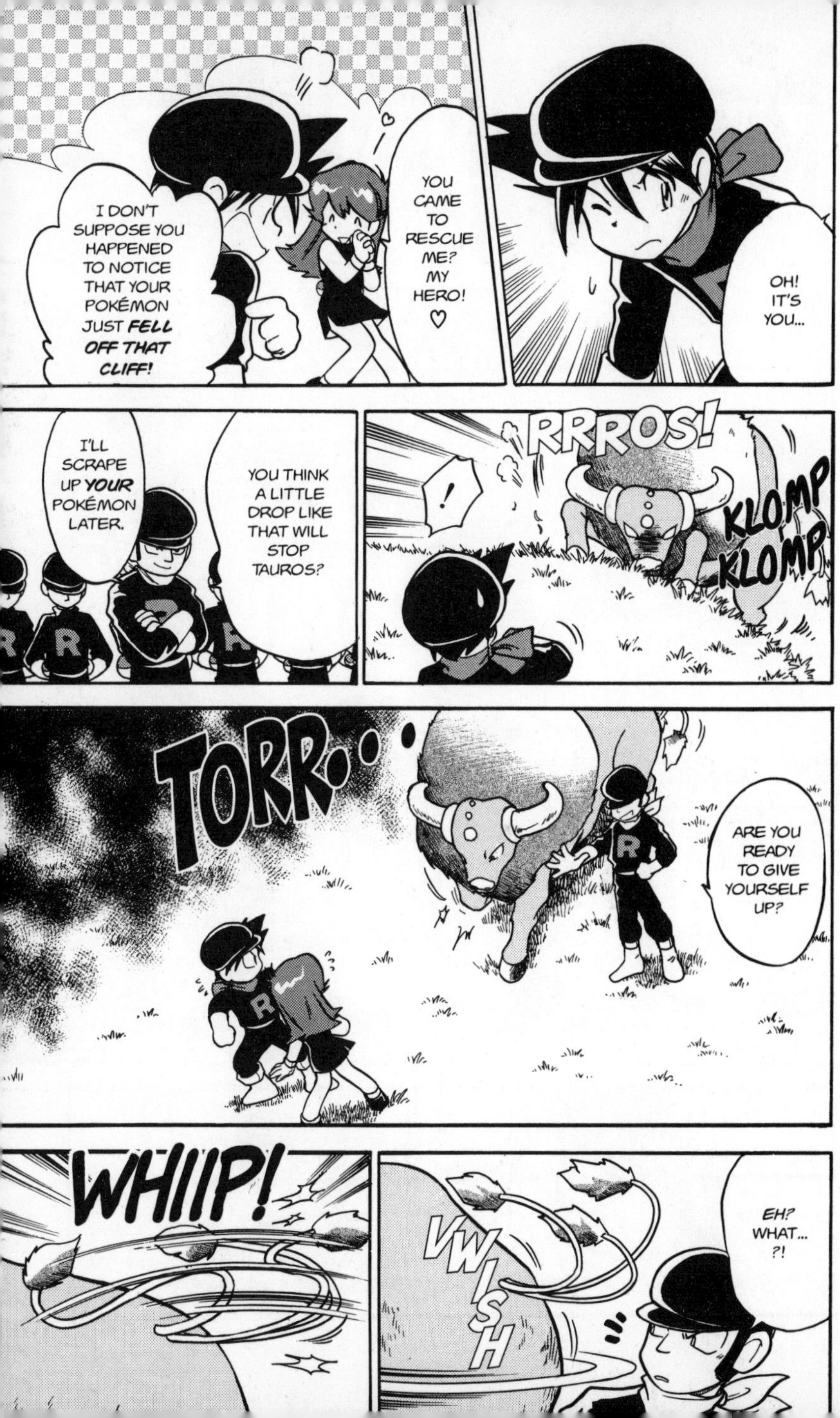
OH! IT'S YOU...
YOU CAME TO RESCUE ME? MY HERO! ♡
I DON'T SUPPOSE YOU HAPPENED TO NOTICE THAT YOUR POKÉMON JUST **FELL OFF THAT CLIFF!**
RRROS!
KLOMP KLOMP
!
YOU THINK A LITTLE DROP LIKE THAT WILL STOP TAUROS?
I'LL SCRAPE UP **YOUR** POKÉMON LATER.
ARE YOU READY TO GIVE YOURSELF UP?
TORR...
EH? WHAT... ?!
VWISH
WHIIP!

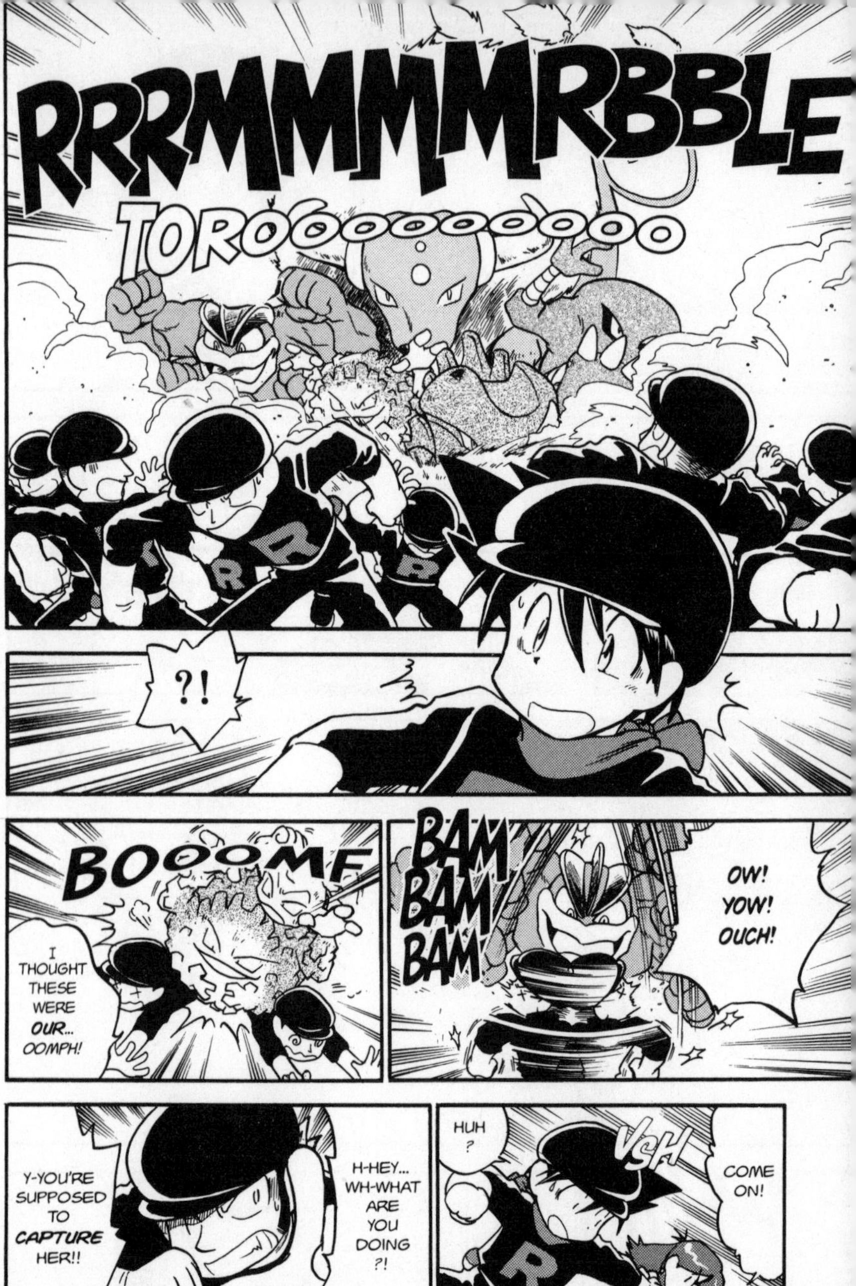
RRRMMMMMRBBLE
TOROOOOOOOOOOO
?!
BAM BAM BAM
OW! YOW! OUCH!
BOOOMF
I THOUGHT THESE WERE OUR... OOMPH!
VSH
HUH?
COME ON!
H-HEY... WH-WHAT ARE YOU DOING?!
Y-YOU'RE SUPPOSED TO CAPTURE HER!!

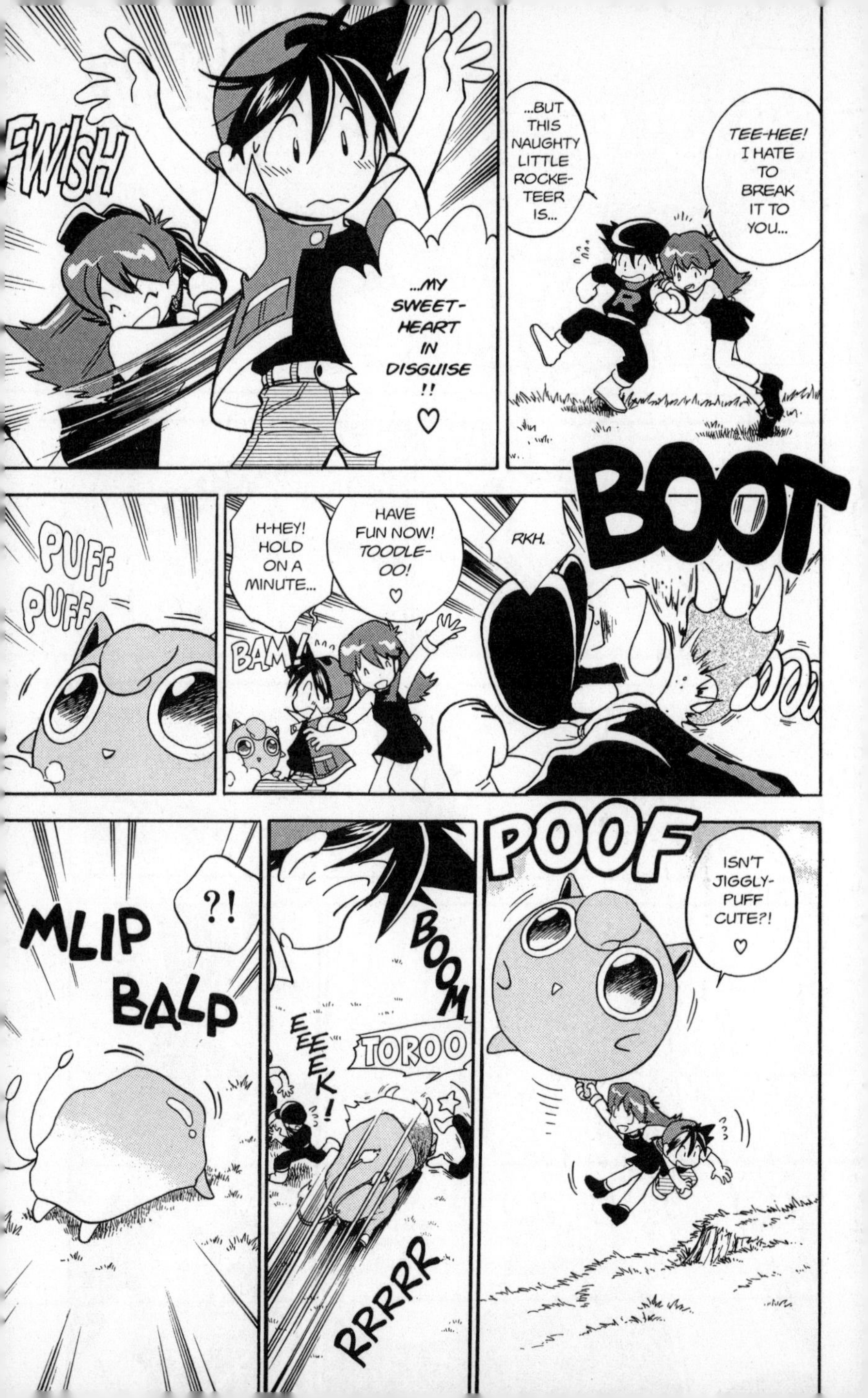
TEE-HEE! I HATE TO BREAK IT TO YOU...
...BUT THIS NAUGHTY LITTLE ROCKE-TEER IS...
FWISH
...MY SWEET-HEART IN DISGUISE!! ♡
BOOT
RKH.
HAVE FUN NOW! TOODLE-OO! ♡
H-HEY! HOLD ON A MINUTE...
BAM
PUFF PUFF
POOF
ISN'T JIGGLY-PUFF CUTE?! ♡
BOOM
EEEEK!
TOROO
RRRRR
?!
MLIP
BALP

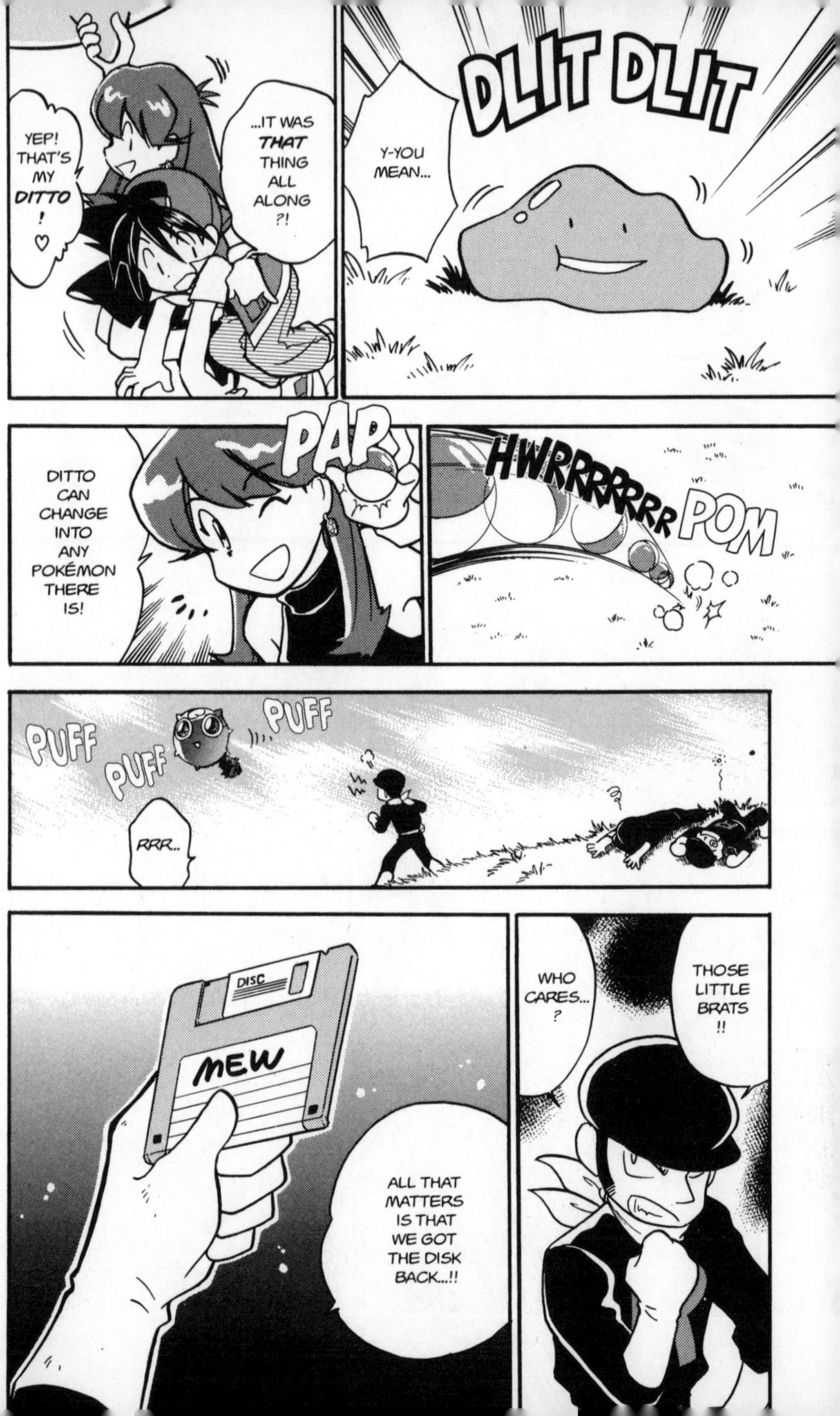
DLIT DLIT
Y-YOU MEAN...
...IT WAS THAT THING ALL ALONG ?!
YEP! THAT'S MY DITTO! ♡
HWRRRRRRRR POM
PAP
DITTO CAN CHANGE INTO ANY POKÉMON THERE IS!
PUFF
PUFF
PUFF
RRR...
THOSE LITTLE BRATS !!
WHO CARES... ?
ALL THAT MATTERS IS THAT WE GOT THE DISK BACK...!!
DISC
MEW

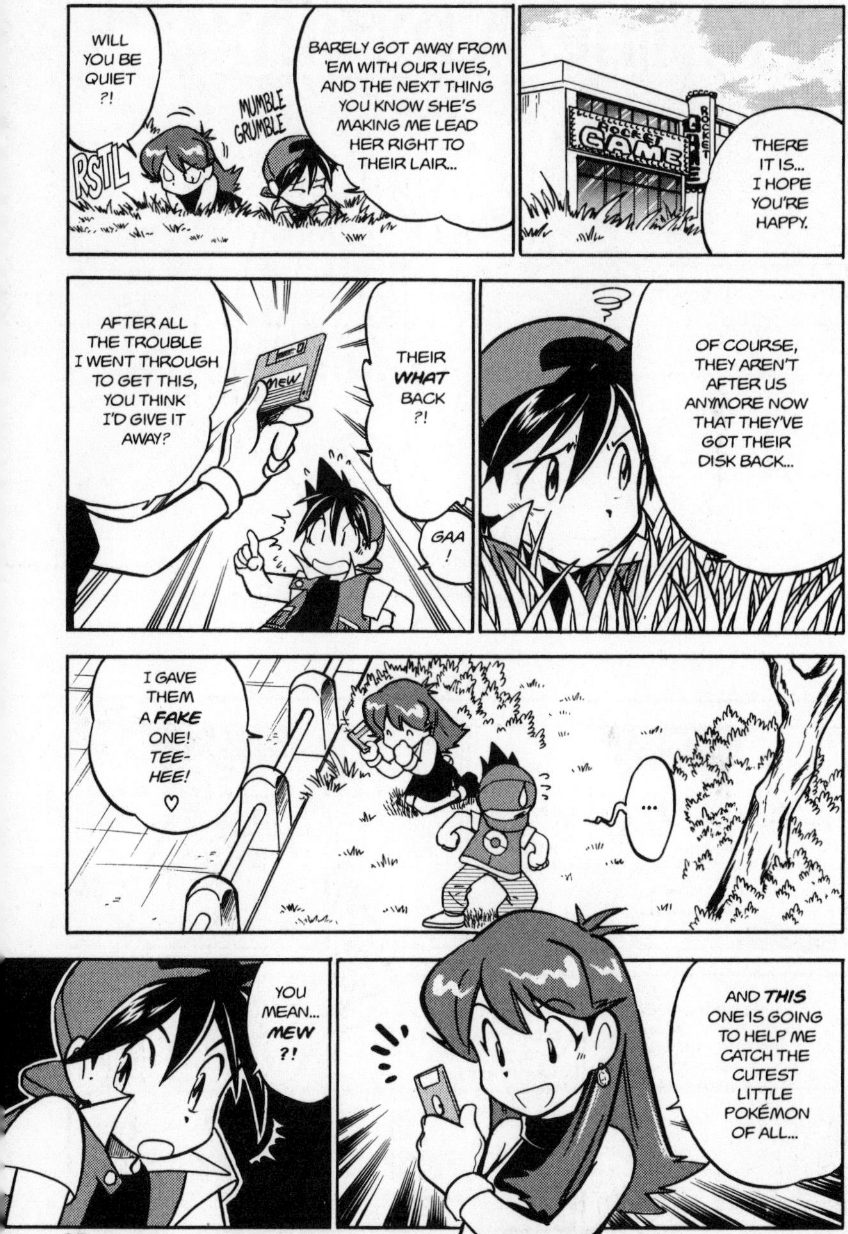
THERE IT IS... I HOPE YOU'RE HAPPY.
ROCKET GAME
ROCKET
BARELY GOT AWAY FROM 'EM WITH OUR LIVES, AND THE NEXT THING YOU KNOW SHE'S MAKING ME LEAD HER RIGHT TO THEIR LAIR...
MUMBLE GRUMBLE
WILL YOU BE QUIET ?!
RSTL
OF COURSE, THEY AREN'T AFTER US ANYMORE NOW THAT THEY'VE GOT THEIR DISK BACK...
THEIR **WHAT** BACK ?!
GAA !
AFTER ALL THE TROUBLE I WENT THROUGH TO GET THIS, YOU THINK I'D GIVE IT AWAY?
MEW
...
I GAVE THEM A **FAKE** ONE! **TEE-HEE!** ♡
AND **THIS** ONE IS GOING TO HELP ME CATCH THE CUTEST LITTLE POKÉMON OF ALL...
YOU MEAN... **MEW** ?!

17 The Jynx Jinx

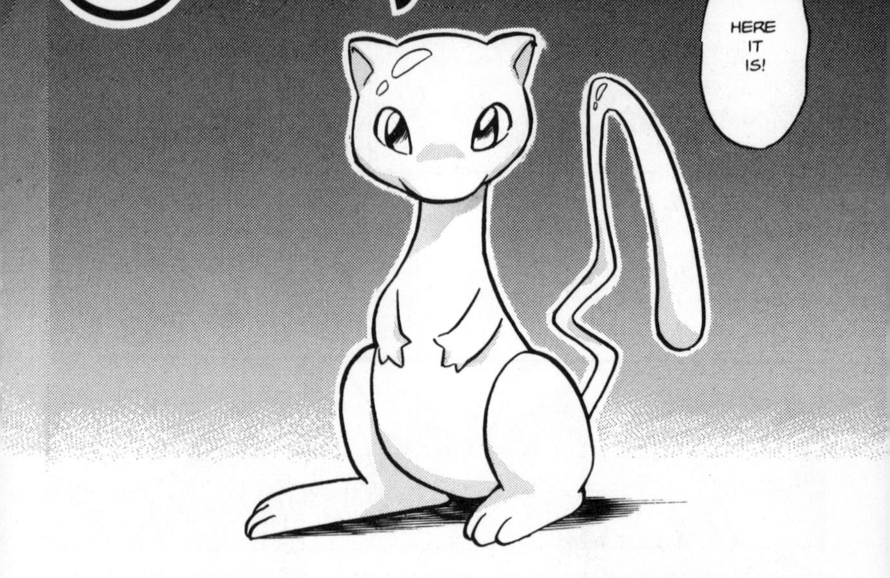
HERE IT IS!

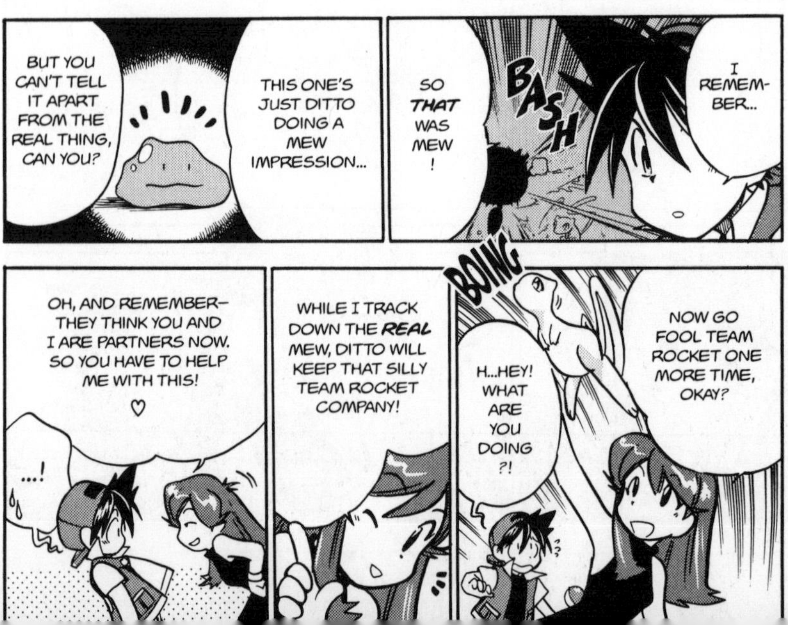
I REMEM-BER...
BASH
SO *THAT* WAS MEW!
THIS ONE'S JUST DITTO DOING A MEW IMPRESSION...
BUT YOU CAN'T TELL IT APART FROM THE REAL THING, CAN YOU?
NOW GO FOOL TEAM ROCKET ONE MORE TIME, OKAY?
BOING
H...HEY! WHAT ARE YOU DOING?!
WHILE I TRACK DOWN THE *REAL* MEW, DITTO WILL KEEP THAT SILLY TEAM ROCKET COMPANY!
OH, AND REMEMBER— THEY THINK YOU AND I ARE PARTNERS NOW. SO YOU HAVE TO HELP ME WITH THIS! ♡
...!

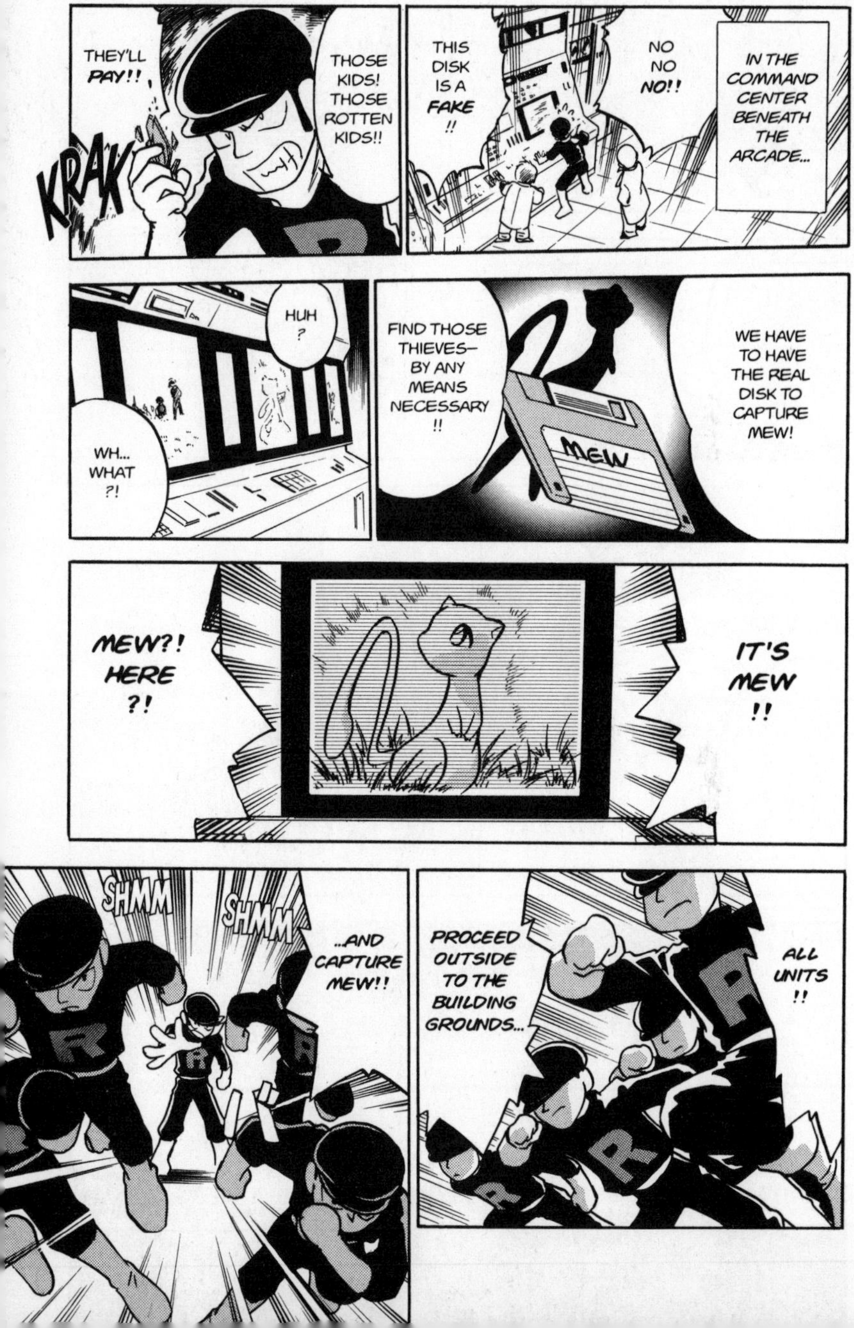
IN THE COMMAND CENTER BENEATH THE ARCADE...
NO NO NO!!
THIS DISK IS A FAKE!!
THOSE KIDS! THOSE ROTTEN KIDS!!
THEY'LL PAY!!
KRAK
WE HAVE TO HAVE THE REAL DISK TO CAPTURE MEW!
FIND THOSE THIEVES— BY ANY MEANS NECESSARY!!
MEW
HUH?
WH... WHAT?!
IT'S MEW!!
MEW?! HERE?!
ALL UNITS!!
PROCEED OUTSIDE TO THE BUILDING GROUNDS...
...AND CAPTURE MEW!!
SHMM
SHMM

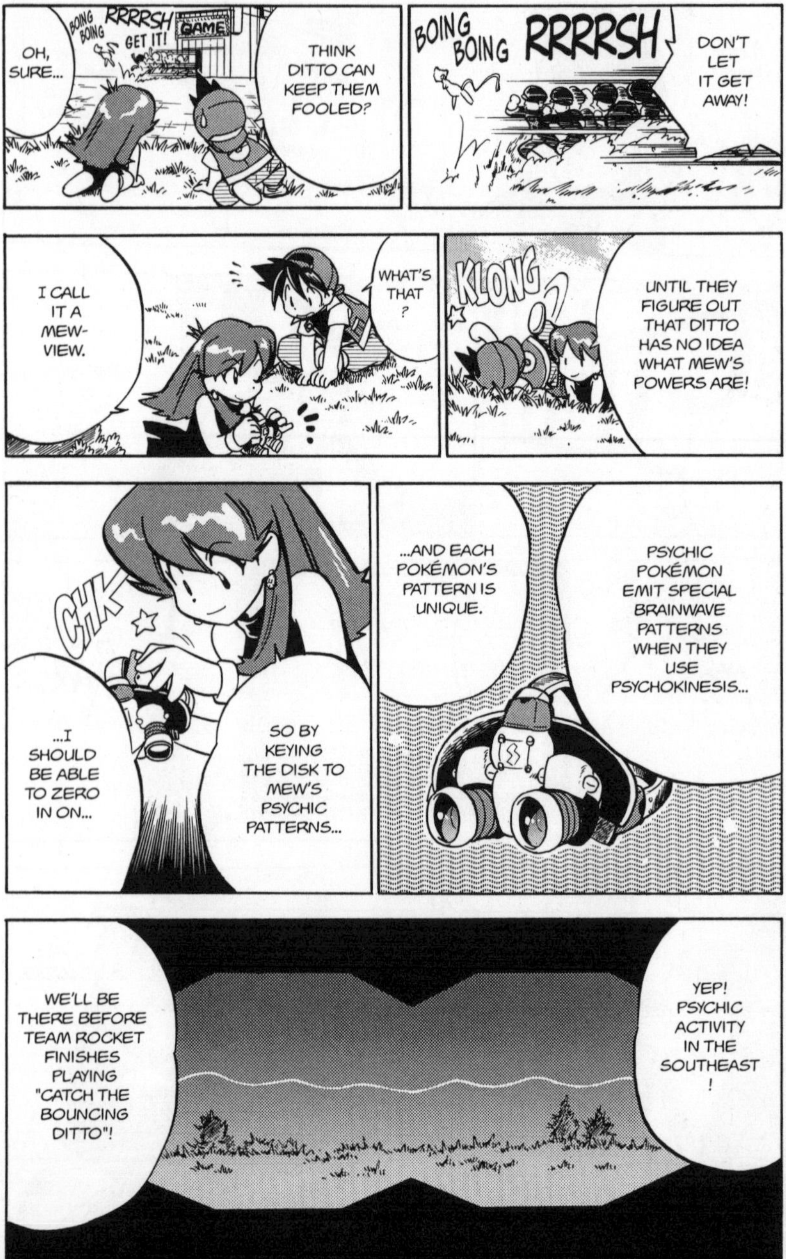
BOING BOING RRRRSH
DON'T LET IT GET AWAY!
THINK DITTO CAN KEEP THEM FOOLED?
BOING BOING RRRRSH
GET IT!
GAME
OH, SURE...
KLONG
UNTIL THEY FIGURE OUT THAT DITTO HAS NO IDEA WHAT MEW'S POWERS ARE!
WHAT'S THAT ?
I CALL IT A MEW-VIEW.
PSYCHIC POKÉMON EMIT SPECIAL BRAINWAVE PATTERNS WHEN THEY USE PSYCHOKINESIS...
...AND EACH POKÉMON'S PATTERN IS UNIQUE.
CHK
SO BY KEYING THE DISK TO MEW'S PSYCHIC PATTERNS...
...I SHOULD BE ABLE TO ZERO IN ON...
YEP! PSYCHIC ACTIVITY IN THE SOUTHEAST !
WE'LL BE THERE BEFORE TEAM ROCKET FINISHES PLAYING "CATCH THE BOUNCING DITTO"!

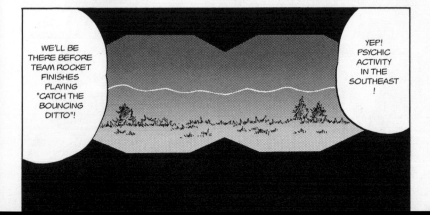

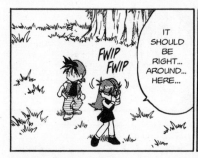

HYOOOOOOOO
FWIP FWIP
IT SHOULD BE RIGHT... AROUND... HERE...
K-CHIK
Ppp... Ppp...
I...UM... I SAW SOMETHING STRANGE AT TEAM ROCKET'S HIDEOUT...
THEY'RE TRYING TO USE MEW TO CREATE SOME KIND OF... OF...MONSTER POKÉMON.
UH-HUH.
SO WHY ARE YOU LOOKING FOR MEW?
?
ISN'T IT OBVIOUS?
FOR M-O-N-E-Y! ♡
M-M-M-MONEY?!
DO YOU HAVE ANY IDEA HOW MANY DIFFERENT TYPES OF POKÉMON HAVE BEEN DISCOVERED?

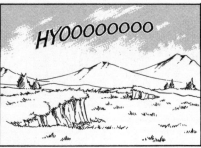

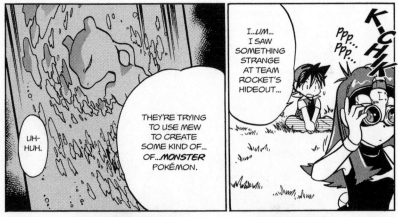

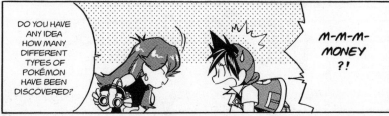

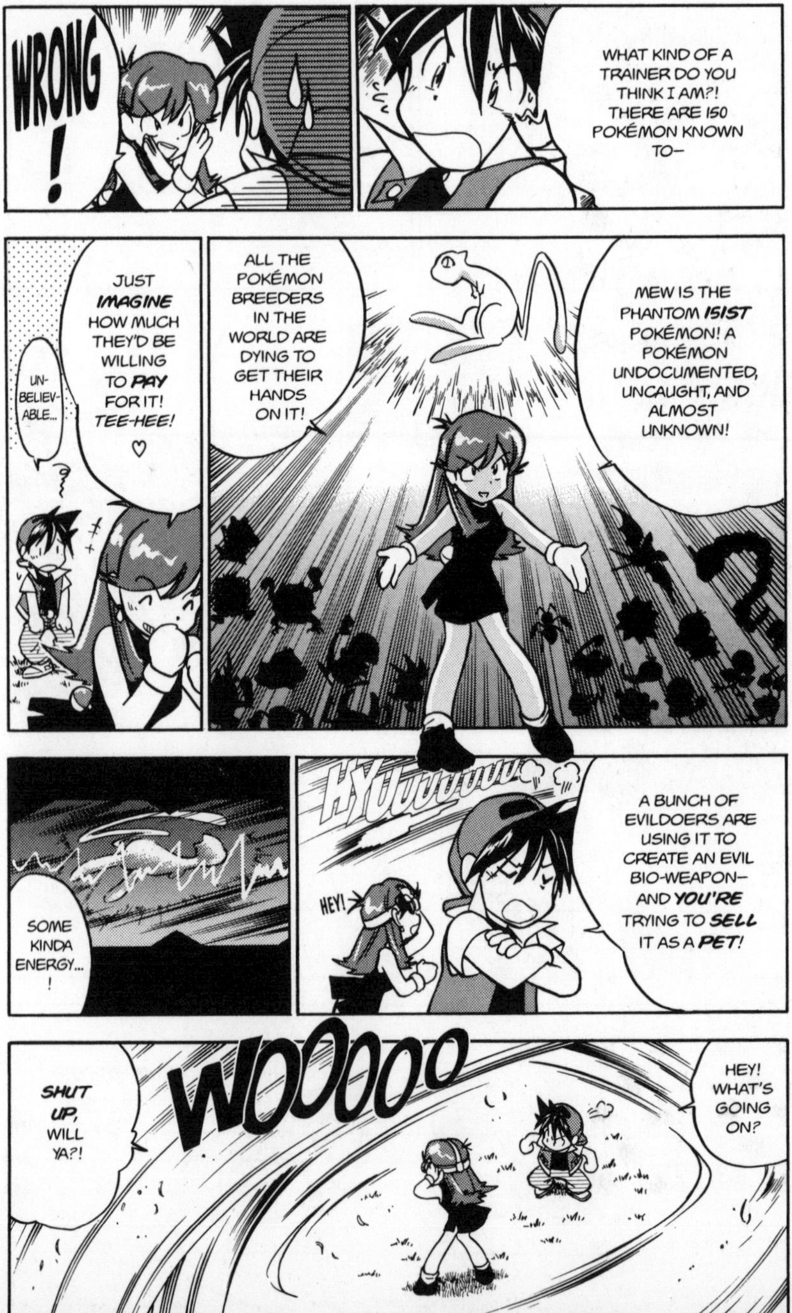
WHAT KIND OF A TRAINER DO YOU THINK I AM?! THERE ARE 150 POKÉMON KNOWN TO—
WRONG !
MEW IS THE PHANTOM *ISIST* POKÉMON! A POKÉMON UNDOCUMENTED, UNCAUGHT, AND ALMOST UNKNOWN!
ALL THE POKÉMON BREEDERS IN THE WORLD ARE DYING TO GET THEIR HANDS ON IT!
JUST *IMAGINE* HOW MUCH THEY'D BE WILLING TO *PAY* FOR IT! *TEE-HEE!* ♡
UN-BELIEV-ABLE...
HYUUUUUUU
A BUNCH OF EVILDOERS ARE USING IT TO CREATE AN EVIL BIO-WEAPON—AND *YOU'RE* TRYING TO *SELL* IT AS A *PET*!
HEY!
SOME KINDA ENERGY... !
HEY! WHAT'S GOING ON?
WOOOOO
SHUT UP, WILL YA?!

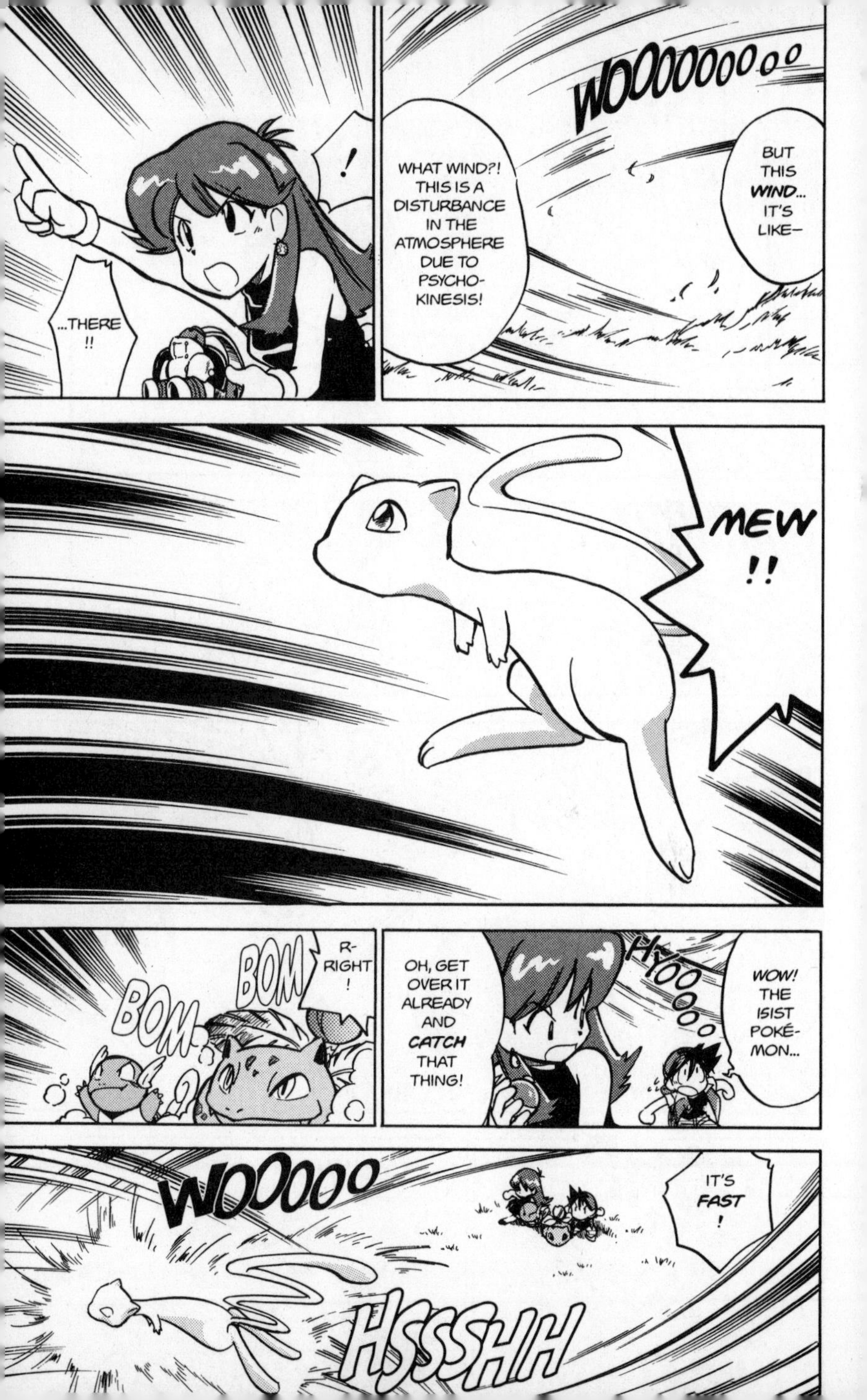
WOOOOOOOoo
BUT THIS WIND... IT'S LIKE–
WHAT WIND?! THIS IS A DISTURBANCE IN THE ATMOSPHERE DUE TO PSYCHO-KINESIS!
!
...THERE !!
MEW !!
WOW! THE ISIST POKÉ-MON...
HYOOOOO
OH, GET OVER IT ALREADY AND CATCH THAT THING!
R-RIGHT !
BOM
BOM
IT'S FAST !
WOOOOO
HSSSHH

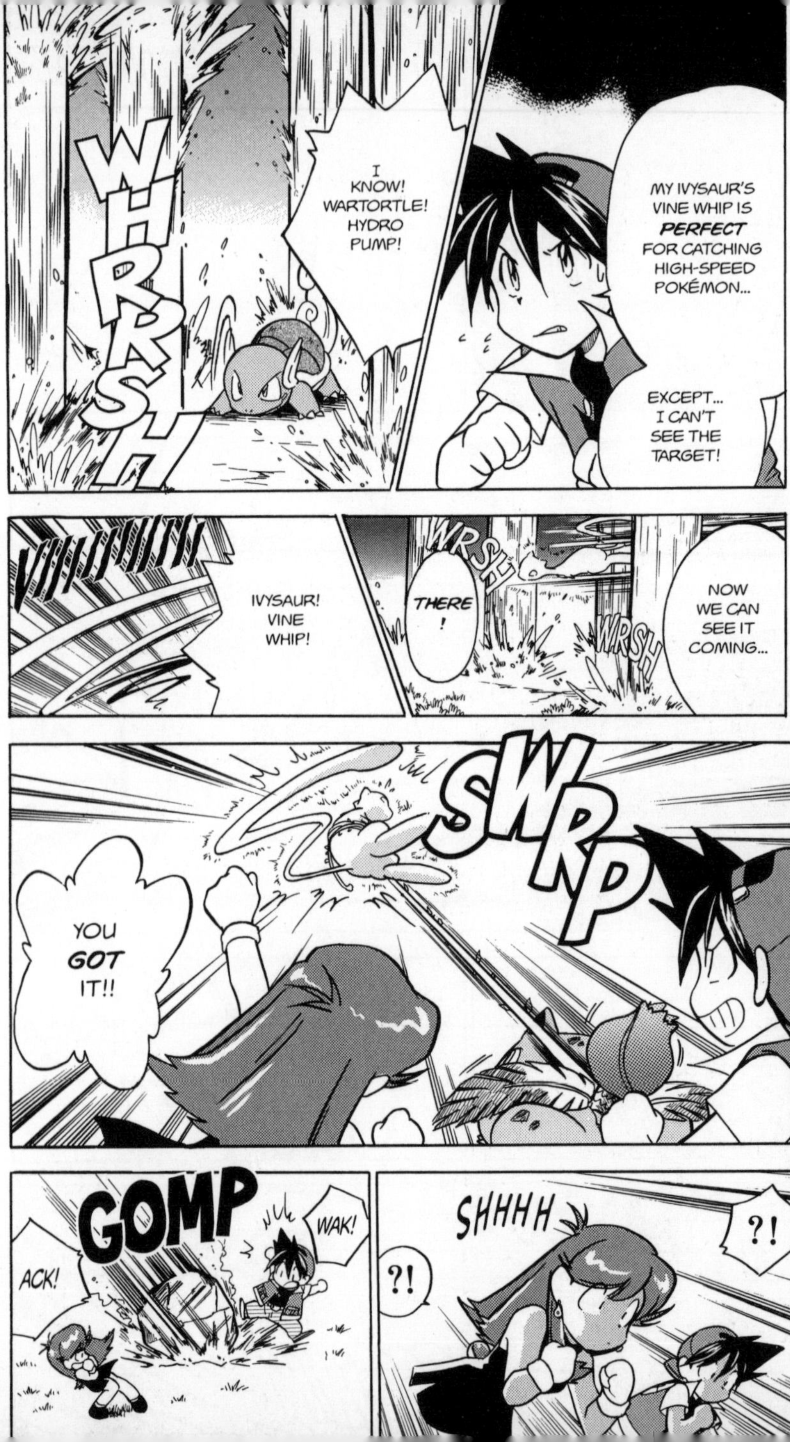
MY IVYSAUR'S VINE WHIP IS **PERFECT** FOR CATCHING HIGH-SPEED POKÉMON...
EXCEPT... I CAN'T SEE THE TARGET!
I KNOW! WARTORTLE! HYDRO PUMP!
WHRRSH
NOW WE CAN SEE IT COMING...
WRSH
WRSH
THERE!
IVYSAUR! VINE WHIP!
SWRP
YOU **GOT** IT!!
?!
SHHHH
?!
WAK!
GOMP
ACK!

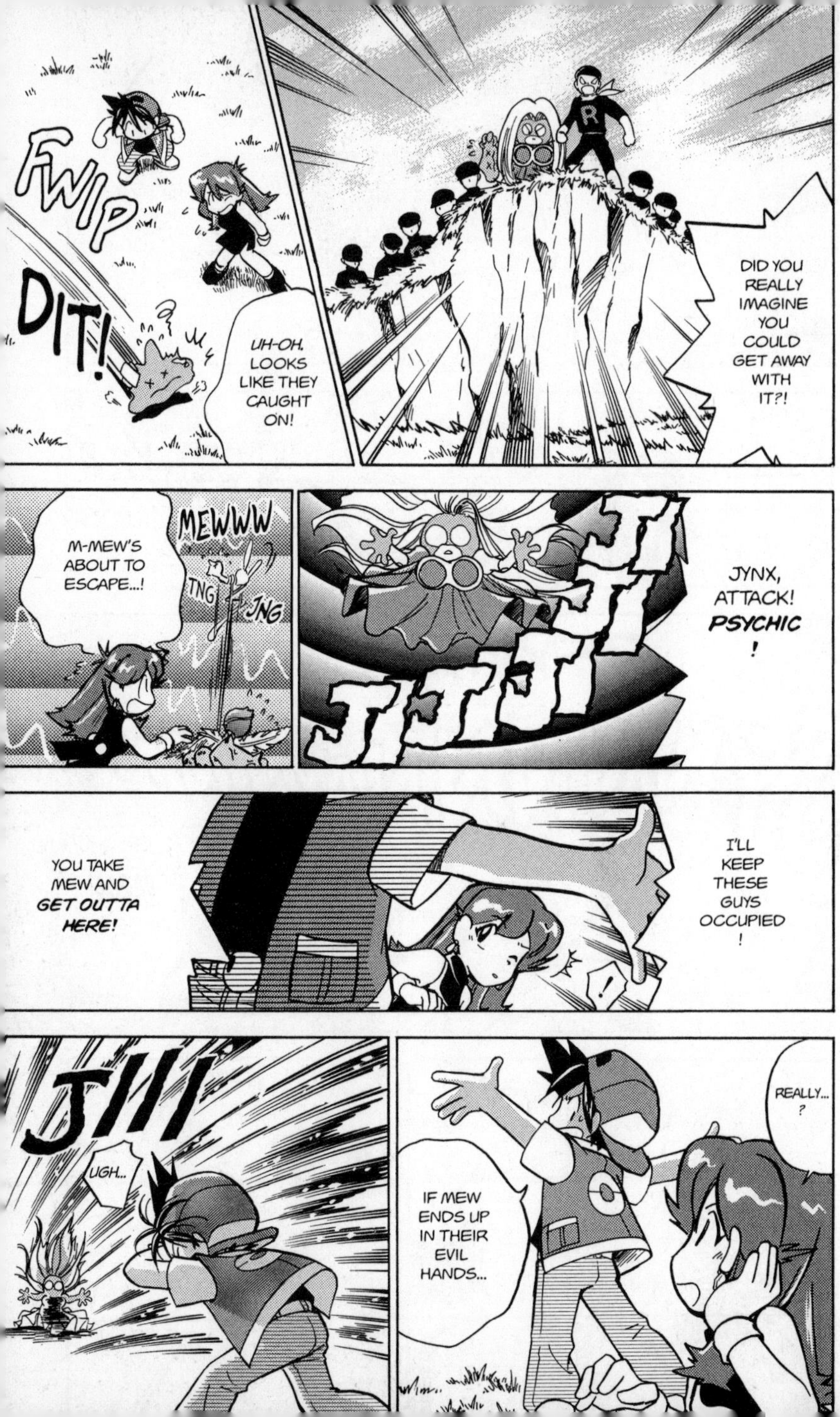
DID YOU REALLY IMAGINE YOU COULD GET AWAY WITH IT?!
FWIP
DIT!
UH-OH. LOOKS LIKE THEY CAUGHT ON!
JYNX, ATTACK! **PSYCHIC**!
JIJIJI
MEWWW
TNG
JNG
M-MEW'S ABOUT TO ESCAPE...!
I'LL KEEP THESE GUYS OCCUPIED!
YOU TAKE MEW AND **GET OUTTA HERE!**
!
REALLY...?
IF MEW ENDS UP IN THEIR EVIL HANDS...
JIII
UGH...

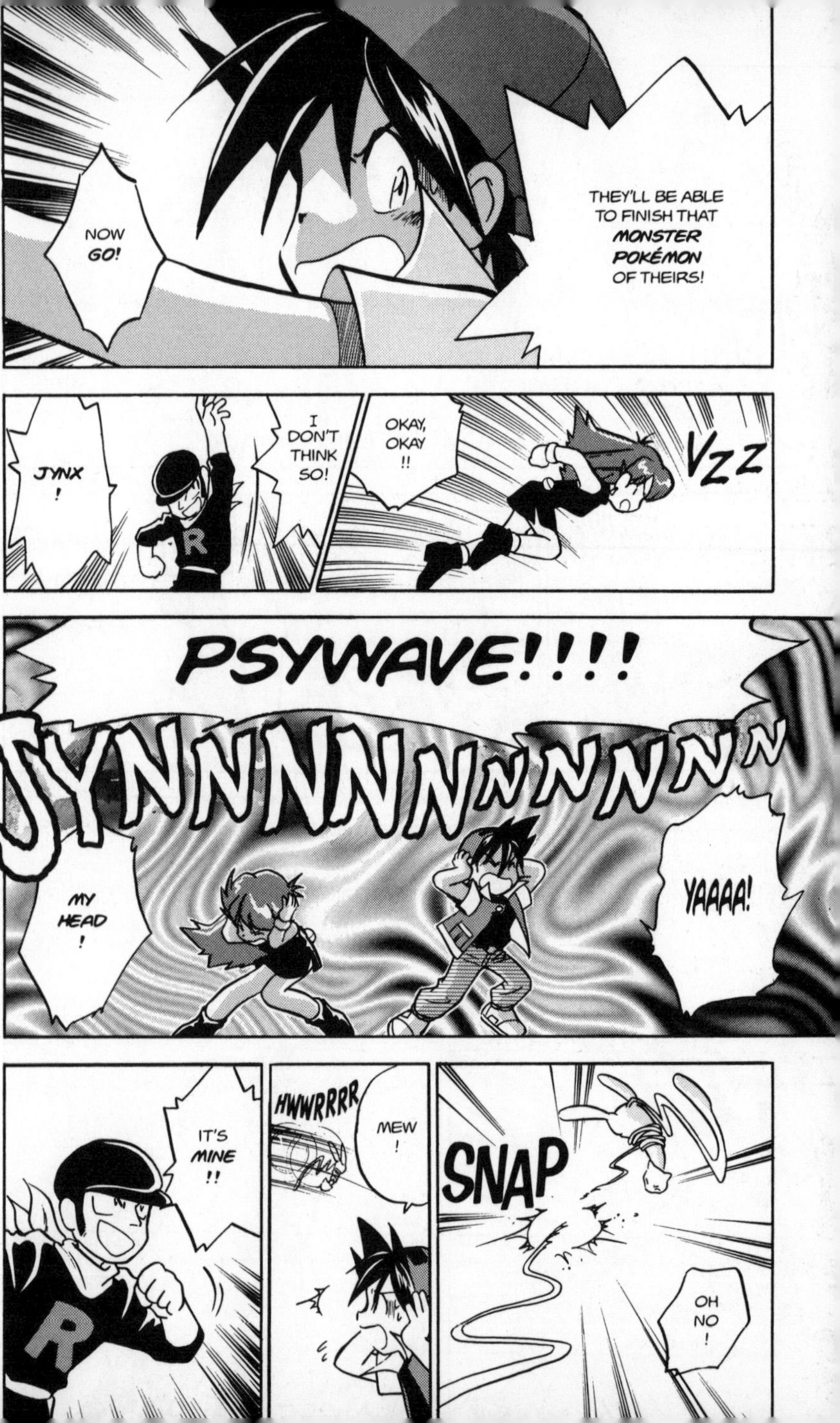
THEY'LL BE ABLE TO FINISH THAT MONSTER POKÉMON OF THEIRS!
NOW GO!
VZZ
OKAY, OKAY !!
I DON'T THINK SO!
JYNX !
PSYWAVE!!!!
JYNNNNNNNNNNNN
YAAAA!
MY HEAD !
SNAP
OH NO !
HWWRRRR
MEW !
IT'S MINE !!

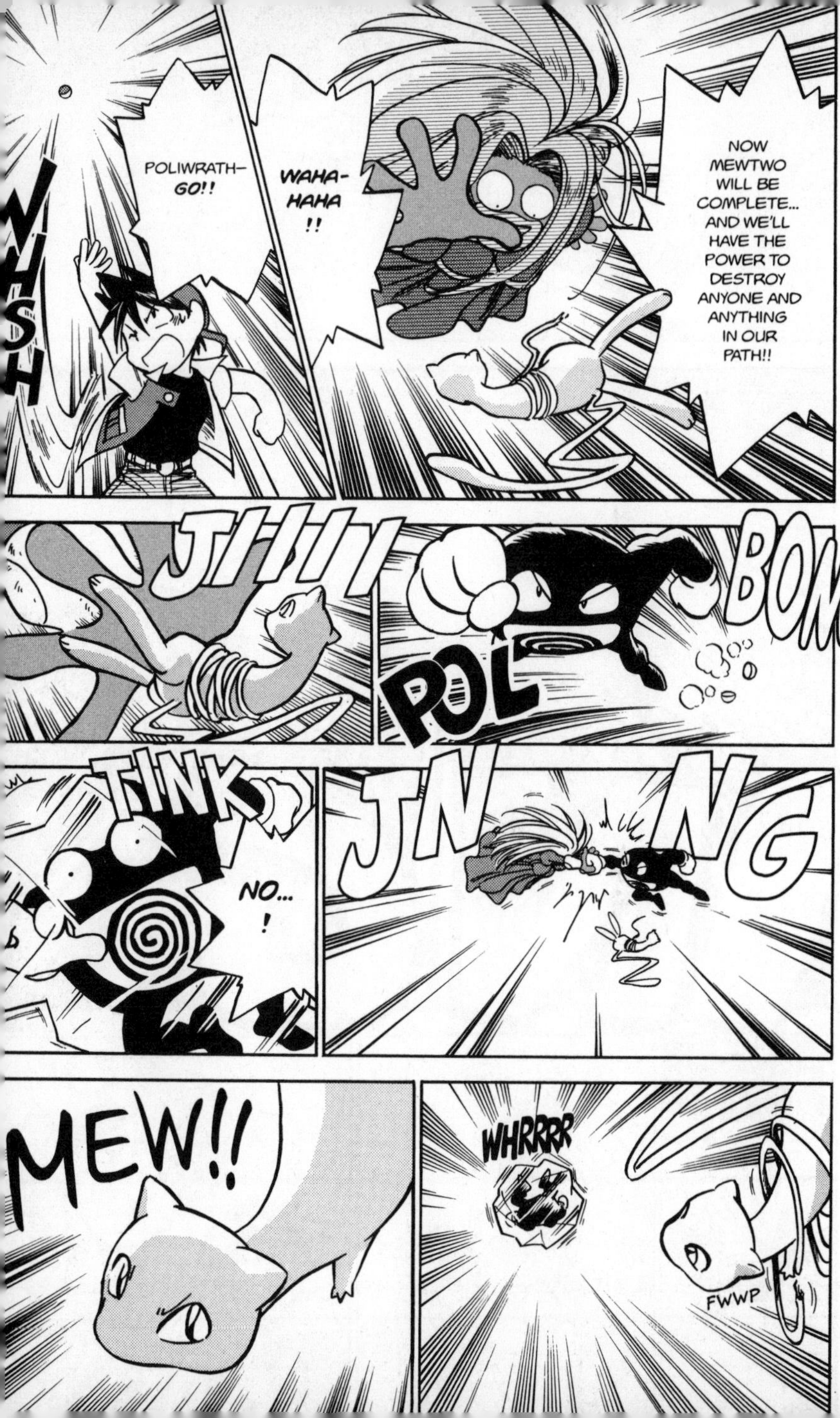
NOW MEWTWO WILL BE COMPLETE... AND WE'LL HAVE THE POWER TO DESTROY ANYONE AND ANYTHING IN OUR PATH!!
WAHA-HAHA !!
POLIWRATH— GO!!
WHSH
BOM
POL
JIIII
JNNG
TINK
NO... !
WHRRRR
FWWP
MEW!!

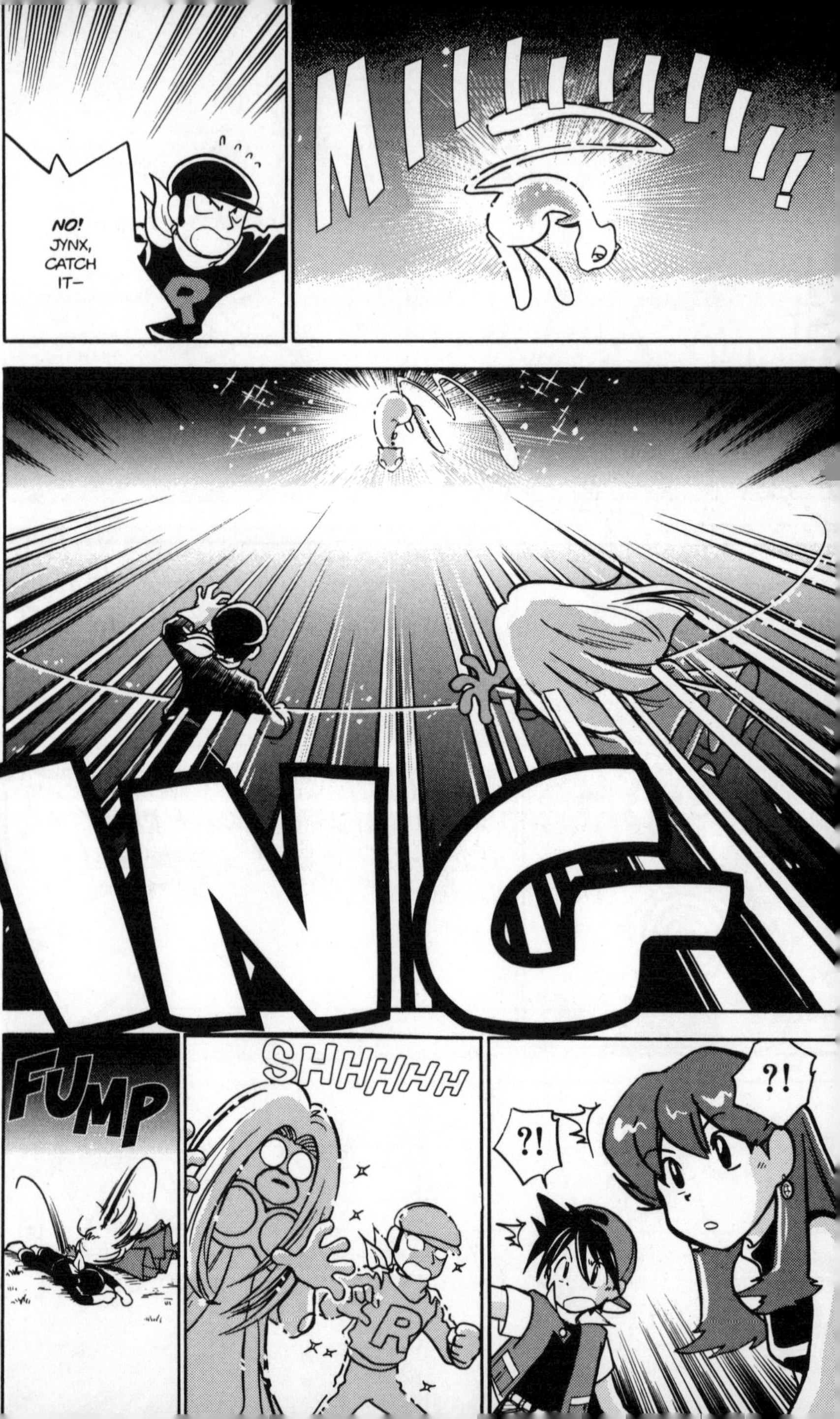
MIIIIIIIIII!
NO! JYNX, CATCH IT—
ING
?!
?!
SHHHHHH
FUMP

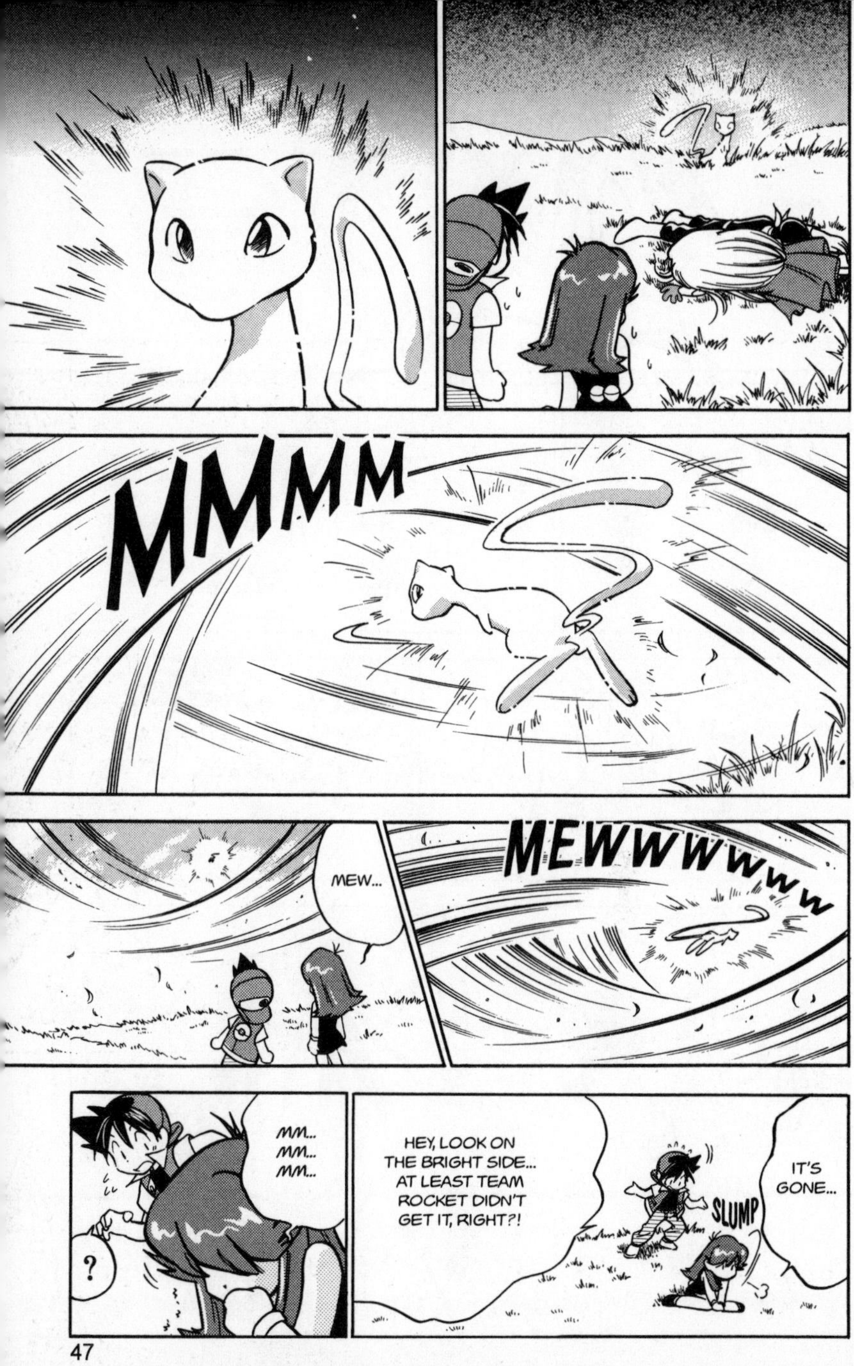
MMMMM
MEWWWWWWWW
MEW...
IT'S GONE...
SLUMP
HEY, LOOK ON THE BRIGHT SIDE... AT LEAST TEAM ROCKET DIDN'T GET IT, RIGHT?!
MM... MM... MM...
?

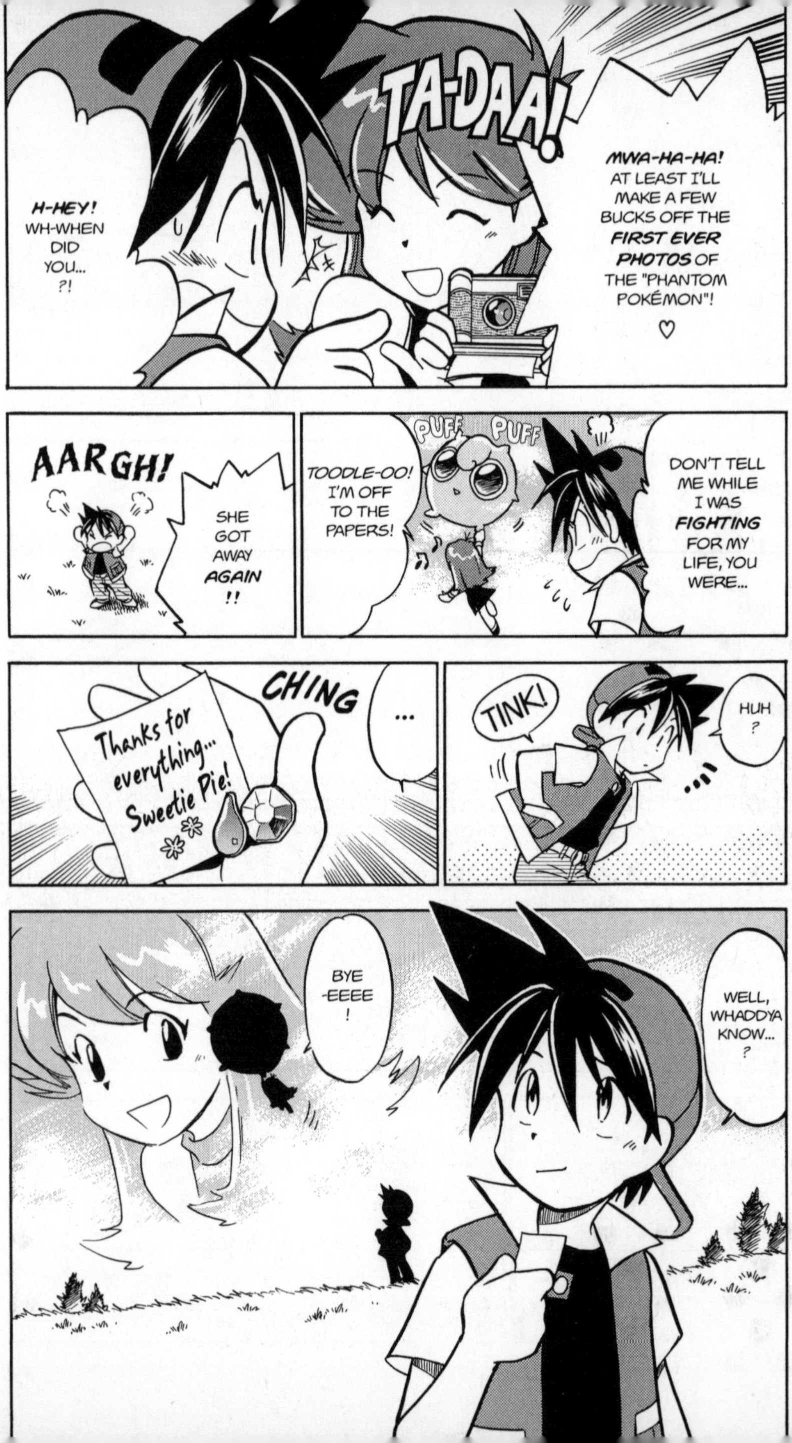
TA-DAA!
MWA-HA-HA! AT LEAST I'LL MAKE A FEW BUCKS OFF THE FIRST EVER PHOTOS OF THE "PHANTOM POKÉMON"! ♡
H-HEY! WH-WHEN DID YOU... ?!
PUFF PUFF
DON'T TELL ME WHILE I WAS FIGHTING FOR MY LIFE, YOU WERE...
TOODLE-OO! I'M OFF TO THE PAPERS!
AARGH!
SHE GOT AWAY AGAIN !!
HUH ?
TINK!
...
...
CHING
Thanks for everything... Sweetie Pie!
WELL, WHADDYA KNOW... ?
BYE -EEEE !

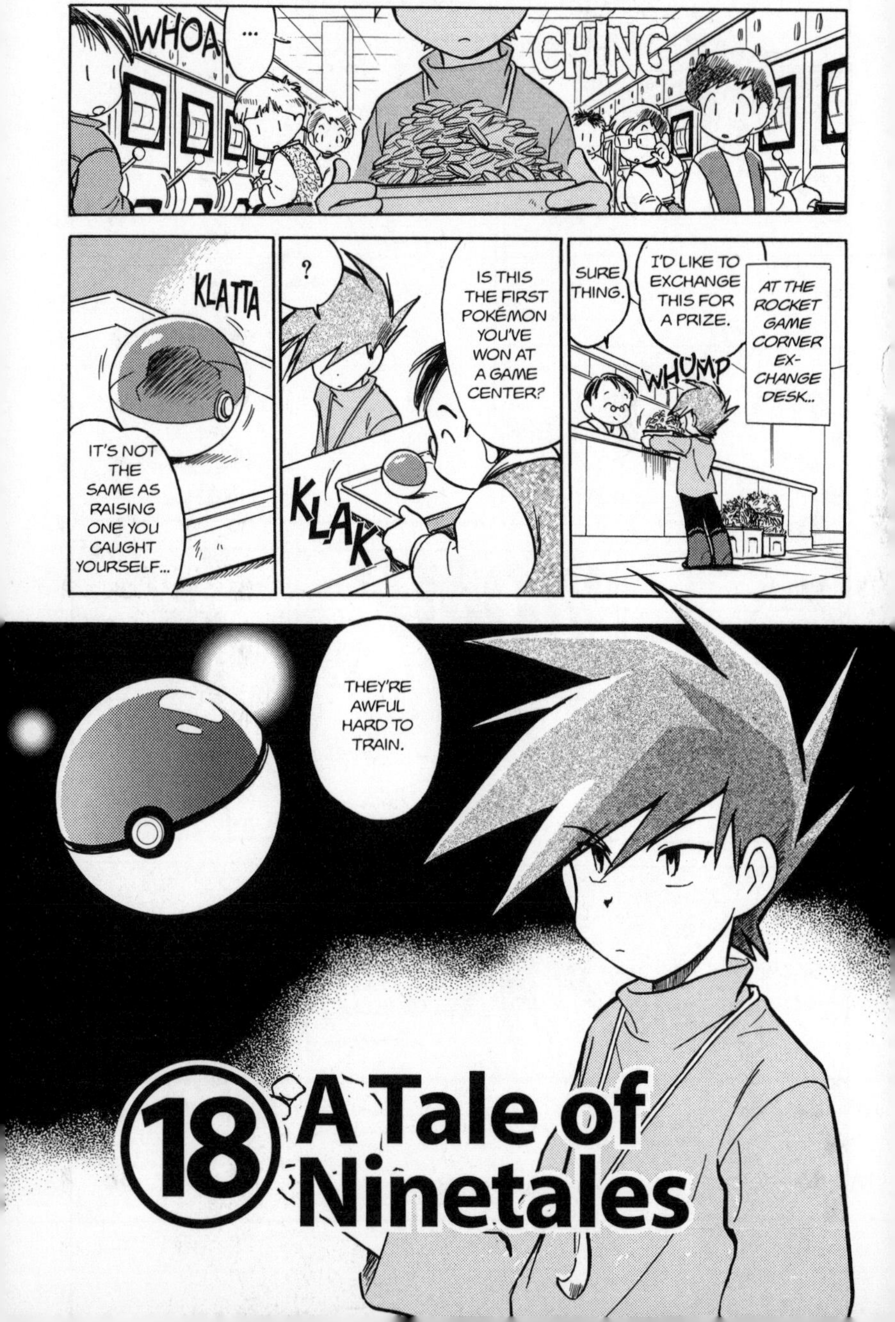
CHING
...
WHOA
AT THE ROCKET GAME CORNER EX-CHANGE DESK...
I'D LIKE TO EXCHANGE THIS FOR A PRIZE.
SURE THING.
WHUMP
IS THIS THE FIRST POKÉMON YOU'VE WON AT A GAME CENTER?
?
KLAK
KLATTA
IT'S NOT THE SAME AS RAISING ONE YOU CAUGHT YOURSELF...
THEY'RE AWFUL HARD TO TRAIN.

18 A Tale of Ninetales

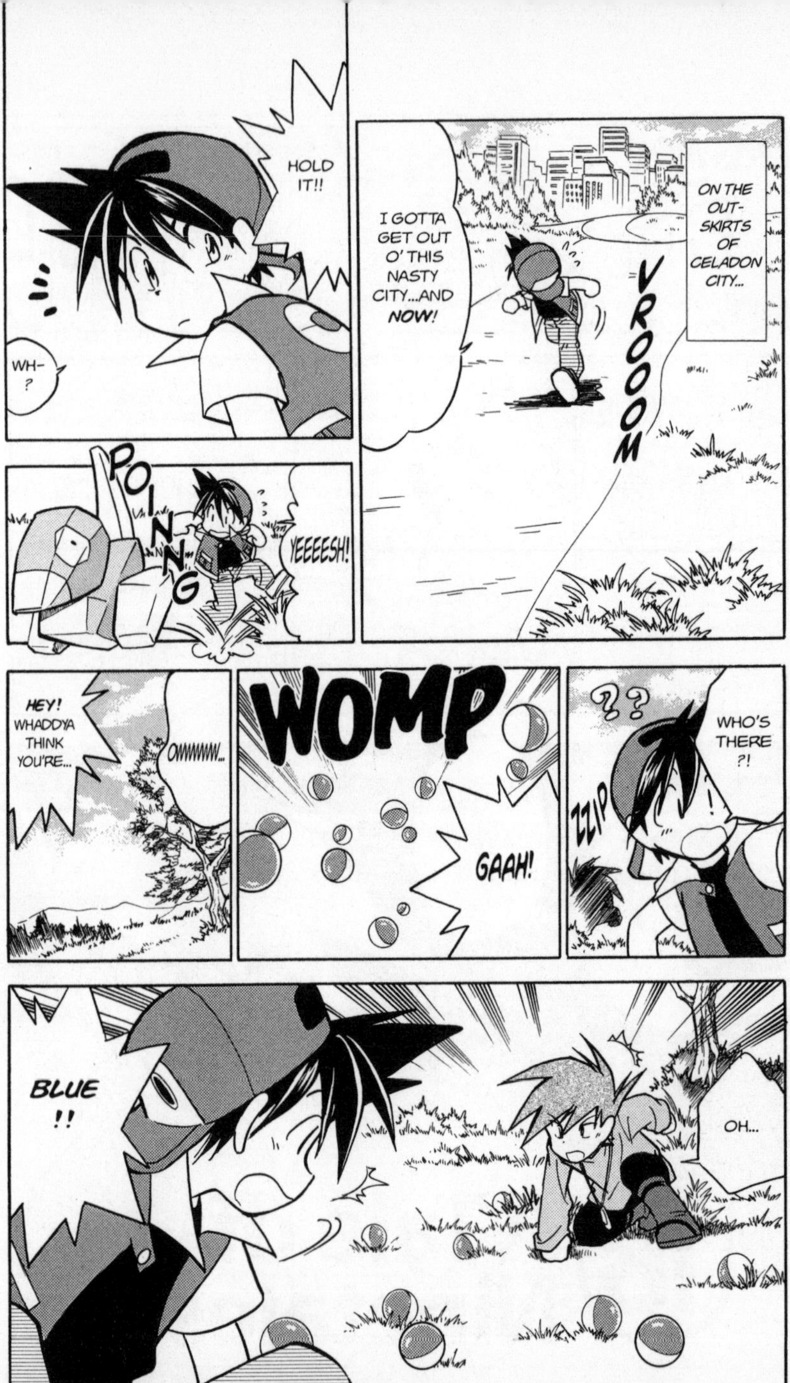
ON THE OUT-SKIRTS OF CELADON CITY...
I GOTTA GET OUT O' THIS NASTY CITY...AND NOW!
VROOOOM
HOLD IT!!
WH-?
POINNG
YEEEESH!
WHO'S THERE ?!
ZZIP
WOMP
GAAH!
HEY! WHADDYA THINK YOU'RE...
OWWWW...
OH...
BLUE !!

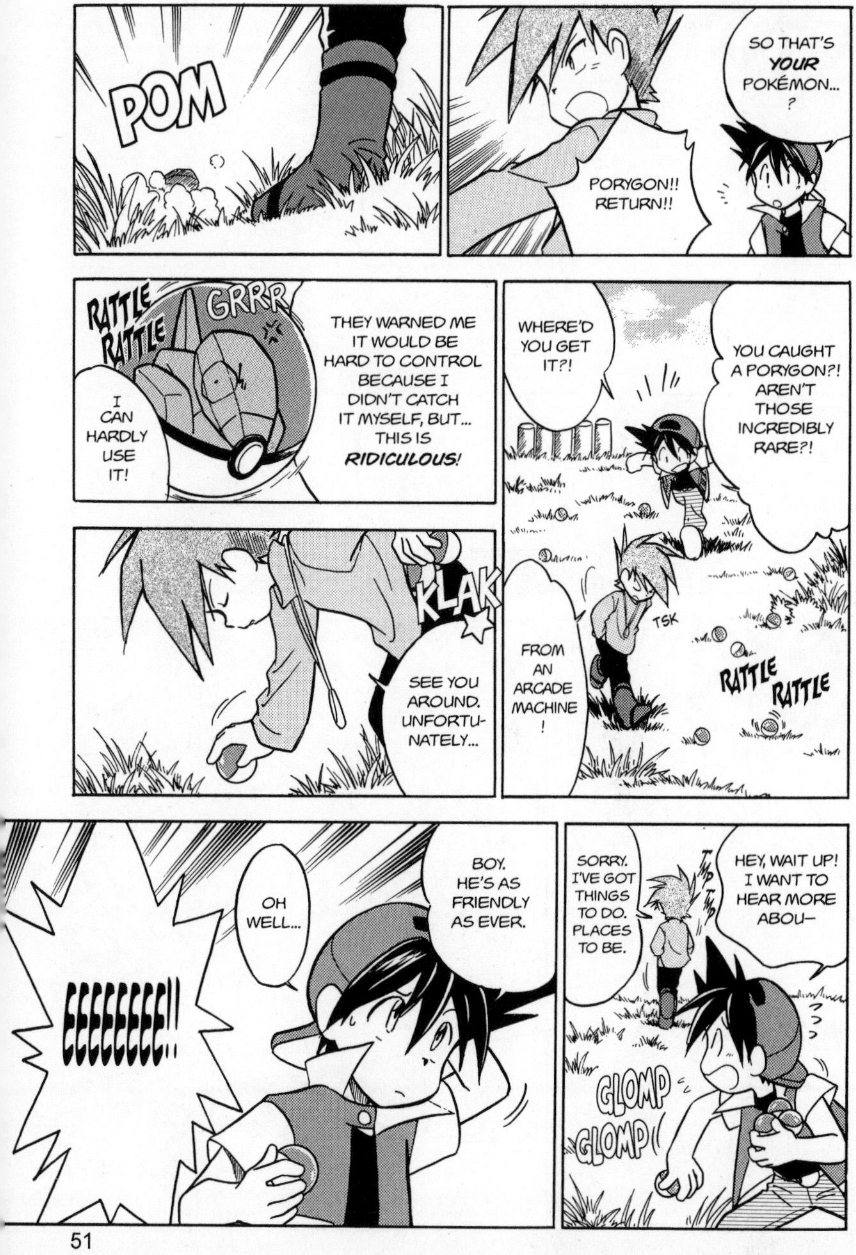
SO THAT'S *YOUR* POKÉMON...?
PORYGON!! RETURN!!
POM
YOU CAUGHT A PORYGON?! AREN'T THOSE INCREDIBLY RARE?!
WHERE'D YOU GET IT?!
FROM AN ARCADE MACHINE!
TSK
RATTLE RATTLE
THEY WARNED ME IT WOULD BE HARD TO CONTROL BECAUSE I DIDN'T CATCH IT MYSELF, BUT... THIS IS *RIDICULOUS*!
GRRR
RATTLE RATTLE
I CAN HARDLY USE IT!
KLAK
SEE YOU AROUND. UNFORTUNATELY...
HEY, WAIT UP! I WANT TO HEAR MORE ABOU—
TMP TMP
SORRY. I'VE GOT THINGS TO DO. PLACES TO BE.
GLOMP GLOMP
BOY. HE'S AS FRIENDLY AS EVER.
OH WELL...
EEEEEEEE!!

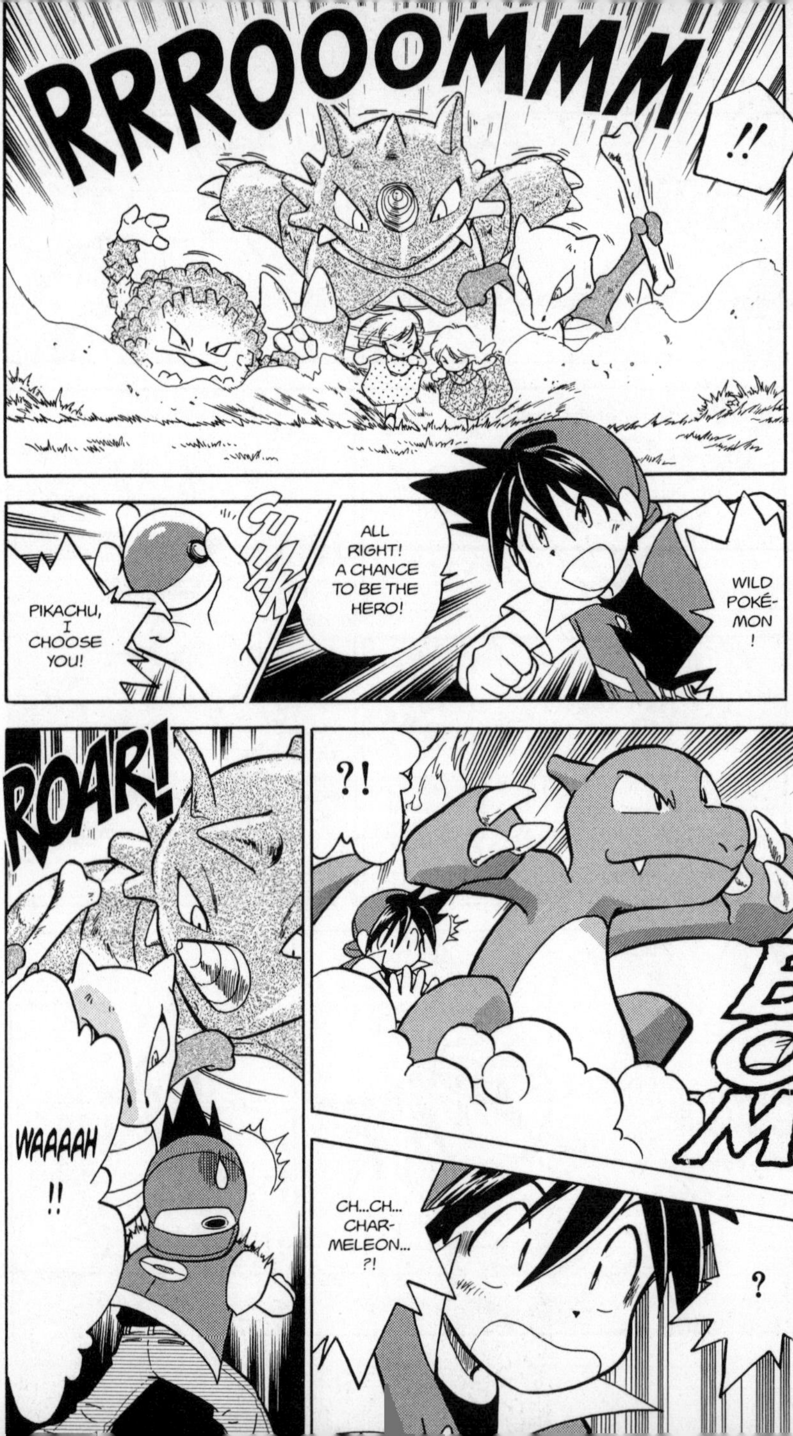
RRROOOMMM
!!
WILD POKÉMON!
ALL RIGHT! A CHANCE TO BE THE HERO!
CHAK
PIKACHU, I CHOOSE YOU!
?!
BOOM
?
CH...CH... CHARMELEON...?!
ROAR!
WAAAAH!!

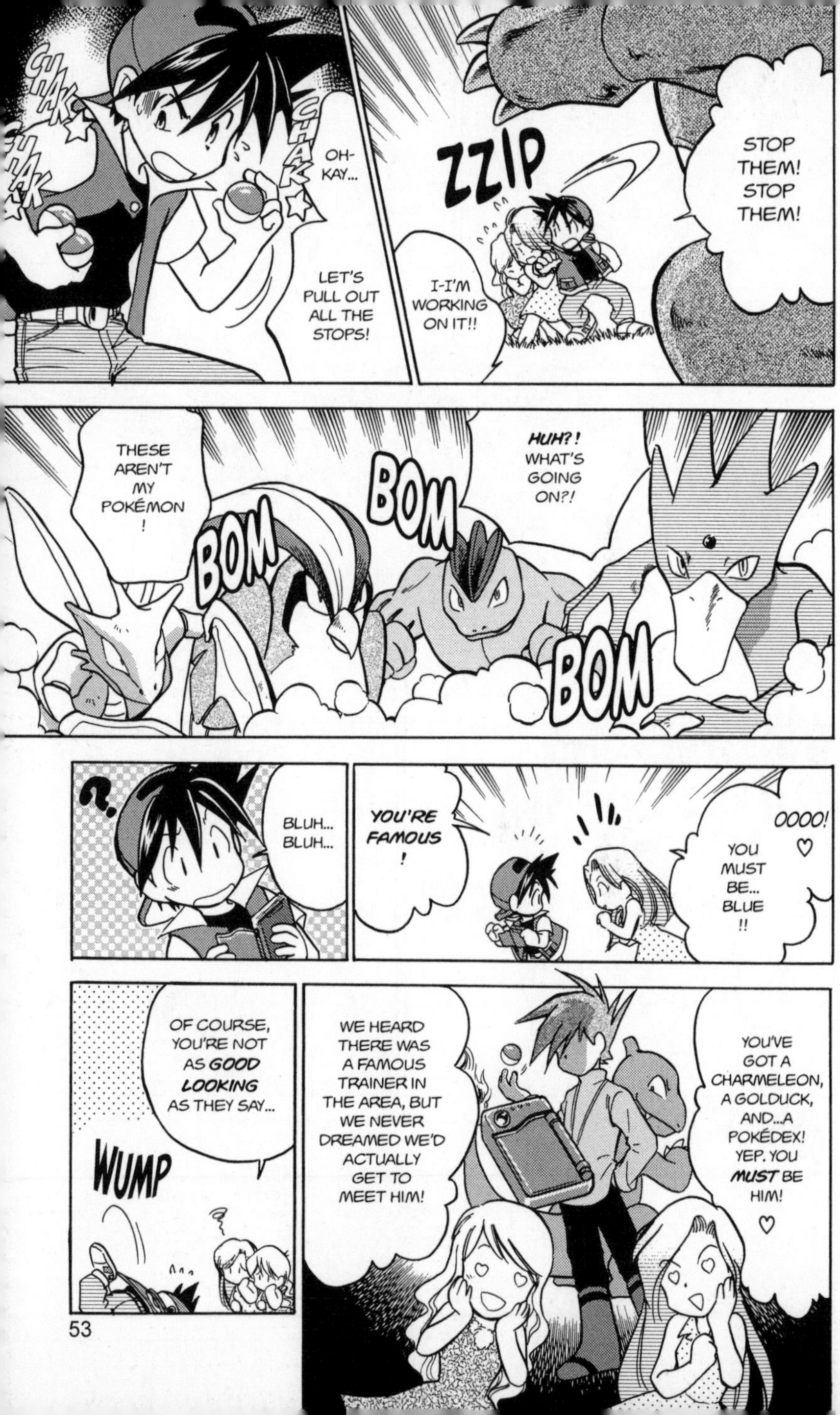
STOP THEM! STOP THEM!
ZZIP
I-I'M WORKING ON IT!!
CHAK CHAK CHAK CHAK
OH-KAY...
LET'S PULL OUT ALL THE STOPS!
HUH?! WHAT'S GOING ON?!
BOM
BOM
BOM
THESE AREN'T MY POKÉMON!
OOOO! ♡
YOU MUST BE... BLUE!!
YOU'RE FAMOUS!
BLUH... BLUH...
YOU'VE GOT A CHARMELEON, A GOLDUCK, AND...A POKÉDEX! YEP. YOU MUST BE HIM! ♡
WE HEARD THERE WAS A FAMOUS TRAINER IN THE AREA, BUT WE NEVER DREAMED WE'D ACTUALLY GET TO MEET HIM!
OF COURSE, YOU'RE NOT AS GOOD LOOKING AS THEY SAY...
WUMP

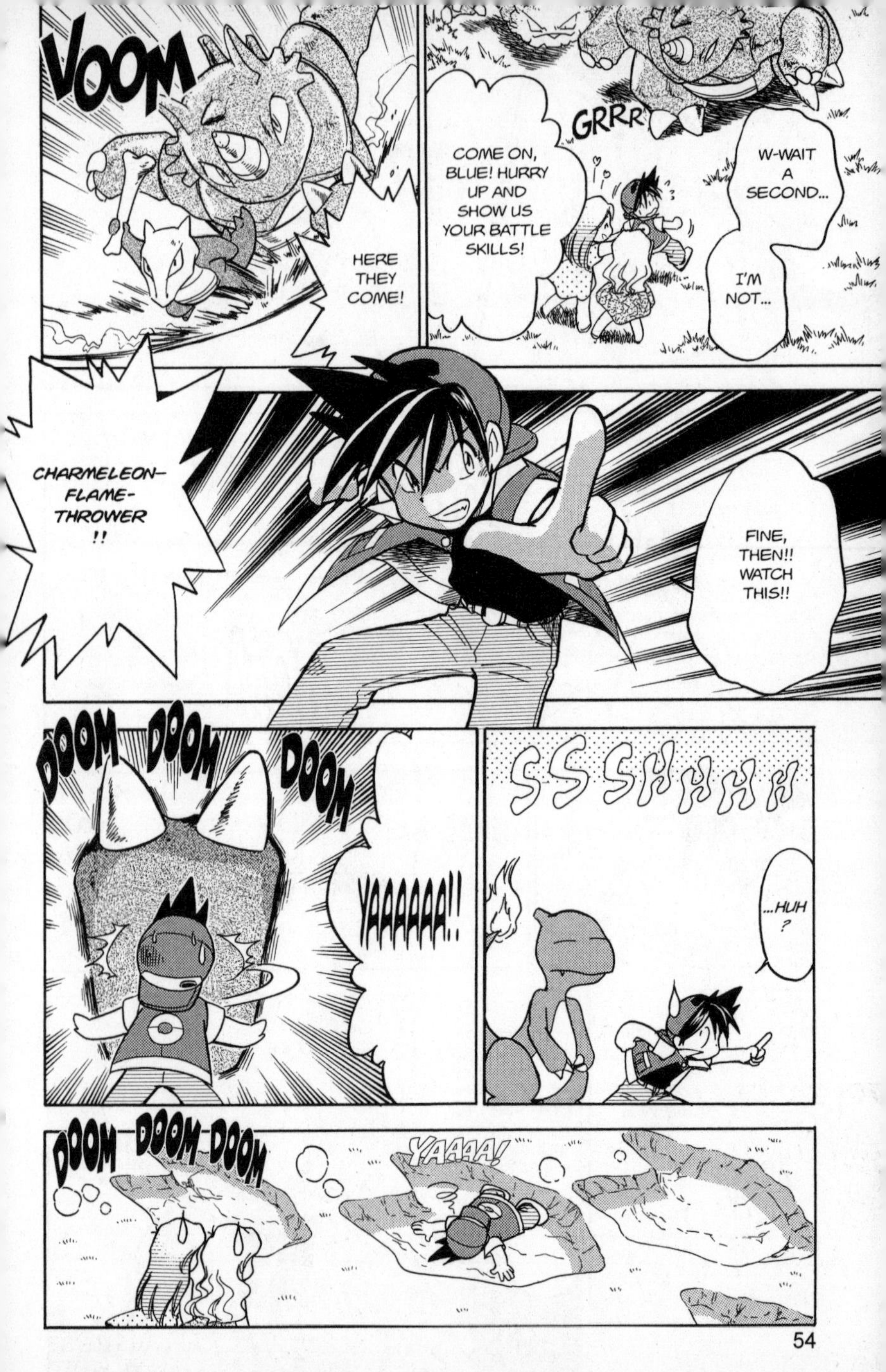
GRRR
COME ON, BLUE! HURRY UP AND SHOW US YOUR BATTLE SKILLS!
W-WAIT A SECOND...
I'M NOT...
VOOM
HERE THEY COME!
FINE, THEN!! WATCH THIS!!
CHARMELEON-FLAME-THROWER!!
SSSHHHHH
...HUH?
DOOM DOOM DOOM
YAAAAAA!!
YAAAA!
DOOM-DOOM-DOOM

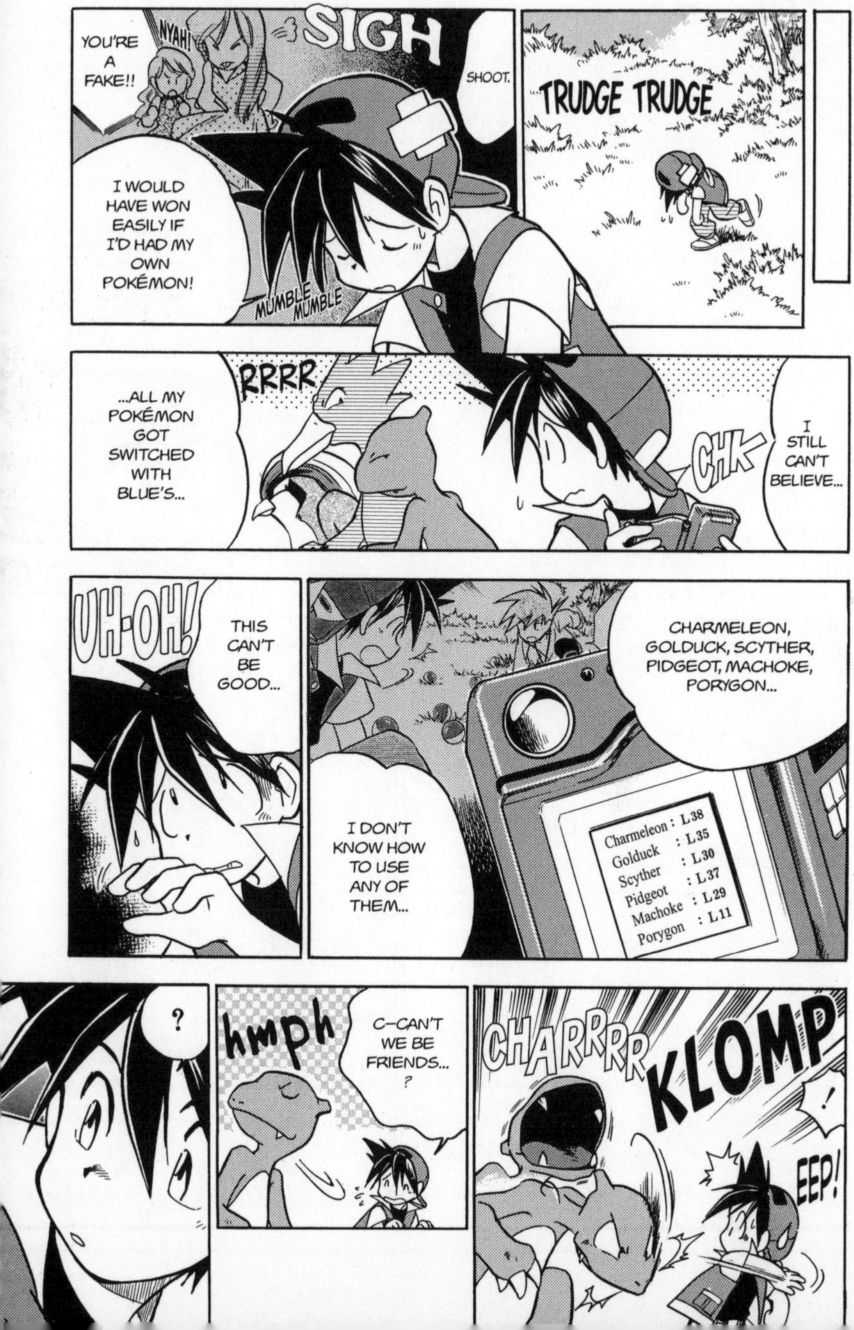

TRUDGE TRUDGE
SHOOT.
SIGH
NYAH!
YOU'RE A FAKE!!
I WOULD HAVE WON EASILY IF I'D HAD MY OWN POKÉMON!
MUMBLE MUMBLE
I STILL CAN'T BELIEVE...
CHK
RRRR
...ALL MY POKÉMON GOT SWITCHED WITH BLUE'S...
CHARMELEON, GOLDUCK, SCYTHER, PIDGEOT, MACHOKE, PORYGON...
Charmeleon : L38
Golduck : L35
Scyther : L30
Pidgeot : L37
Machoke : L29
Porygon : L11
I DON'T KNOW HOW TO USE ANY OF THEM...
THIS CAN'T BE GOOD...
UH-OH!
KLOMP
CHARRRR
!
EEP!
C-CAN'T WE BE FRIENDS...?
hmph
?

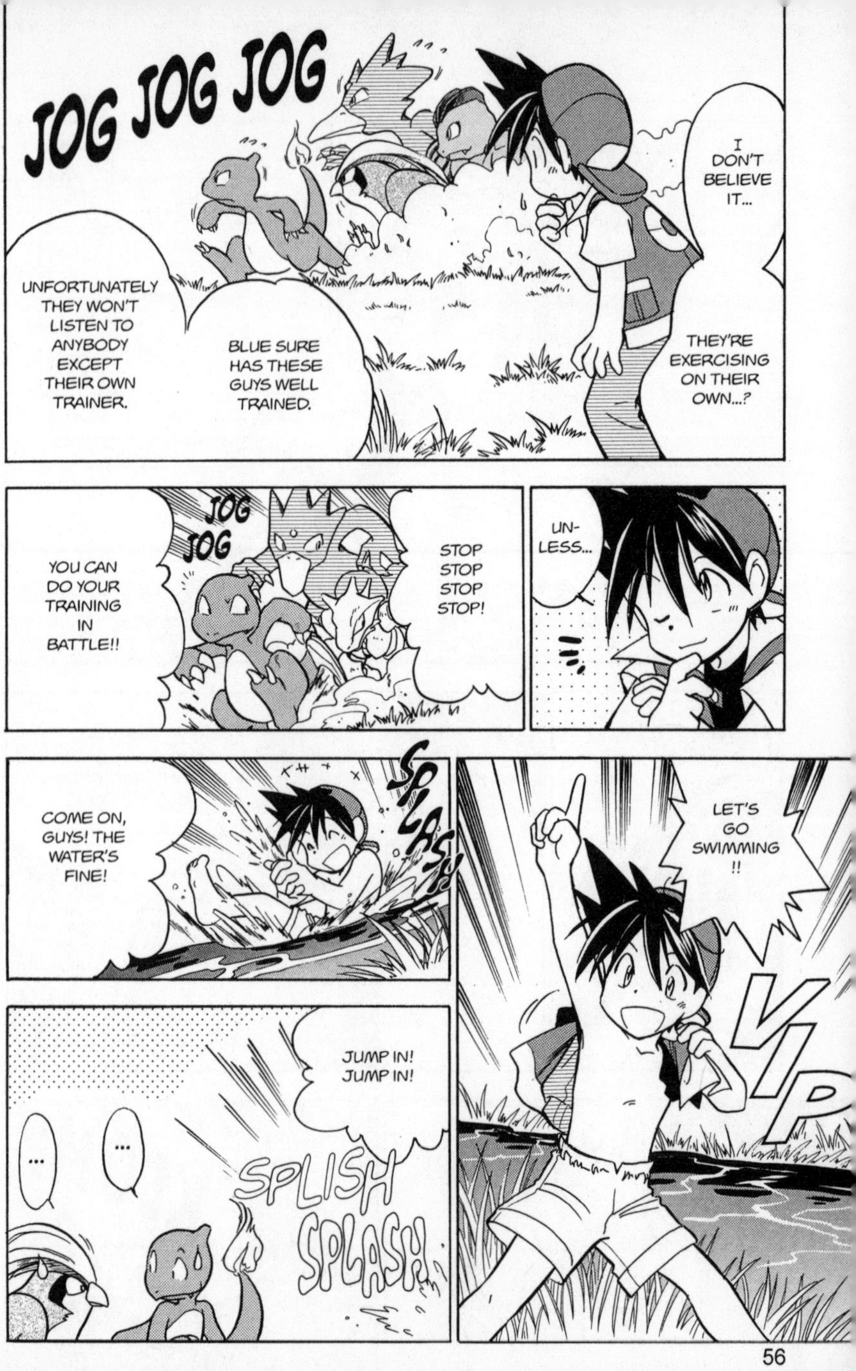
I DON'T BELIEVE IT...
THEY'RE EXERCISING ON THEIR OWN...?
JOG JOG JOG
BLUE SURE HAS THESE GUYS WELL TRAINED.
UNFORTUNATELY THEY WON'T LISTEN TO ANYBODY EXCEPT THEIR OWN TRAINER.
UN-LESS...
STOP STOP STOP STOP!
JOG JOG
YOU CAN DO YOUR TRAINING IN BATTLE!!
LET'S GO SWIMMING!!
VIP
SPLASH
COME ON, GUYS! THE WATER'S FINE!
JUMP IN! JUMP IN!
SPLISH SPLASH
...
...

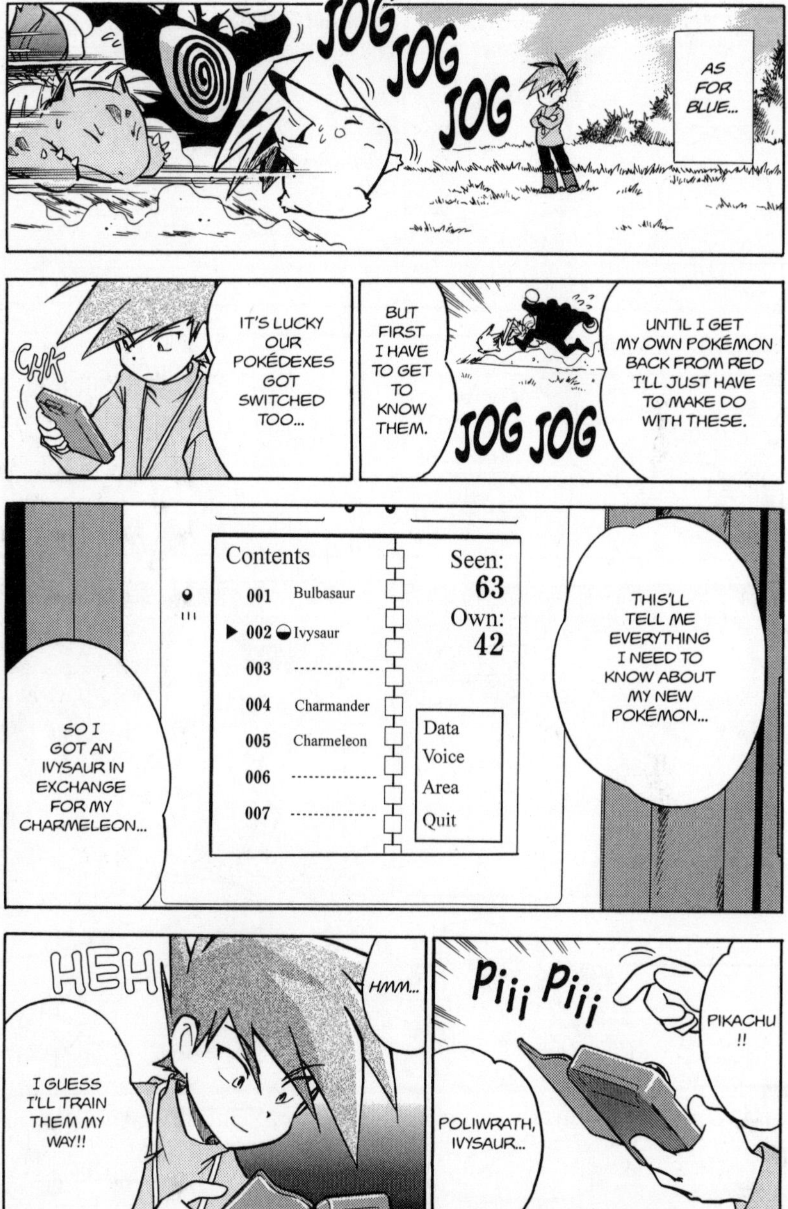
AS FOR BLUE...
JOG JOG JOG
UNTIL I GET MY OWN POKÉMON BACK FROM RED I'LL JUST HAVE TO MAKE DO WITH THESE.
BUT FIRST I HAVE TO GET TO KNOW THEM.
JOG JOG
IT'S LUCKY OUR POKÉDEXES GOT SWITCHED TOO...
CHK
THIS'LL TELL ME EVERYTHING I NEED TO KNOW ABOUT MY NEW POKÉMON...
Contents
001 Bulbasaur
002 Ivysaur
003
004 Charmander
005 Charmeleon
006
007
Seen: 63
Own: 42
Data
Voice
Area
Quit
SO I GOT AN IVYSAUR IN EXCHANGE FOR MY CHARMELEON...
PIKACHU !!
Piii Piii
POLIWRATH, IVYSAUR...
HMM...
HEH
I GUESS I'LL TRAIN THEM MY WAY!!

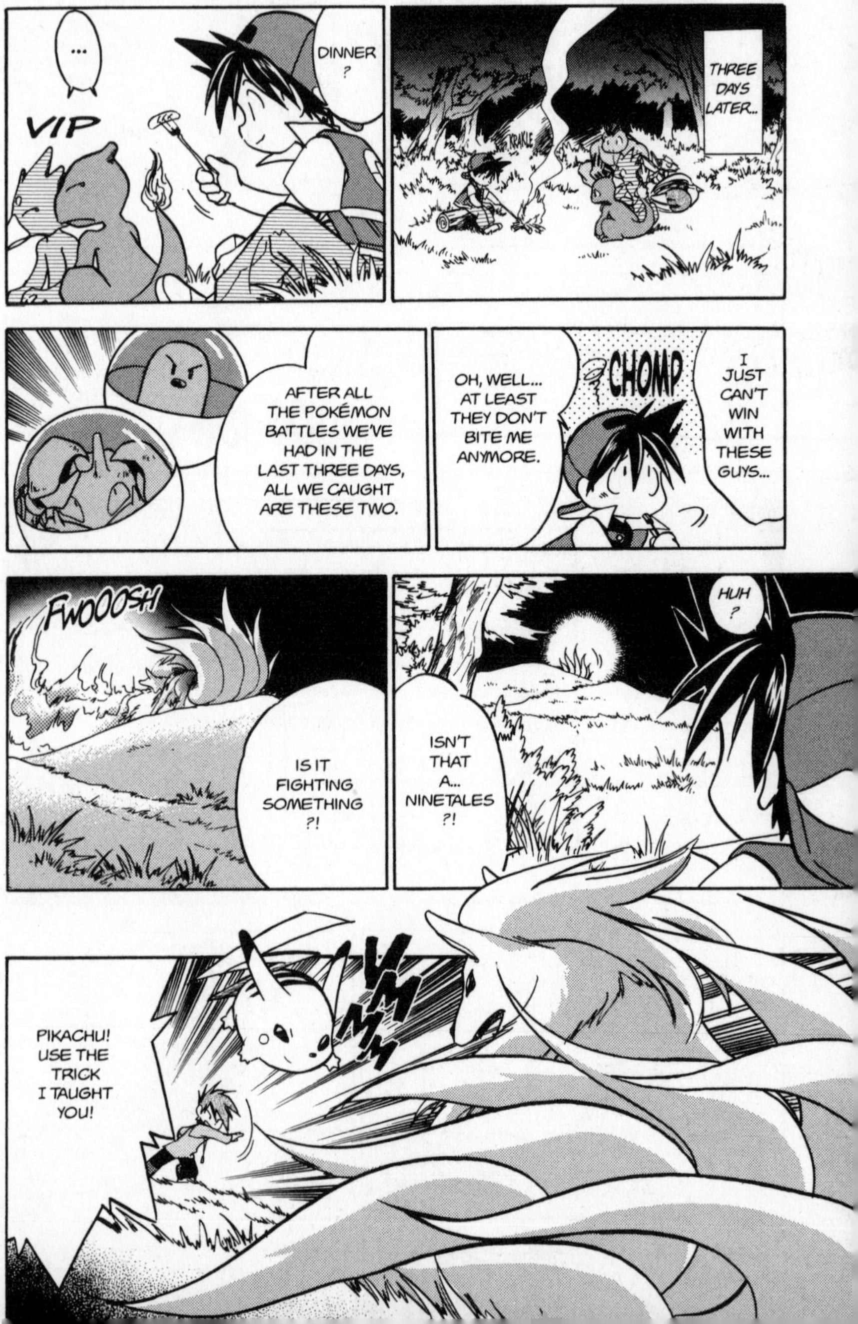
THREE DAYS LATER...
KRAKLE
DINNER ?
...
VIP
I JUST CAN'T WIN WITH THESE GUYS...
CHOMP
OH, WELL... AT LEAST THEY DON'T BITE ME ANYMORE.
AFTER ALL THE POKÉMON BATTLES WE'VE HAD IN THE LAST THREE DAYS, ALL WE CAUGHT ARE THESE TWO.
HUH ?
ISN'T THAT A... NINETALES ?!
FWOOOSH
IS IT FIGHTING SOMETHING ?!
VMMM
PIKACHU! USE THE TRICK I TAUGHT YOU!

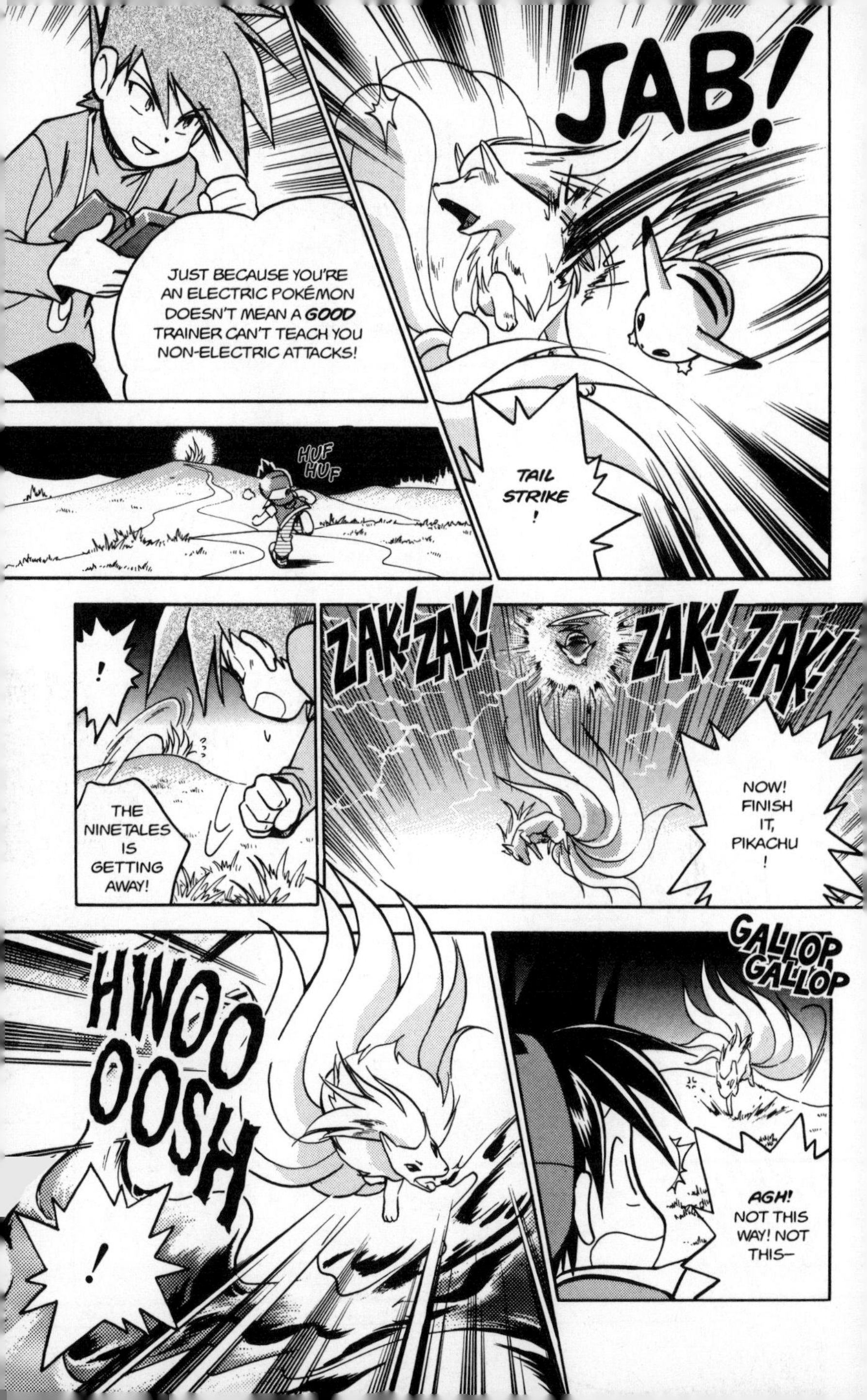
JAB!
TAIL STRIKE!
JUST BECAUSE YOU'RE AN ELECTRIC POKÉMON DOESN'T MEAN A **GOOD** TRAINER CAN'T TEACH YOU NON-ELECTRIC ATTACKS!
HUF HUF
ZAK! ZAK! ZAK! ZAK!
NOW! FINISH IT, PIKACHU!
!
THE NINETALES IS GETTING AWAY!
GALLOP GALLOP
AGH! NOT THIS WAY! NOT THIS—
HWOOOOSH
!

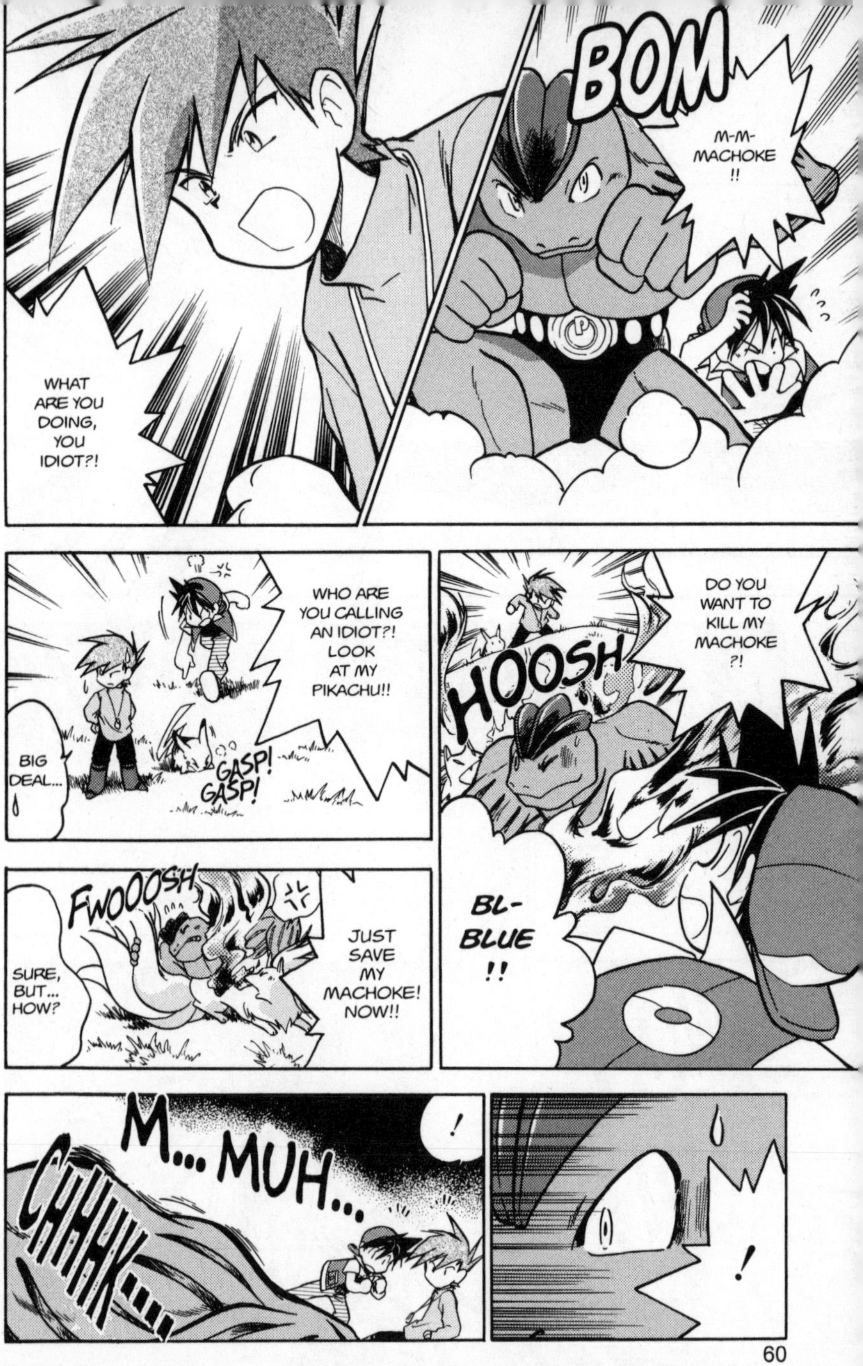
BOM
M-M-MACHOKE!!
WHAT ARE YOU DOING, YOU IDIOT?!
DO YOU WANT TO KILL MY MACHOKE?!
HOOSH
BL-BLUE!!
WHO ARE YOU CALLING AN IDIOT?! LOOK AT MY PIKACHU!!
GASP! GASP!
BIG DEAL...
JUST SAVE MY MACHOKE! NOW!!
FWOOOSH
SURE, BUT... HOW?
!
M... MUH...
!
CHHHK....

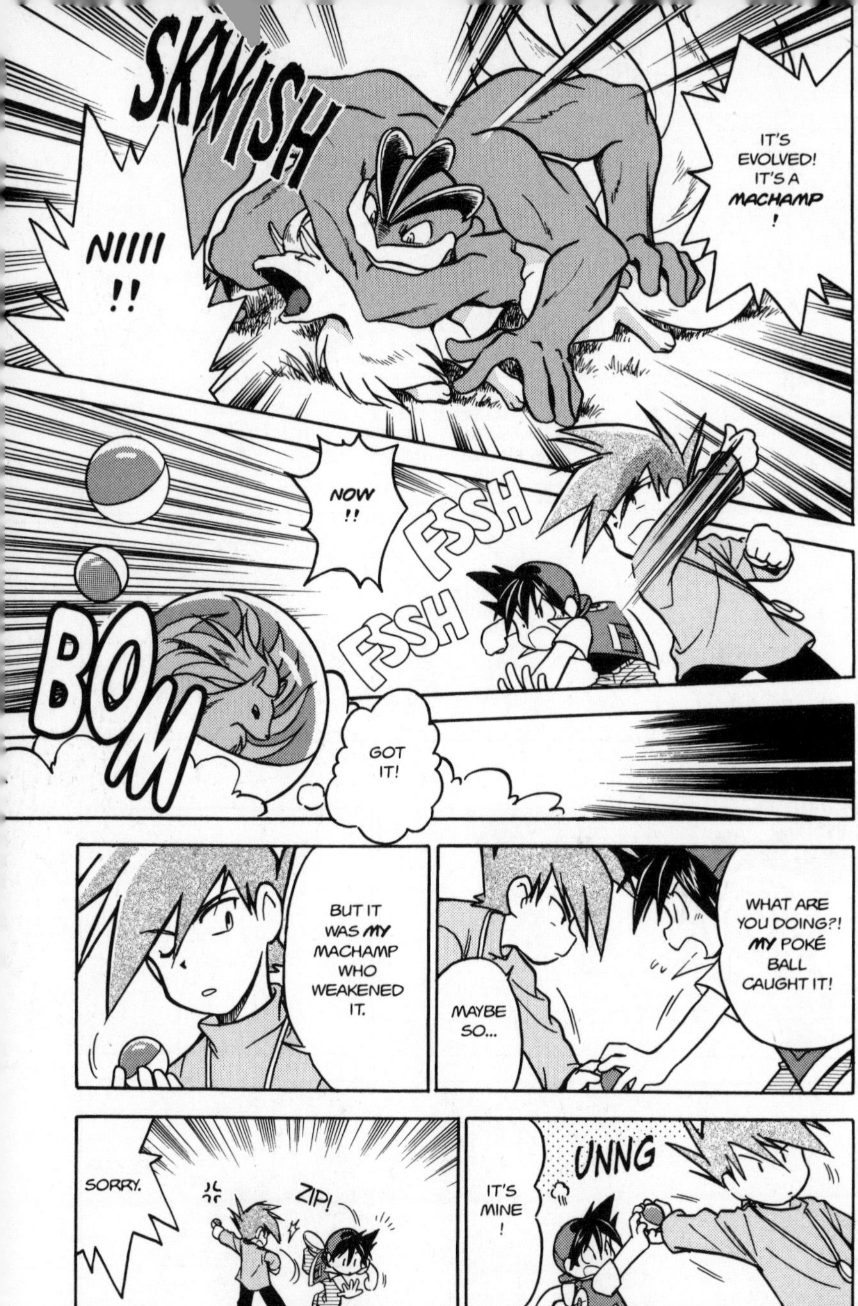
IT'S EVOLVED! IT'S A MACHAMP!
SKWISH
NIIII!!
NOW!!
FSSH
FSSH
BOM
GOT IT!
WHAT ARE YOU DOING?! MY POKÉ BALL CAUGHT IT!
MAYBE SO...
BUT IT WAS MY MACHAMP WHO WEAKENED IT.
UNNG
IT'S MINE!
ZIP!
SORRY.

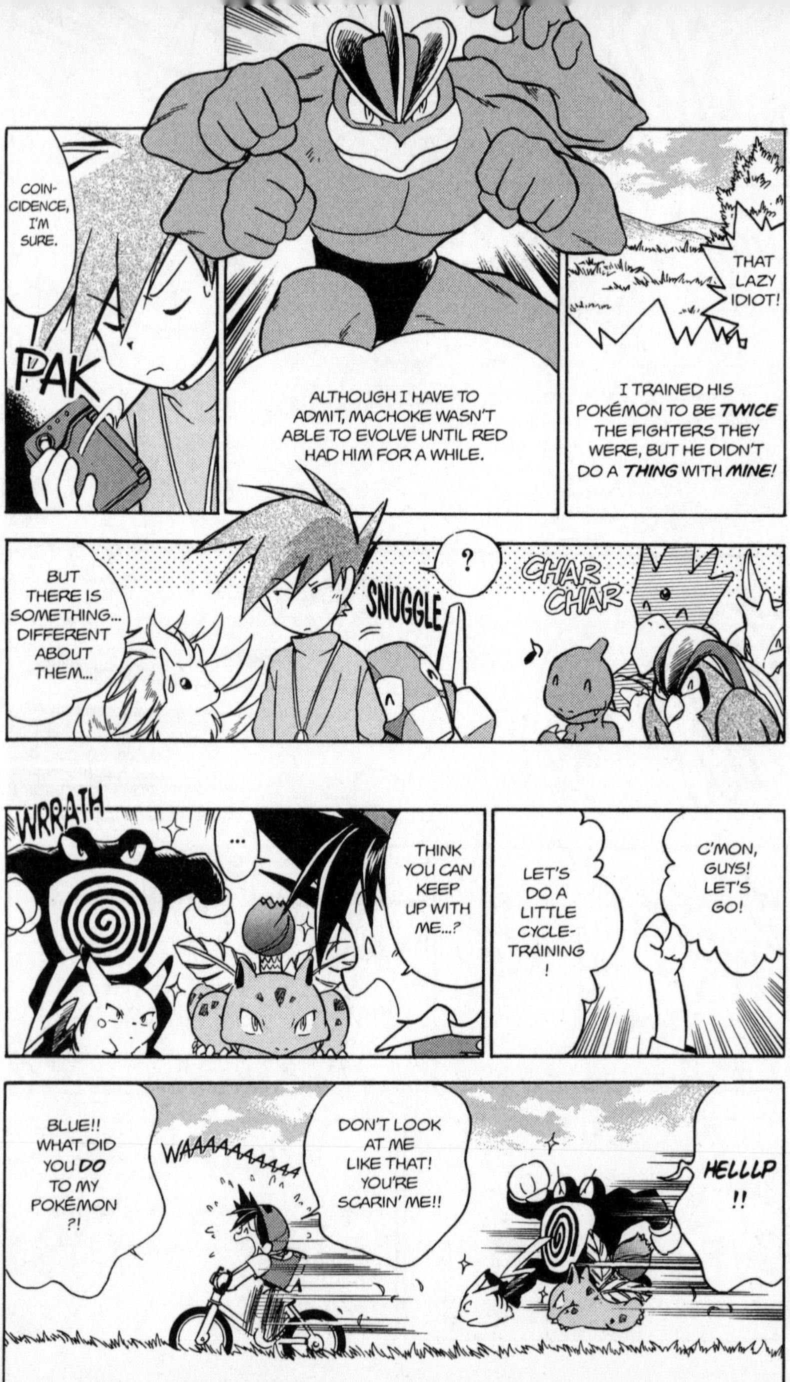
THAT LAZY IDIOT!
I TRAINED HIS POKéMON TO BE **TWICE** THE FIGHTERS THEY WERE, BUT HE DIDN'T DO A **THING** WITH **MINE**!
ALTHOUGH I HAVE TO ADMIT, MACHOKE WASN'T ABLE TO EVOLVE UNTIL RED HAD HIM FOR A WHILE.
COIN-CIDENCE, I'M SURE.
PAK
CHAR CHAR
?
SNUGGLE
BUT THERE IS SOMETHING... DIFFERENT ABOUT THEM...
C'MON, GUYS! LET'S GO!
LET'S DO A LITTLE CYCLE-TRAINING!
THINK YOU CAN KEEP UP WITH ME...?
...
WRRATH
HELLLP!!
DON'T LOOK AT ME LIKE THAT! YOU'RE SCARIN' ME!!
WAAAAAAAAAA
BLUE!! WHAT DID YOU **DO** TO MY POKéMON?!

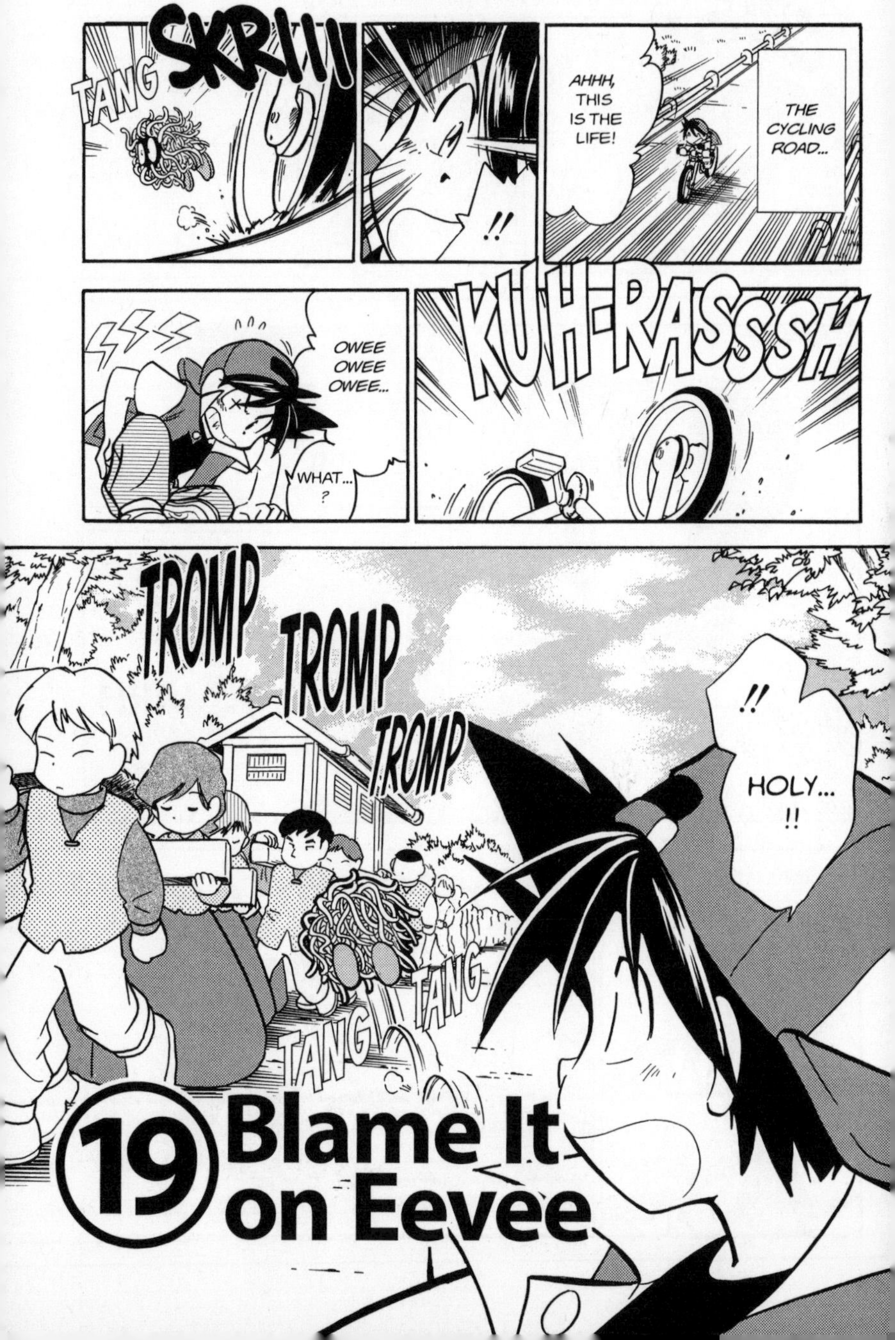
THE CYCLING ROAD...
AHHH, THIS IS THE LIFE!
!!
TANG
SKRIII
KUH-RASSSH
OWEE OWEE OWEE...
WHAT... ?
!!
HOLY... !!
TROMP
TROMP
TROMP
TANG
TANG
19 Blame It on Eevee

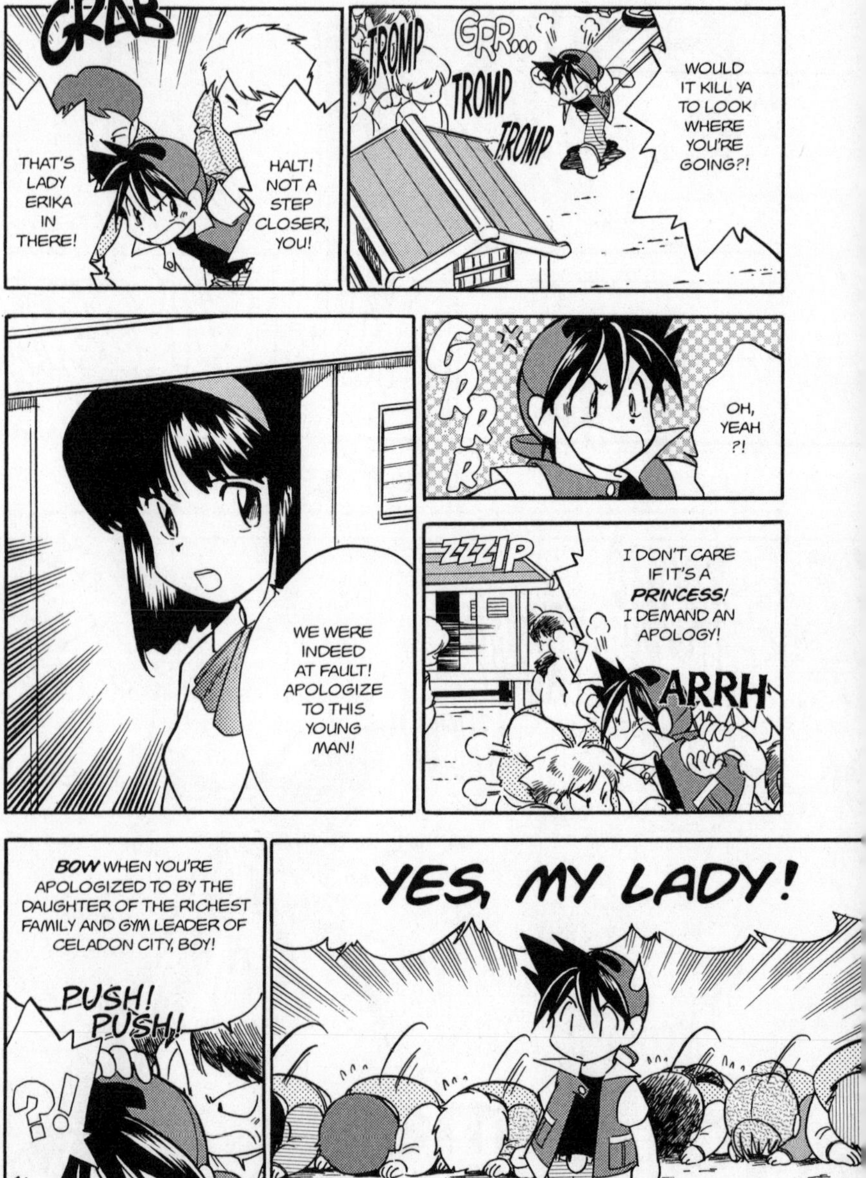
WOULD IT KILL YA TO LOOK WHERE YOU'RE GOING?!
GRR...
TROMP
TROMP
TROMP
HALT! NOT A STEP CLOSER, YOU!
GRAB
THAT'S LADY ERIKA IN THERE!
OH, YEAH?!
GRRR
I DON'T CARE IF IT'S A *PRINCESS*! I DEMAND AN APOLOGY!
ZZZIP
ARRH
WE WERE INDEED AT FAULT! APOLOGIZE TO THIS YOUNG MAN!
YES, MY LADY!
BOW WHEN YOU'RE APOLOGIZED TO BY THE DAUGHTER OF THE RICHEST FAMILY AND GYM LEADER OF CELADON CITY, BOY!
PUSH! PUSH!
?!

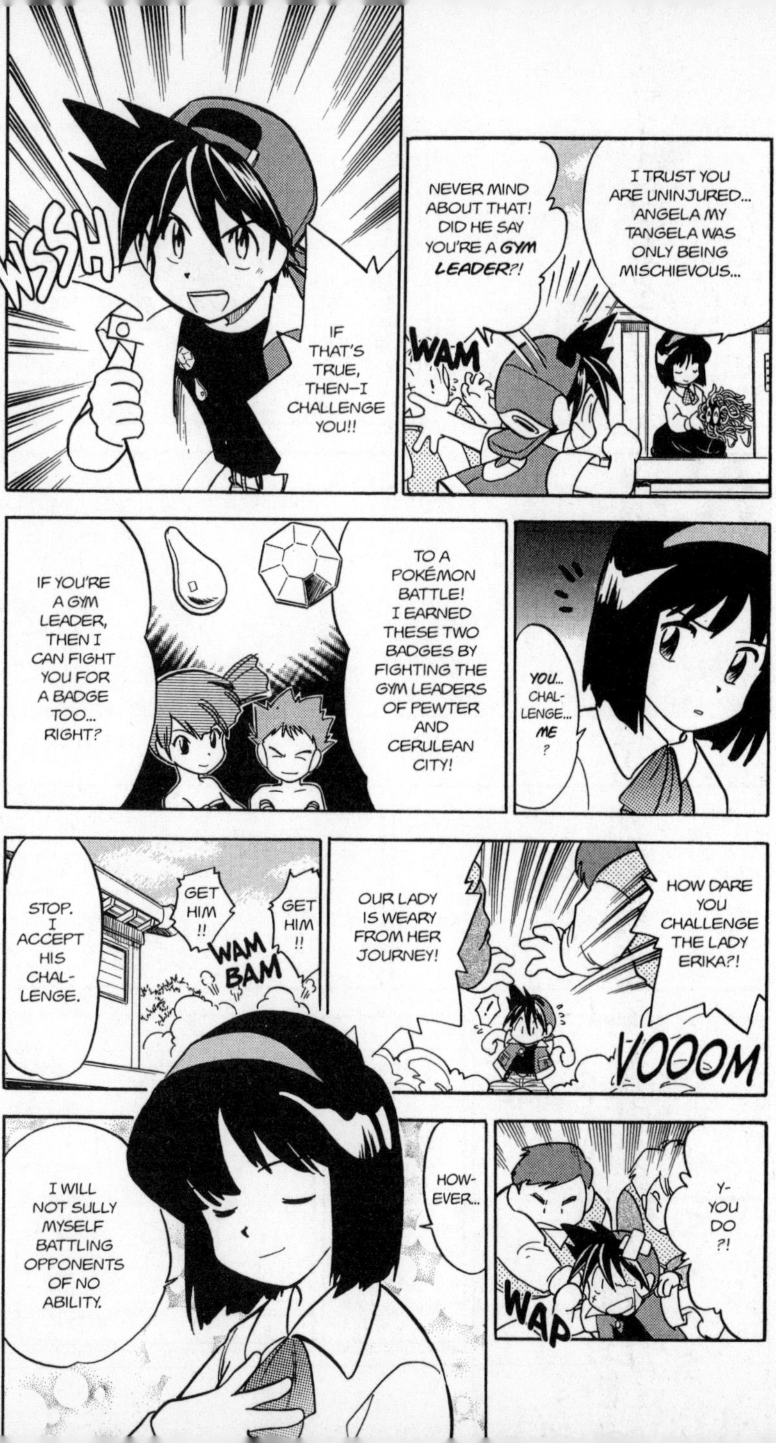
I TRUST YOU ARE UNINJURED... ANGELA MY TANGELA WAS ONLY BEING MISCHIEVOUS...
NEVER MIND ABOUT THAT! DID HE SAY YOU'RE A GYM LEADER?!
WAM
WSSH
IF THAT'S TRUE, THEN—I CHALLENGE YOU!!
YOU... CHAL-LENGE... ME?
TO A POKÉMON BATTLE! I EARNED THESE TWO BADGES BY FIGHTING THE GYM LEADERS OF PEWTER AND CERULEAN CITY!
IF YOU'RE A GYM LEADER, THEN I CAN FIGHT YOU FOR A BADGE TOO... RIGHT?
HOW DARE YOU CHALLENGE THE LADY ERIKA?!
OUR LADY IS WEARY FROM HER JOURNEY!
VOOOM
GET HIM!!
GET HIM!!
WAM BAM
STOP. I ACCEPT HIS CHAL-LENGE.
Y-YOU DO?!
WAP
HOW-EVER...
I WILL NOT SULLY MYSELF BATTLING OPPONENTS OF NO ABILITY.

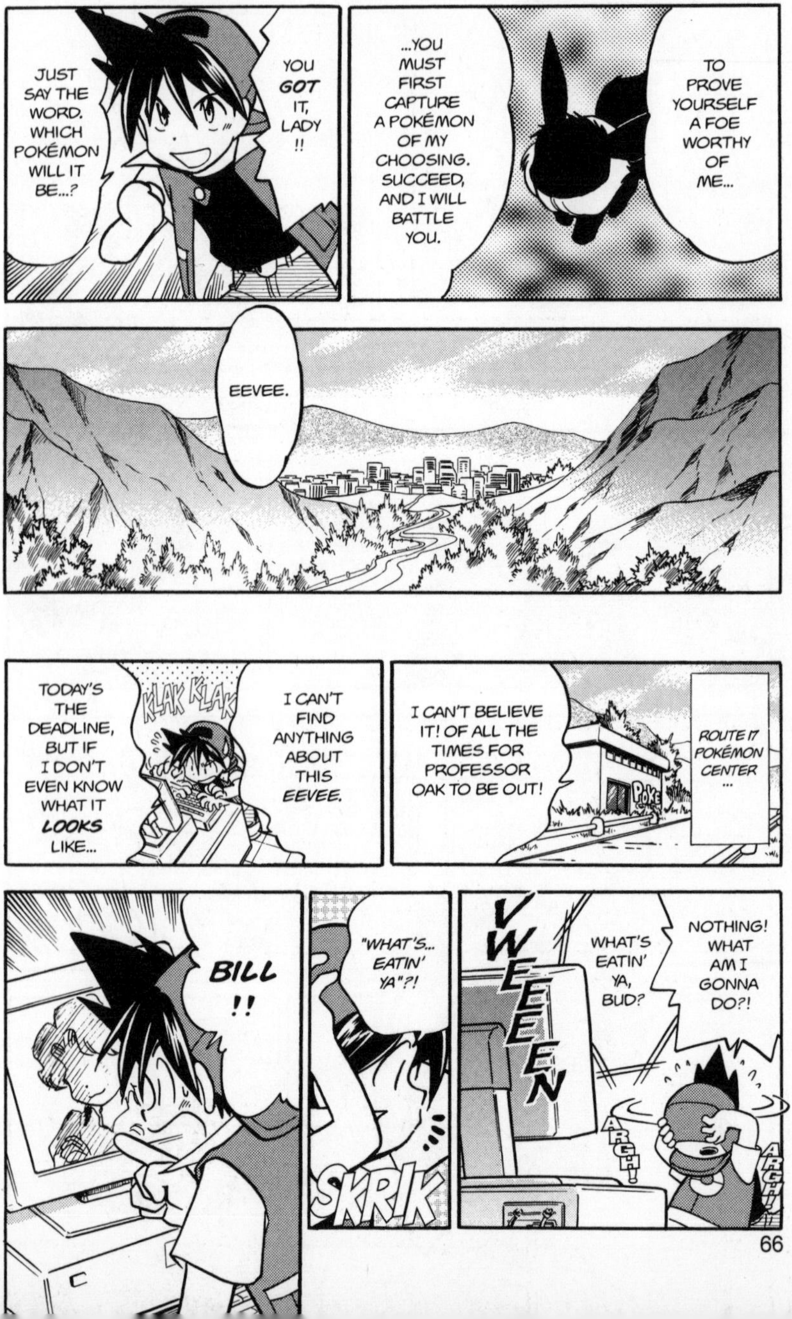
TO PROVE YOURSELF A FOE WORTHY OF ME...
...YOU MUST FIRST CAPTURE A POKÉMON OF MY CHOOSING. SUCCEED, AND I WILL BATTLE YOU.
YOU GOT IT, LADY!!
JUST SAY THE WORD. WHICH POKÉMON WILL IT BE...?
EEVEE.
ROUTE 17 POKÉMON CENTER ...
I CAN'T BELIEVE IT! OF ALL THE TIMES FOR PROFESSOR OAK TO BE OUT!
POKE
I CAN'T FIND ANYTHING ABOUT THIS EEVEE.
KLAK KLAK
TODAY'S THE DEADLINE, BUT IF I DON'T EVEN KNOW WHAT IT LOOKS LIKE...
NOTHING! WHAT AM I GONNA DO?!
WHAT'S EATIN' YA, BUD?
VWEEEEN
ARGH!
ARGH!
"WHAT'S... EATIN' YA"?!
SKRIK
BILL!!

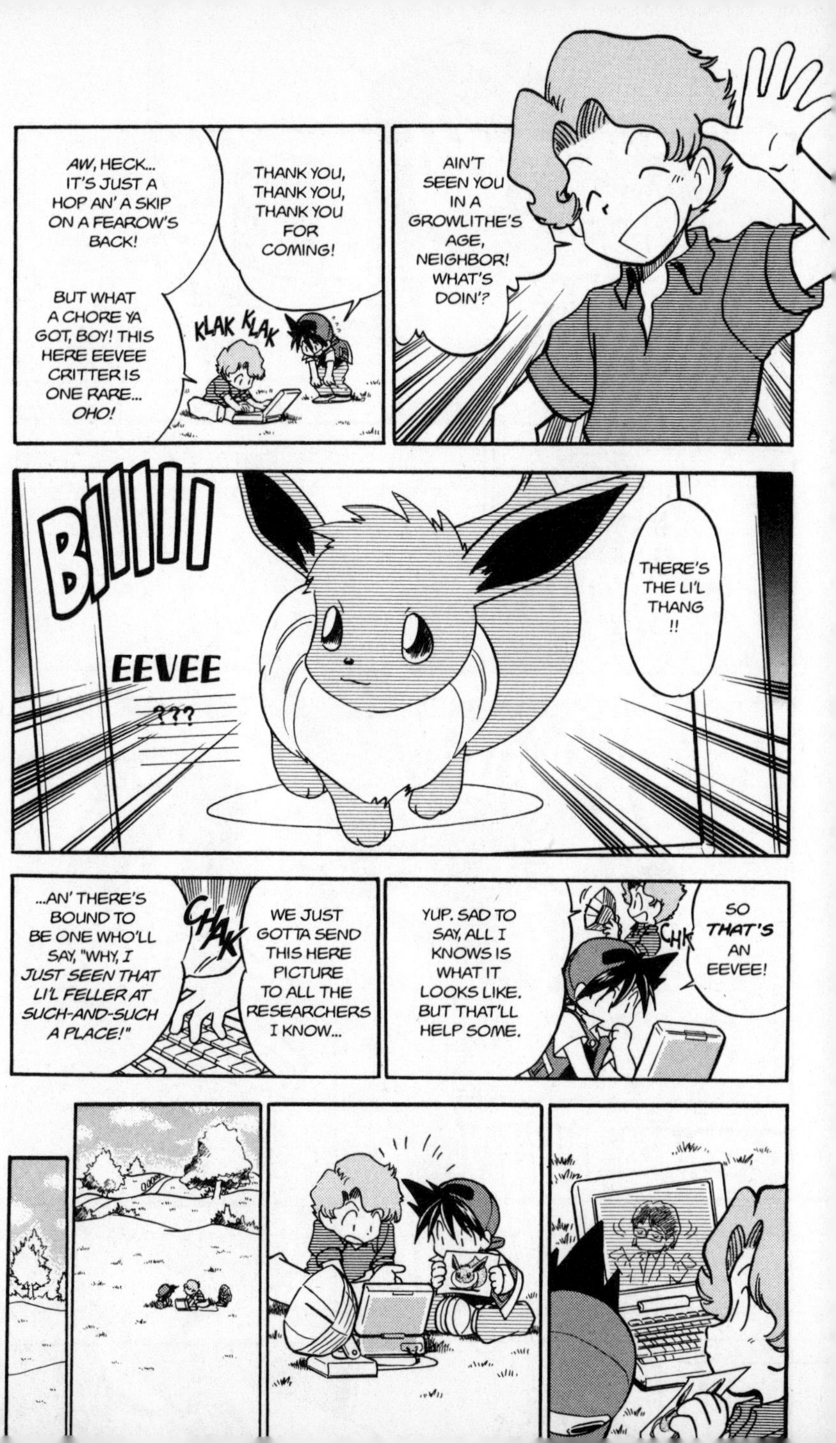
AIN'T SEEN YOU IN A GROWLITHE'S AGE, NEIGHBOR! WHAT'S DOIN'?
THANK YOU, THANK YOU, THANK YOU FOR COMING!
AW, HECK... IT'S JUST A HOP AN' A SKIP ON A FEAROW'S BACK!
KLAK KLAK
BUT WHAT A CHORE YA GOT, BOY! THIS HERE EEVEE CRITTER IS ONE RARE... *OHO!*
THERE'S THE LI'L THANG !!
BIIIIII
EEVEE
???
SO *THAT'S* AN EEVEE!
CHK
YUP. SAD TO SAY, ALL I KNOWS IS WHAT IT LOOKS LIKE. BUT THAT'LL HELP SOME.
WE JUST GOTTA SEND THIS HERE PICTURE TO ALL THE RESEARCHERS I KNOW...
CHAK
...AN' THERE'S BOUND TO BE ONE WHO'LL SAY, "WHY, *I JUST SEEN THAT LI'L FELLER AT SUCH-AND-SUCH A PLACE!*"

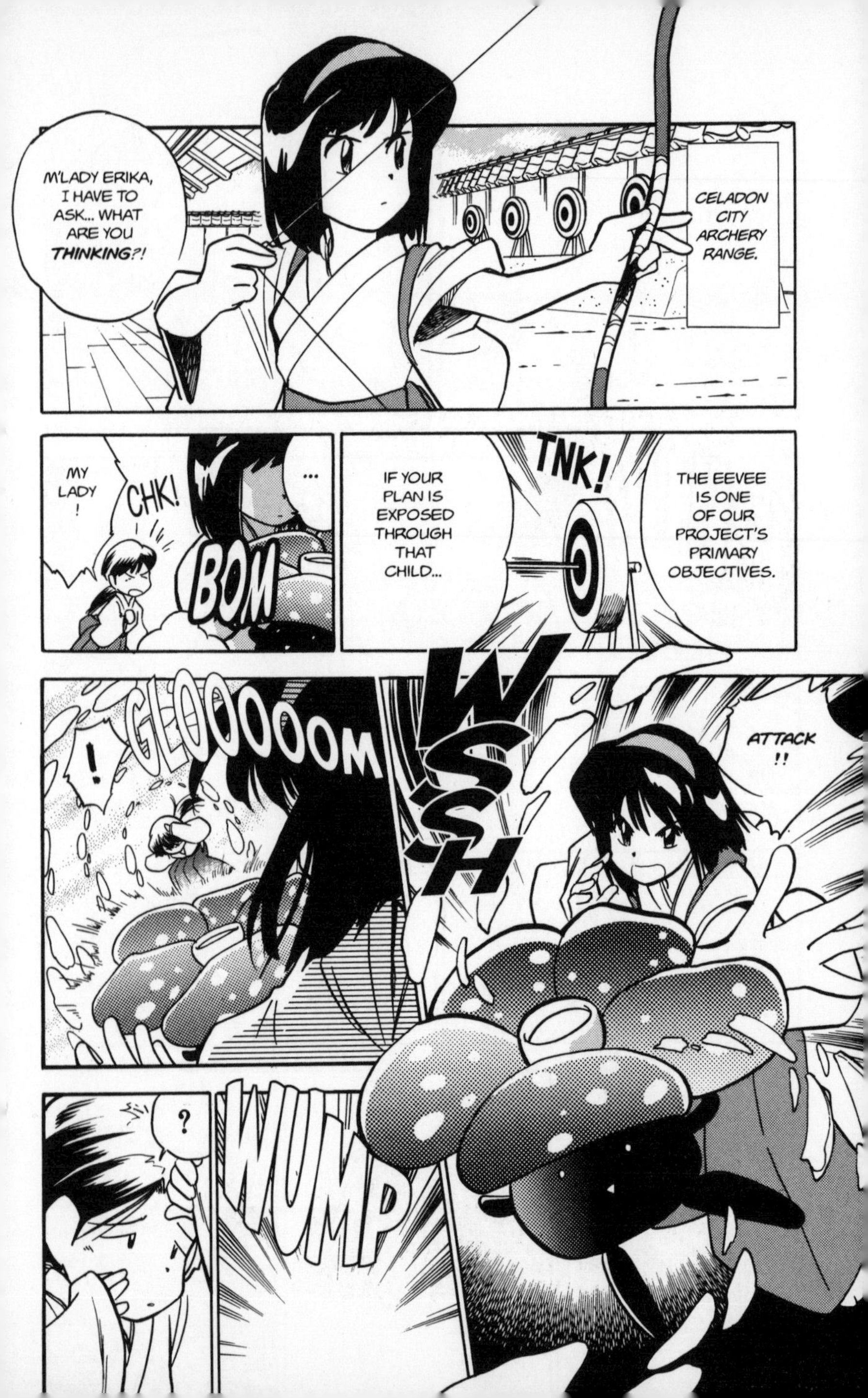

CELADON CITY ARCHERY RANGE.
M'LADY ERIKA, I HAVE TO ASK... WHAT ARE YOU **THINKING**?!
THE EEVEE IS ONE OF OUR PROJECT'S PRIMARY OBJECTIVES.
TNK!
IF YOUR PLAN IS EXPOSED THROUGH THAT CHILD...
...
CHK!
MY LADY !
BOM
ATTACK !!
WSH
GLOOOOOM
!
WUMP
?

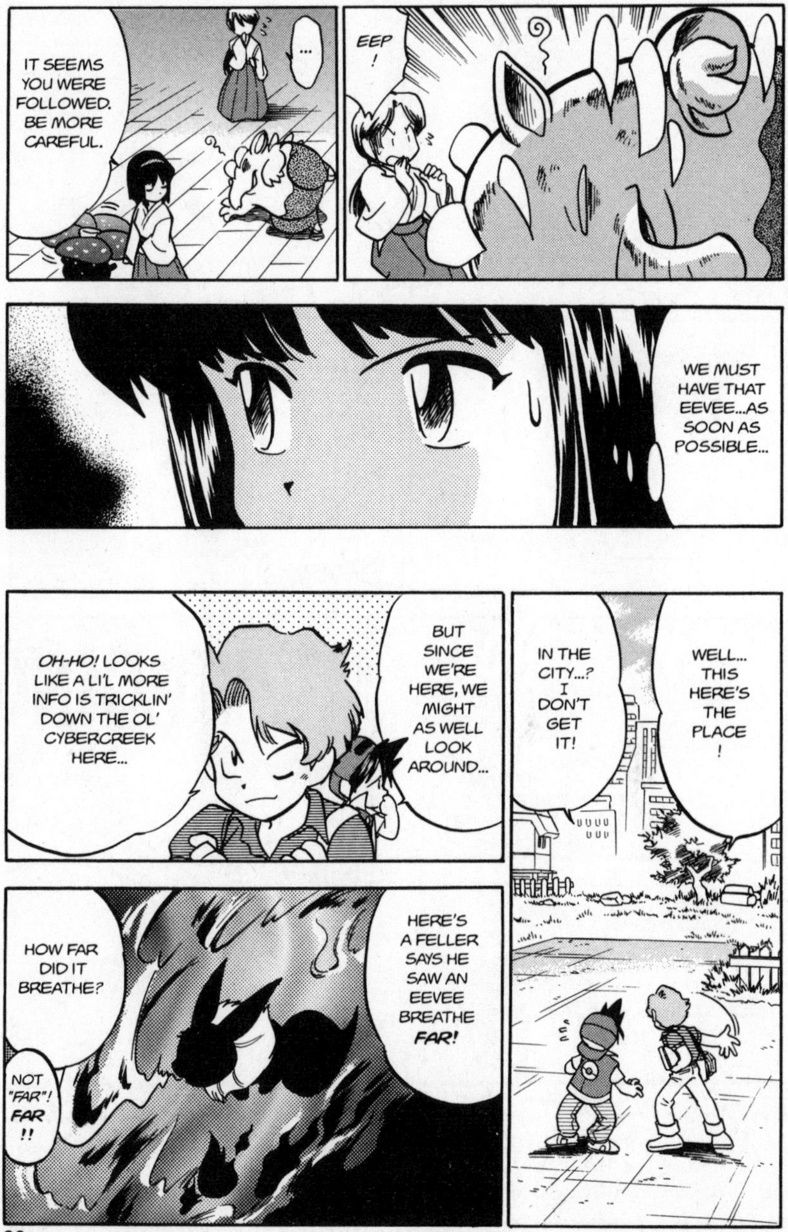
EEP!
...
IT SEEMS YOU WERE FOLLOWED. BE MORE CAREFUL.
WE MUST HAVE THAT EEVEE...AS SOON AS POSSIBLE...
WELL... THIS HERE'S THE PLACE!
IN THE CITY...? I DON'T GET IT!
BUT SINCE WE'RE HERE, WE MIGHT AS WELL LOOK AROUND...
OH-HO! LOOKS LIKE A LI'L MORE INFO IS TRICKLIN' DOWN THE OL' CYBERCREEK HERE...
HERE'S A FELLER SAYS HE SAW AN EEVEE BREATHE ***FAR!***
HOW FAR DID IT BREATHE?
NOT *"FAR"*! ***FAR!!***

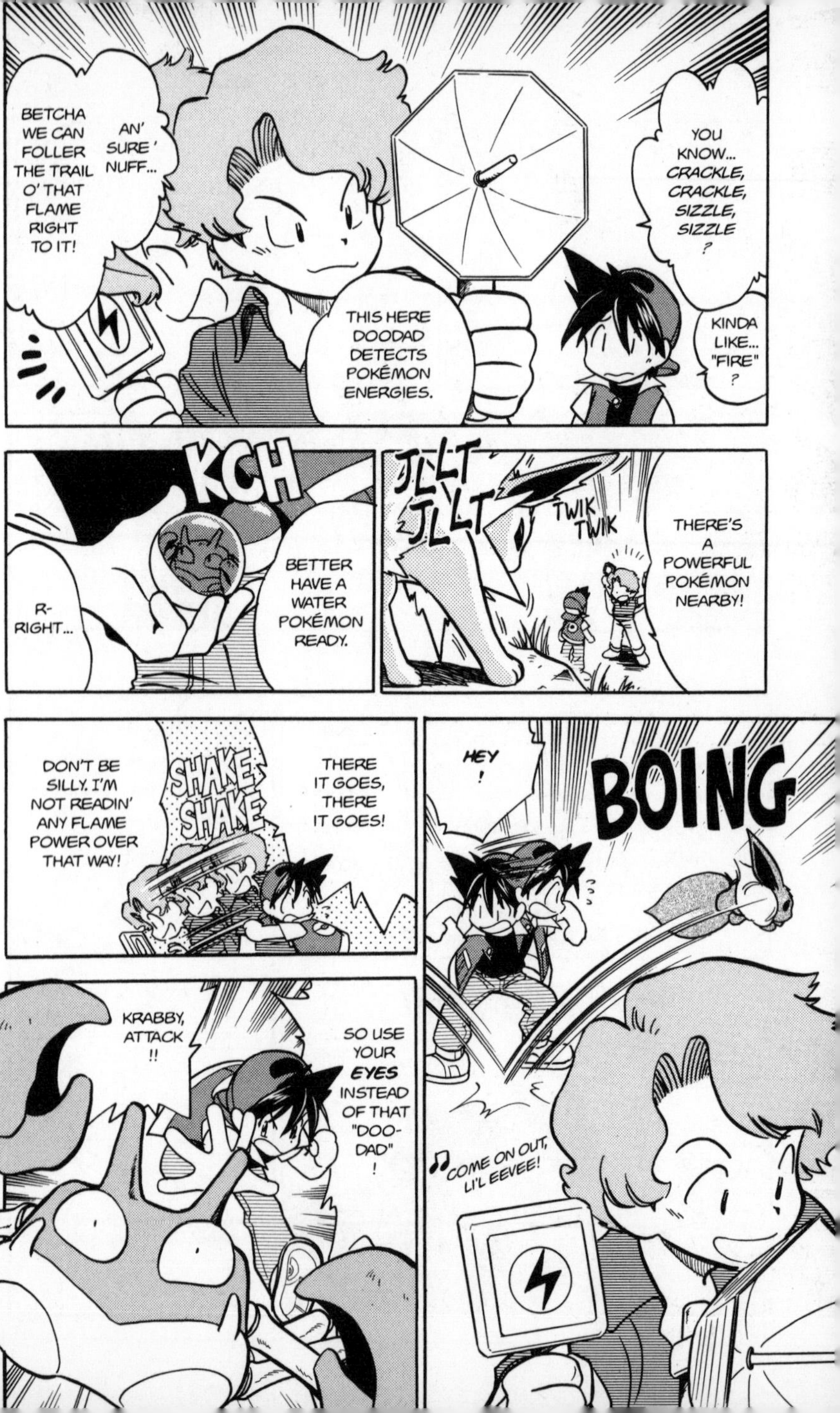
YOU KNOW... *CRACKLE, CRACKLE, SIZZLE, SIZZLE*?
KINDA LIKE... "FIRE"?
AN' SURE 'NUFF...
BETCHA WE CAN FOLLER THE TRAIL O' THAT FLAME RIGHT TO IT!
THIS HERE DOODAD DETECTS POKÉMON ENERGIES.
JLLT JLLT
TWIK TWIK
THERE'S A POWERFUL POKÉMON NEARBY!
KCH
BETTER HAVE A WATER POKÉMON READY.
R-RIGHT...
HEY!
BOING
COME ON OUT, LI'L EEVEE!
THERE IT GOES, THERE IT GOES!
SHAKE SHAKE
DON'T BE SILLY. I'M NOT READIN' ANY FLAME POWER OVER THAT WAY!
SO USE YOUR *EYES* INSTEAD OF THAT "DOO-DAD"!
KRABBY, ATTACK!!

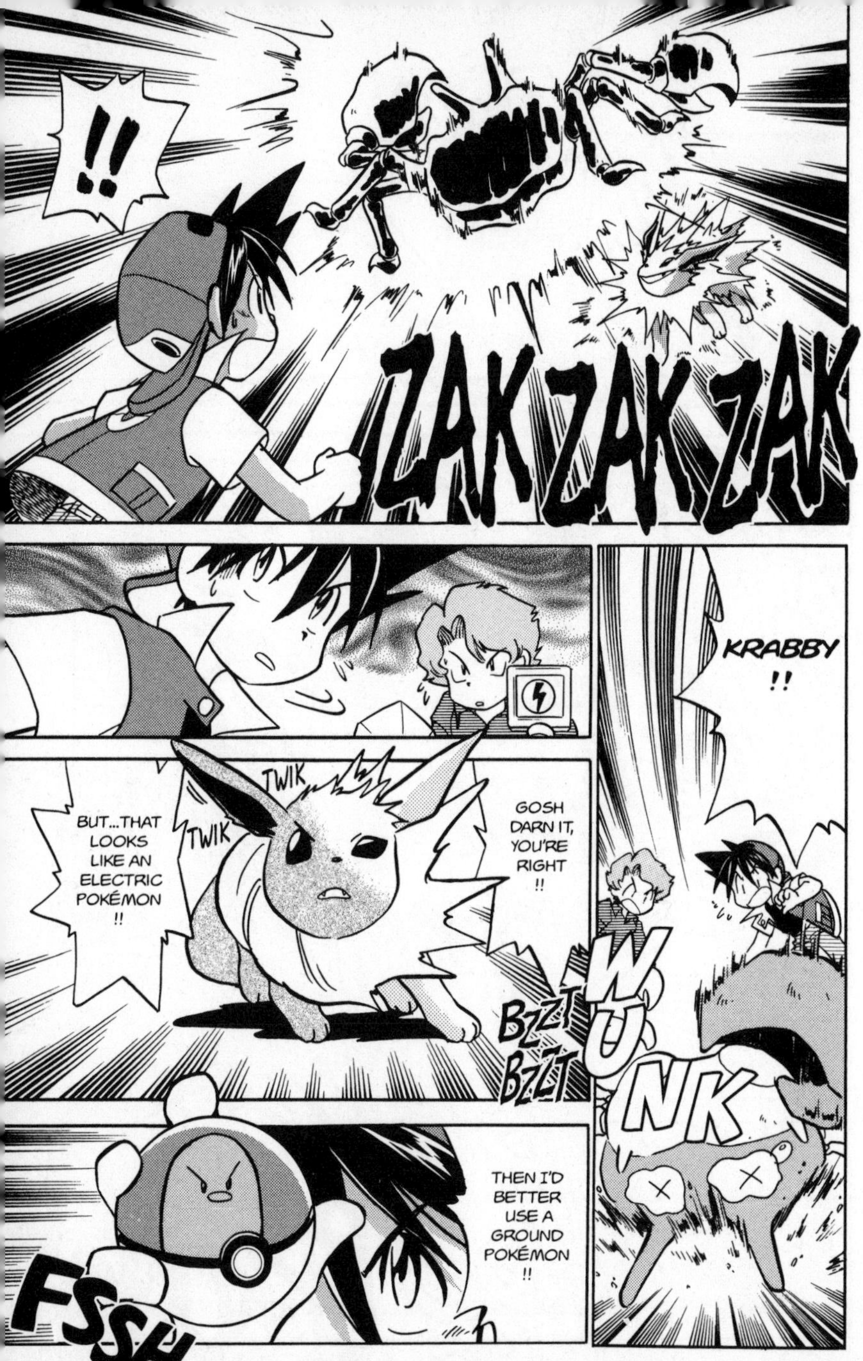
!!
ZAK ZAK ZAK
KRABBY !!
WUNK
GOSH DARN IT, YOU'RE RIGHT !!
TWIK
TWIK
BUT...THAT LOOKS LIKE AN ELECTRIC POKÉMON !!
BZZT BZZT
THEN I'D BETTER USE A GROUND POKÉMON !!
FSSH

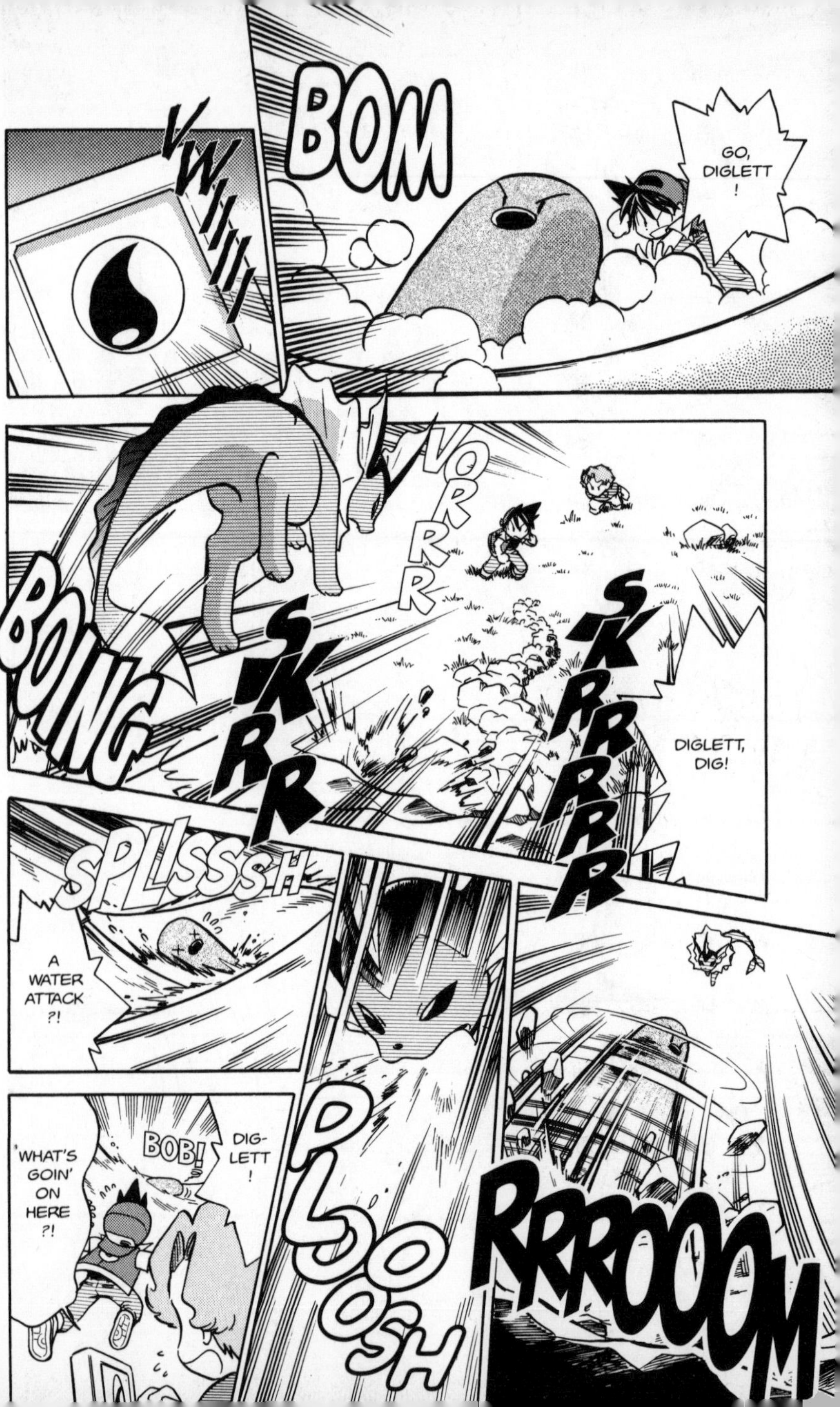
GO, DIGLETT!
BOM
VWIIIIII
DIGLETT, DIG!
SKRRRRRR
VORRR
SKRR
BOING
RRROOOM
PLOOOSH
SPLISSSH
A WATER ATTACK?!
DIG-LETT!
BOB!
WHAT'S GOIN' ON HERE?!

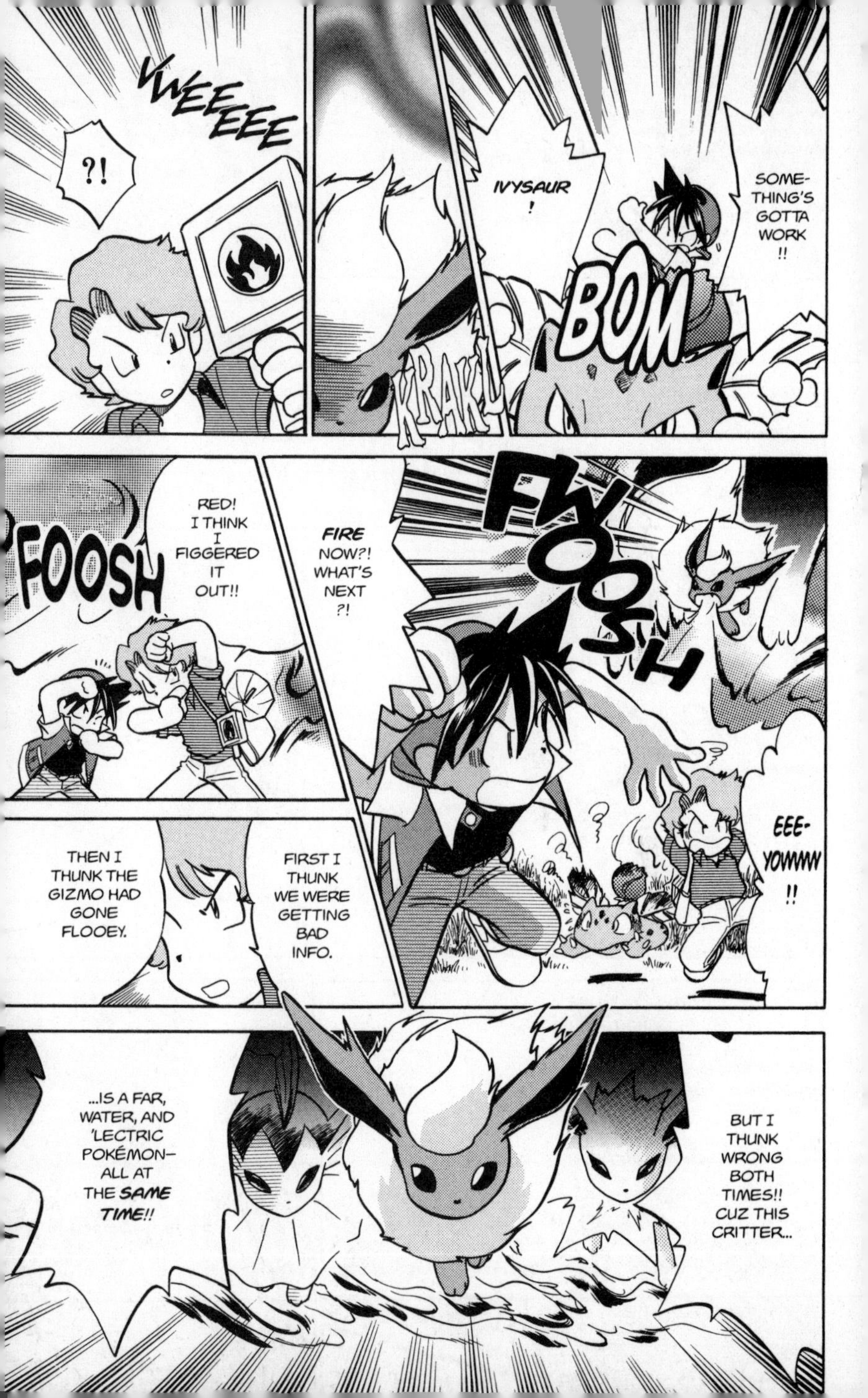

SOME-THING'S GOTTA WORK!!
IVYSAUR!
BOM
KRAKL
VWEEEEEE
?!
FWOOSH
FIRE NOW?! WHAT'S NEXT?!
EEE-YOWWW!!
RED! I THINK I FIGGERED IT OUT!!
FOOSH
FIRST I THUNK WE WERE GETTING BAD INFO.
THEN I THUNK THE GIZMO HAD GONE FLOOEY.
BUT I THUNK WRONG BOTH TIMES!! CUZ THIS CRITTER...
...IS A FAR, WATER, AND 'LECTRIC POKÉMON—ALL AT THE SAME TIME!!

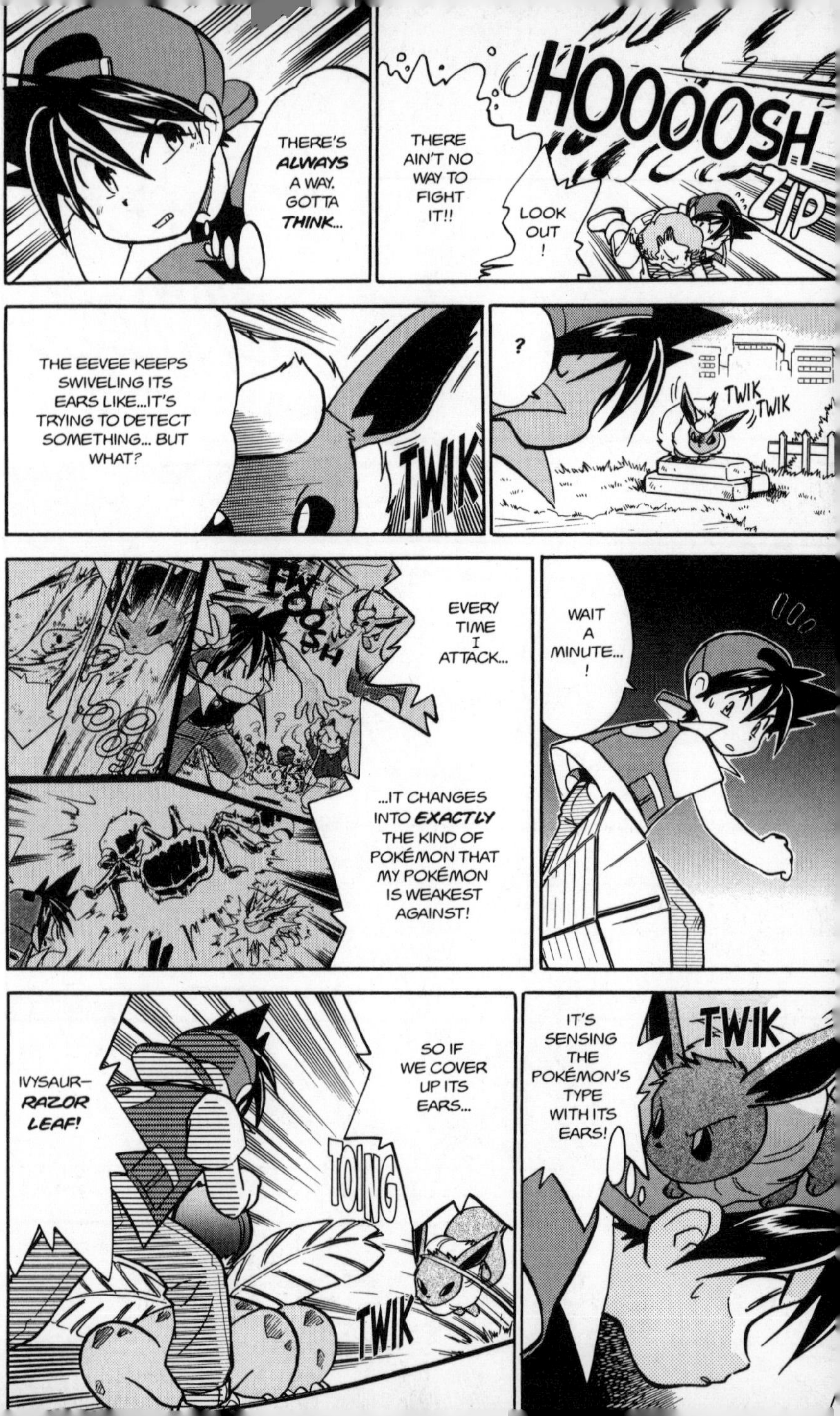
HOOOOSH
ZIP
THERE AIN'T NO WAY TO FIGHT IT!!
LOOK OUT!
THERE'S *ALWAYS* A WAY. GOTTA *THINK*...
?
TWIK TWIK
THE EEVEE KEEPS SWIVELING ITS EARS LIKE...IT'S TRYING TO DETECT SOMETHING... BUT WHAT?
TWIK
WAIT A MINUTE...!
EVERY TIME I ATTACK...
FWOOSH
...IT CHANGES INTO *EXACTLY* THE KIND OF POKÉMON THAT MY POKÉMON IS WEAKEST AGAINST!
TWIK
IT'S SENSING THE POKÉMON'S TYPE WITH ITS EARS!
SO IF WE COVER UP ITS EARS...
IVYSAUR— *RAZOR LEAF!*
TOING
TWIK

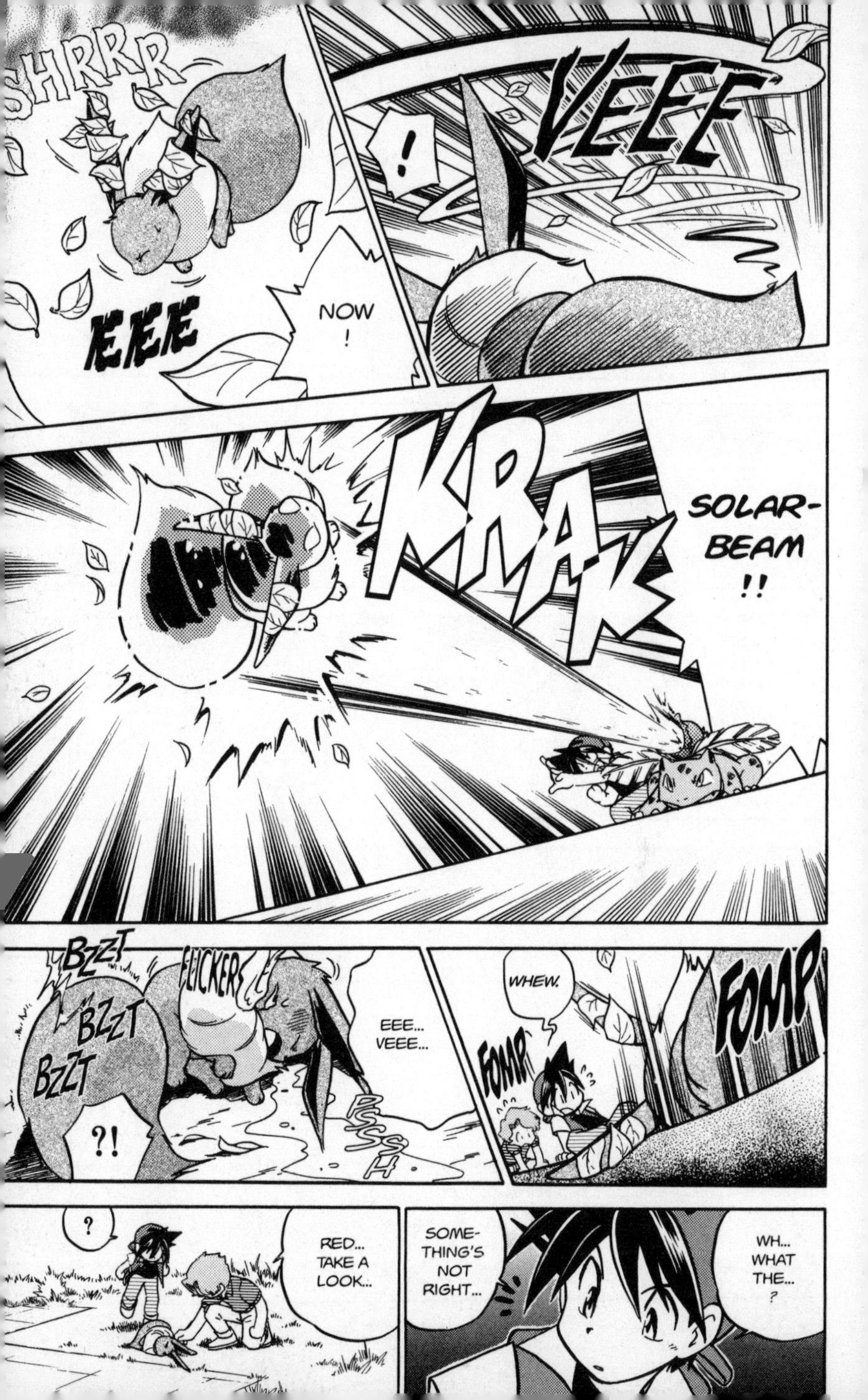
!
VEEE
SHRRR
NOW !
SOLAR-BEAM !!
KRAK
FOMP
WHEW.
FOMP
FLICKER
BZZT
EEE... VEEE...
BZZT
BZZT
PSSSH
?!
WH... WHAT THE... ?
SOME-THING'S NOT RIGHT...
RED... TAKE A LOOK...
?

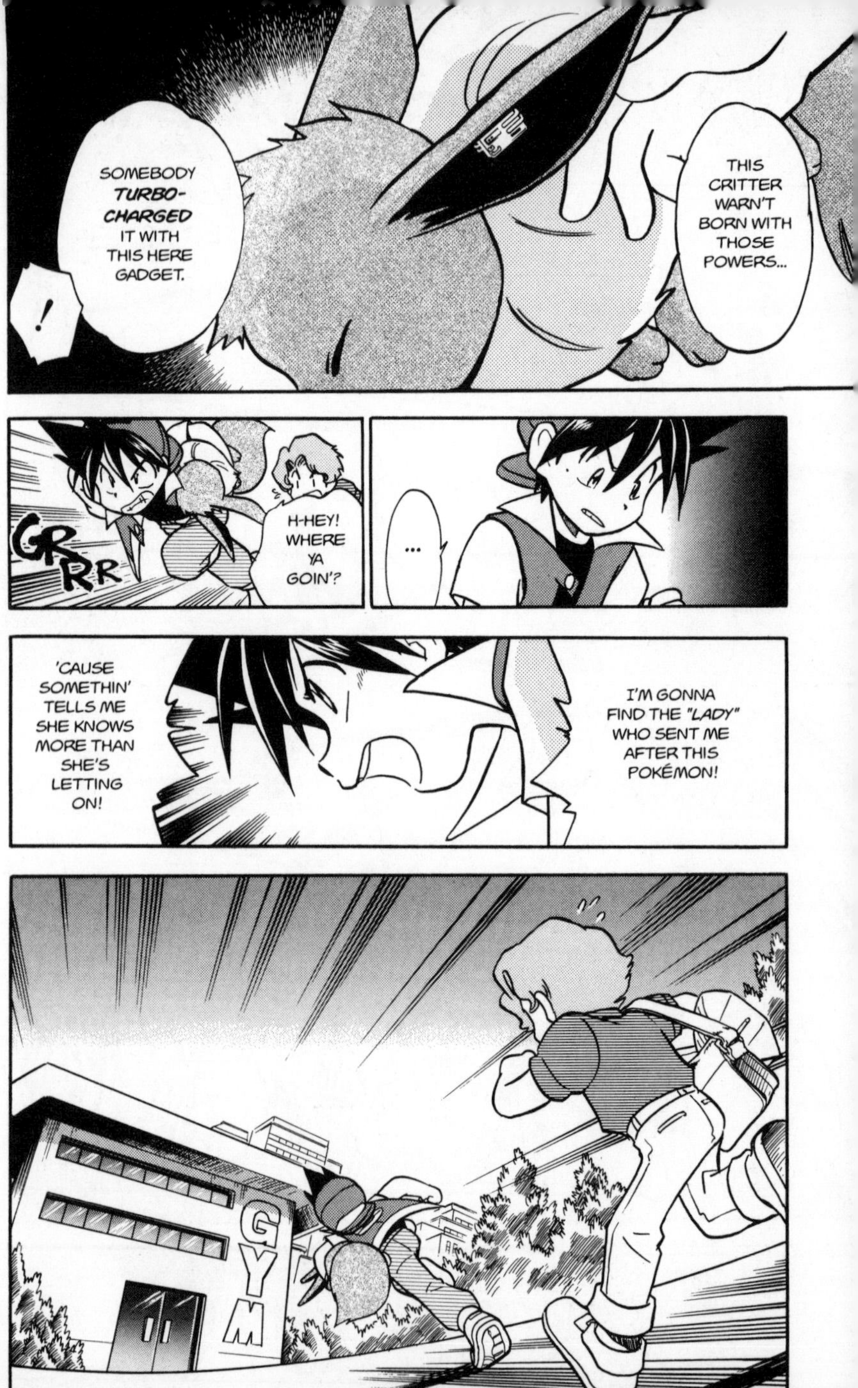
THIS CRITTER WARN'T BORN WITH THOSE POWERS...
SOMEBODY ***TURBO-CHARGED*** IT WITH THIS HERE GADGET.
!
...
H-HEY! WHERE YA GOIN'?
GRRR
I'M GONNA FIND THE *"LADY"* WHO SENT ME AFTER THIS POKÉMON!
'CAUSE SOMETHIN' TELLS ME SHE KNOWS MORE THAN SHE'S LETTING ON!
GYM

⑳ Meanwhile...Vileplume!

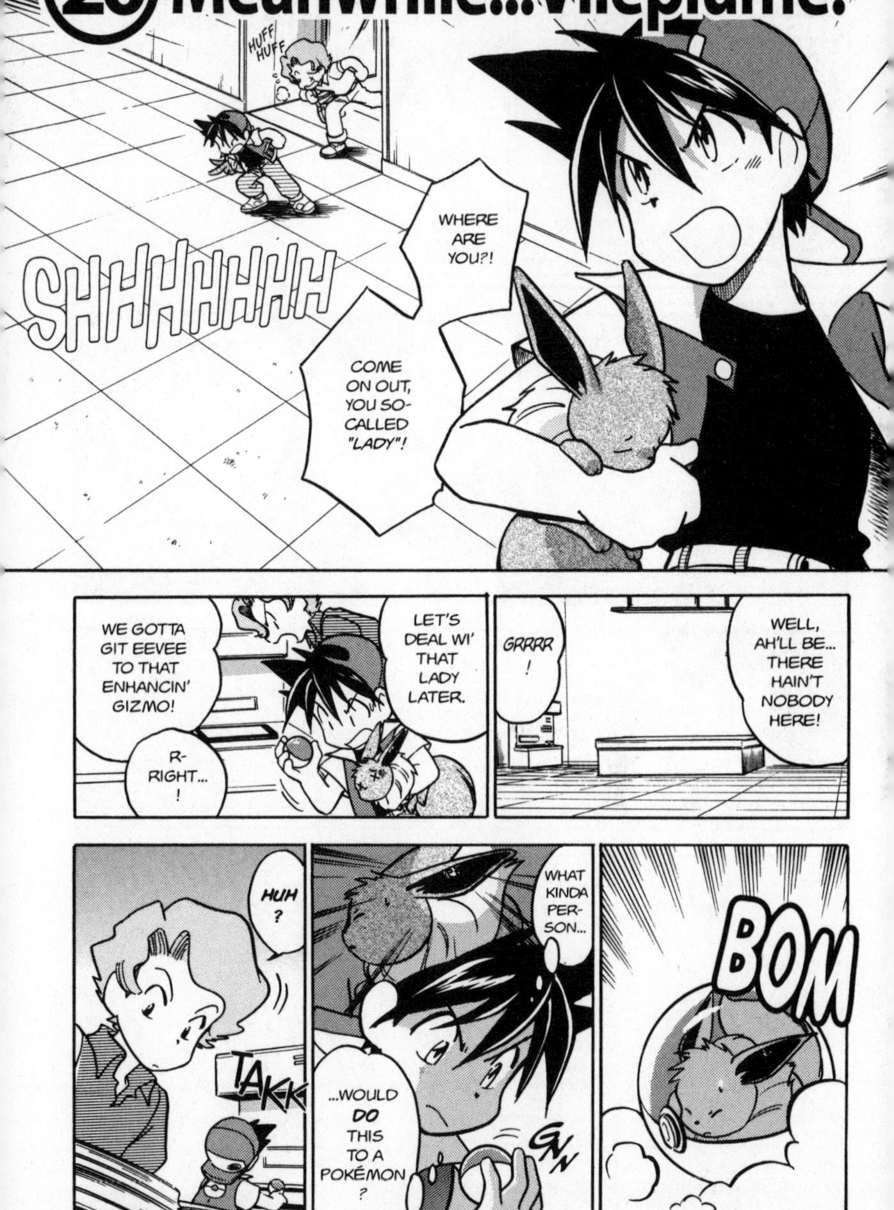

WHERE ARE YOU?!
COME ON OUT, YOU SO-CALLED "LADY"!
HUFF HUFF
SHHHHHHHH
WELL, AH'LL BE... THERE HAIN'T NOBODY HERE!
GRRRR!
LET'S DEAL WI' THAT LADY LATER.
WE GOTTA GIT EEVEE TO THAT ENHANCIN' GIZMO!
R-RIGHT...!
BOM
WHAT KINDA PERSON...
...WOULD DO THIS TO A POKÉMON?
GNN
HUH?
TAKK

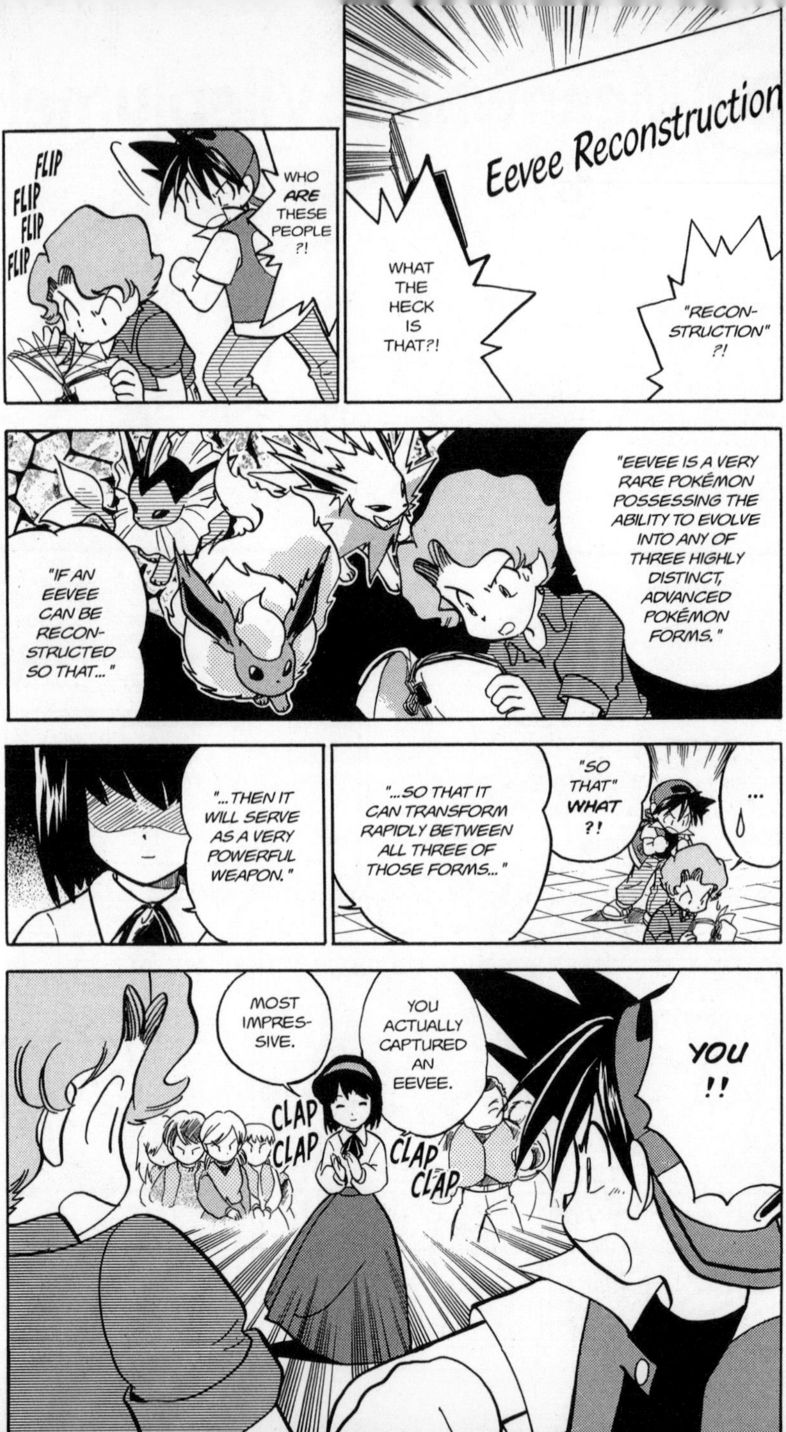
Eevee Reconstruction
"RECON-STRUCTION"?!
WHAT THE HECK IS THAT?!
WHO ARE THESE PEOPLE?!
FLIP FLIP FLIP FLIP
"EEVEE IS A VERY RARE POKÉMON POSSESSING THE ABILITY TO EVOLVE INTO ANY OF THREE HIGHLY DISTINCT, ADVANCED POKÉMON FORMS."
"IF AN EEVEE CAN BE RECON-STRUCTED SO THAT..."
...
"SO THAT" WHAT ?!
"...SO THAT IT CAN TRANSFORM RAPIDLY BETWEEN ALL THREE OF THOSE FORMS..."
"...THEN IT WILL SERVE AS A VERY POWERFUL WEAPON."
YOU !!
YOU ACTUALLY CAPTURED AN EEVEE.
CLAP CLAP
MOST IMPRES-SIVE.
CLAP CLAP

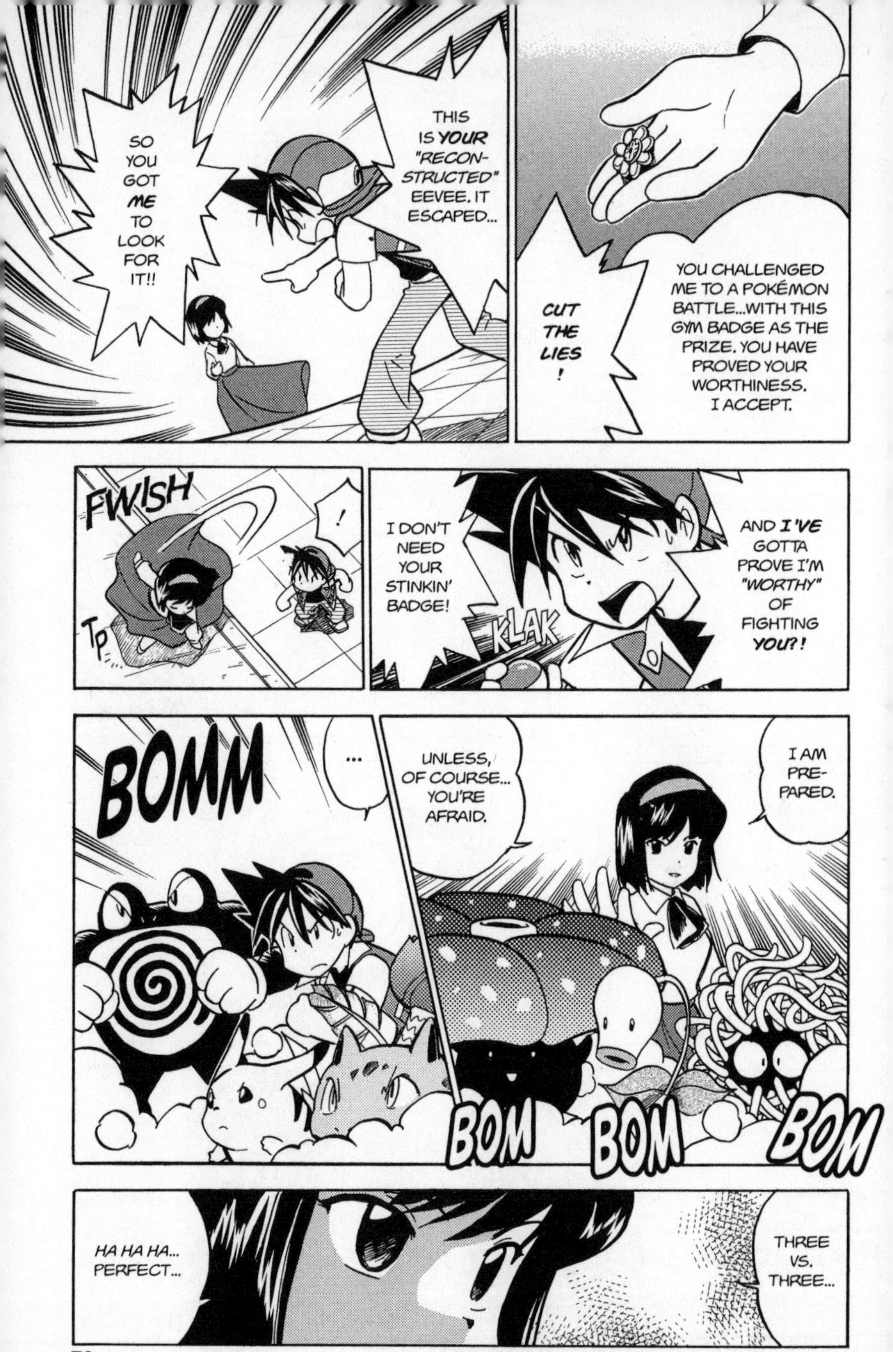
YOU CHALLENGED ME TO A POKÉMON BATTLE...WITH THIS GYM BADGE AS THE PRIZE. YOU HAVE PROVED YOUR WORTHINESS. I ACCEPT.
CUT THE LIES!
THIS IS YOUR "RECONSTRUCTED" EEVEE. IT ESCAPED...
SO YOU GOT ME TO LOOK FOR IT!!
AND I'VE GOTTA PROVE I'M "WORTHY" OF FIGHTING YOU?!
I DON'T NEED YOUR STINKIN' BADGE!
KLAK
!
FWISH
Tp
I AM PREPARED.
UNLESS, OF COURSE... YOU'RE AFRAID.
...
BOMM
BOM
BOM
BOM
THREE VS. THREE...
HA HA HA... PERFECT...

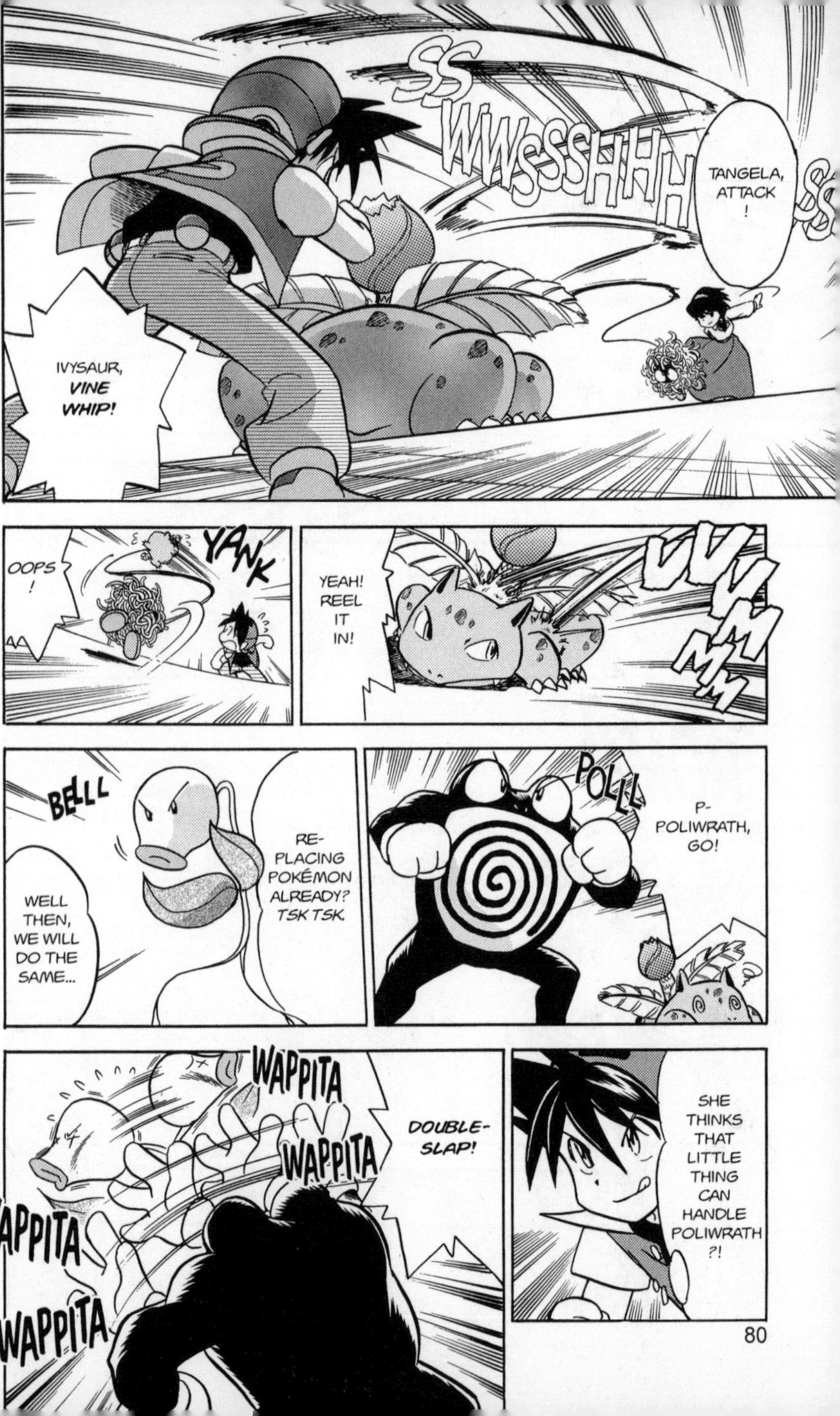
SSWWSSHHHSS
TANGELA, ATTACK!
IVYSAUR, VINE WHIP!
VVVMMMM
YEAH! REEL IT IN!
YANK
OOPS!
POLLL
P-POLIWRATH, GO!
BELLL
RE-PLACING POKÉMON ALREADY? TSK TSK.
WELL THEN, WE WILL DO THE SAME...
SHE THINKS THAT LITTLE THING CAN HANDLE POLIWRATH?!
WAPPITA
DOUBLE-SLAP!
WAPPITA
WAPPITA
WAPPITA

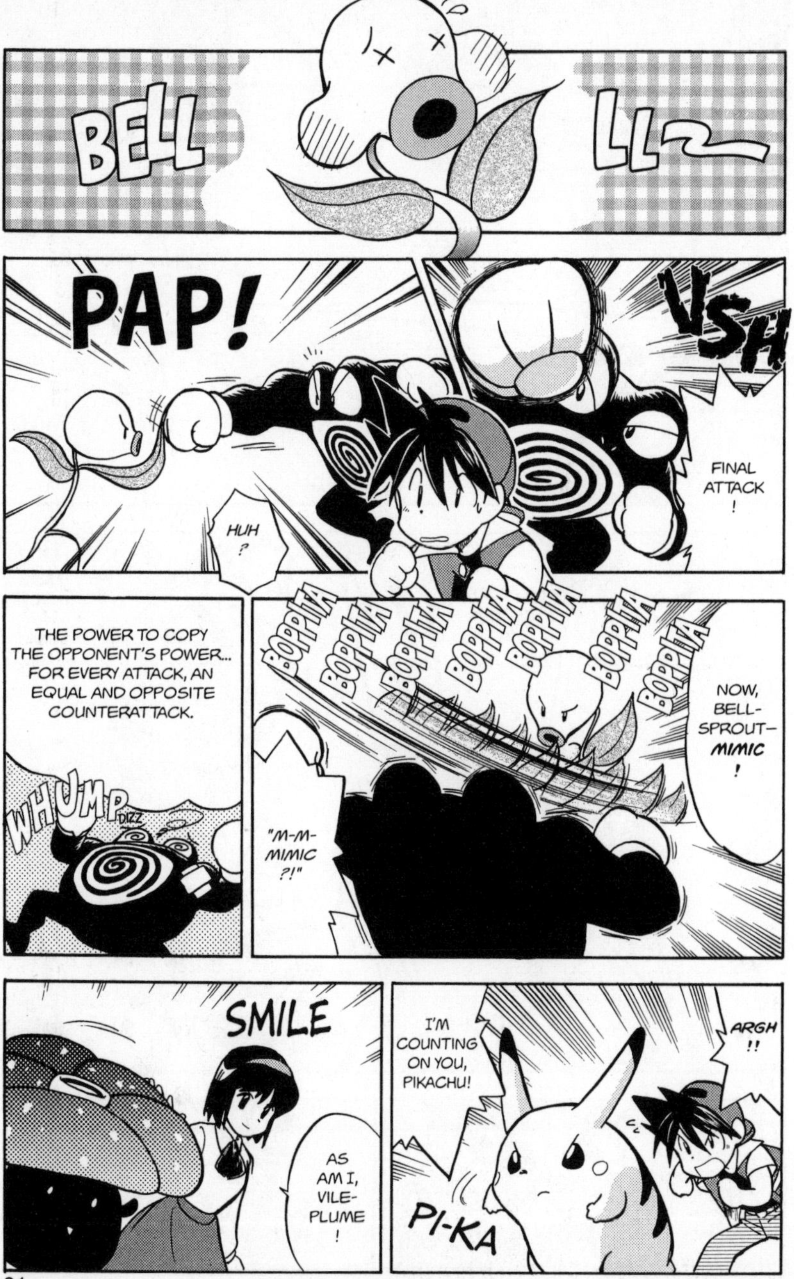
BELL LL~
VSH
FINAL ATTACK!
PAP!
HUH?
NOW, BELL-SPROUT—MIMIC!
BOPPITA BOPPITA BOPPITA BOPPITA BOPPITA BOPPITA BOPPITA BOPPITA
"M-M-MIMIC?!"
THE POWER TO COPY THE OPPONENT'S POWER... FOR EVERY ATTACK, AN EQUAL AND OPPOSITE COUNTERATTACK.
WHUMP
DIZZ
ARGH!!
I'M COUNTING ON YOU, PIKACHU!
PI-KA
SMILE
AS AM I, VILE-PLUME!

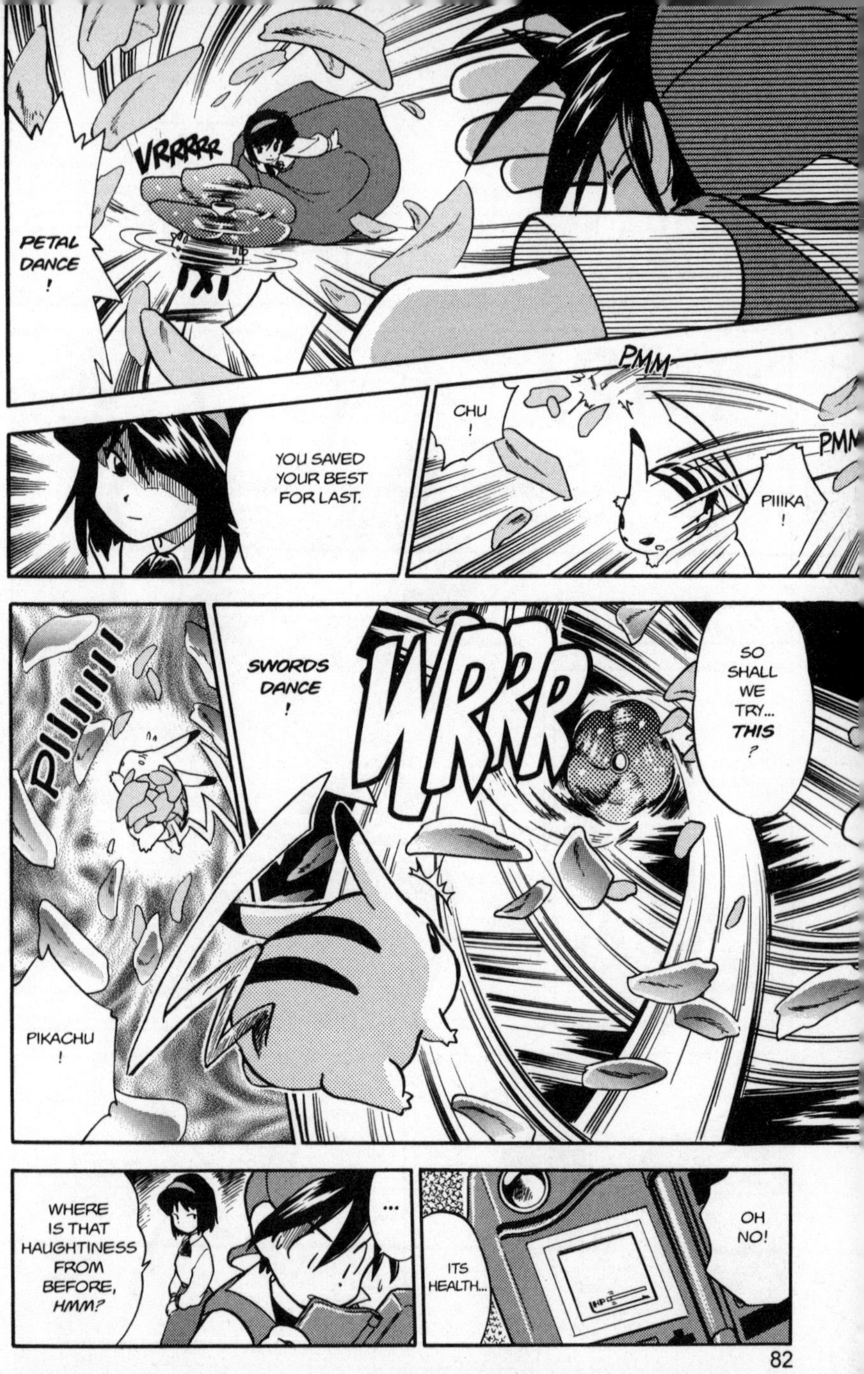
VRRRRR
PETAL DANCE!
PMM
CHU!
PMM
PIIIKA!
YOU SAVED YOUR BEST FOR LAST.
SO SHALL WE TRY... THIS?
WRRR
SWORDS DANCE!
PIIIIII
PIKACHU!
OH NO!
ITS HEALTH...
...
WHERE IS THAT HAUGHTINESS FROM BEFORE, HMM?

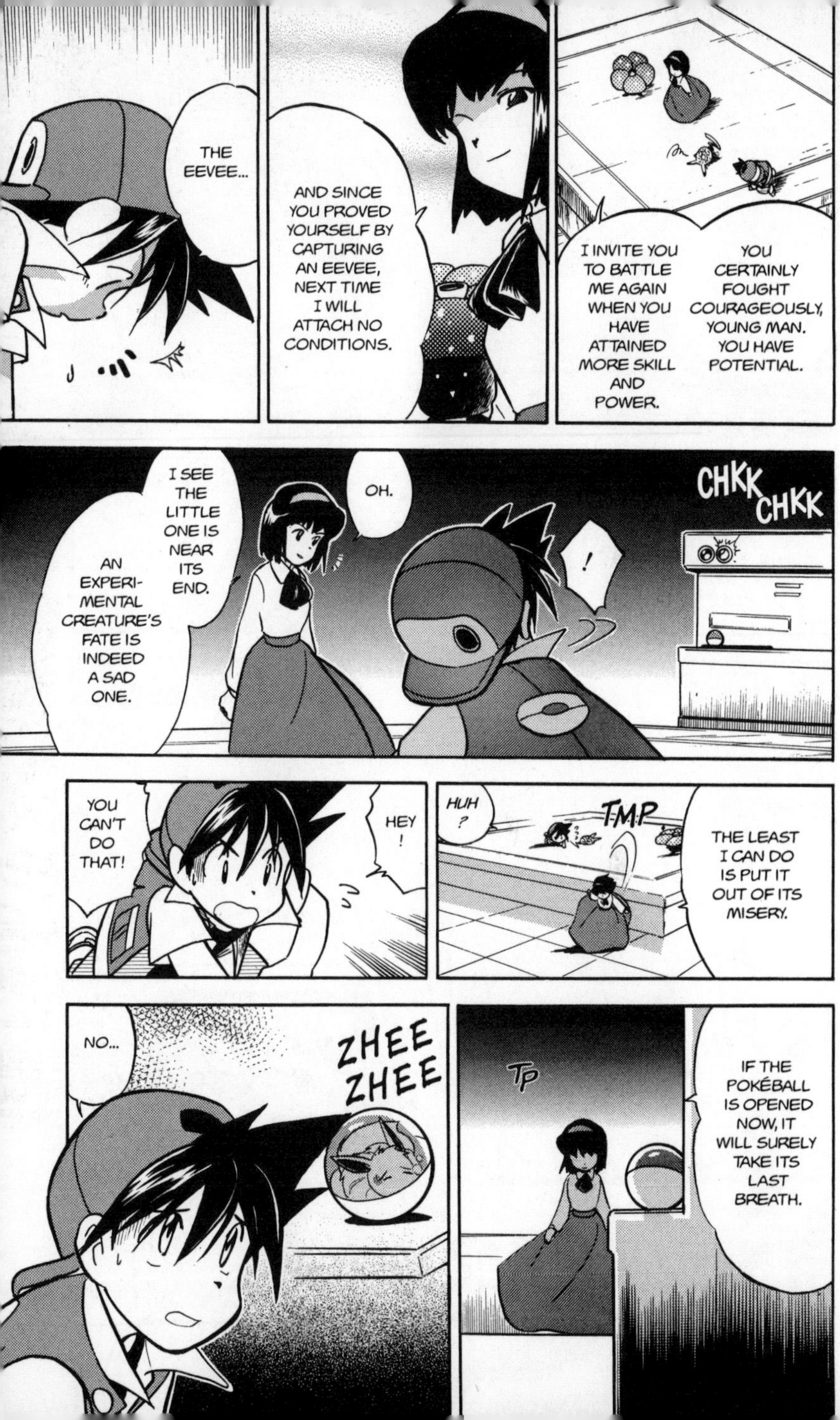
YOU CERTAINLY FOUGHT COURAGEOUSLY, YOUNG MAN. YOU HAVE POTENTIAL.
I INVITE YOU TO BATTLE ME AGAIN WHEN YOU HAVE ATTAINED MORE SKILL AND POWER.
AND SINCE YOU PROVED YOURSELF BY CAPTURING AN EEVEE, NEXT TIME I WILL ATTACH NO CONDITIONS.
THE EEVEE...
CHKK CHKK
!
OH.
I SEE THE LITTLE ONE IS NEAR ITS END.
AN EXPERI-MENTAL CREATURE'S FATE IS INDEED A SAD ONE.
THE LEAST I CAN DO IS PUT IT OUT OF ITS MISERY.
TMP
HUH?
HEY!
YOU CAN'T DO THAT!
IF THE POKÉBALL IS OPENED NOW, IT WILL SURELY TAKE ITS LAST BREATH.
TP
ZHEE ZHEE
NO...

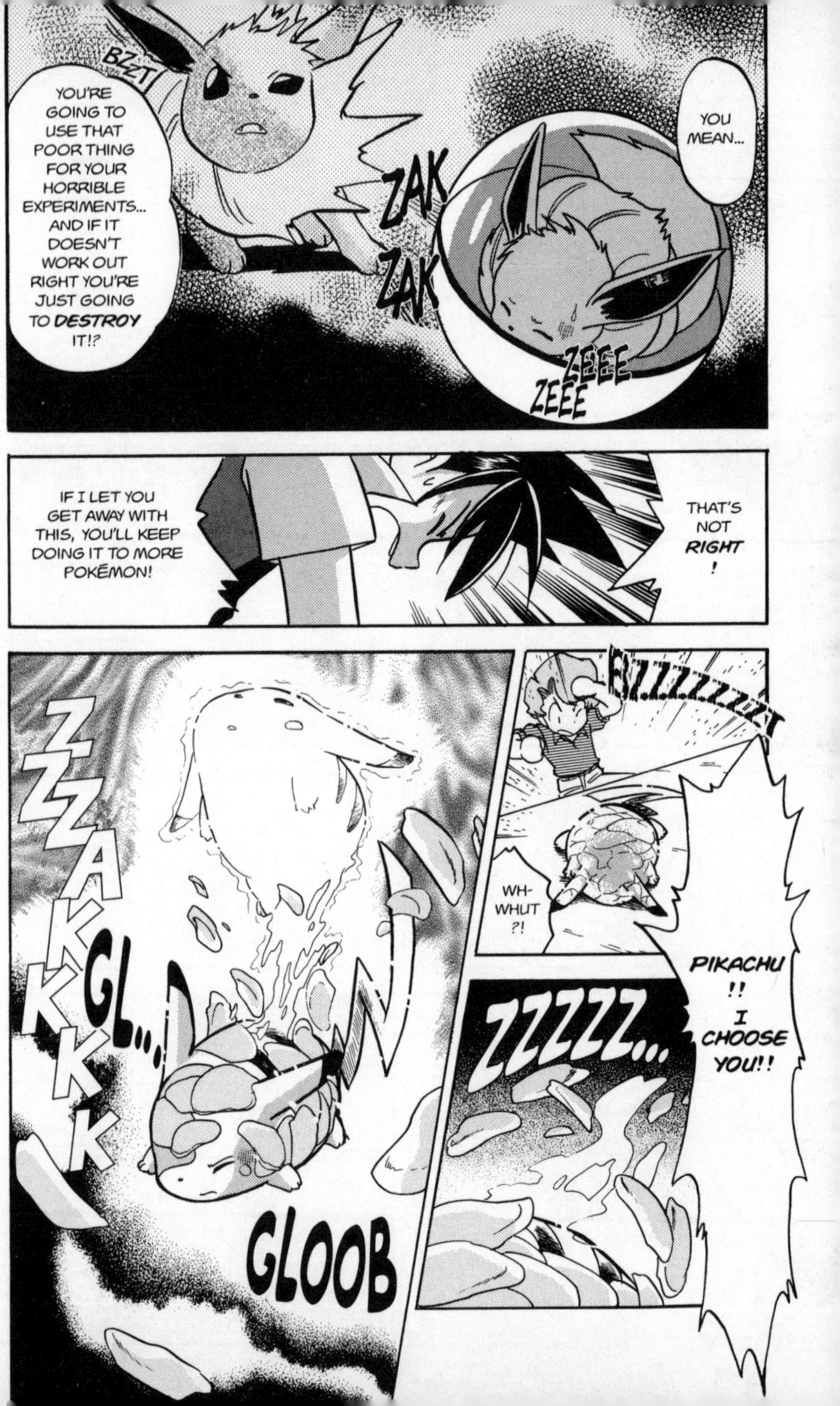
YOU MEAN...
ZAK
ZAK
BZZT
YOU'RE GOING TO USE THAT POOR THING FOR YOUR HORRIBLE EXPERIMENTS... AND IF IT DOESN'T WORK OUT RIGHT YOU'RE JUST GOING TO **DESTROY** IT!?
ZEEE
ZEEE
THAT'S NOT **RIGHT**!
IF I LET YOU GET AWAY WITH THIS, YOU'LL KEEP DOING IT TO MORE POKÉMON!
BZZZZZZZZT
WH-WHUT?!
PIKACHU!! I CHOOSE YOU!!
ZZZZZ...
ZZZAKKKKK
GL...
GLOOB

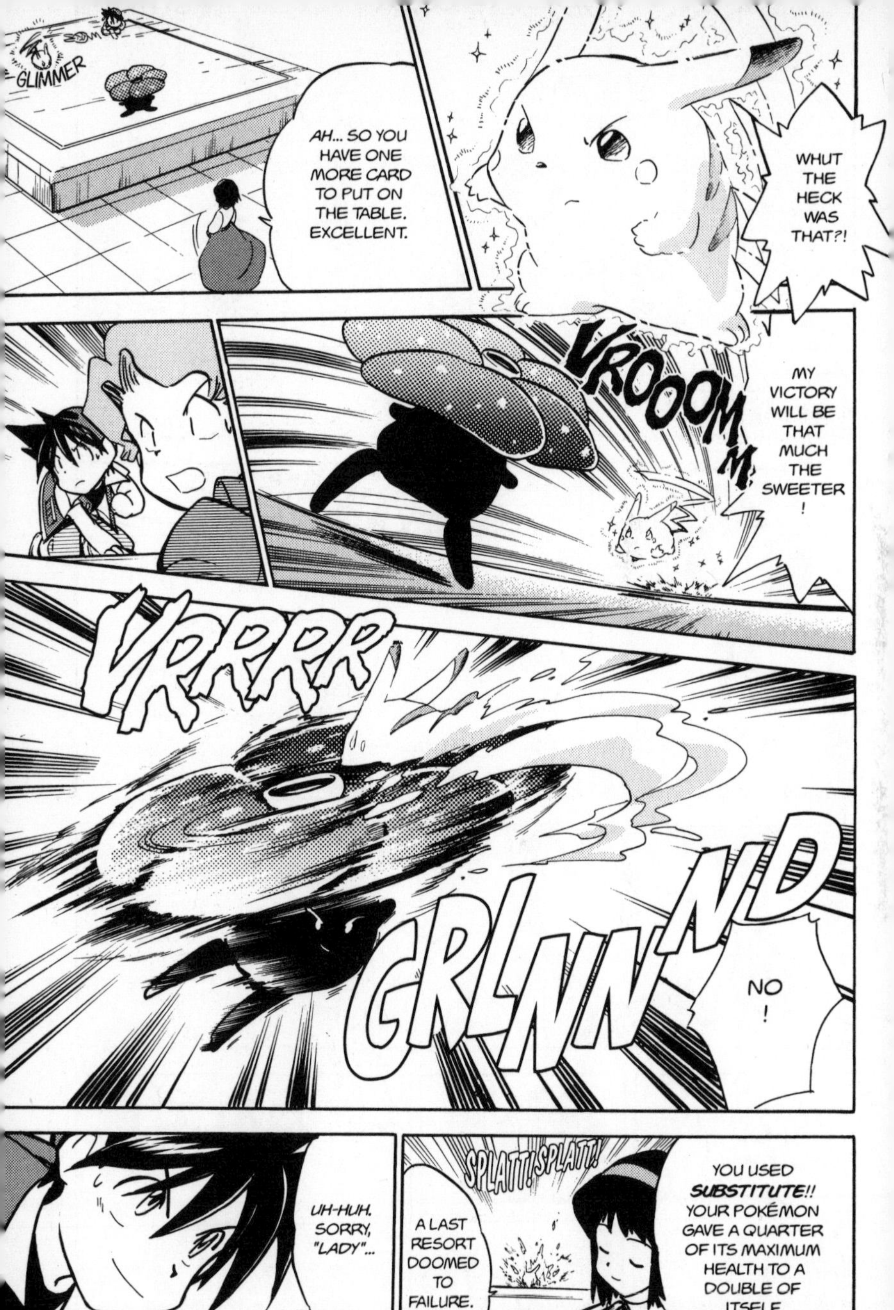
WHUT THE HECK WAS THAT?!
GLIMMER
AH... SO YOU HAVE ONE MORE CARD TO PUT ON THE TABLE. EXCELLENT.
VROOOMM
MY VICTORY WILL BE THAT MUCH THE SWEETER!
VRRRRR
GRINNND
NO!
SPLATT! SPLATT!
YOU USED **SUBSTITUTE!!** YOUR POKÉMON GAVE A QUARTER OF ITS MAXIMUM HEALTH TO A DOUBLE OF ITSELF.
A LAST RESORT DOOMED TO FAILURE.
UH-HUH. SORRY, "LADY"...

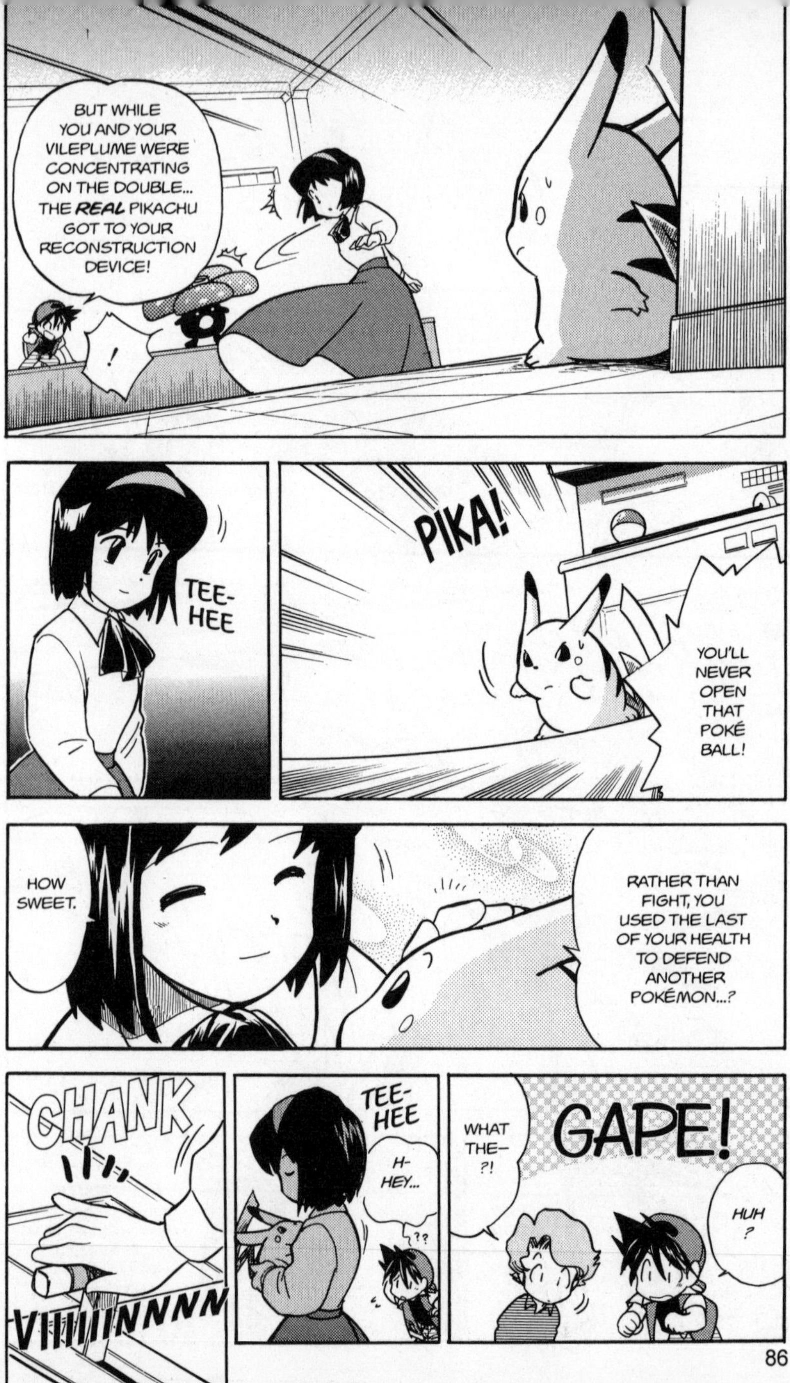
BUT WHILE YOU AND YOUR VILEPLUME WERE CONCENTRATING ON THE DOUBLE... THE REAL PIKACHU GOT TO YOUR RECONSTRUCTION DEVICE!
!
PIKA!
YOU'LL NEVER OPEN THAT POKÉ BALL!
TEE-HEE
RATHER THAN FIGHT, YOU USED THE LAST OF YOUR HEALTH TO DEFEND ANOTHER POKÉMON...?
HOW SWEET.
GAPE!
HUH?
WHAT THE—?!
TEE-HEE
H-HEY...
??
CHANK
VIIIIIINNNNN

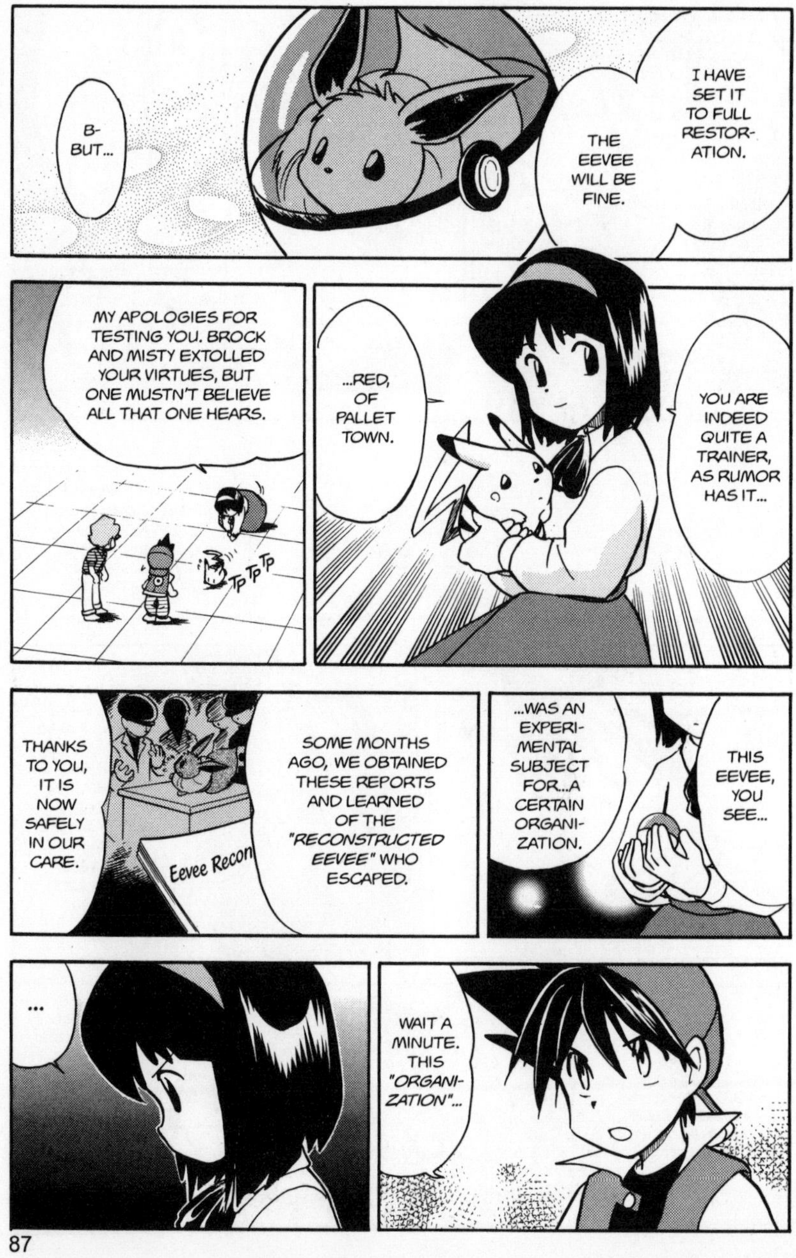
I HAVE SET IT TO FULL RESTOR-ATION.
THE EEVEE WILL BE FINE.
B-BUT...
YOU ARE INDEED QUITE A TRAINER, AS RUMOR HAS IT...
...RED, OF PALLET TOWN.
MY APOLOGIES FOR TESTING YOU. BROCK AND MISTY EXTOLLED YOUR VIRTUES, BUT ONE MUSTN'T BELIEVE ALL THAT ONE HEARS.
TP TP TP
THIS EEVEE, YOU SEE...
...WAS AN EXPERI-MENTAL SUBJECT FOR...A CERTAIN ORGANI-ZATION.
SOME MONTHS AGO, WE OBTAINED THESE REPORTS AND LEARNED OF THE "RECONSTRUCTED EEVEE" WHO ESCAPED.
THANKS TO YOU, IT IS NOW SAFELY IN OUR CARE.
Eevee Recon
WAIT A MINUTE. THIS "ORGANI-ZATION"...
...

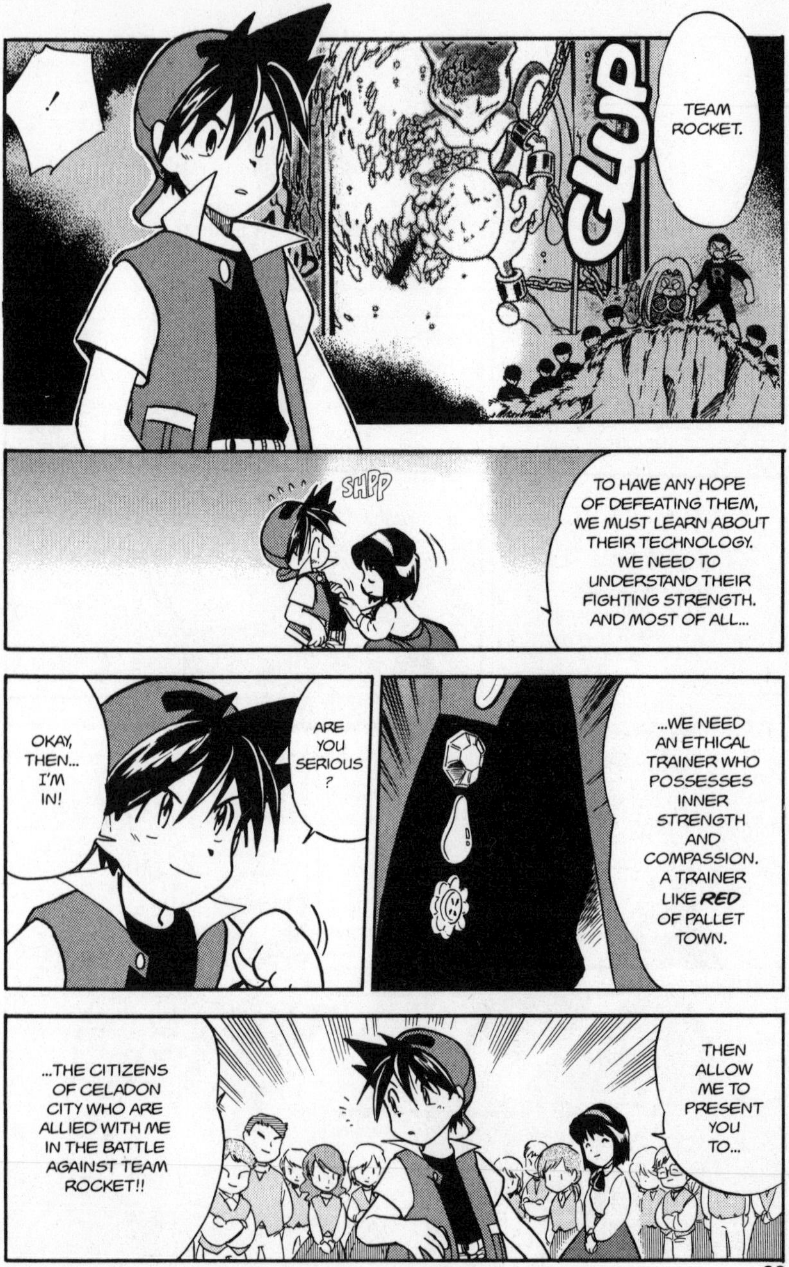
TEAM ROCKET.
GLUP
!
TO HAVE ANY HOPE OF DEFEATING THEM, WE MUST LEARN ABOUT THEIR TECHNOLOGY. WE NEED TO UNDERSTAND THEIR FIGHTING STRENGTH. AND MOST OF ALL...
SHPP
...WE NEED AN ETHICAL TRAINER WHO POSSESSES INNER STRENGTH AND COMPASSION. A TRAINER LIKE **RED** OF PALLET TOWN.
ARE YOU SERIOUS?
OKAY, THEN... I'M IN!
THEN ALLOW ME TO PRESENT YOU TO...
...THE CITIZENS OF CELADON CITY WHO ARE ALLIED WITH ME IN THE BATTLE AGAINST TEAM ROCKET!!

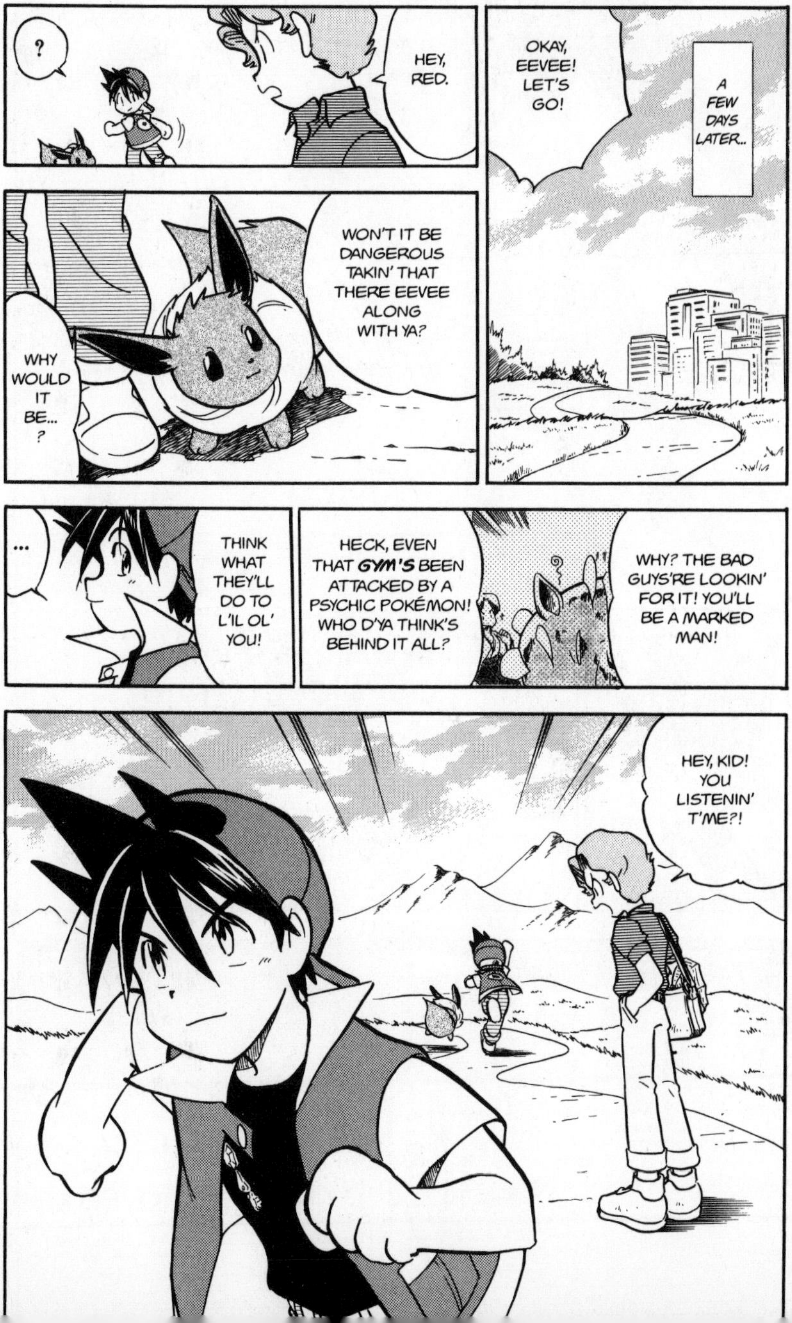
A FEW DAYS LATER...
OKAY, EEVEE! LET'S GO!
HEY, RED.
?
WON'T IT BE DANGEROUS TAKIN' THAT THERE EEVEE ALONG WITH YA?
WHY WOULD IT BE...?
WHY? THE BAD GUYS'RE LOOKIN' FOR IT! YOU'LL BE A MARKED MAN!
HECK, EVEN THAT GYM'S BEEN ATTACKED BY A PSYCHIC POKÉMON! WHO D'YA THINK'S BEHIND IT ALL?
THINK WHAT THEY'LL DO TO L'IL OL' YOU!
...
HEY, KID! YOU LISTENIN' T'ME?!

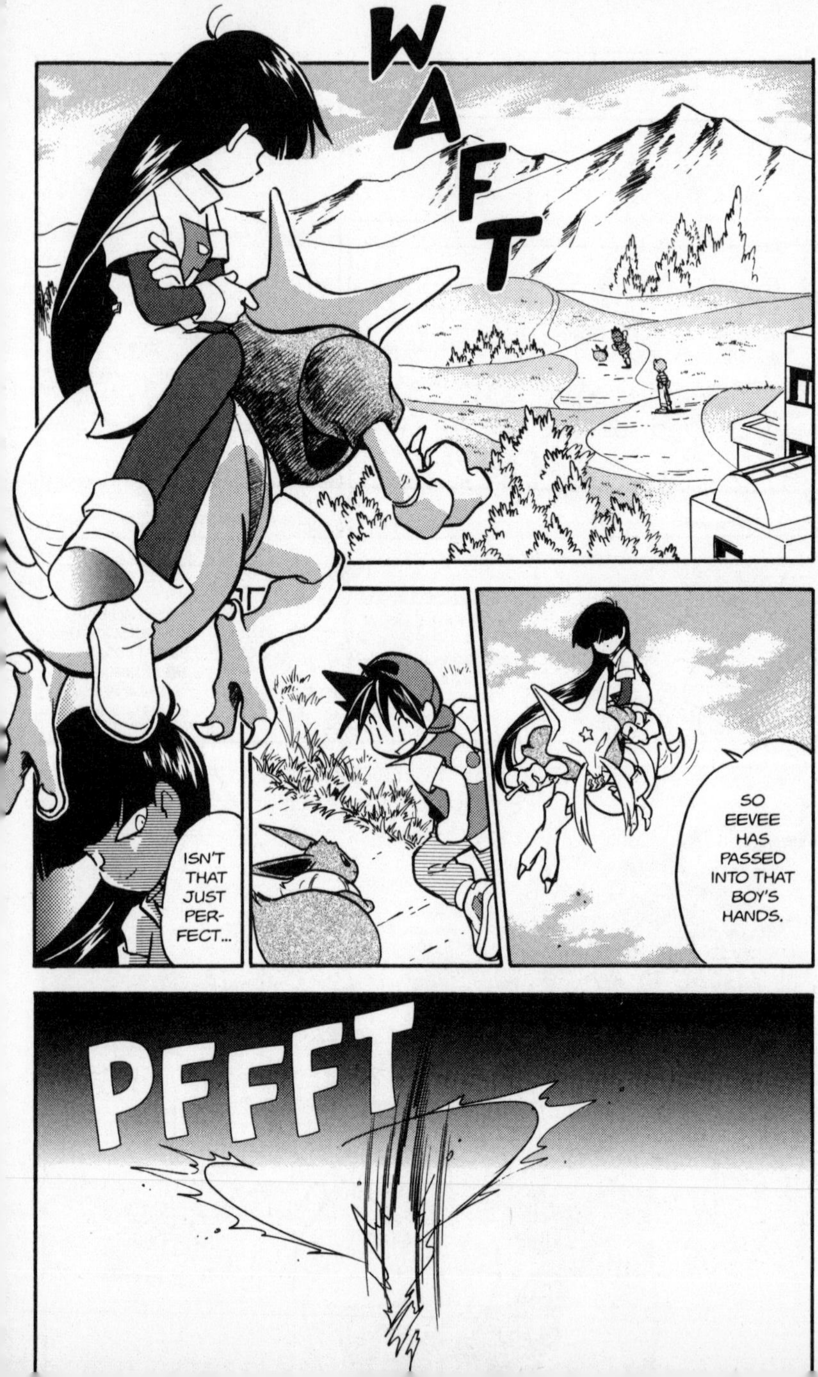
WAFT
SO EEVEE HAS PASSED INTO THAT BOY'S HANDS.
ISN'T THAT JUST PER-FECT...
PFFFT

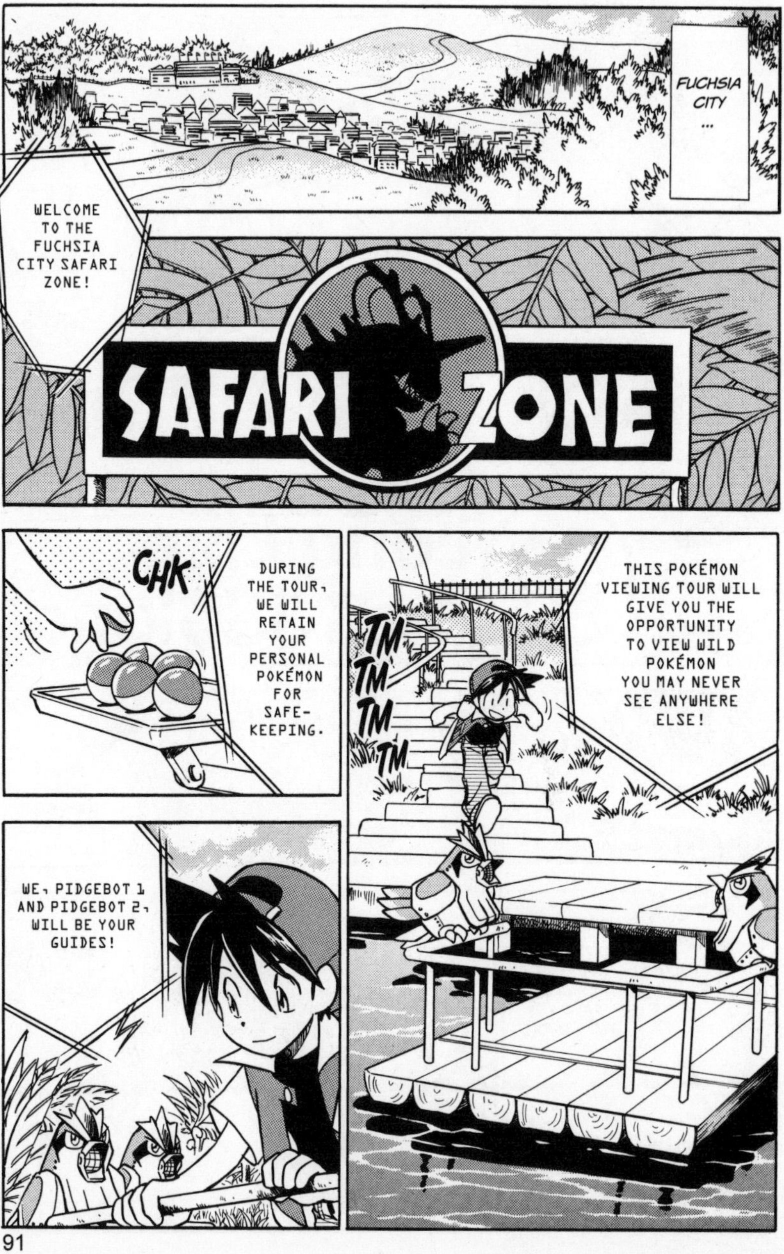
FUCHSIA CITY ...
WELCOME TO THE FUCHSIA CITY SAFARI ZONE!
SAFARI ZONE
THIS POKÉMON VIEWING TOUR WILL GIVE YOU THE OPPORTUNITY TO VIEW WILD POKÉMON YOU MAY NEVER SEE ANYWHERE ELSE!
TM TM TM TM
CHK
DURING THE TOUR, WE WILL RETAIN YOUR PERSONAL POKÉMON FOR SAFE-KEEPING.
WE, PIDGEBOT 1 AND PIDGEBOT 2, WILL BE YOUR GUIDES!

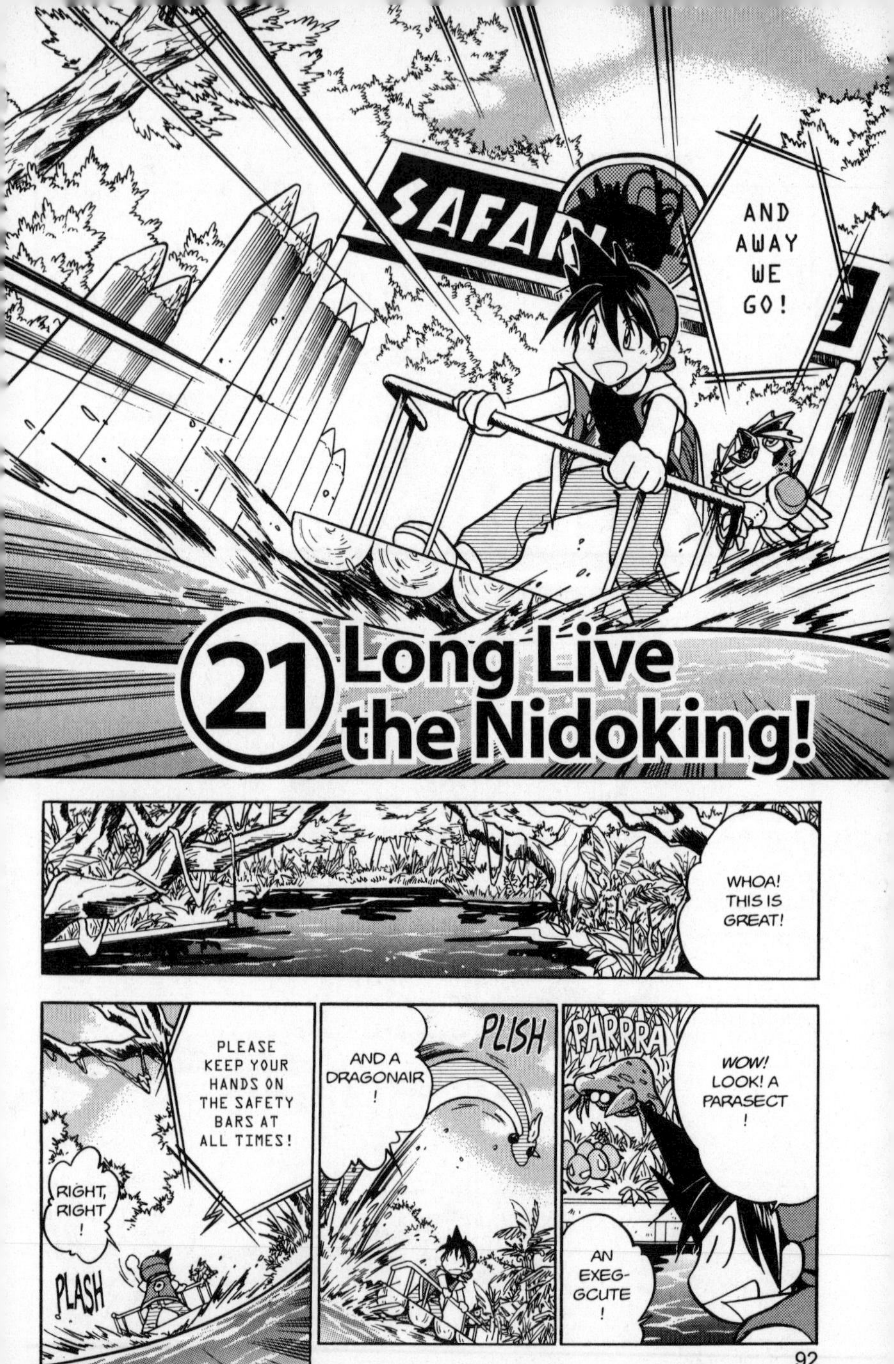
SAFARI
AND AWAY WE GO!
21 Long Live the Nidoking!
WHOA! THIS IS GREAT!
PARRRA
WOW! LOOK! A PARASECT!
AN EXEG-GCUTE!
PLISH
AND A DRAGONAIR!
PLEASE KEEP YOUR HANDS ON THE SAFETY BARS AT ALL TIMES!
RIGHT, RIGHT!
PLASH

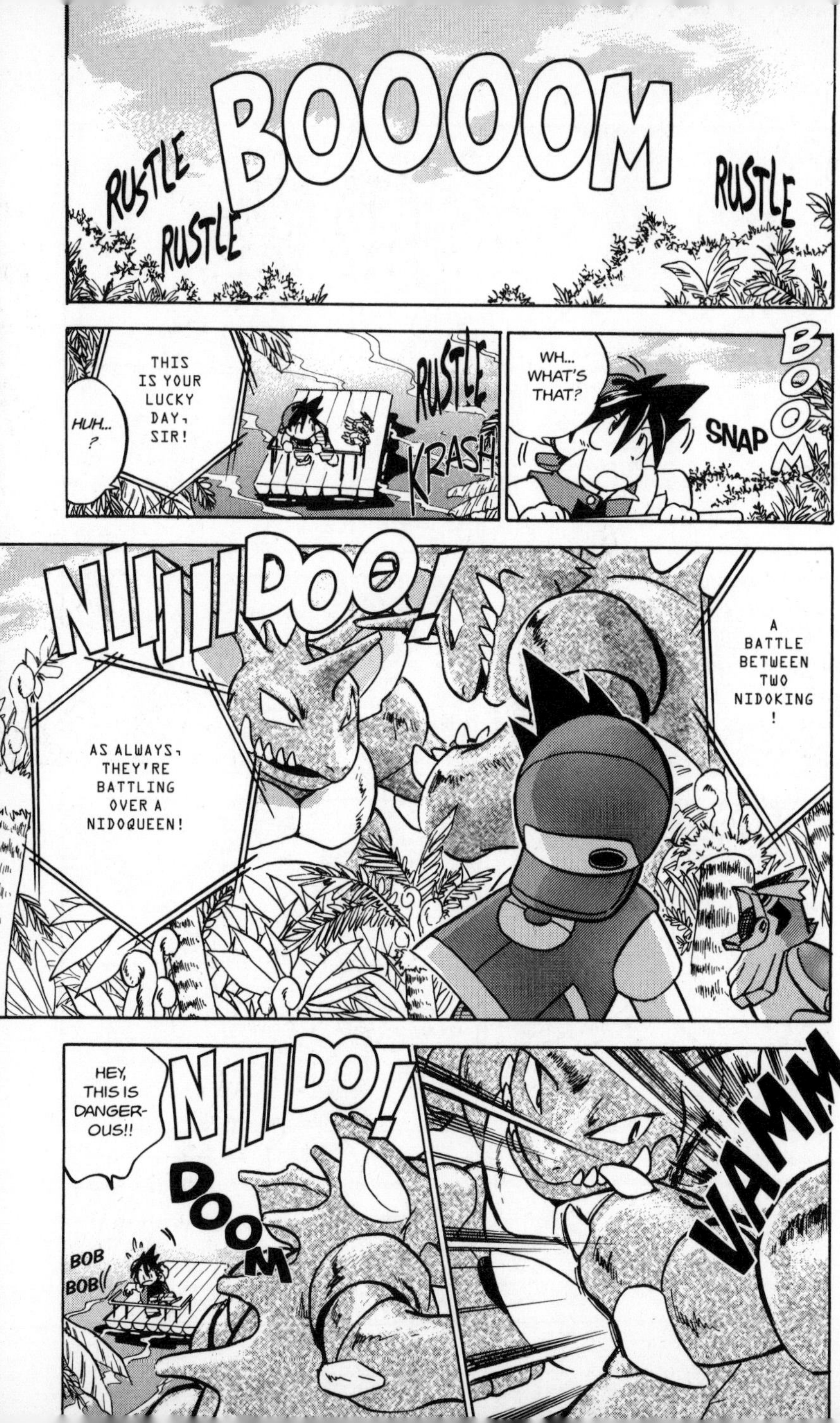
RUSTLE
BOOOOM
RUSTLE
RUSTLE
WH... WHAT'S THAT?
BOOOM
SNAP
RUSTLE
THIS IS YOUR LUCKY DAY, SIR!
KRASH
HUH... ?
A BATTLE BETWEEN TWO NIDOKING!
NIIIIIDOO!
AS ALWAYS, THEY'RE BATTLING OVER A NIDOQUEEN!
VAMM
NIIIDO!
HEY, THIS IS DANGEROUS!!
DOOM
BOB BOB

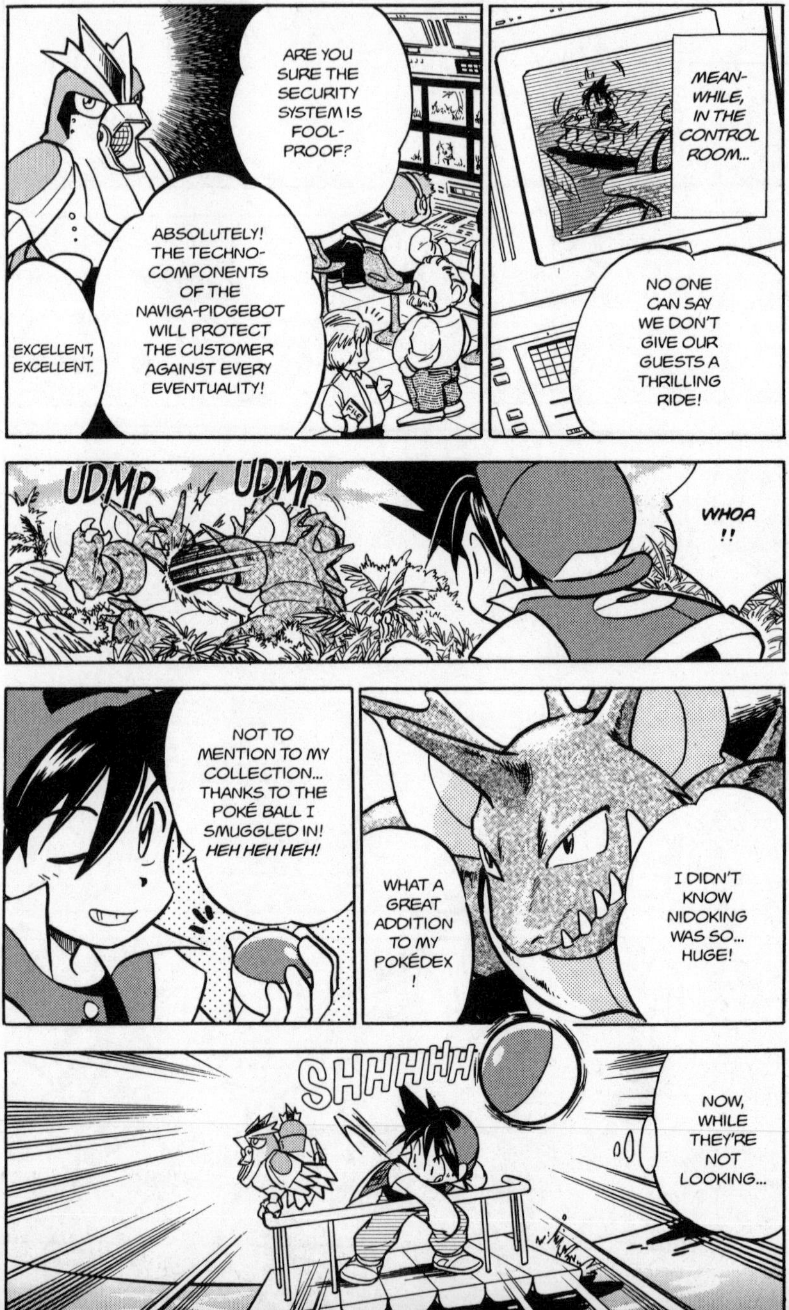
MEAN-WHILE, IN THE CONTROL ROOM...
NO ONE CAN SAY WE DON'T GIVE OUR GUESTS A THRILLING RIDE!
ARE YOU SURE THE SECURITY SYSTEM IS FOOL-PROOF?
ABSOLUTELY! THE TECHNO-COMPONENTS OF THE NAVIGA-PIDGEBOT WILL PROTECT THE CUSTOMER AGAINST EVERY EVENTUALITY!
EXCELLENT, EXCELLENT.
WHOA !!
UDMP
UDMP
I DIDN'T KNOW NIDOKING WAS SO... HUGE!
WHAT A GREAT ADDITION TO MY POKÉDEX !
NOT TO MENTION TO MY COLLECTION... THANKS TO THE POKÉ BALL I SMUGGLED IN! HEH HEH HEH!
NOW, WHILE THEY'RE NOT LOOKING...
SHHHHHH

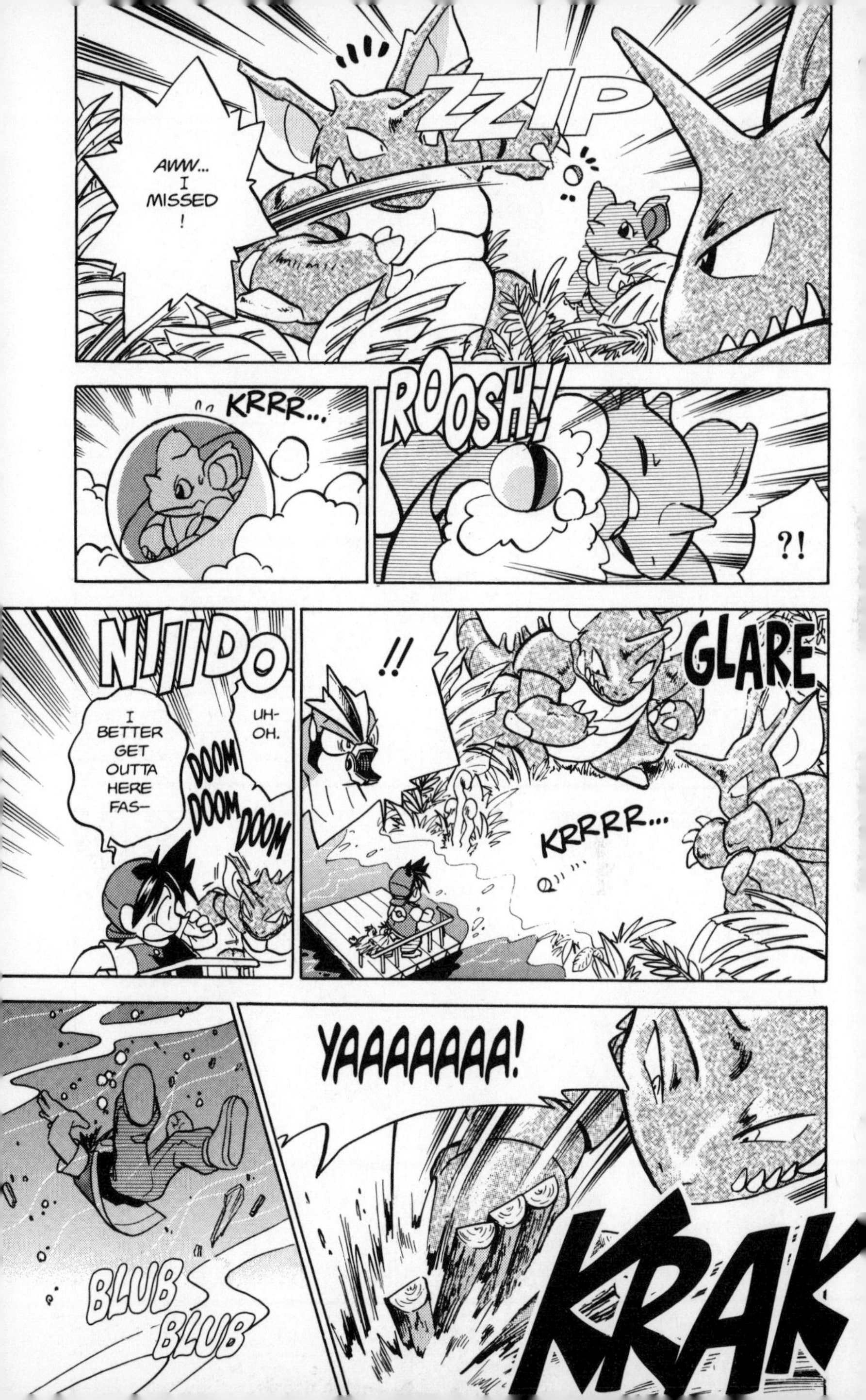
ZZIP
AWW... I MISSED!
ROOSH!
?!
KRRR...
GLARE
!!
KRRRR...
NIIIDO
UH-OH.
I BETTER GET OUTTA HERE FAS—
DOOM DOOM DOOM
YAAAAAAA!
KRAK
BLUB BLUB

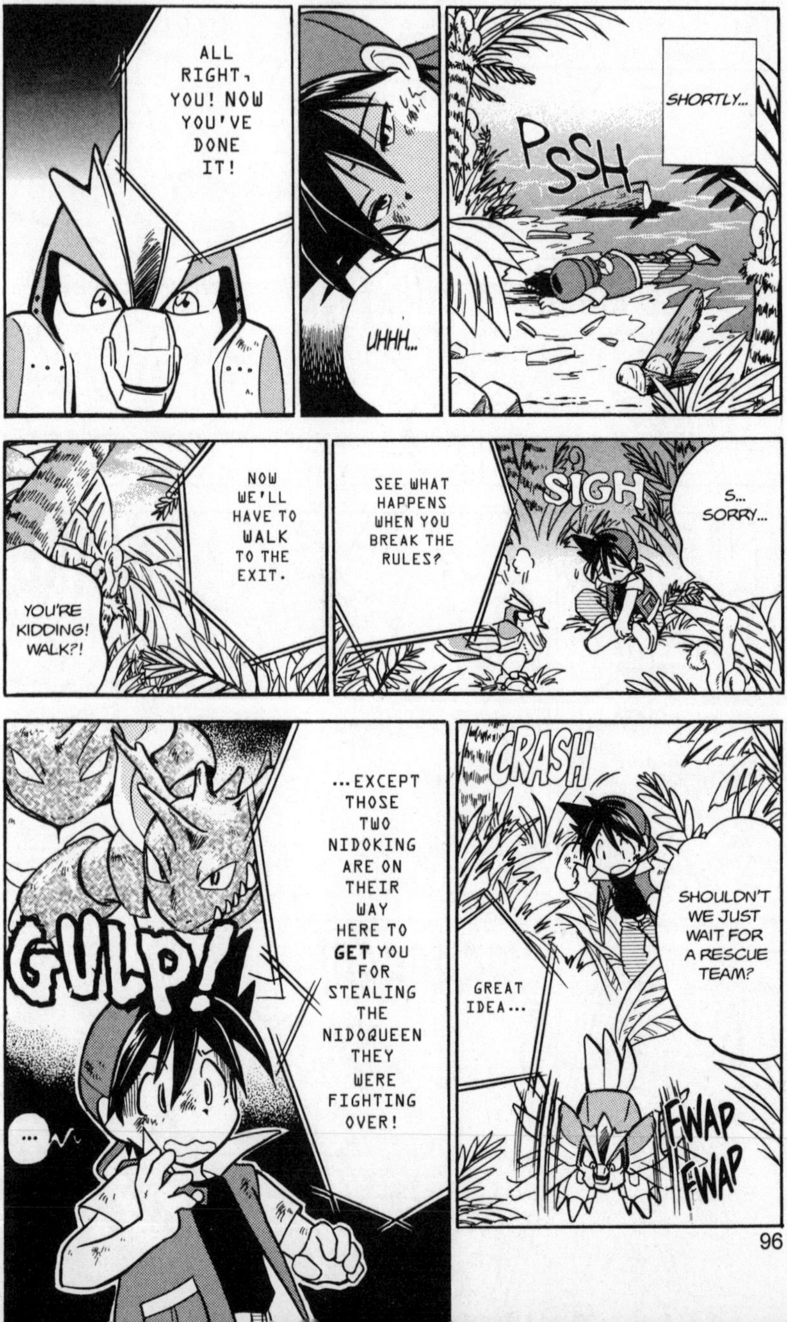
SHORTLY...
PSSH
UHHH...
ALL RIGHT, YOU! NOW YOU'VE DONE IT!
...
...
SIGH
S... SORRY...
SEE WHAT HAPPENS WHEN YOU BREAK THE RULES?
NOW WE'LL HAVE TO WALK TO THE EXIT.
YOU'RE KIDDING! WALK?!
CRASH
SHOULDN'T WE JUST WAIT FOR A RESCUE TEAM?
GREAT IDEA...
FWAP FWAP
...EXCEPT THOSE TWO NIDOKING ARE ON THEIR WAY HERE TO **GET** YOU FOR STEALING THE NIDOQUEEN THEY WERE FIGHTING OVER!
GULP!
...

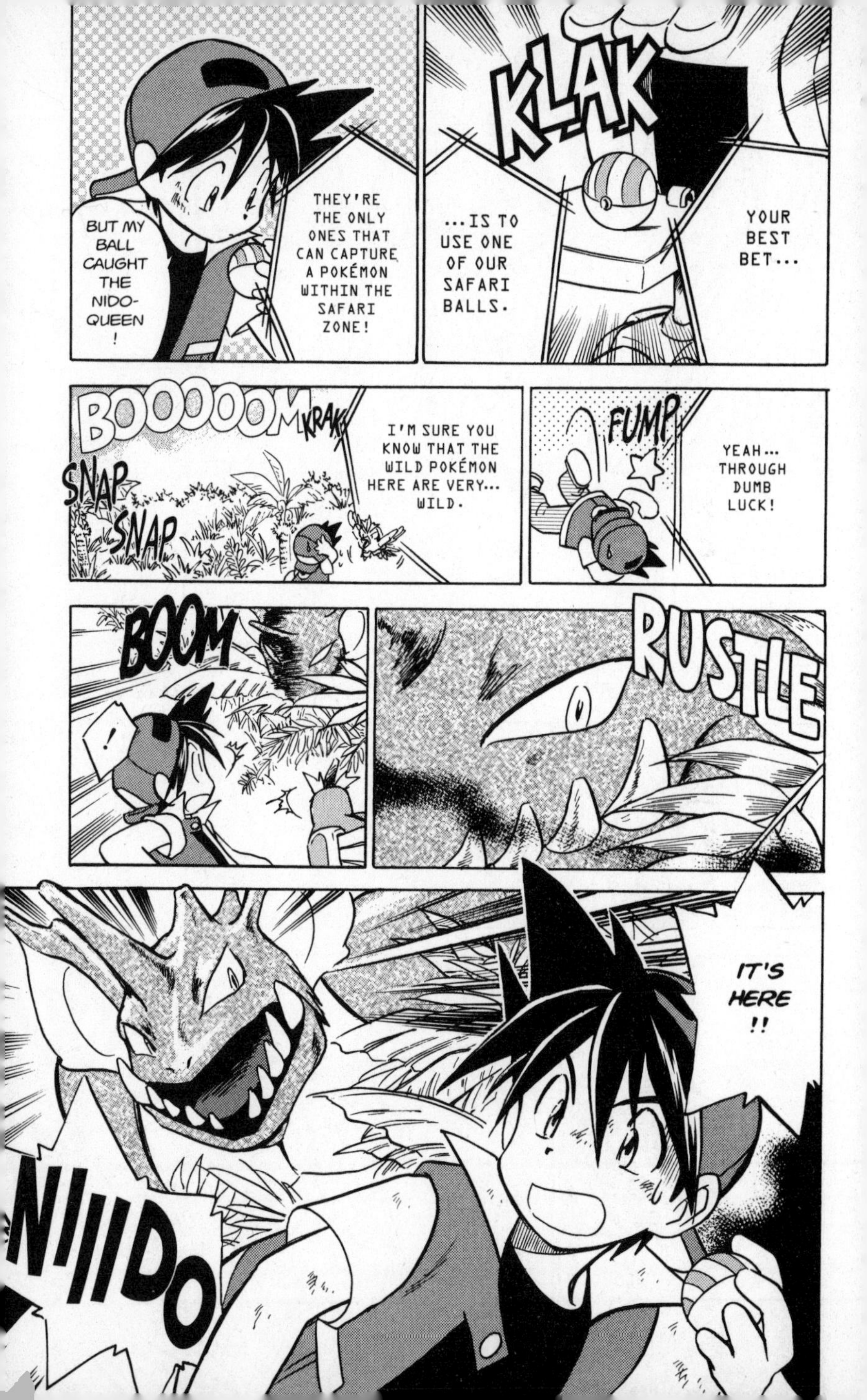
KLAK
YOUR BEST BET...
...IS TO USE ONE OF OUR SAFARI BALLS.
THEY'RE THE ONLY ONES THAT CAN CAPTURE A POKÉMON WITHIN THE SAFARI ZONE!
BUT MY BALL CAUGHT THE NIDO-QUEEN!
FUMP
YEAH... THROUGH DUMB LUCK!
I'M SURE YOU KNOW THAT THE WILD POKÉMON HERE ARE VERY... WILD.
KRAK
BOOOOOM
SNAP
SNAP
RUSTLE
BOOM
!
IT'S HERE!!
NIIIDO

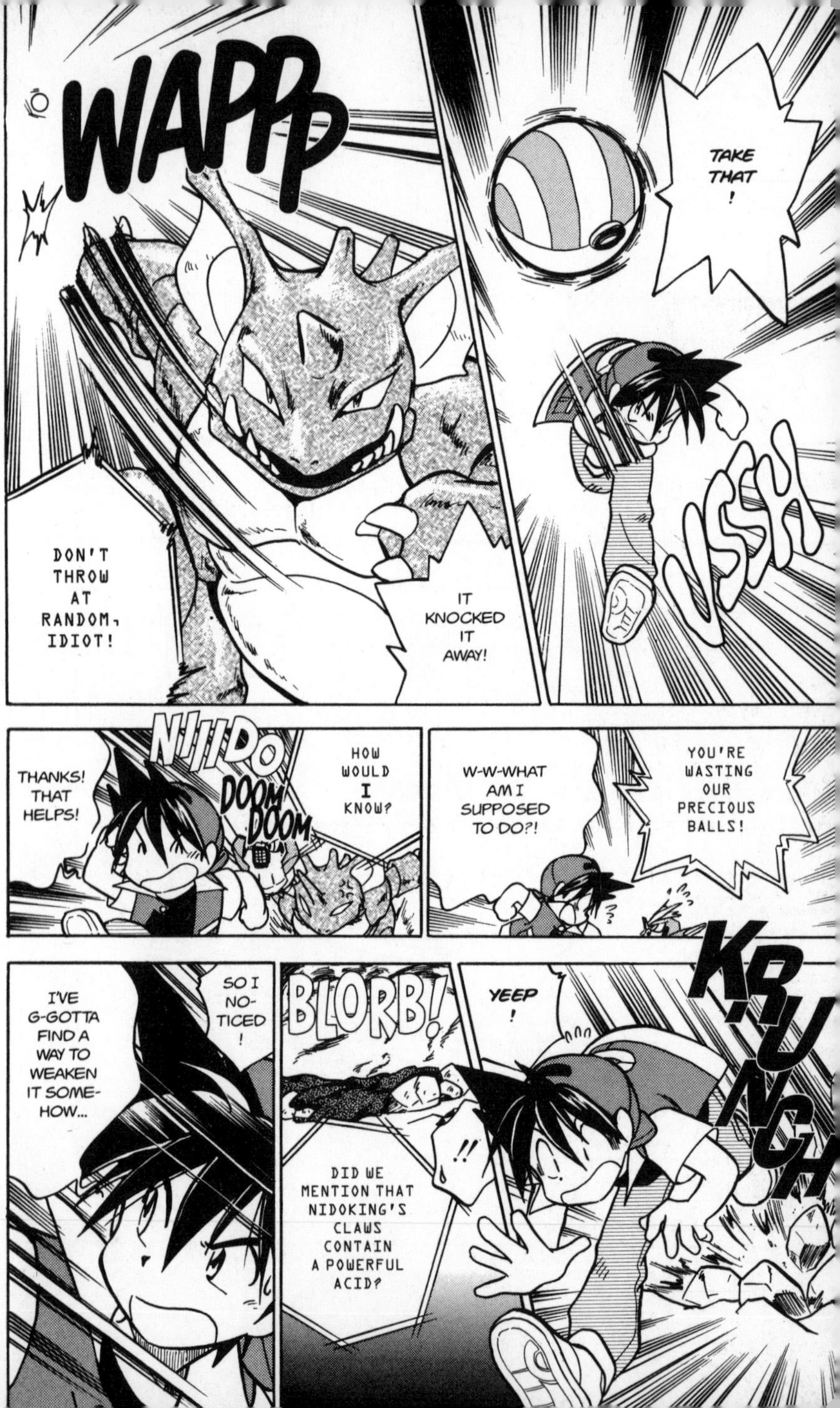
TAKE THAT!
VSSH
WAPP
IT KNOCKED IT AWAY!
DON'T THROW AT RANDOM, IDIOT!
YOU'RE WASTING OUR PRECIOUS BALLS!
W-W-WHAT AM I SUPPOSED TO DO?!
HOW WOULD I KNOW?
NIIIDO
DOOM DOOM
THANKS! THAT HELPS!
KRUNCH
YEEP!
BLORB!
DID WE MENTION THAT NIDOKING'S CLAWS CONTAIN A POWERFUL ACID?
SO I NO-TICED!
I'VE G-GOTTA FIND A WAY TO WEAKEN IT SOME-HOW...

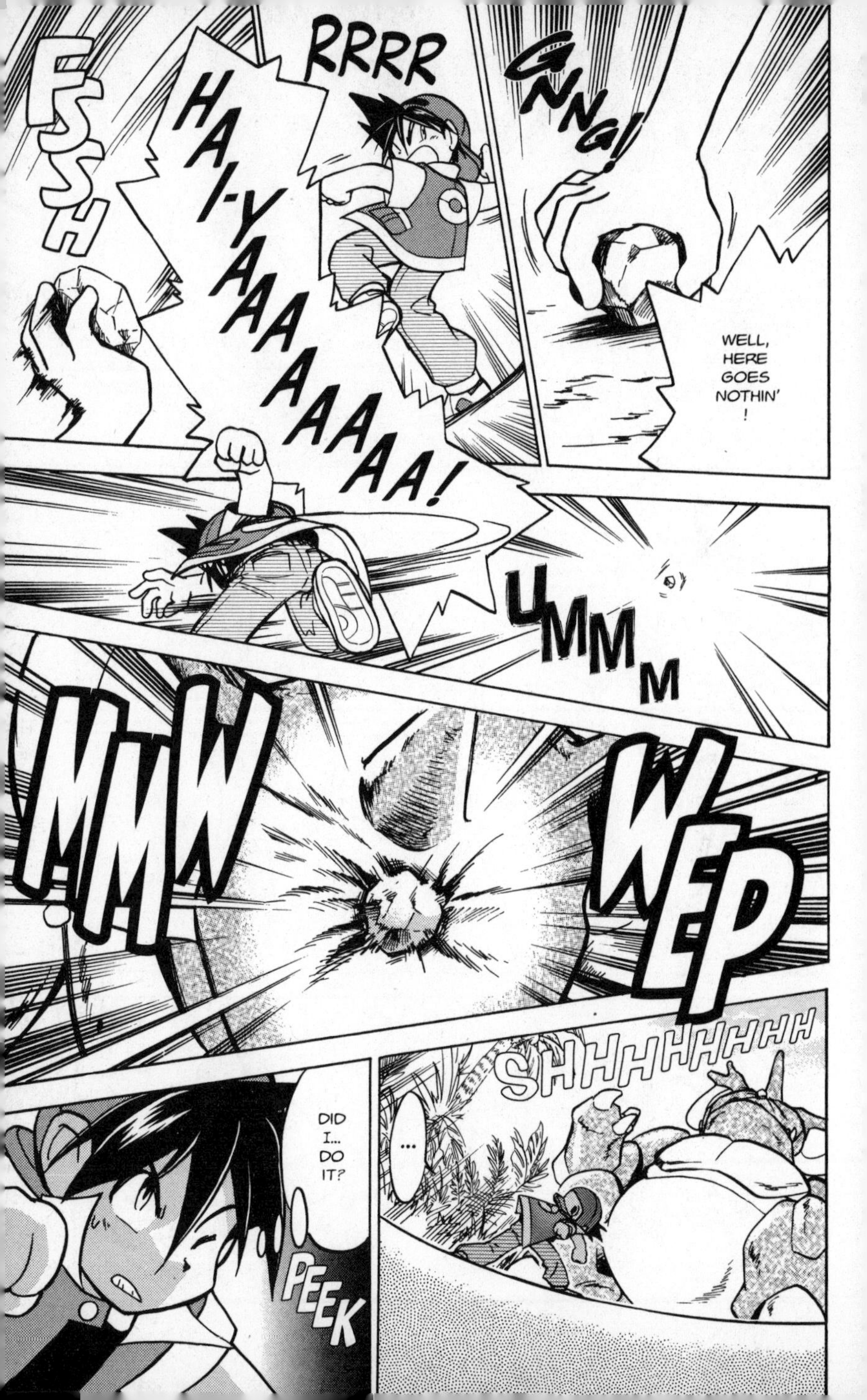
GNNG!
WELL, HERE GOES NOTHIN'!
RRRR
HAI-YAAAAAAAAAA!
FSSH
UMMMM
MMWEP
SHHHHHHHHH
...
DID I... DO IT?
PEEK

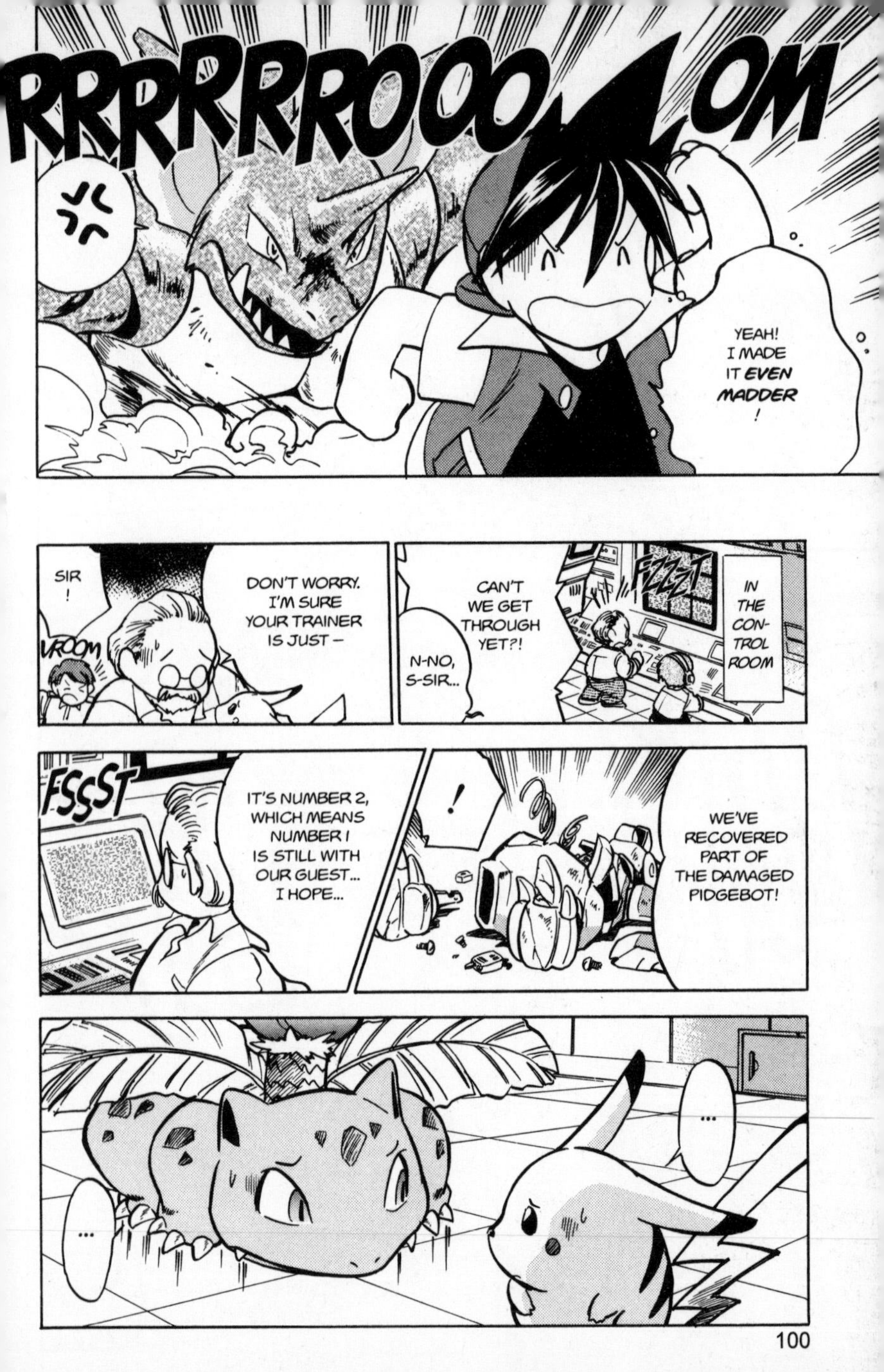
RRRRRROOOOOM
YEAH! I MADE IT EVEN MADDER!
IN THE CONTROL ROOM
FZZZT
CAN'T WE GET THROUGH YET?!
N-NO, S-SIR...
SIR!
DON'T WORRY. I'M SURE YOUR TRAINER IS JUST –
VROOM
WE'VE RECOVERED PART OF THE DAMAGED PIDGEBOT!
!
IT'S NUMBER 2, WHICH MEANS NUMBER 1 IS STILL WITH OUR GUEST... I HOPE...
FSSST
...
...

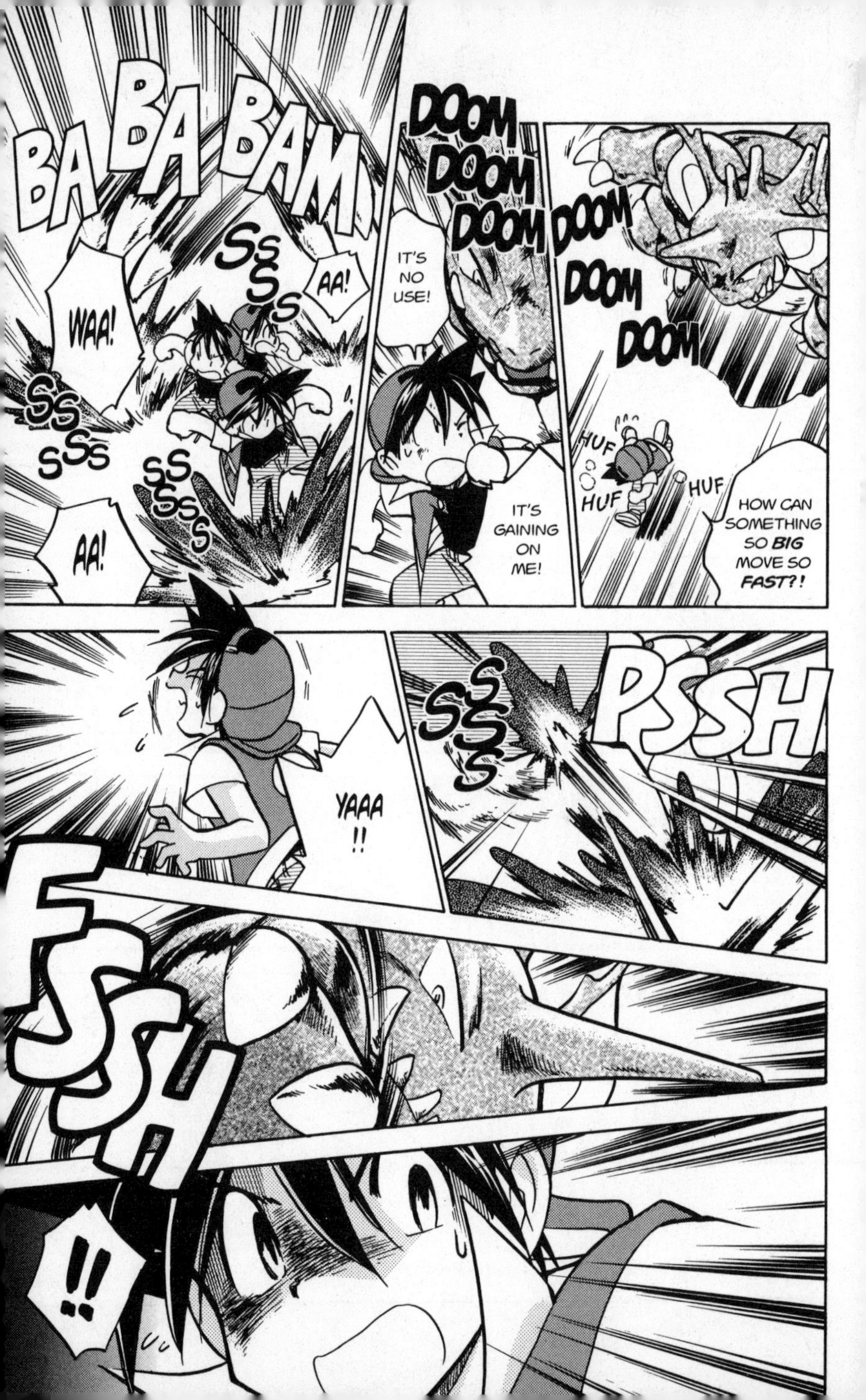
DOOM
DOOM
DOOM
HUF
HUF
HUF
HOW CAN SOMETHING SO **BIG** MOVE SO ***FAST?!***
DOOM
DOOM
DOOM
IT'S NO USE!
IT'S GAINING ON ME!
BA BA BAM
SSSS
AA!
WAA!
SSSSS
SSSSS
AA!
PSSH
SSSSS
YAAA !!
FSSH
!!

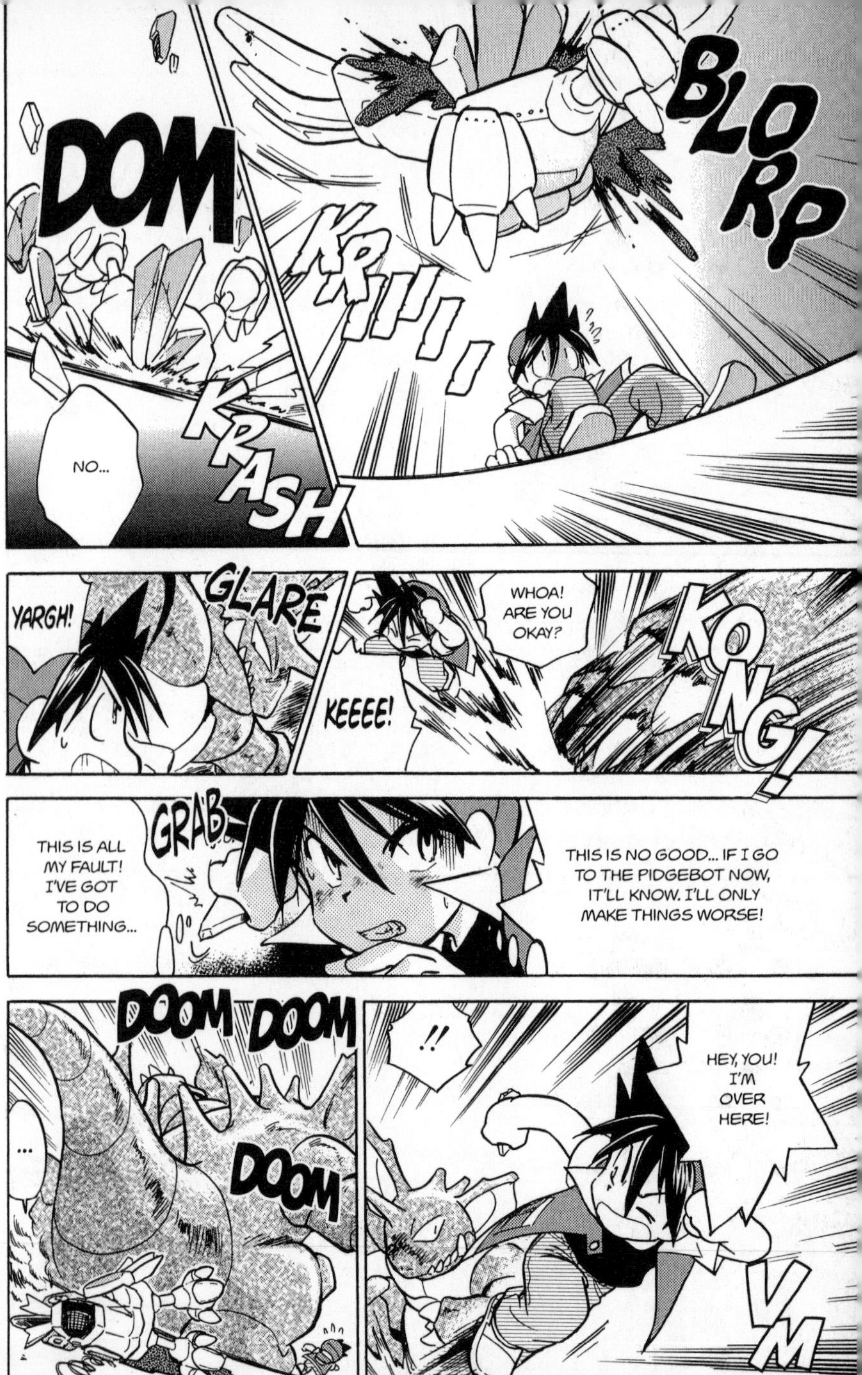
BLORP
KRIIIII
DOM
KRASH
NO...
KONG!
WHOA! ARE YOU OKAY?
KEEEE!
GLARE
YARGH!
THIS IS NO GOOD... IF I GO TO THE PIDGEBOT NOW, IT'LL KNOW. I'LL ONLY MAKE THINGS WORSE!
GRAB
THIS IS ALL MY FAULT! I'VE GOT TO DO SOMETHING...
!!
HEY, YOU! I'M OVER HERE!
VMMM
DOOM DOOM
DOOM
...

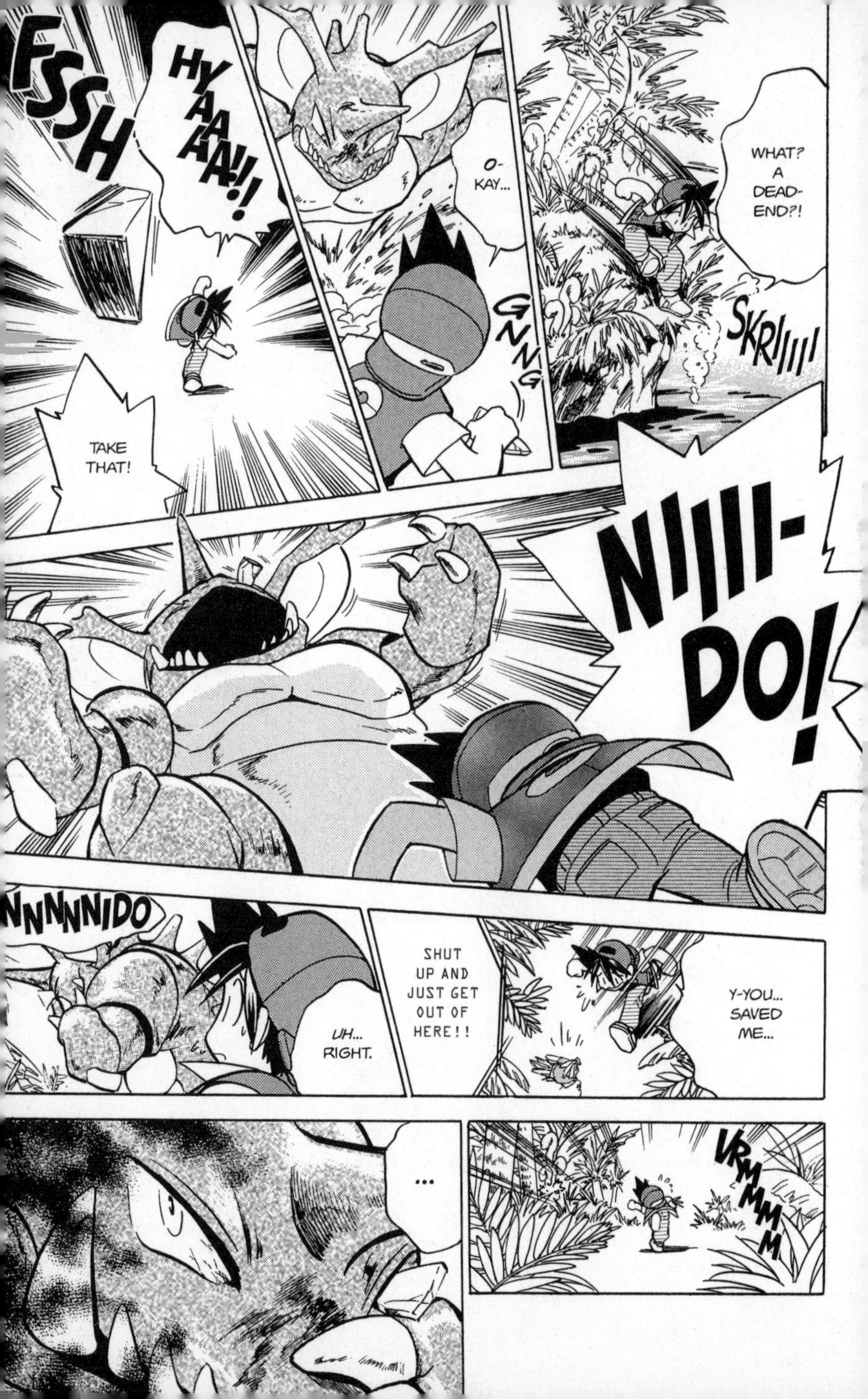
WHAT? A DEAD-END?!
SKRIIIIII
O-KAY...
GNNG
FSSH
HYAAAA!!
TAKE THAT!
NIIII-DO!
Y-YOU... SAVED ME...
SHUT UP AND JUST GET OUT OF HERE!!
UH... RIGHT.
NNNNNIDO
VRMMMMM
...

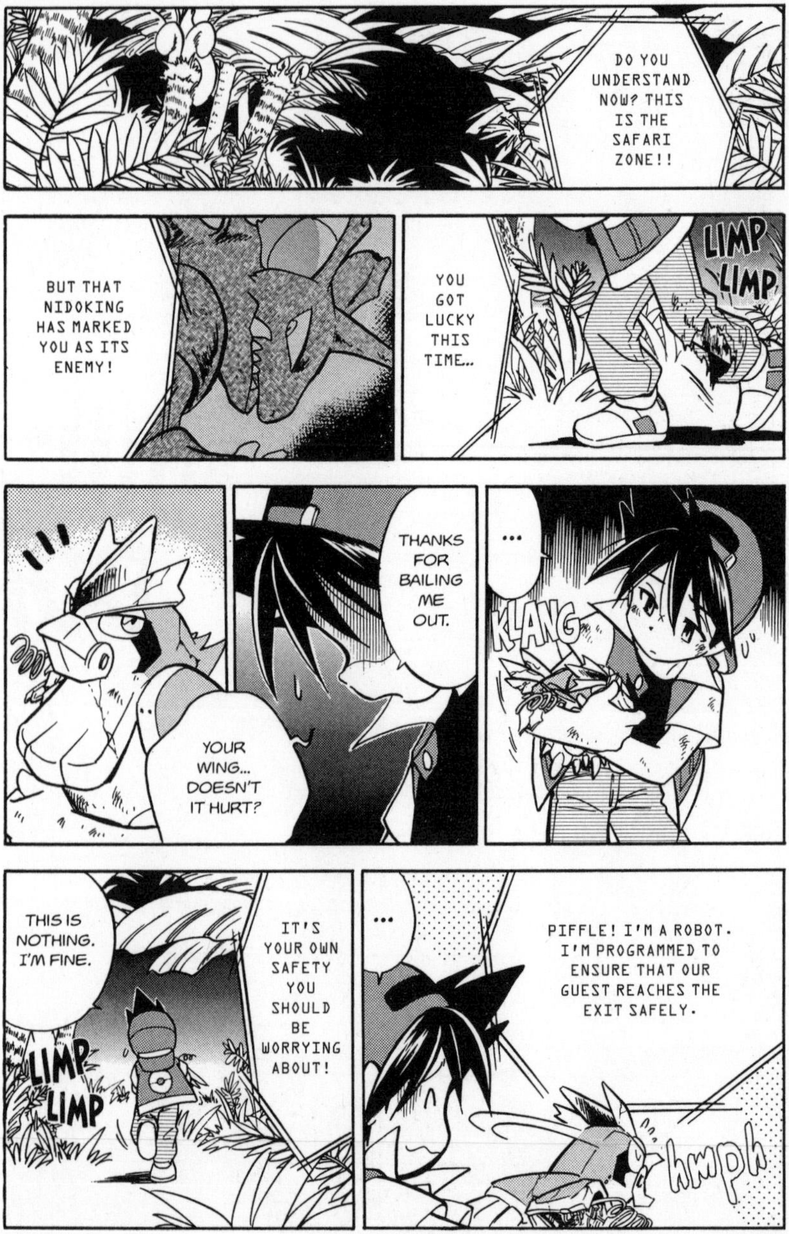
DO YOU UNDERSTAND NOW? THIS IS THE SAFARI ZONE!!
LIMP LIMP
YOU GOT LUCKY THIS TIME...
BUT THAT NIDOKING HAS MARKED YOU AS ITS ENEMY!
...
KLANG
THANKS FOR BAILING ME OUT.
YOUR WING... DOESN'T IT HURT?
...
PIFFLE! I'M A ROBOT. I'M PROGRAMMED TO ENSURE THAT OUR GUEST REACHES THE EXIT SAFELY.
hmph
IT'S YOUR OWN SAFETY YOU SHOULD BE WORRYING ABOUT!
THIS IS NOTHING. I'M FINE.
LIMP LIMP

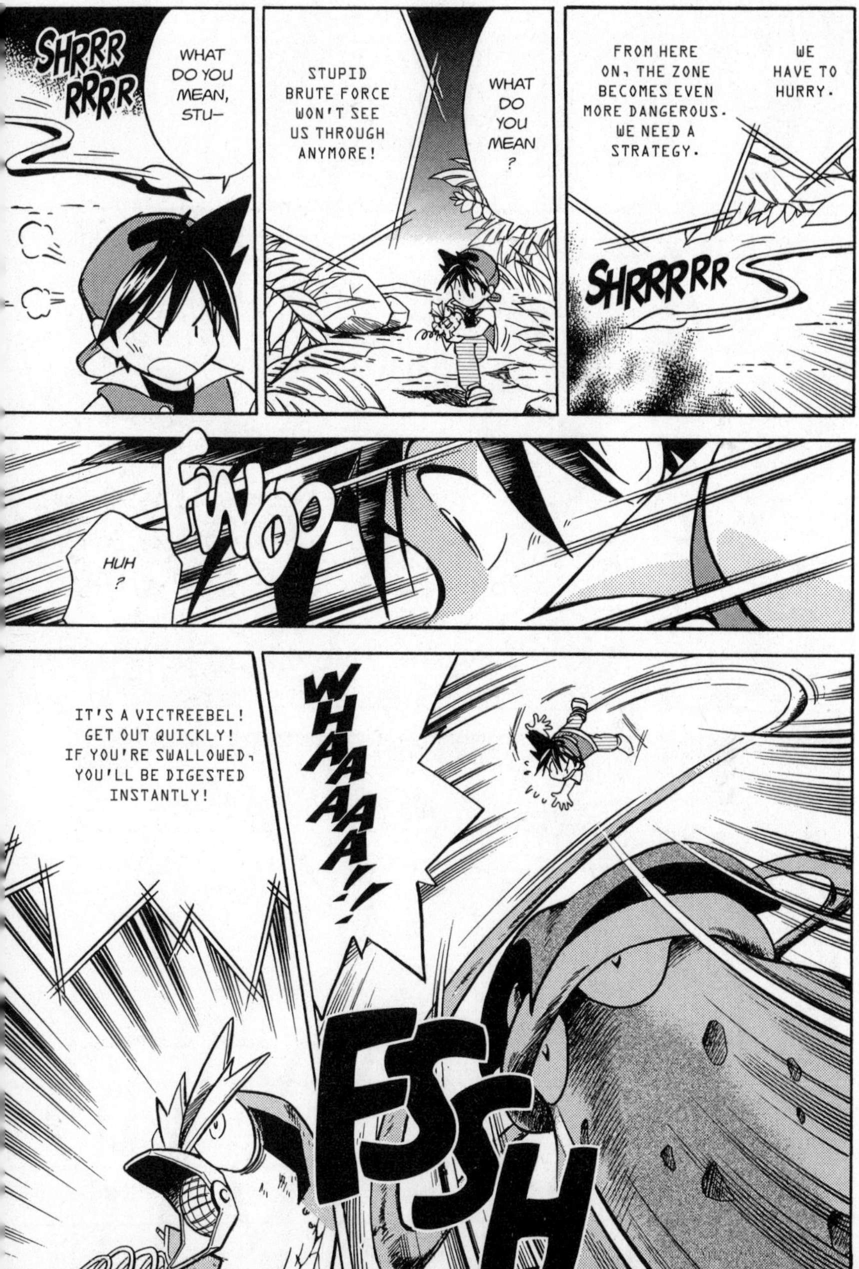
WE HAVE TO HURRY.
FROM HERE ON, THE ZONE BECOMES EVEN MORE DANGEROUS. WE NEED A STRATEGY.
SHRRRRR
WHAT DO YOU MEAN?
STUPID BRUTE FORCE WON'T SEE US THROUGH ANYMORE!
WHAT DO YOU MEAN, STU—
SHRRR RRRR
FWOO
HUH?
WHAAAAA!!
FSSH
IT'S A VICTREEBEL! GET OUT QUICKLY! IF YOU'RE SWALLOWED, YOU'LL BE DIGESTED INSTANTLY!

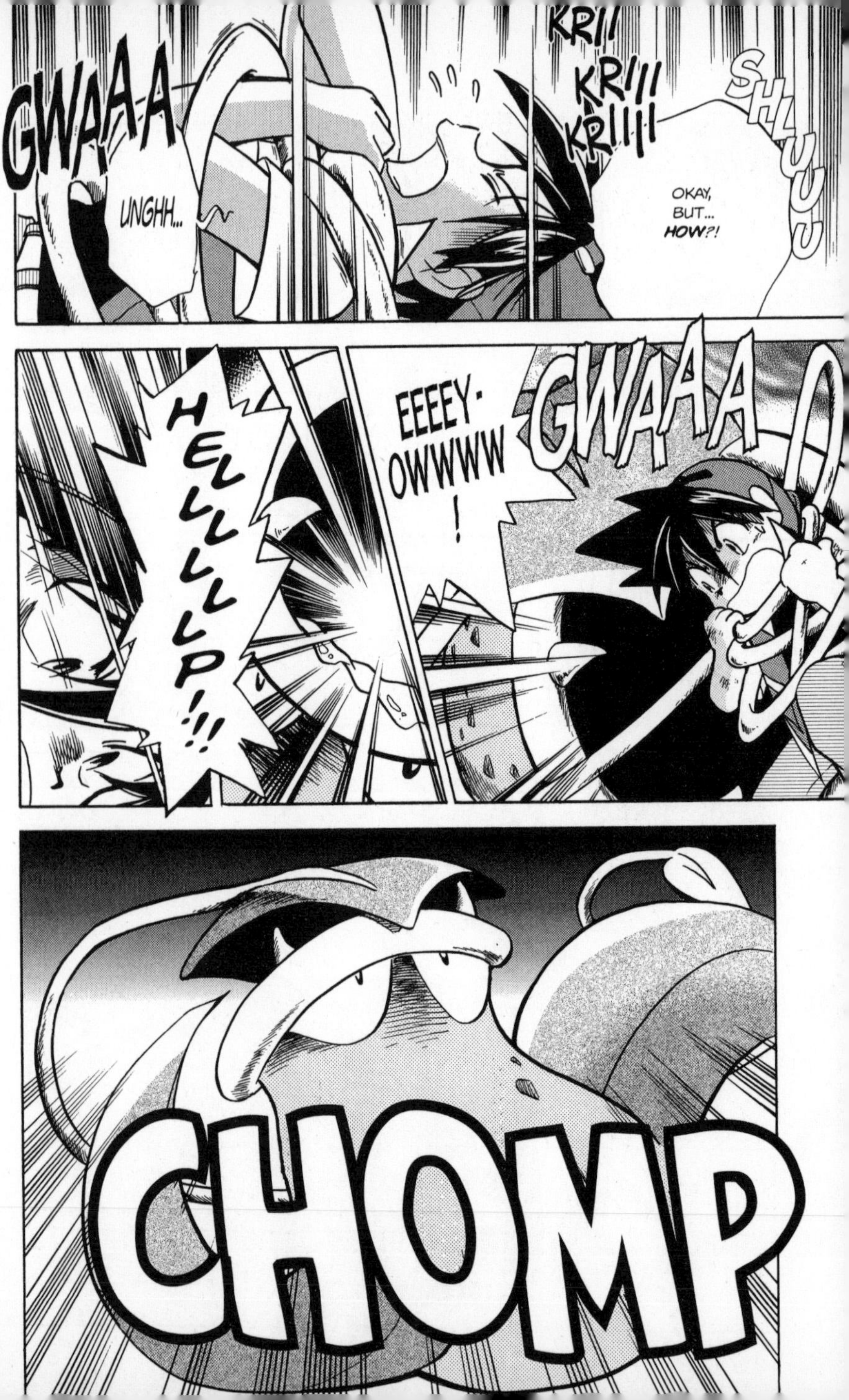
SHLUUUU
KRII KRIII KRIIII
OKAY, BUT... HOW?!
GWAAA
UNGHH...
GWAAAA
EEEEY-OWWWW!
HELLLLLLP!!!
CHOMP

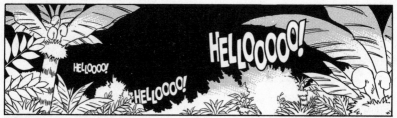

HELLOOOOO!
HELLOOOO!
HELLOOOO!
STILL NO SIGN OF HIM?
SHFFFF
NO, SIR. AND NO WORD FROM THE MAIN GATE.
SHFFFF
THEN ALL WE CAN DO IS...
GULP
...PRAY HE IS SAFE.
!
PI...
PIKACHUU! (WHERE ARE YOU?!)
PIKACHUU!
PIKACHU!!

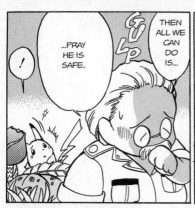

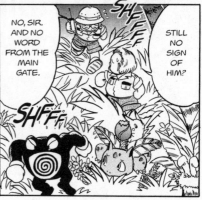

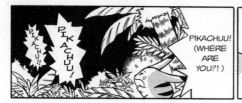

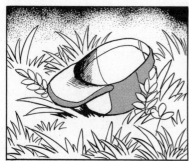

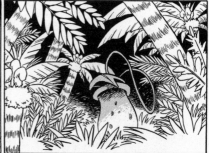

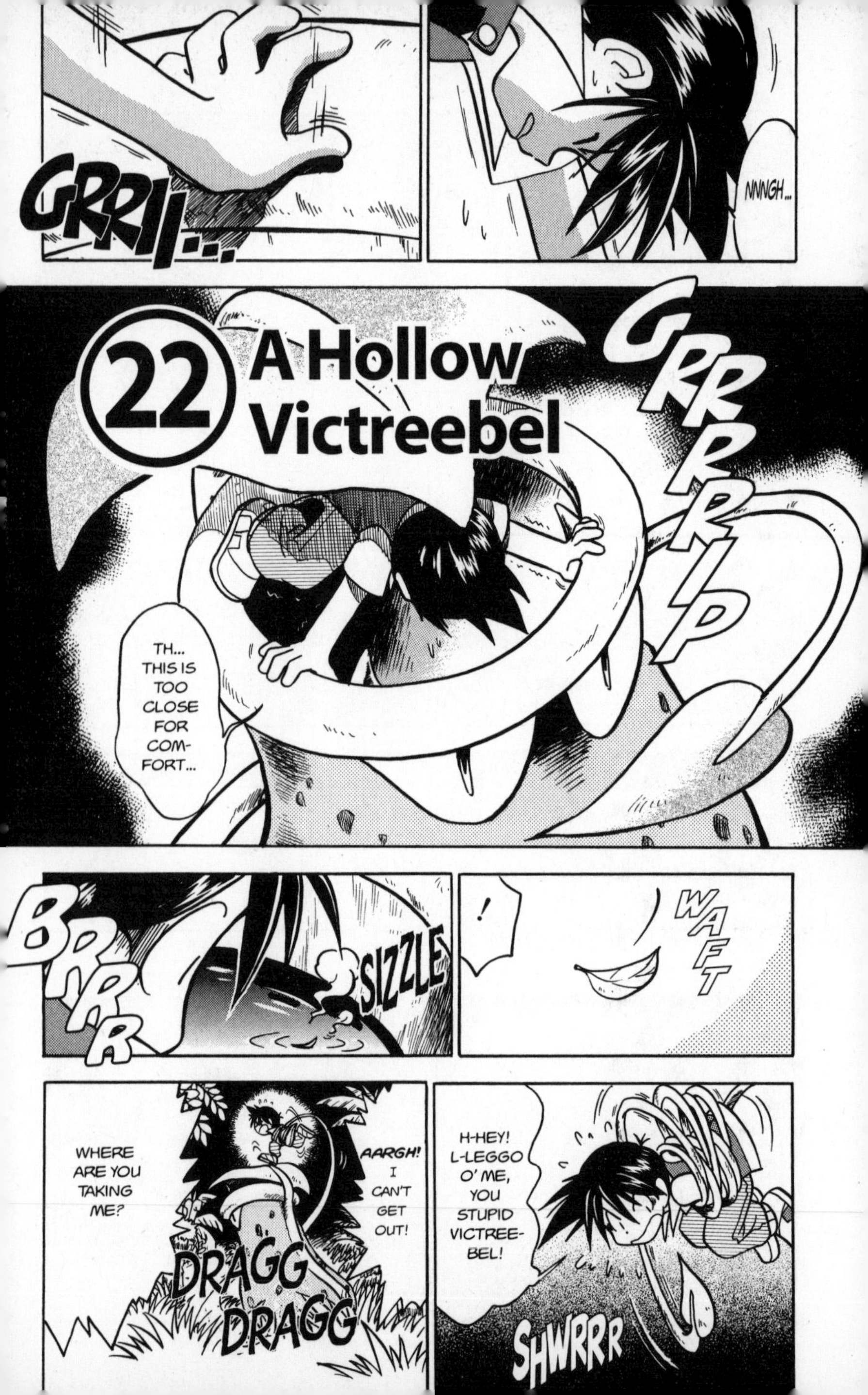
NNNGH...
GRRI...
22 A Hollow Victreebel
GRRRRIP
TH... THIS IS TOO CLOSE FOR COM-FORT...
!
WAFT
BRRRR
SIZZLE
H-HEY! L-LEGGO O' ME, YOU STUPID VICTREE-BEL!
SHWRRR
AARGH! I CAN'T GET OUT!
WHERE ARE YOU TAKING ME?
DRAGG
DRAGG

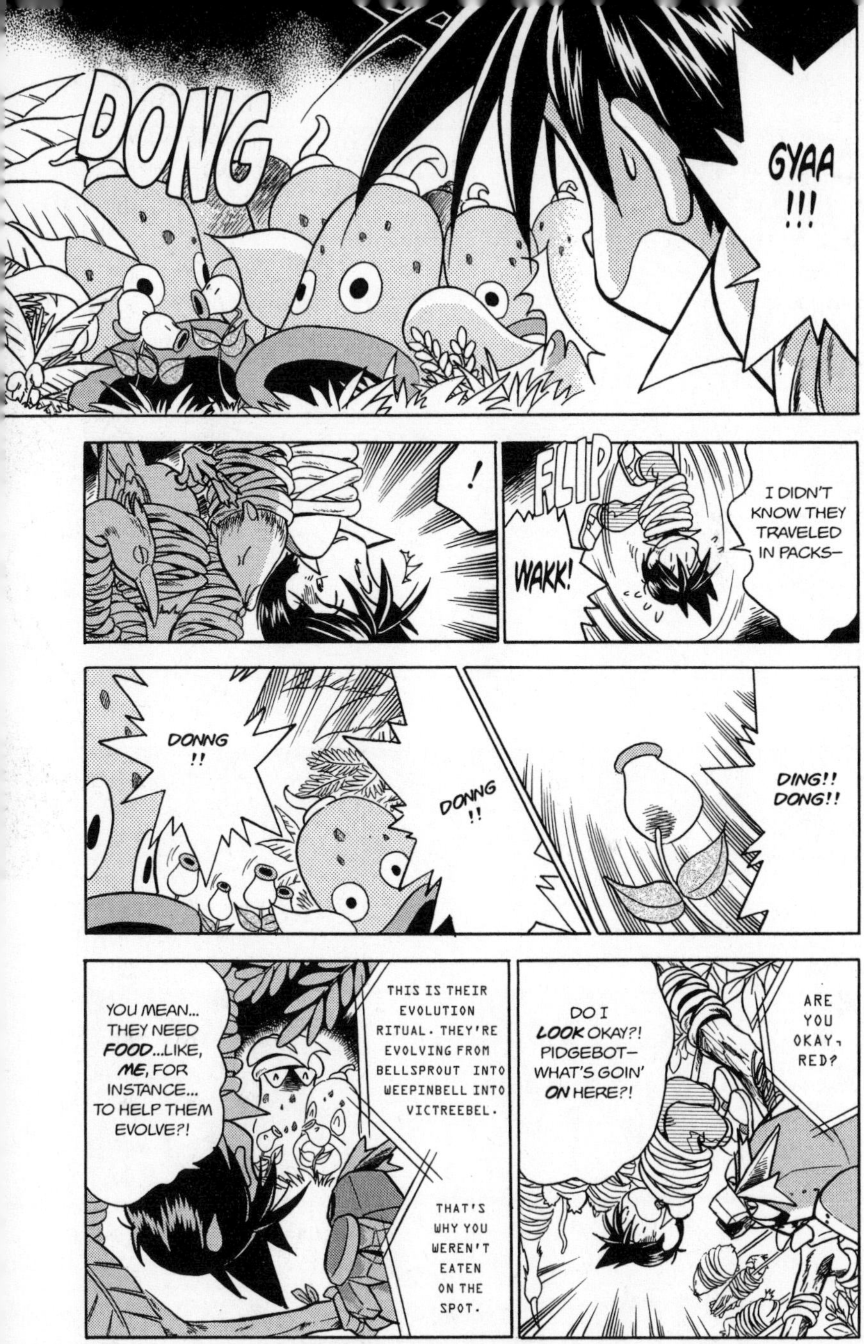
DONG
GYAA!!!
FLIP
I DIDN'T KNOW THEY TRAVELED IN PACKS—
WAKK!
!
DING!! DONG!!
DONNG!!
DONNG!!
ARE YOU OKAY, RED?
DO I LOOK OKAY?! PIDGEBOT— WHAT'S GOIN' ON HERE?!
THIS IS THEIR EVOLUTION RITUAL. THEY'RE EVOLVING FROM BELLSPROUT INTO WEEPINBELL INTO VICTREEBEL.
YOU MEAN... THEY NEED FOOD...LIKE, ME, FOR INSTANCE... TO HELP THEM EVOLVE?!
THAT'S WHY YOU WEREN'T EATEN ON THE SPOT.

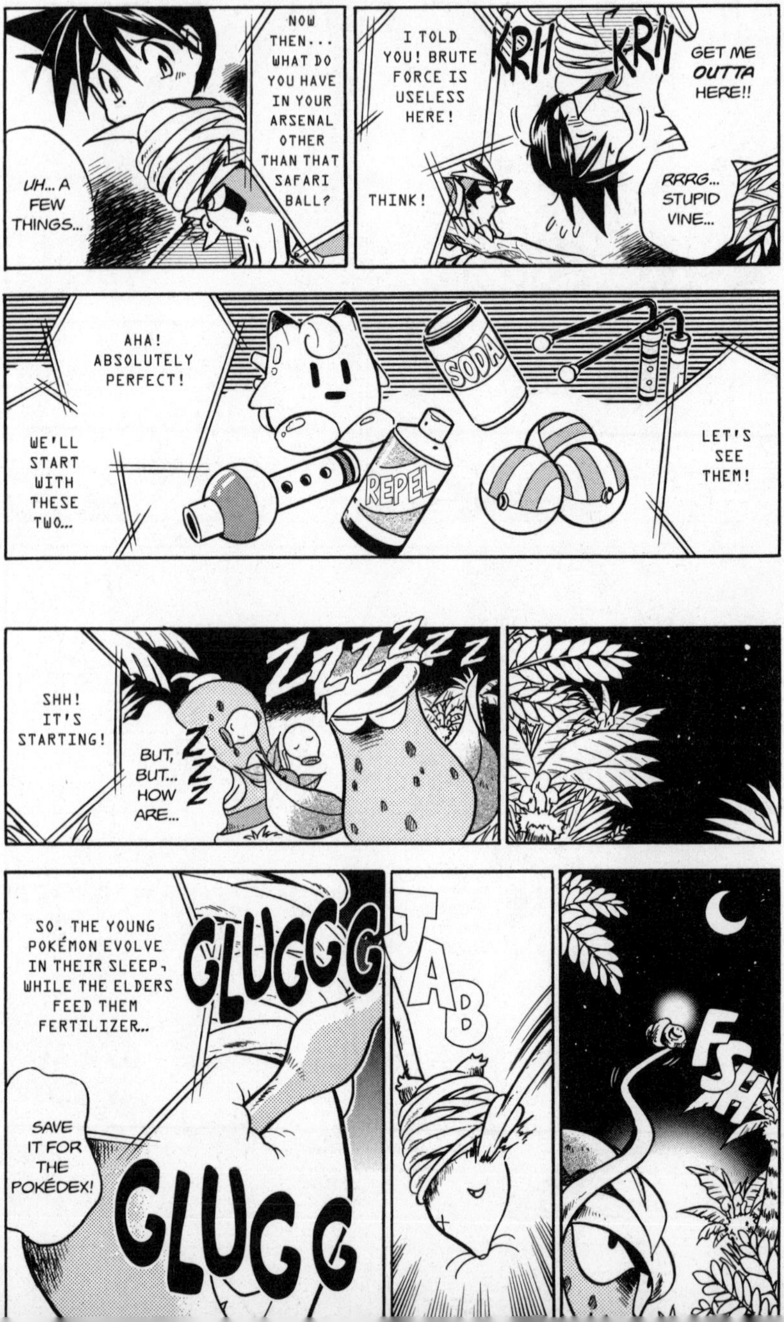
GET ME OUTTA HERE!!
KRII KRII
I TOLD YOU! BRUTE FORCE IS USELESS HERE!
RRRG... STUPID VINE...
THINK!
NOW THEN... WHAT DO YOU HAVE IN YOUR ARSENAL OTHER THAN THAT SAFARI BALL?
UH... A FEW THINGS...
LET'S SEE THEM!
SODA
REPEL
AHA! ABSOLUTELY PERFECT!
WE'LL START WITH THESE TWO...
ZZZZZZZ
SHH! IT'S STARTING!
ZZZ
BUT, BUT... HOW ARE...
FSH
JAB
GLUGGG
SO. THE YOUNG POKÉMON EVOLVE IN THEIR SLEEP, WHILE THE ELDERS FEED THEM FERTILIZER..
SAVE IT FOR THE POKÉDEX!
GLUGG

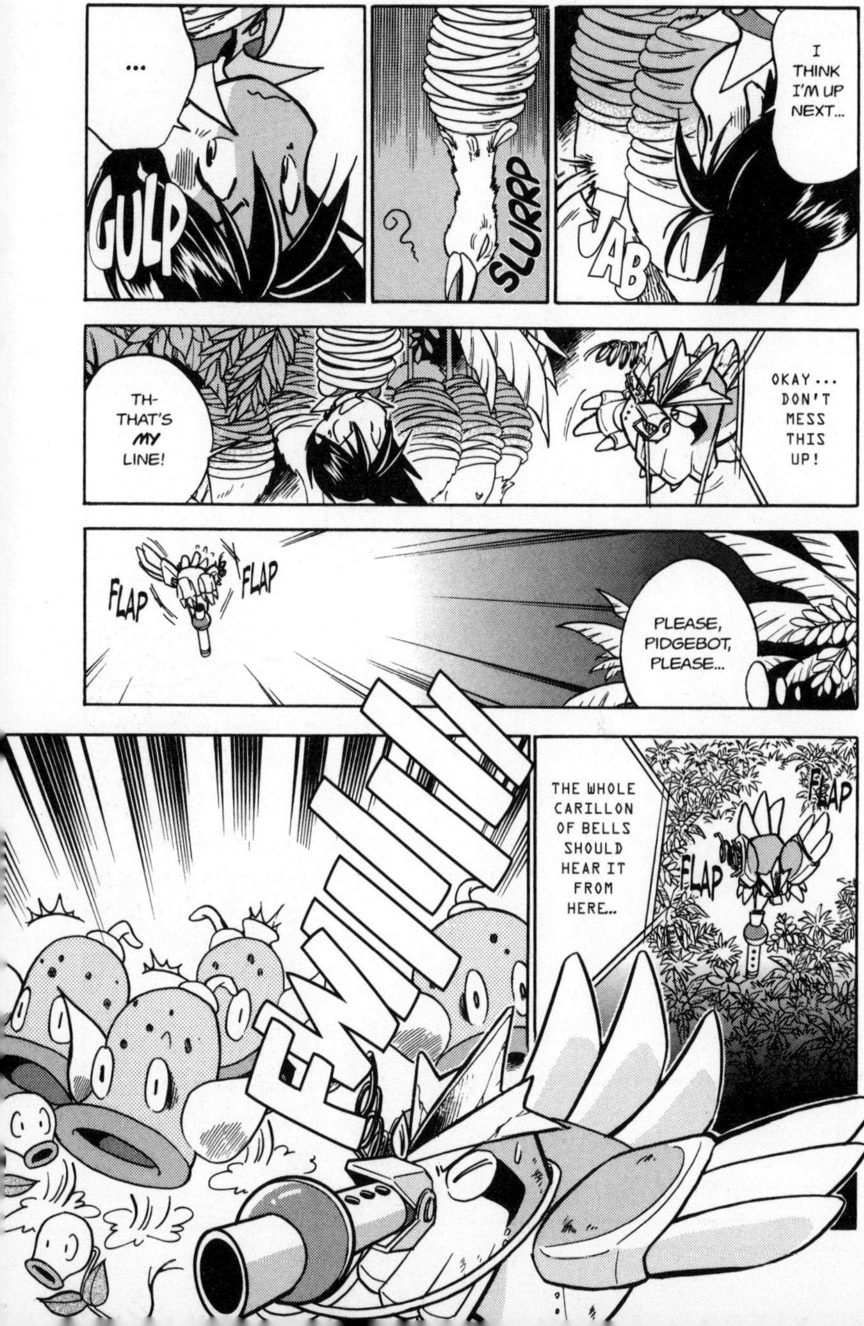

I THINK I'M UP NEXT...
JAB
SLURRP
...
GULP
OKAY... DON'T MESS THIS UP!
TH-THAT'S MY LINE!
PLEASE, PIDGEBOT, PLEASE...
FLAP
FLAP
THE WHOLE CARILLON OF BELLS SHOULD HEAR IT FROM HERE..
FLAP
FLAP

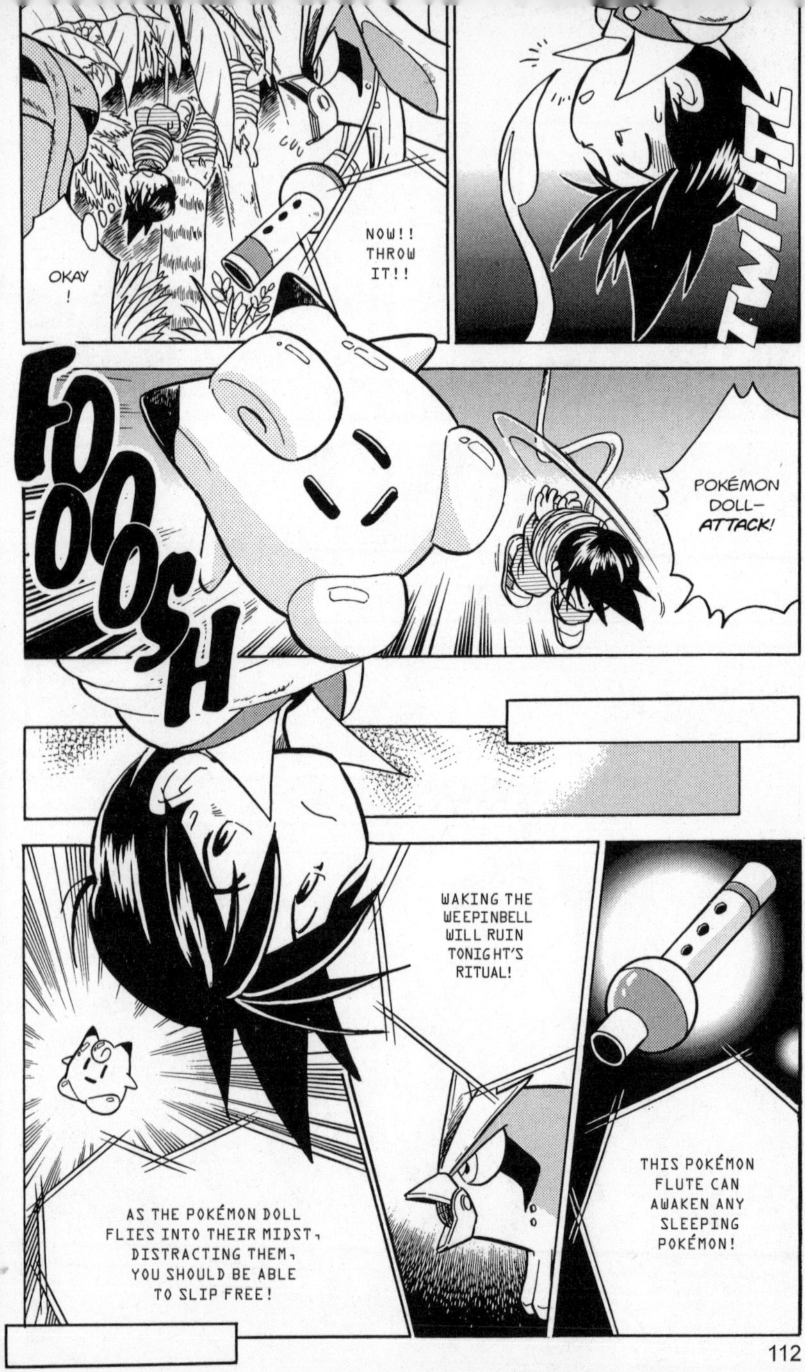
TWIIIT
NOW!! THROW IT!!
OKAY !
POKÉMON DOLL—ATTACK!
FOOOOSH
THIS POKÉMON FLUTE CAN AWAKEN ANY SLEEPING POKÉMON!
WAKING THE WEEPINBELL WILL RUIN TONIGHT'S RITUAL!
AS THE POKÉMON DOLL FLIES INTO THEIR MIDST, DISTRACTING THEM, YOU SHOULD BE ABLE TO SLIP FREE!

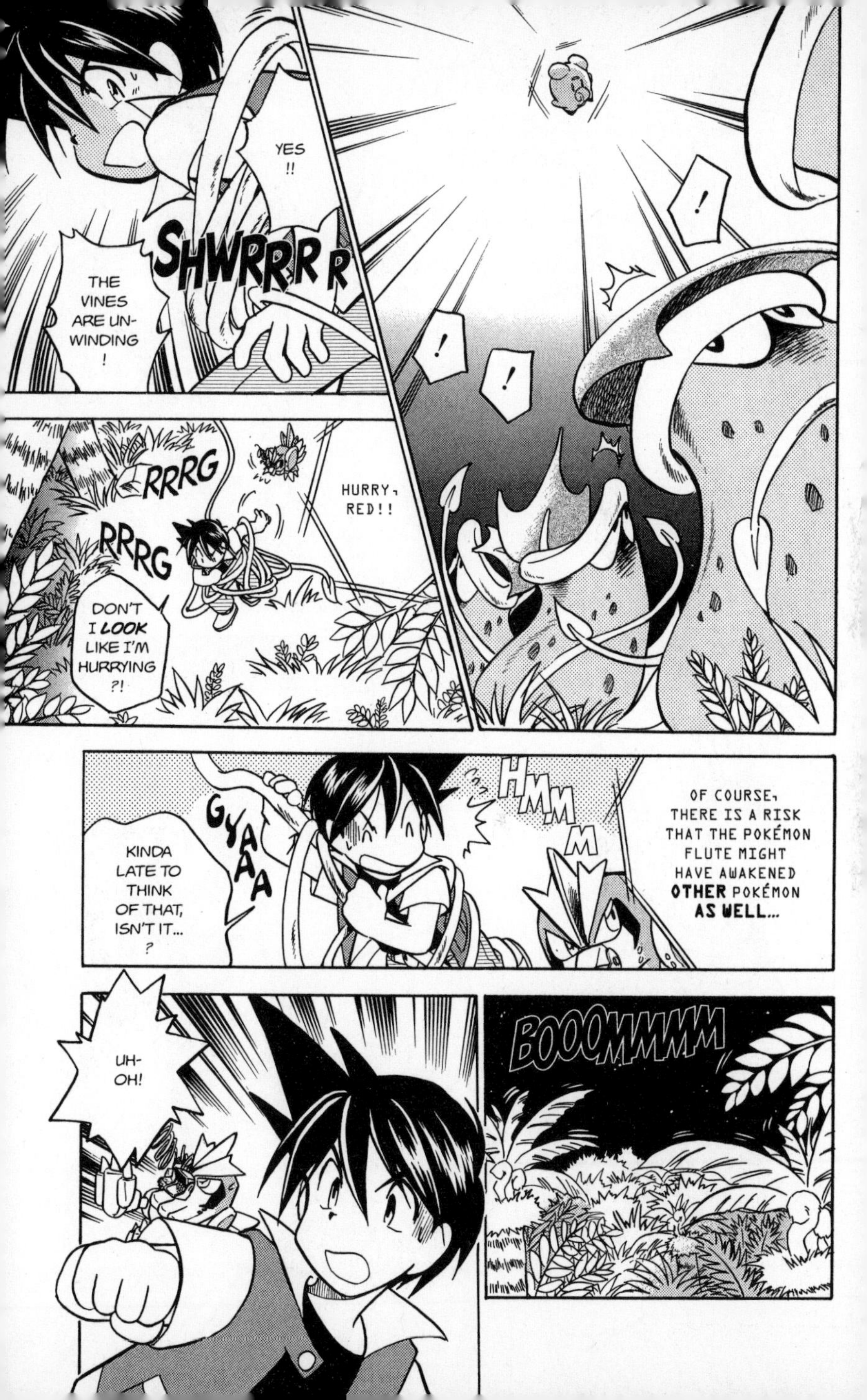
!
!
!
YES!!
SHWRRRR
THE VINES ARE UN-WINDING!
HURRY, RED!!
RRRG
RRRG
DON'T I LOOK LIKE I'M HURRYING?!
OF COURSE, THERE IS A RISK THAT THE POKÉMON FLUTE MIGHT HAVE AWAKENED OTHER POKÉMON AS WELL...
HMMMM
GYAAA
KINDA LATE TO THINK OF THAT, ISN'T IT...?
BOOOMMMM
UH-OH!

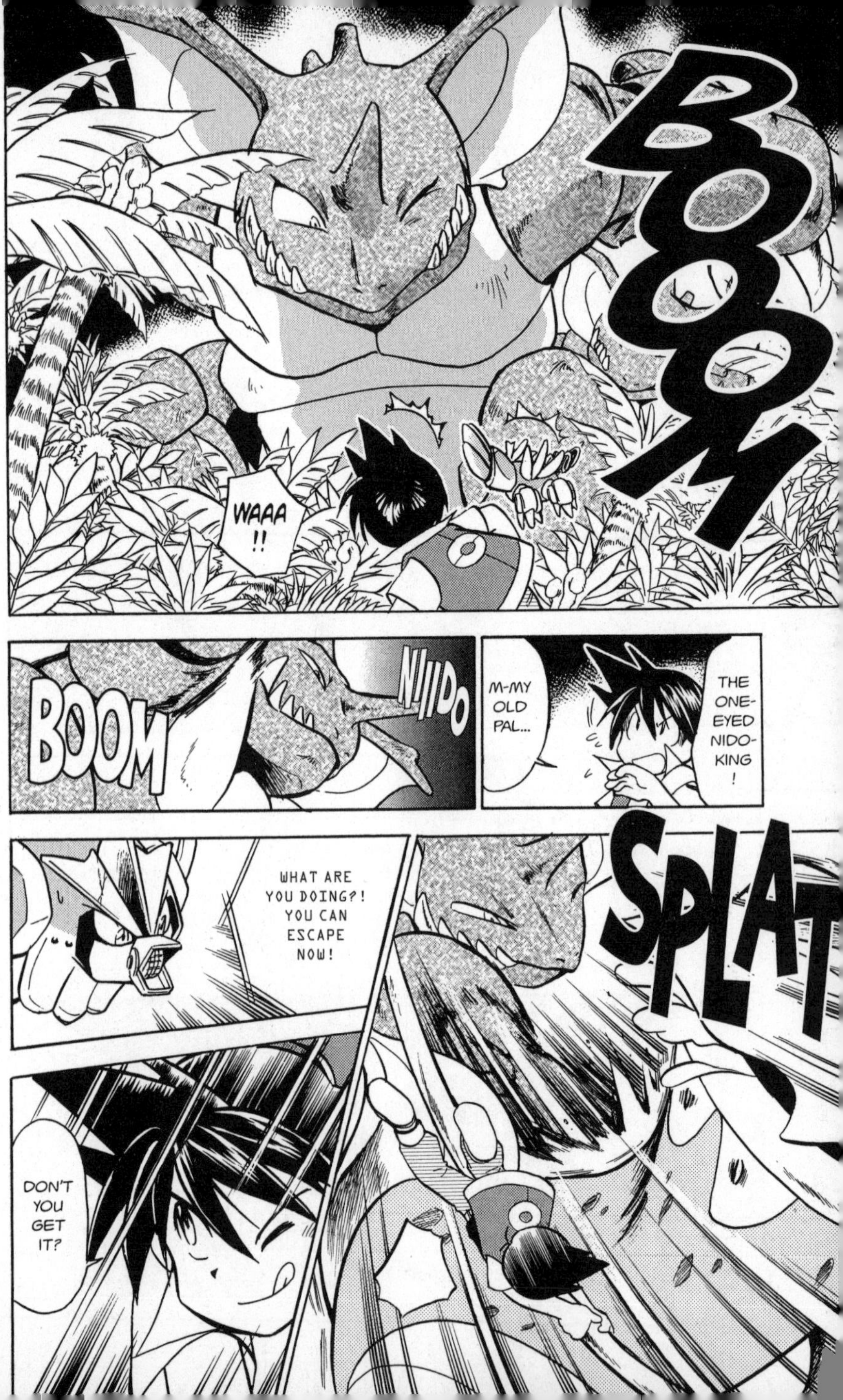
BOOOM
WAAA !!
THE ONE-EYED NIDO-KING !
M-MY OLD PAL...
NIIIDO
BOOM
SPLAT
WHAT ARE YOU DOING?! YOU CAN ESCAPE NOW!
DON'T YOU GET IT?

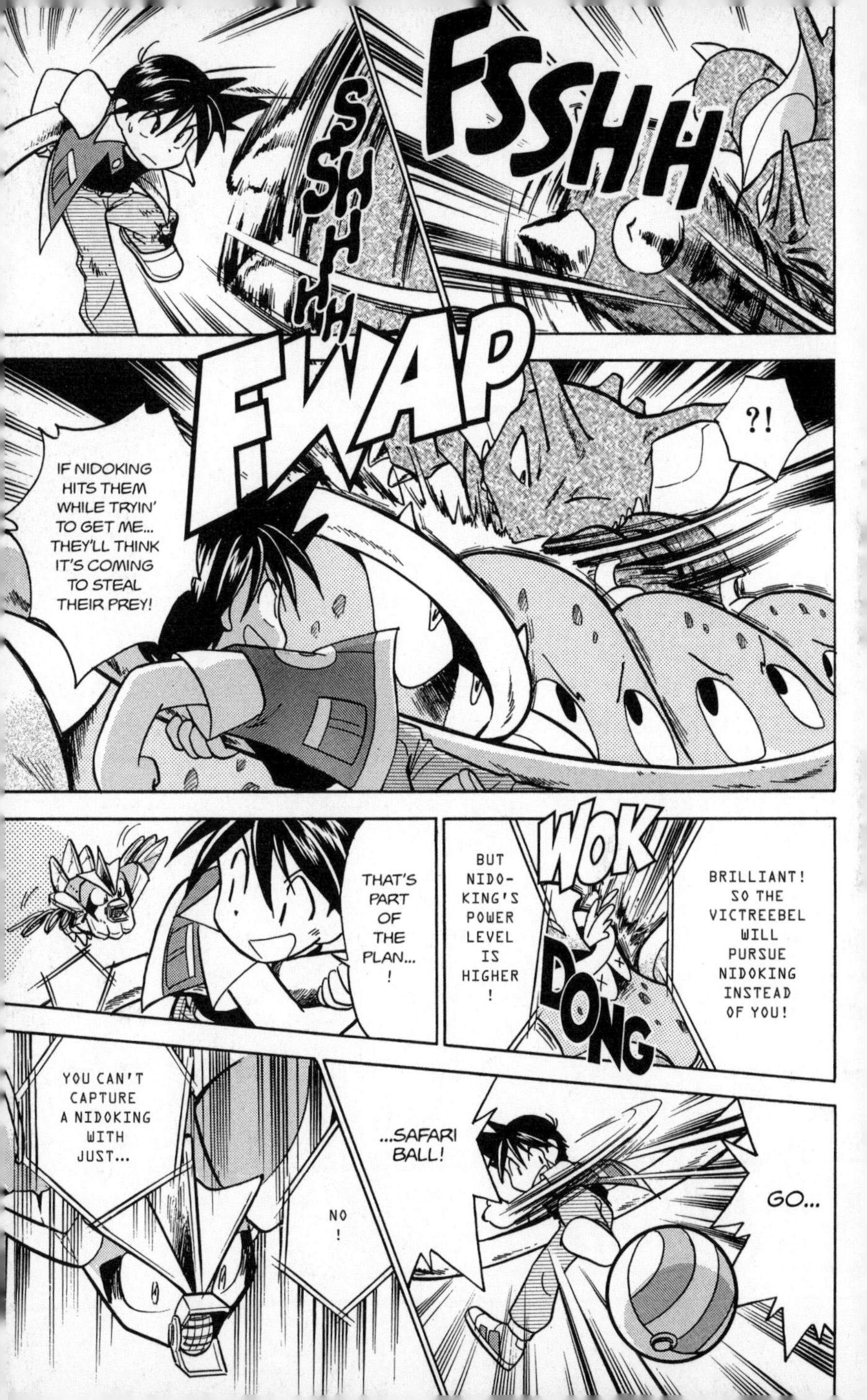
FSSHH
SSHHHH
FWAP
?!
IF NIDOKING HITS THEM WHILE TRYIN' TO GET ME... THEY'LL THINK IT'S COMING TO STEAL THEIR PREY!
BRILLIANT! SO THE VICTREEBEL WILL PURSUE NIDOKING INSTEAD OF YOU!
WOK
DONG
BUT NIDO-KING'S POWER LEVEL IS HIGHER!
THAT'S PART OF THE PLAN...!
GO...
...SAFARI BALL!
NO!
YOU CAN'T CAPTURE A NIDOKING WITH JUST...

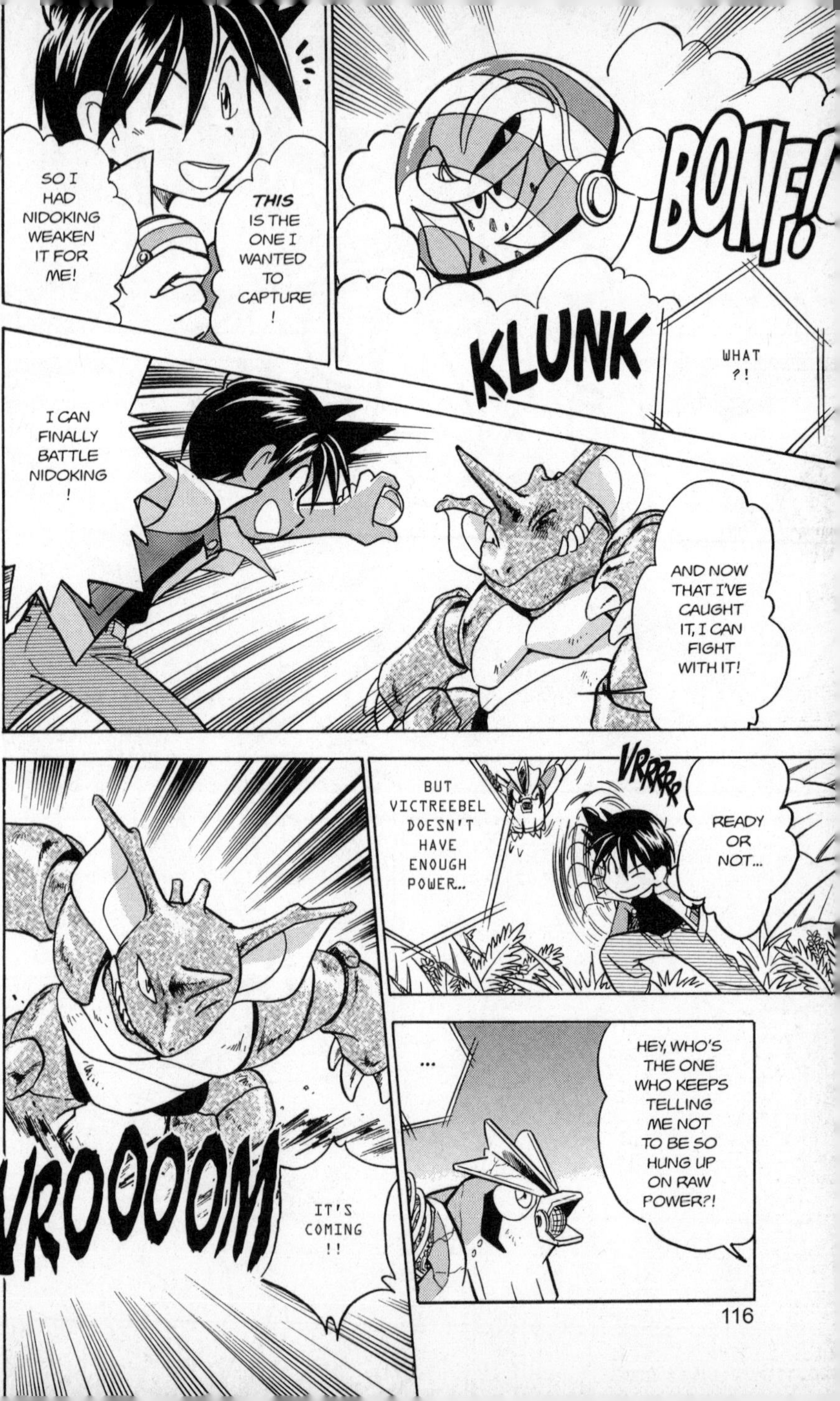
BONF!!
THIS IS THE ONE I WANTED TO CAPTURE!
SO I HAD NIDOKING WEAKEN IT FOR ME!
KLUNK
WHAT?!
AND NOW THAT I'VE CAUGHT IT, I CAN FIGHT WITH IT!
I CAN FINALLY BATTLE NIDOKING!
VRRRRR
READY OR NOT...
BUT VICTREEBEL DOESN'T HAVE ENOUGH POWER..
HEY, WHO'S THE ONE WHO KEEPS TELLING ME NOT TO BE SO HUNG UP ON RAW POWER?!
...
VROOOOM
IT'S COMING!!

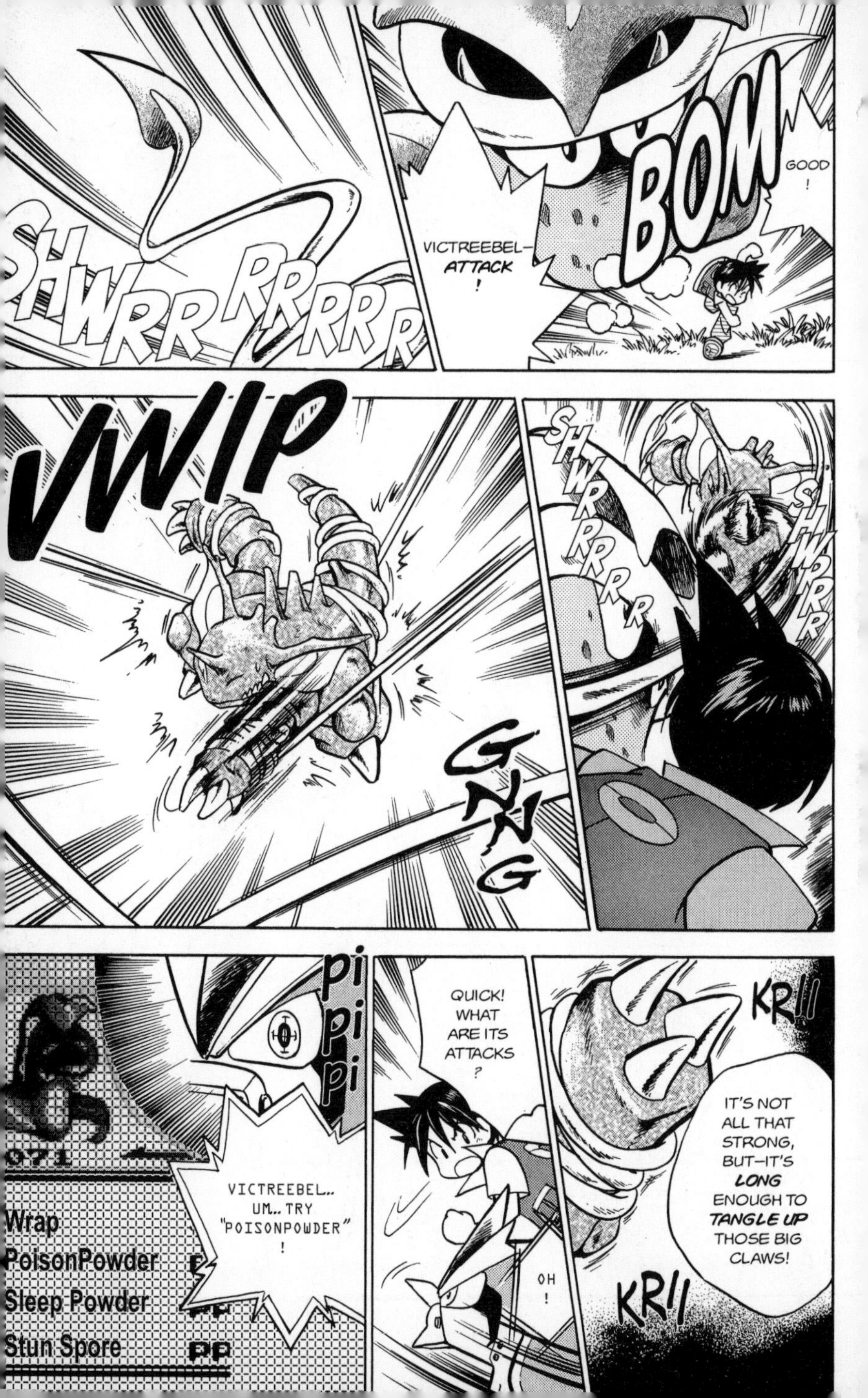
GOOD!
BOM
VICTREEBEL—ATTACK!
SHWRRRRRRRRR
SHWRRRRR
SHWRRR
VWIP
GNNG
KRII
IT'S NOT ALL THAT STRONG, BUT—IT'S LONG ENOUGH TO TANGLE UP THOSE BIG CLAWS!
KRII
QUICK! WHAT ARE ITS ATTACKS?
OH!
pipipi
VICTREEBEL.. UM.. TRY "POISONPOWDER"!
071
Wrap
PoisonPowder
Sleep Powder
Stun Spore

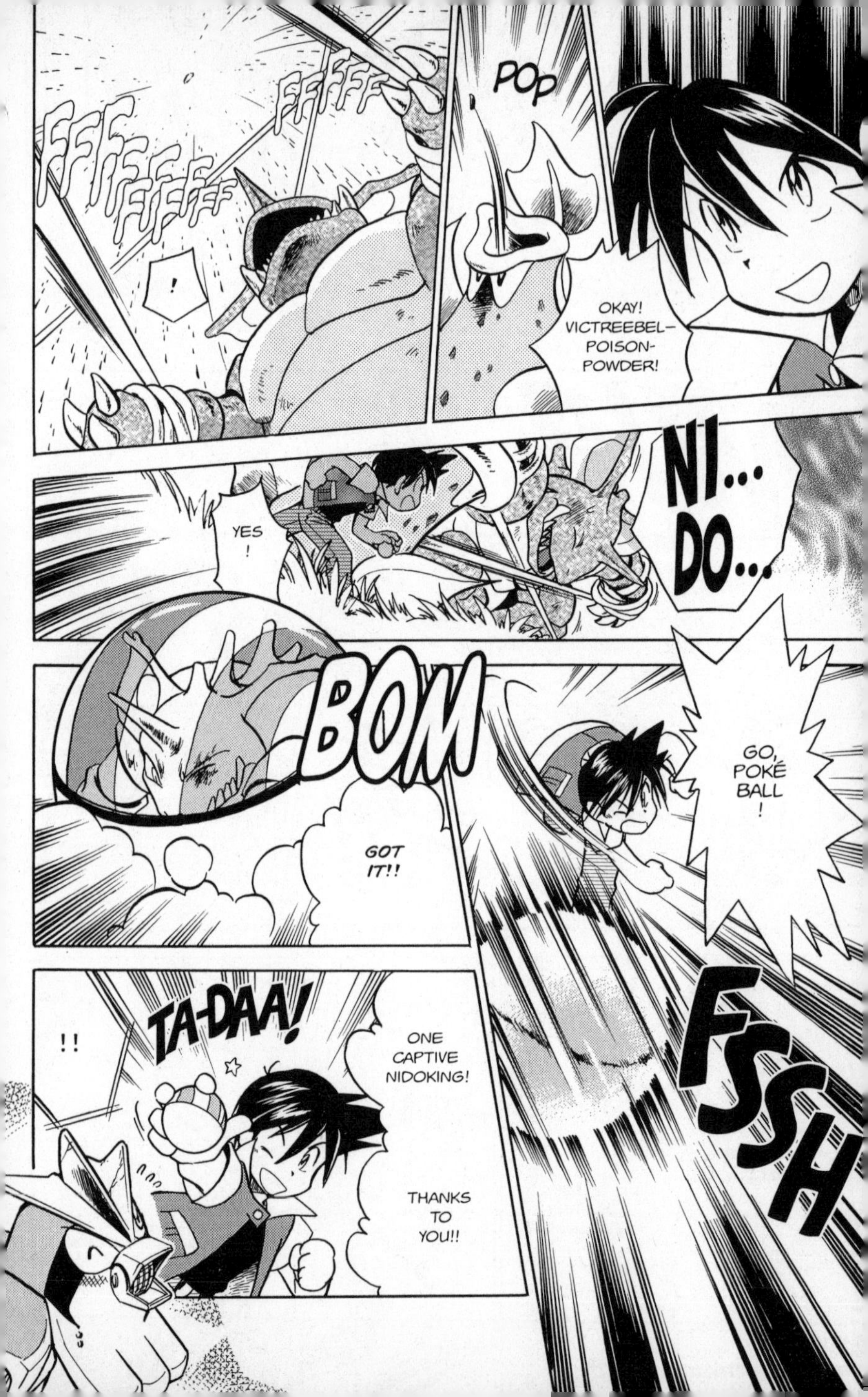
POP
OKAY! VICTREEBEL-POISON-POWDER!
FFFFFF
FFFFFFFFFFFFFF
!
NI... DO...
YES!
GO, POKÉ BALL!
FSSH
BOM
GOT IT!!
TA-DAA!
ONE CAPTIVE NIDOKING!
THANKS TO YOU!!
!!

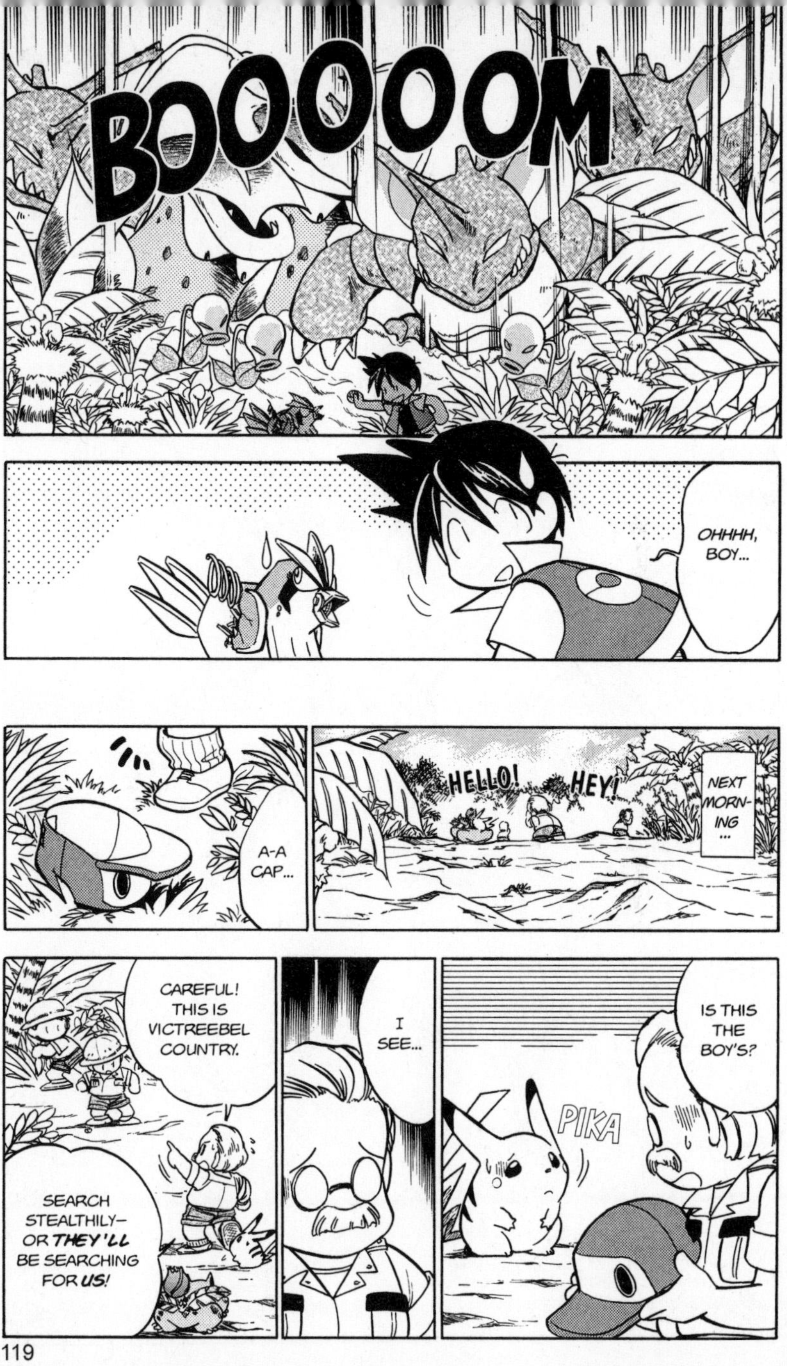
BOOOOOM
OHHHH, BOY...
NEXT MORNING...
HEY!
HELLO!
A-A CAP...
IS THIS THE BOY'S?
PIKA
I SEE...
CAREFUL! THIS IS VICTREEBEL COUNTRY.
SEARCH STEALTHILY—OR THEY'LL BE SEARCHING FOR US!

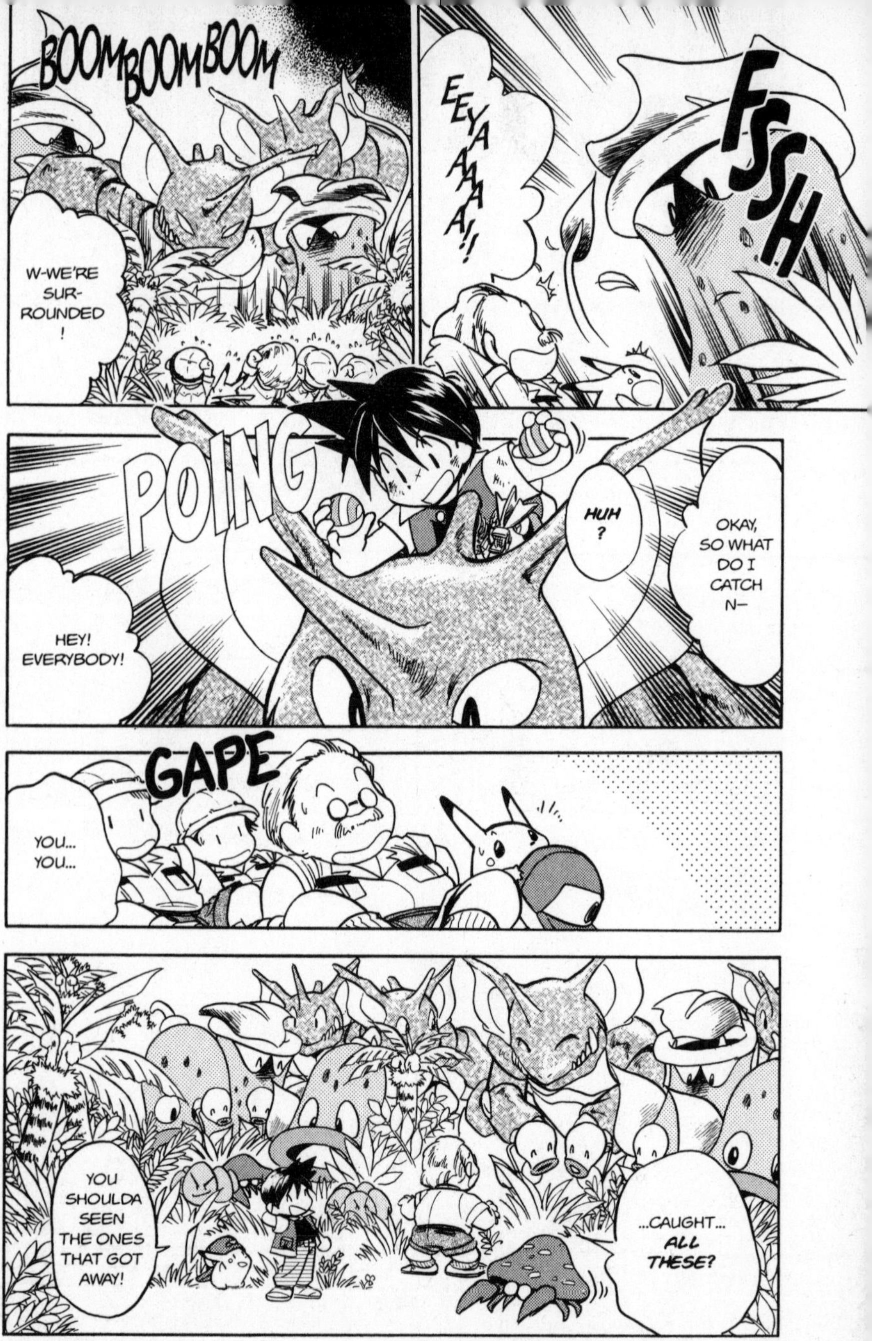
FSSH
EEYAAAAA!!
BOOMBOOMBOOM
W-WE'RE SURROUNDED!
OKAY, SO WHAT DO I CATCH N—
HUH?
POING
HEY! EVERYBODY!
GAPE
YOU... YOU...
...CAUGHT... **ALL THESE?**
YOU SHOULDA SEEN THE ONES THAT GOT AWAY!

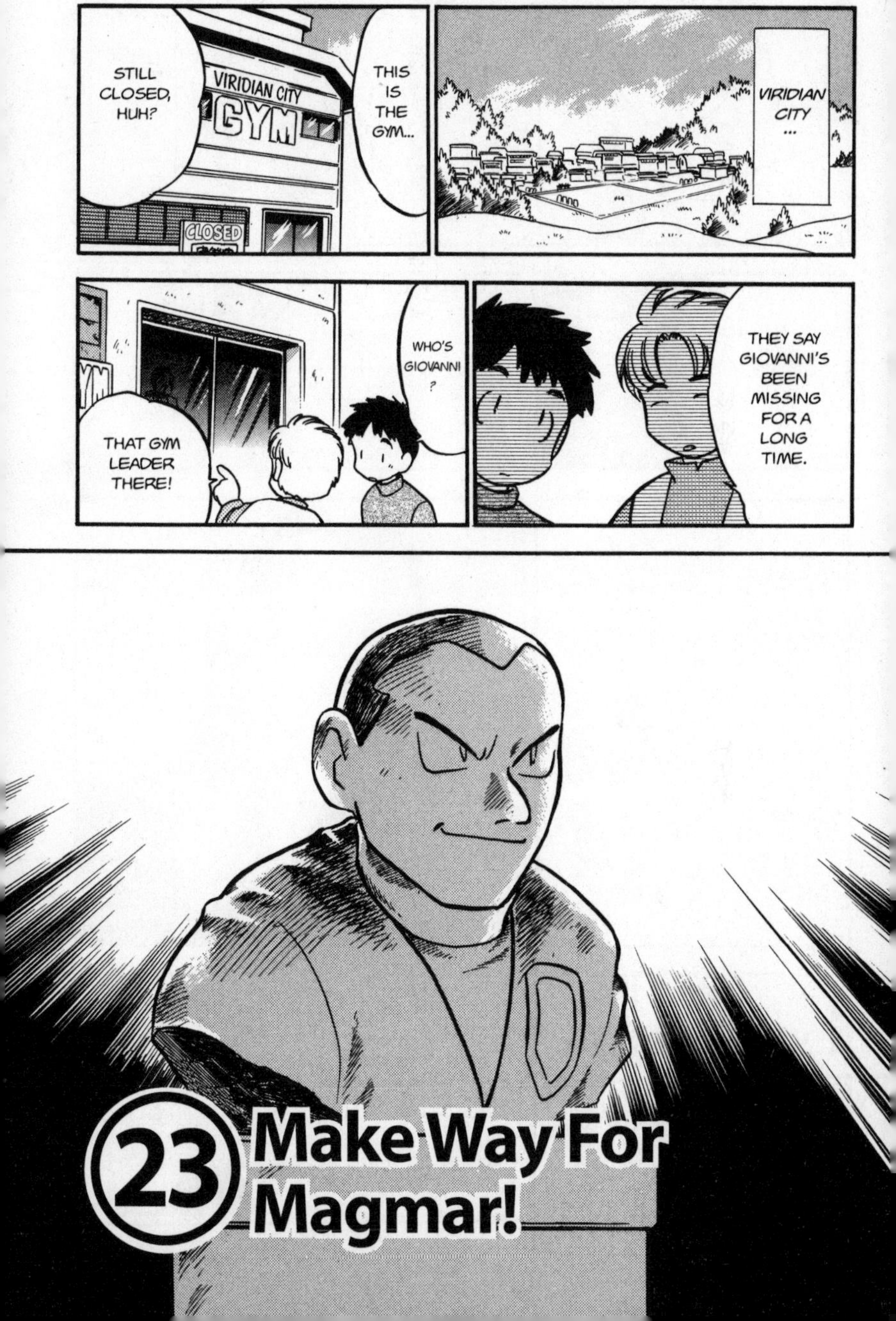
VIRIDIAN CITY ...
THIS IS THE GYM...
STILL CLOSED, HUH?
VIRIDIAN CITY GYM
CLOSED
THEY SAY GIOVANNI'S BEEN MISSING FOR A LONG TIME.
WHO'S GIOVANNI ?
THAT GYM LEADER THERE!
23 Make Way For Magmar!

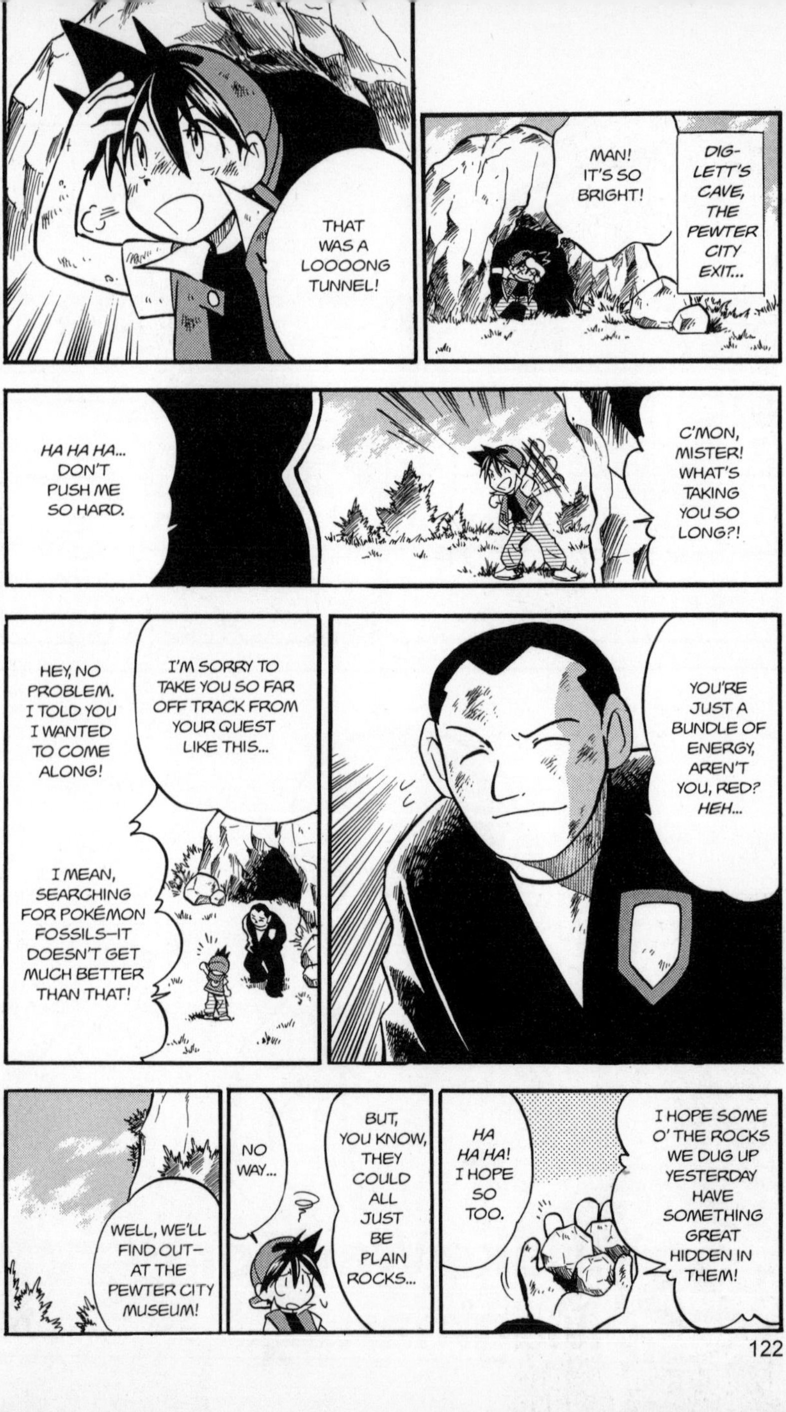
DIG-LETT'S CAVE, THE PEWTER CITY EXIT...
MAN! IT'S SO BRIGHT!
THAT WAS A LOOOONG TUNNEL!
C'MON, MISTER! WHAT'S TAKING YOU SO LONG?!
HA HA HA... DON'T PUSH ME SO HARD.
YOU'RE JUST A BUNDLE OF ENERGY, AREN'T YOU, RED? HEH...
I'M SORRY TO TAKE YOU SO FAR OFF TRACK FROM YOUR QUEST LIKE THIS...
HEY, NO PROBLEM. I TOLD YOU I WANTED TO COME ALONG!
I MEAN, SEARCHING FOR POKÉMON FOSSILS—IT DOESN'T GET MUCH BETTER THAN THAT!
I HOPE SOME O' THE ROCKS WE DUG UP YESTERDAY HAVE SOMETHING GREAT HIDDEN IN THEM!
HA HA HA! I HOPE SO TOO.
BUT, YOU KNOW, THEY COULD ALL JUST BE PLAIN ROCKS...
NO WAY...
WELL, WE'LL FIND OUT—AT THE PEWTER CITY MUSEUM!

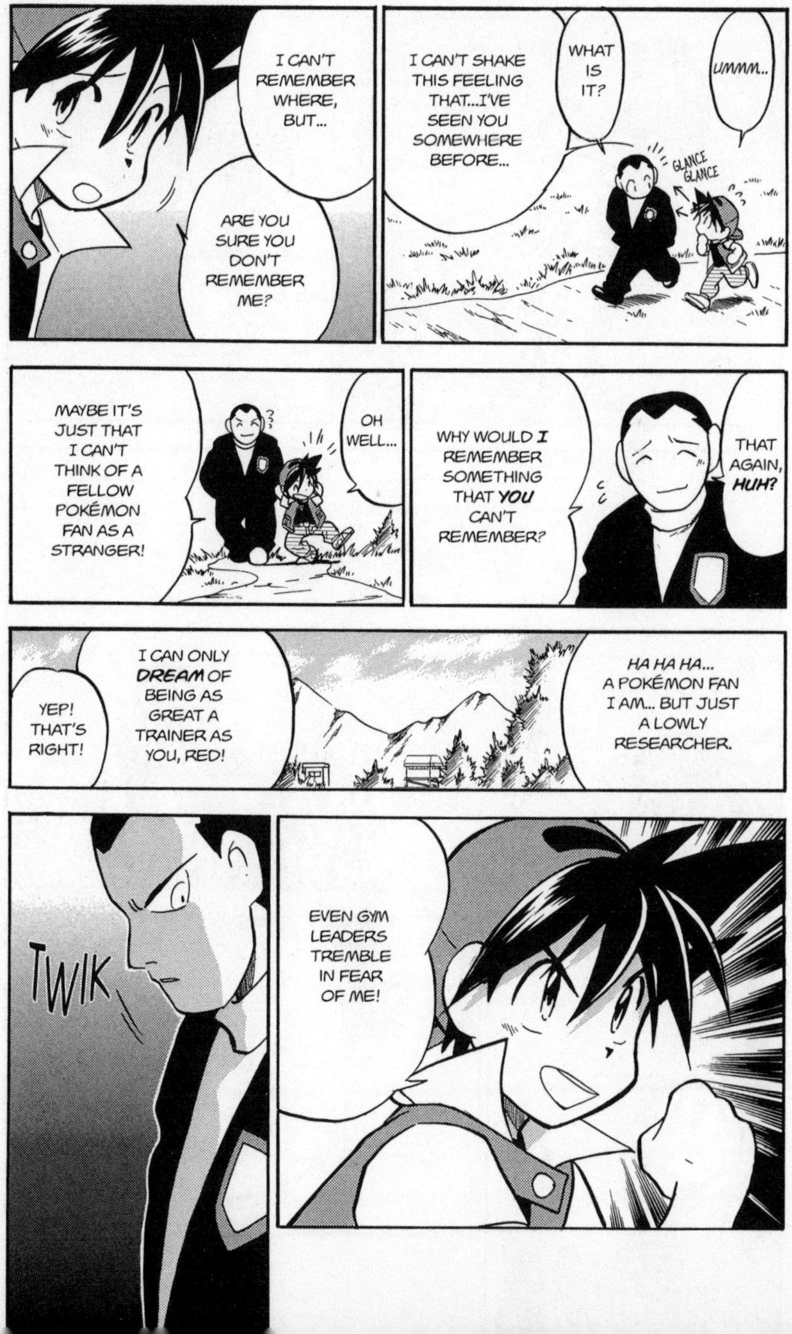
UMMM...
WHAT IS IT?
I CAN'T SHAKE THIS FEELING THAT...I'VE SEEN YOU SOMEWHERE BEFORE...
GLANCE GLANCE
I CAN'T REMEMBER WHERE, BUT...
ARE YOU SURE YOU DON'T REMEMBER ME?
THAT AGAIN, HUH?
WHY WOULD I REMEMBER SOMETHING THAT YOU CAN'T REMEMBER?
OH WELL...
MAYBE IT'S JUST THAT I CAN'T THINK OF A FELLOW POKÉMON FAN AS A STRANGER!
HA HA HA... A POKÉMON FAN I AM... BUT JUST A LOWLY RESEARCHER.
I CAN ONLY DREAM OF BEING AS GREAT A TRAINER AS YOU, RED!
YEP! THAT'S RIGHT!
EVEN GYM LEADERS TREMBLE IN FEAR OF ME!
TWIK

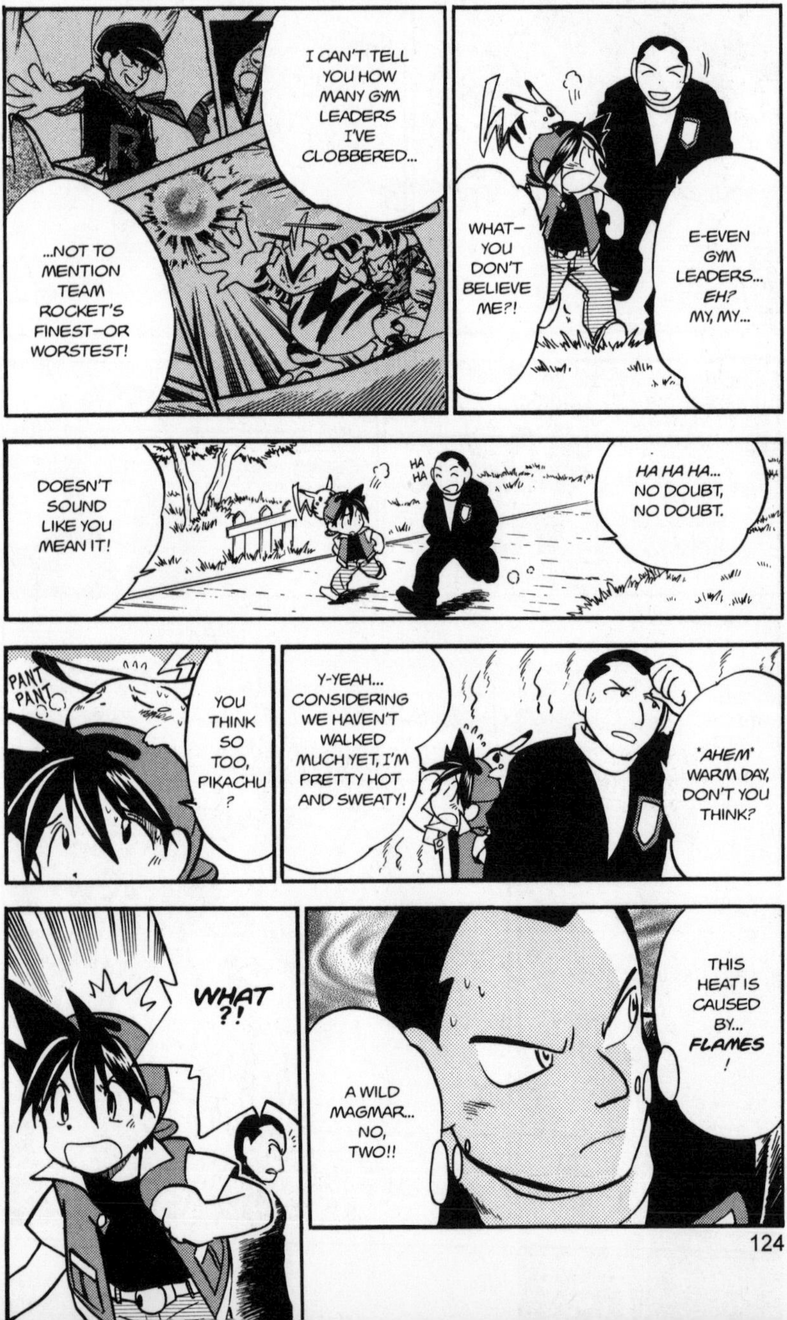
E-EVEN GYM LEADERS... EH? MY, MY...
WHAT— YOU DON'T BELIEVE ME?!
I CAN'T TELL YOU HOW MANY GYM LEADERS I'VE CLOBBERED...
...NOT TO MENTION TEAM ROCKET'S FINEST—OR WORSTEST!
HA HA HA... NO DOUBT, NO DOUBT.
HA HA
DOESN'T SOUND LIKE YOU MEAN IT!
AHEM WARM DAY, DON'T YOU THINK?
Y-YEAH... CONSIDERING WE HAVEN'T WALKED MUCH YET, I'M PRETTY HOT AND SWEATY!
YOU THINK SO TOO, PIKACHU?
PANT PANT
THIS HEAT IS CAUSED BY... FLAMES!
A WILD MAGMAR... NO, TWO!!
WHAT?!

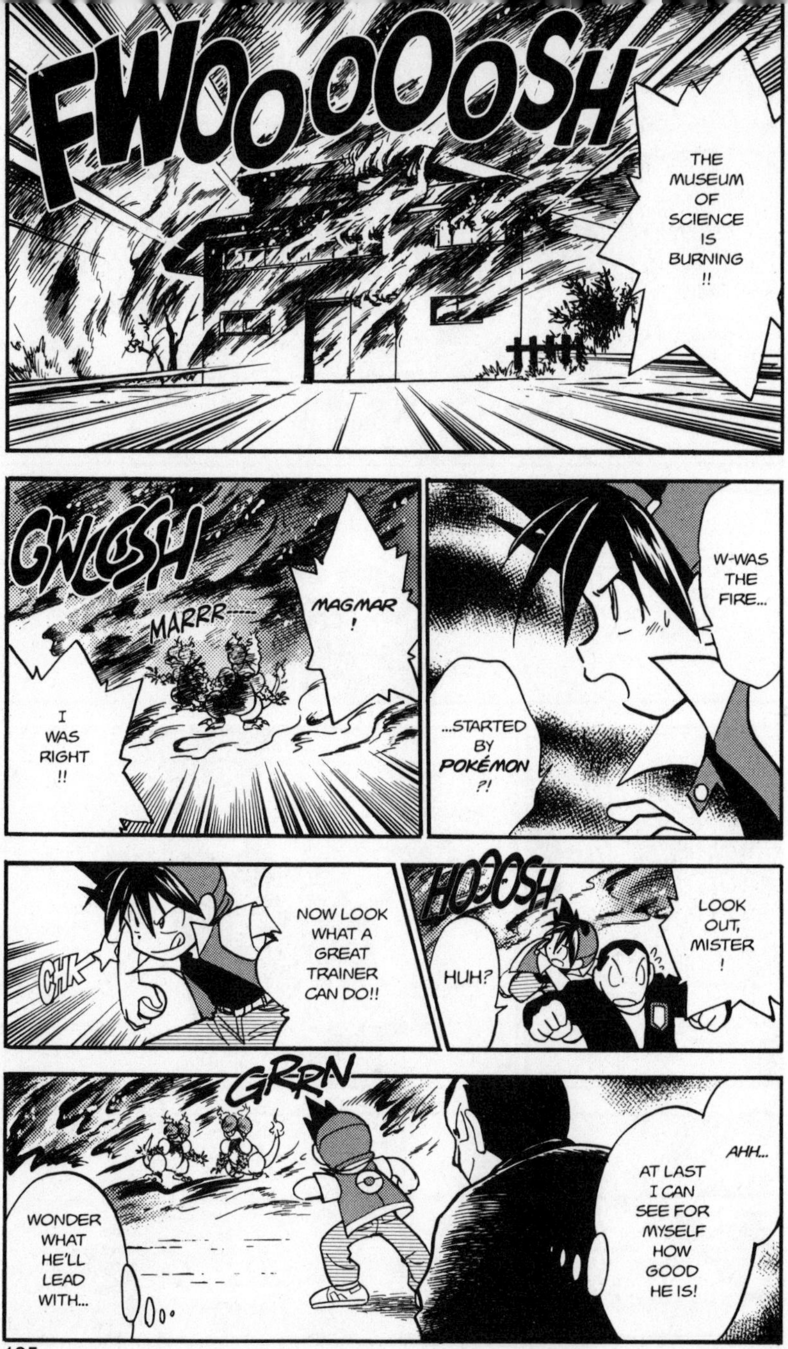
FWOOOOOSH
THE MUSEUM OF SCIENCE IS BURNING!!
W-WAS THE FIRE...
...STARTED BY POKÉMON?!
MAGMAR!
GWOOSH
MARRR-----
I WAS RIGHT!!
HOOOSH
LOOK OUT, MISTER!
HUH?
NOW LOOK WHAT A GREAT TRAINER CAN DO!!
CHK
AHH...
AT LAST I CAN SEE FOR MYSELF HOW GOOD HE IS!
GRRN
WONDER WHAT HE'LL LEAD WITH...

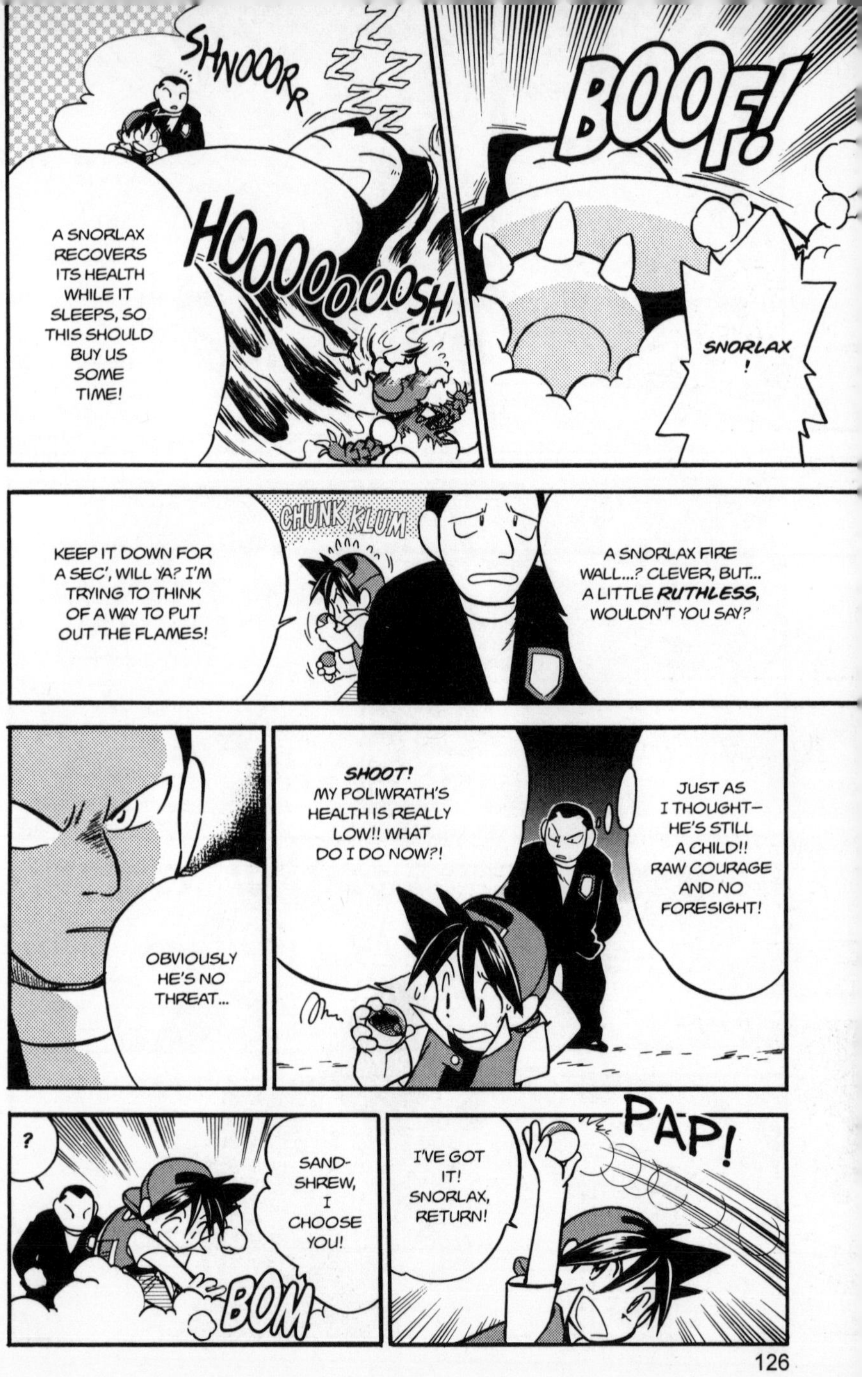
BOOF!
SNORLAX!
Z Z Z Z Z Z
SHNOOORR
HOOOOOOOSH
A SNORLAX RECOVERS ITS HEALTH WHILE IT SLEEPS, SO THIS SHOULD BUY US SOME TIME!
A SNORLAX FIRE WALL...? CLEVER, BUT... A LITTLE **RUTHLESS**, WOULDN'T YOU SAY?
CHUNK KLUM
KEEP IT DOWN FOR A SEC', WILL YA? I'M TRYING TO THINK OF A WAY TO PUT OUT THE FLAMES!
JUST AS I THOUGHT— HE'S STILL A CHILD!! RAW COURAGE AND NO FORESIGHT!
SHOOT! MY POLIWRATH'S HEALTH IS REALLY LOW!! WHAT DO I DO NOW?!
OBVIOUSLY HE'S NO THREAT...
PAP!
I'VE GOT IT! SNORLAX, RETURN!
SAND-SHREW, I CHOOSE YOU!
?
BOM

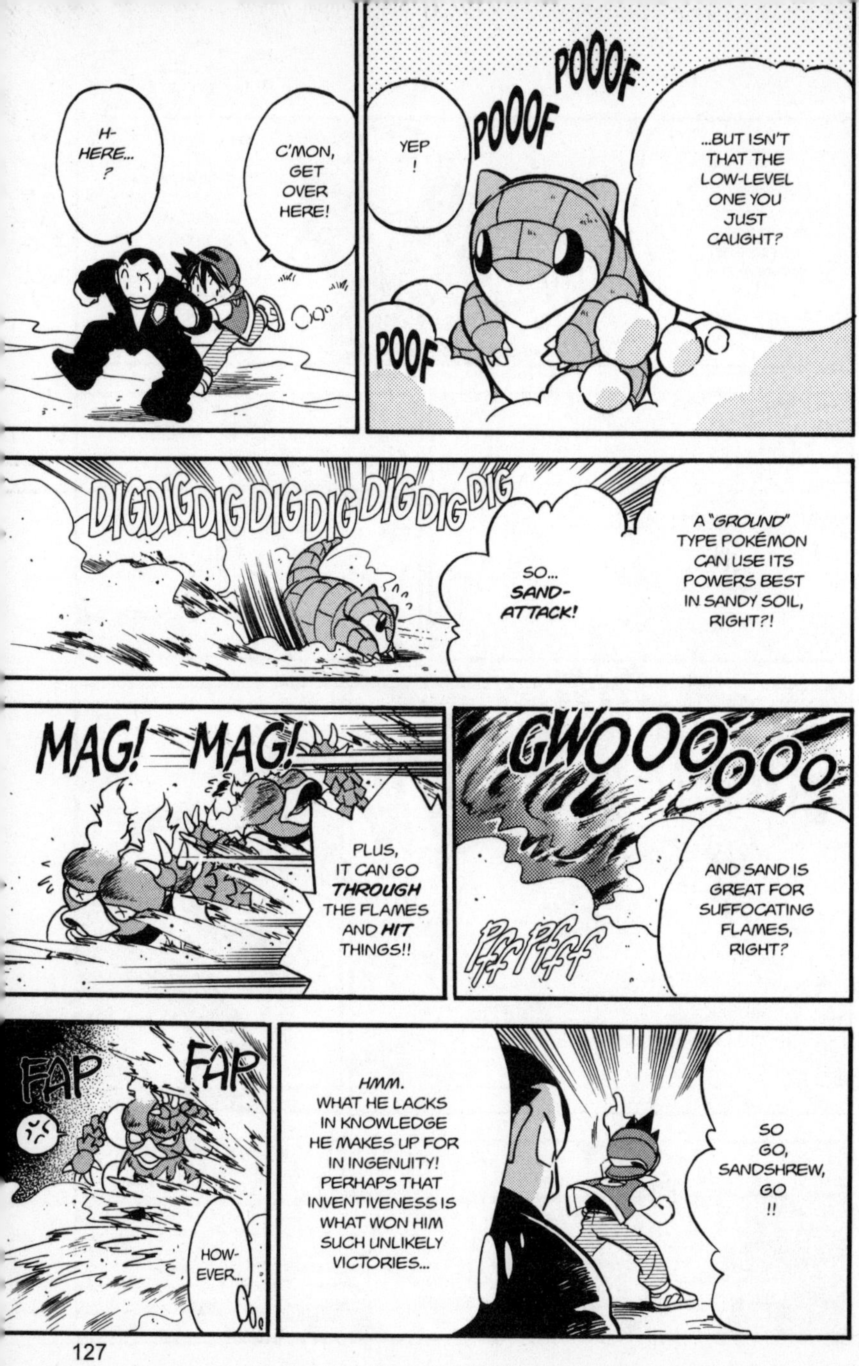

POOOF
...BUT ISN'T THAT THE LOW-LEVEL ONE YOU JUST CAUGHT?
POOOF
YEP!
POOF
C'MON, GET OVER HERE!
H-HERE...?
A "GROUND" TYPE POKÉMON CAN USE ITS POWERS BEST IN SANDY SOIL, RIGHT?!
SO... SAND-ATTACK!
DIGDIGDIGDIGDIGDIGDIGDIG
GWOOOOOOO
AND SAND IS GREAT FOR SUFFOCATING FLAMES, RIGHT?
Pfff Pfff
MAG! MAG!
PLUS, IT CAN GO THROUGH THE FLAMES AND HIT THINGS!!
SO GO, SANDSHREW, GO!!
HMM. WHAT HE LACKS IN KNOWLEDGE HE MAKES UP FOR IN INGENUITY! PERHAPS THAT INVENTIVENESS IS WHAT WON HIM SUCH UNLIKELY VICTORIES...
FAP FAP
HOW-EVER...

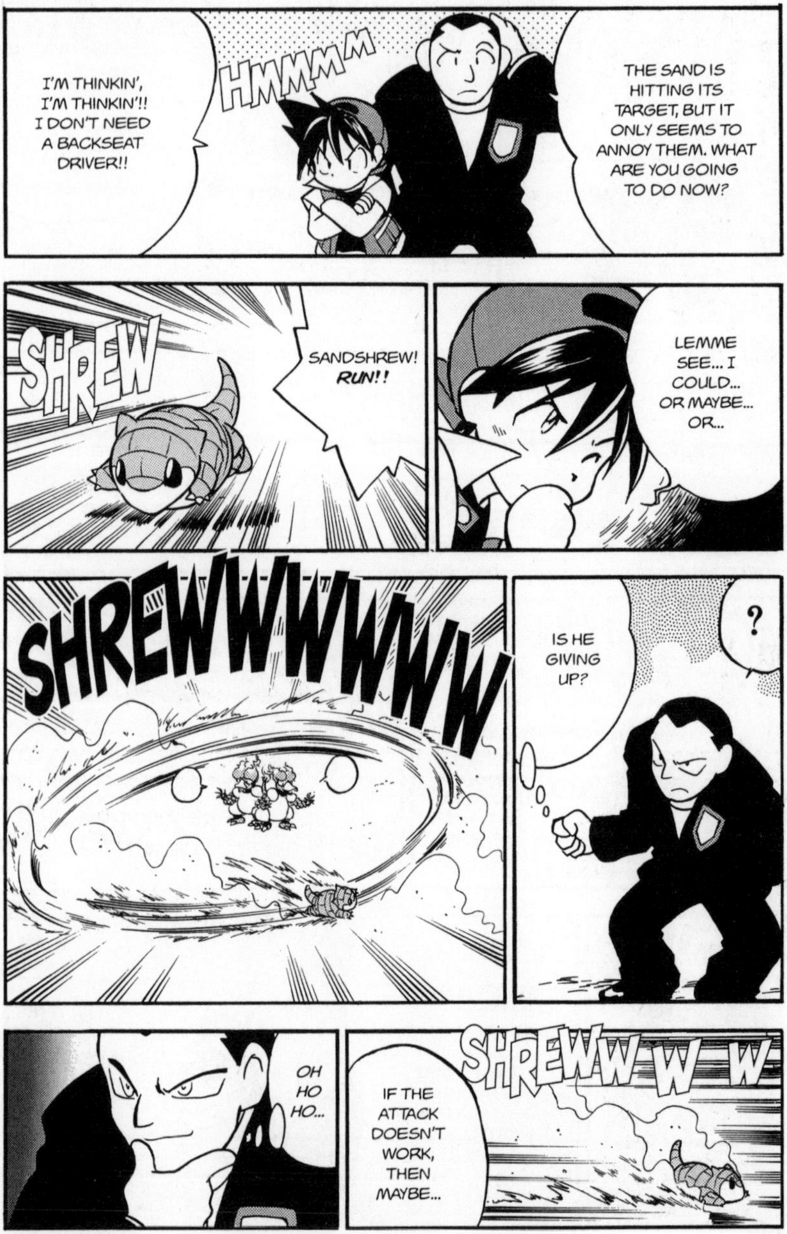
THE SAND IS HITTING ITS TARGET, BUT IT ONLY SEEMS TO ANNOY THEM. WHAT ARE YOU GOING TO DO NOW?
HMMMM
I'M THINKIN', I'M THINKIN'!! I DON'T NEED A BACKSEAT DRIVER!!
LEMME SEE... I COULD... OR MAYBE... OR...
SANDSHREW! RUN!!
SHREW
?
IS HE GIVING UP?
SHREWWWWWWW
SHREWWW W W W
IF THE ATTACK DOESN'T WORK, THEN MAYBE...
OH HO HO...

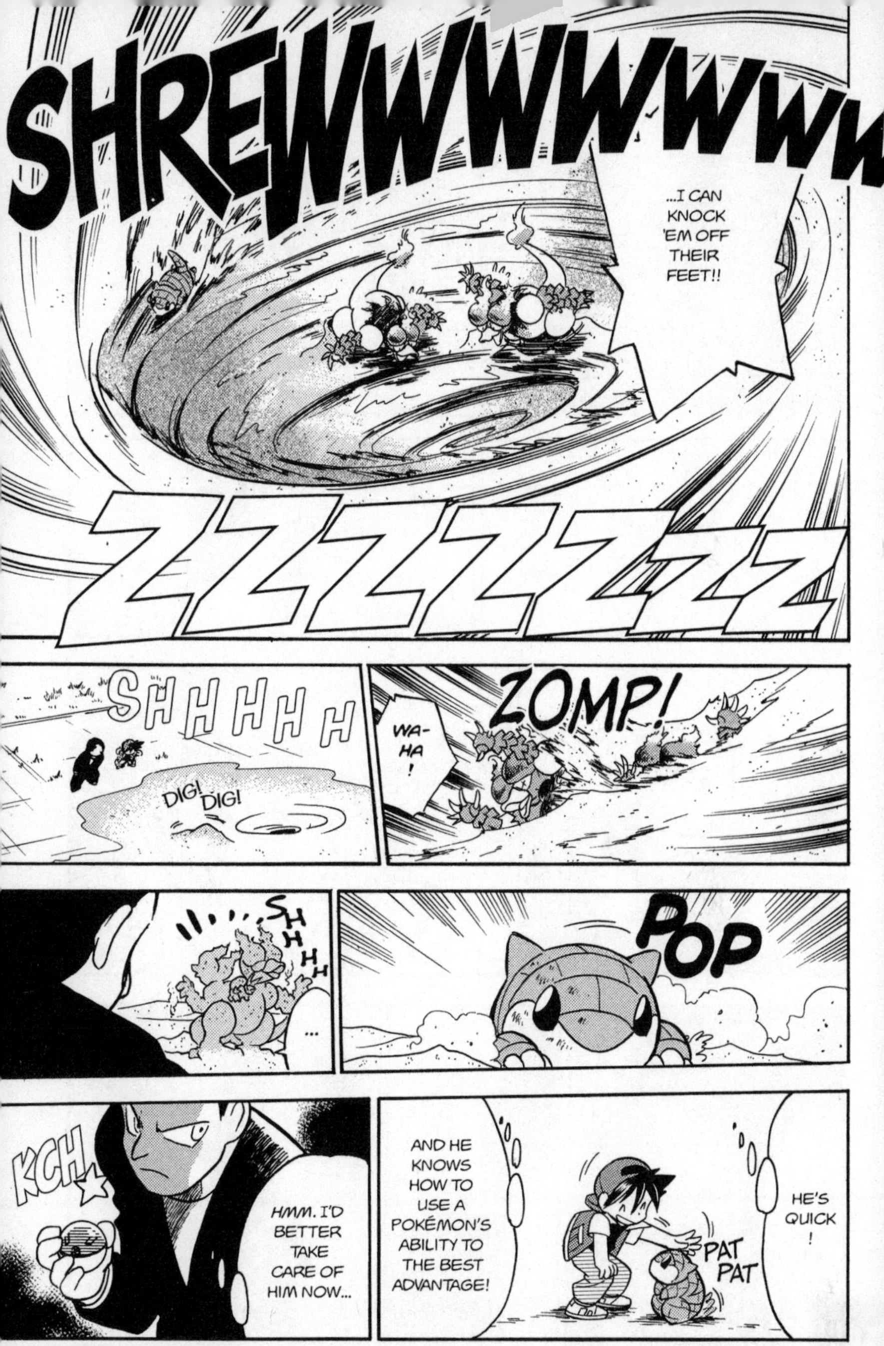
SHREWWWWWWWW
...I CAN KNOCK 'EM OFF THEIR FEET!!
ZZZZZZZZ
ZOMP!
WA-HA!
SHHHHHH
DIG! DIG!
POP
SHHHHH
...
HE'S QUICK!
AND HE KNOWS HOW TO USE A POKÉMON'S ABILITY TO THE BEST ADVANTAGE!
PAT PAT
KCH
HMM. I'D BETTER TAKE CARE OF HIM NOW...

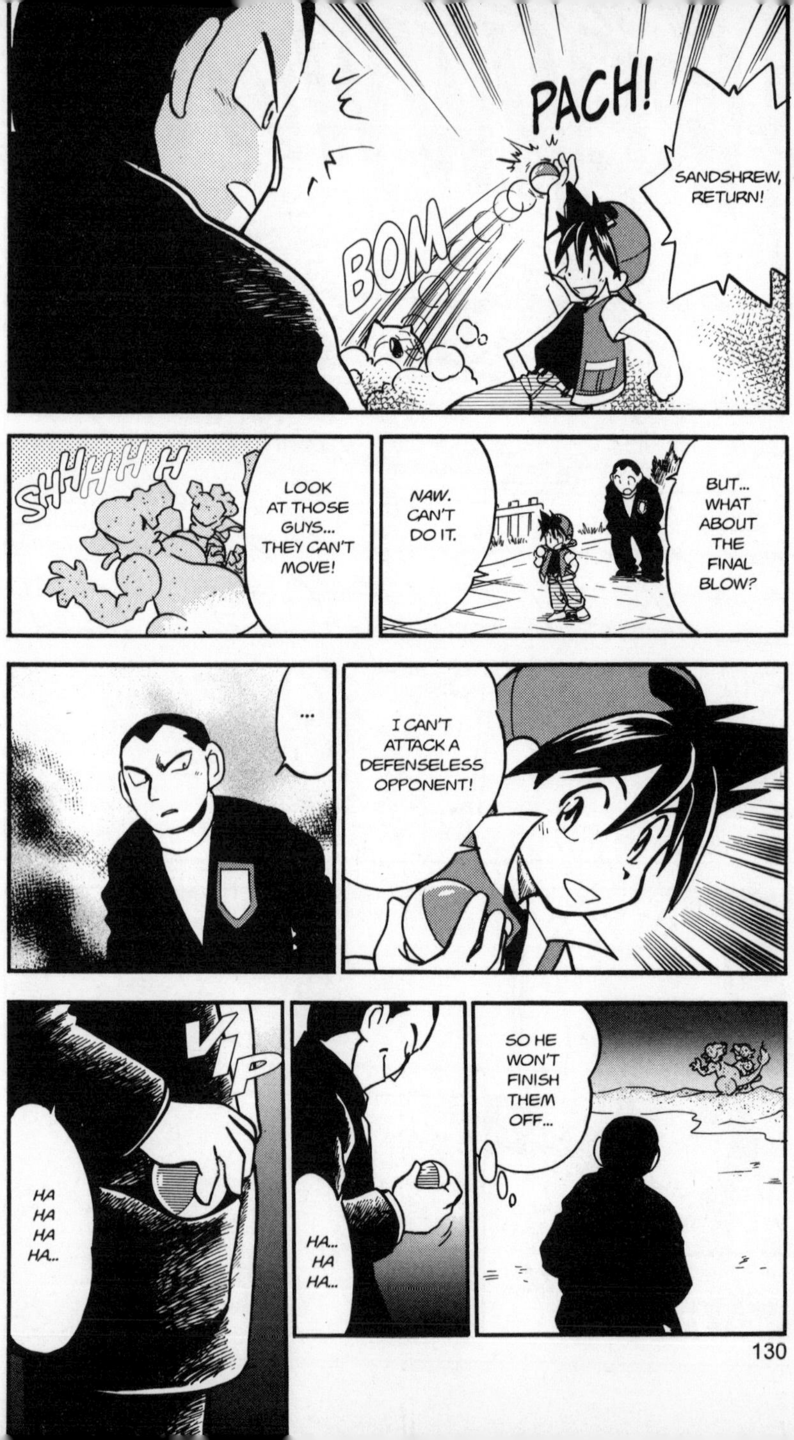
SANDSHREW, RETURN!
PACH!
BOM
BUT... WHAT ABOUT THE FINAL BLOW?
NAW. CAN'T DO IT.
LOOK AT THOSE GUYS... THEY CAN'T MOVE!
SHHHHH
I CAN'T ATTACK A DEFENSELESS OPPONENT!
...
SO HE WON'T FINISH THEM OFF...
HA... HA HA...
VIP
HA HA HA HA...

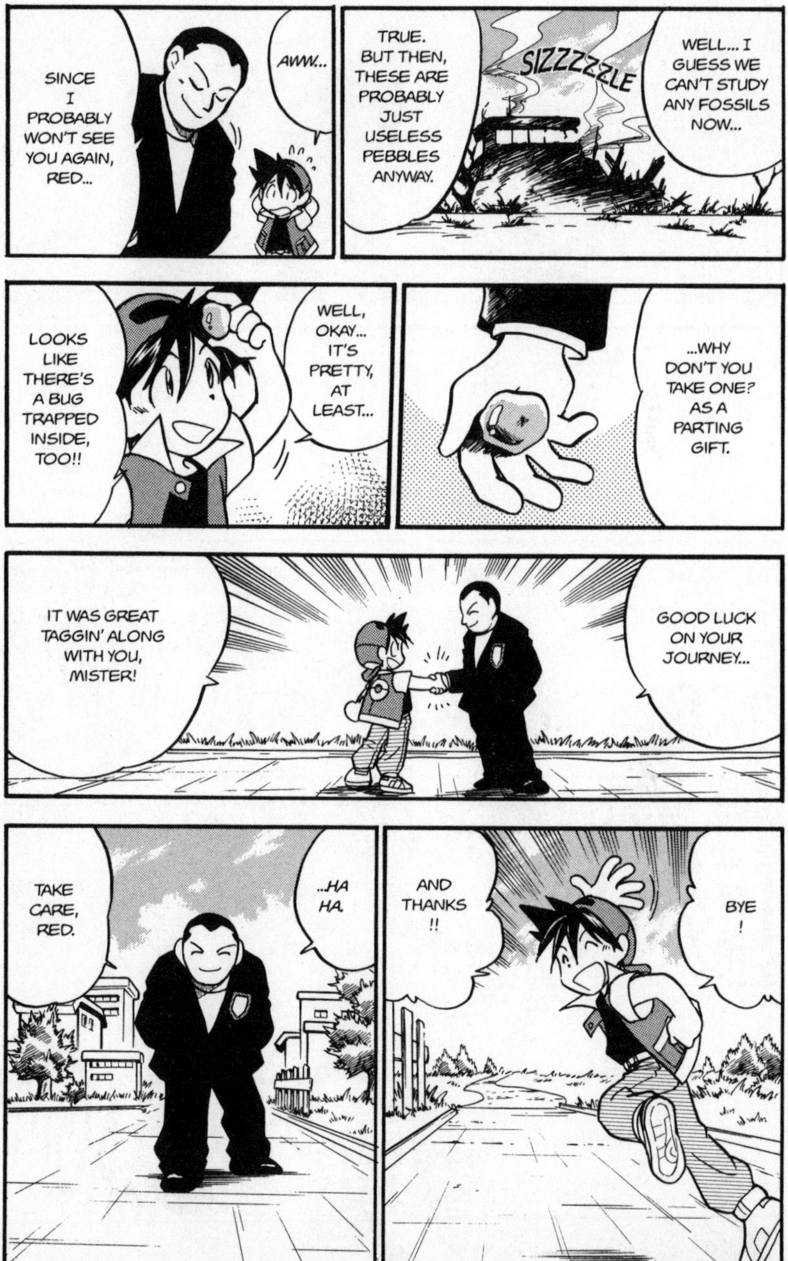
WELL... I GUESS WE CAN'T STUDY ANY FOSSILS NOW...
SIZZZZZLE
TRUE. BUT THEN, THESE ARE PROBABLY JUST USELESS PEBBLES ANYWAY.
AWW...
SINCE I PROBABLY WON'T SEE YOU AGAIN, RED...
...WHY DON'T YOU TAKE ONE? AS A PARTING GIFT.
WELL, OKAY... IT'S PRETTY, AT LEAST...
LOOKS LIKE THERE'S A BUG TRAPPED INSIDE, TOO!!
GOOD LUCK ON YOUR JOURNEY...
IT WAS GREAT TAGGIN' ALONG WITH YOU, MISTER!
BYE!
AND THANKS!!
...HA HA.
TAKE CARE, RED.

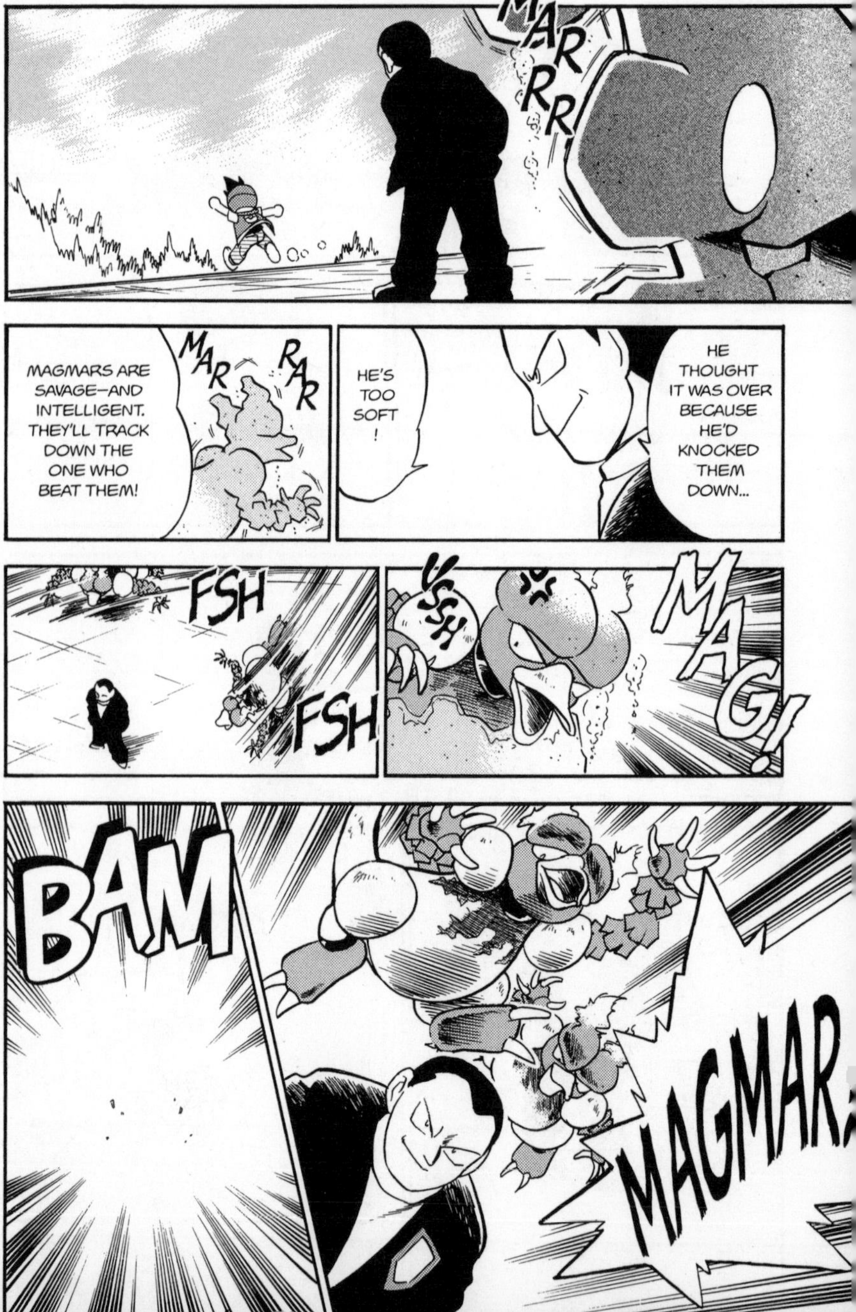
MARRRR
HE THOUGHT IT WAS OVER BECAUSE HE'D KNOCKED THEM DOWN...
HE'S TOO SOFT!
MAR RAR
MAGMARS ARE SAVAGE—AND INTELLIGENT. THEY'LL TRACK DOWN THE ONE WHO BEAT THEM!
MAGI!
VSSH
FSH
FSH
BAM
MAGMAR

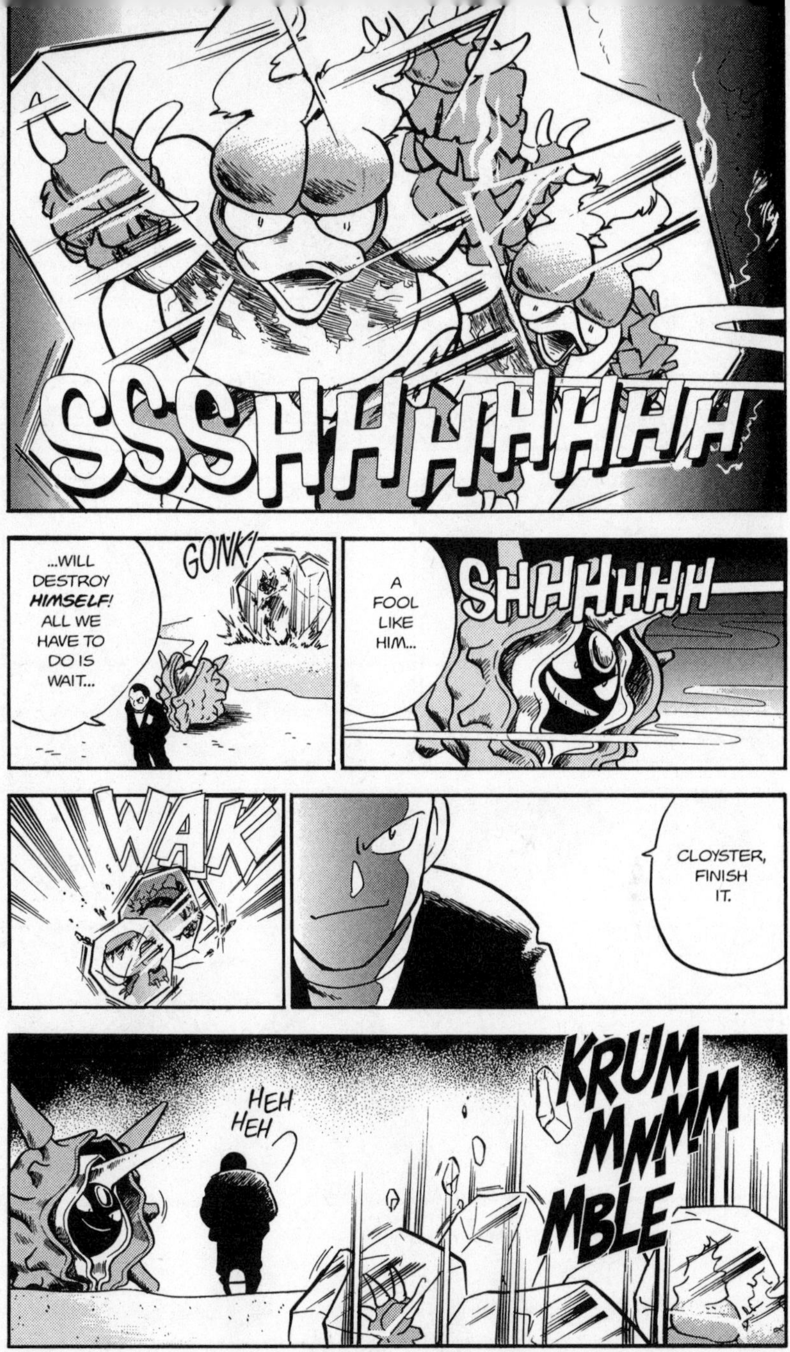
SSSHHHHHHHH
A FOOL LIKE HIM...
SHHHHHH
...WILL DESTROY **HIMSELF**! ALL WE HAVE TO DO IS WAIT...
GONK!
CLOYSTER, FINISH IT.
WAK
KRUM MNMM MBLE
HEH HEH

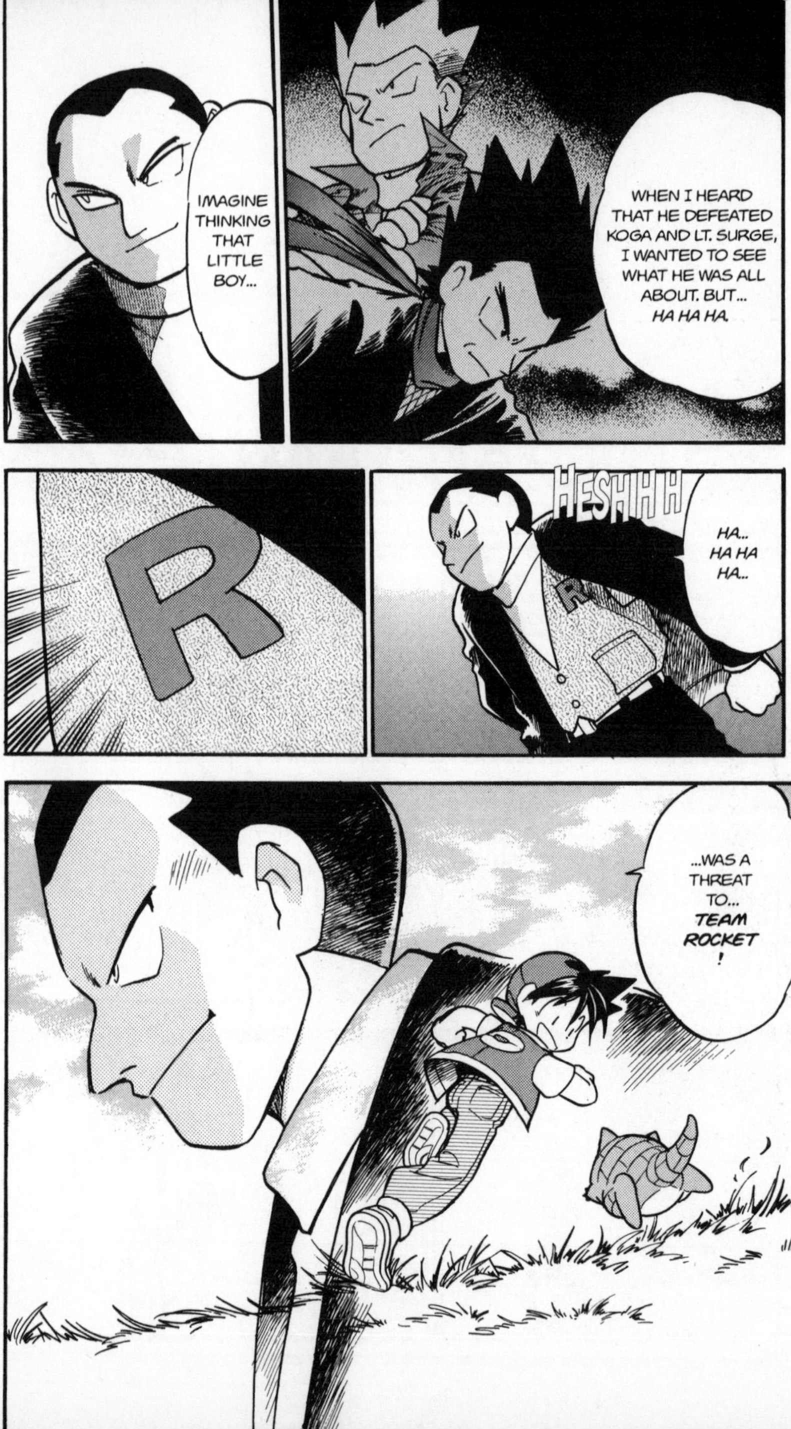
WHEN I HEARD THAT HE DEFEATED KOGA AND LT. SURGE, I WANTED TO SEE WHAT HE WAS ALL ABOUT. BUT... *HA HA HA.*
IMAGINE THINKING THAT LITTLE BOY...
HESHIHH H
HA... HA HA HA...
...WAS A THREAT TO... ***TEAM ROCKET!***

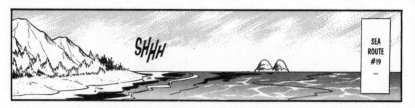

SEA ROUTE #19 ...
SHHH
24 What a Dragonite
PING PING
IT OUGHTA BE AROUND HERE SOME-WHERE...
THE ITEM FINDER'S PINGING LIKE CRAZY! IT'S GOTTA BE CLOSE—
PING PING
AND I'M GONNA MAKE IT MINE!

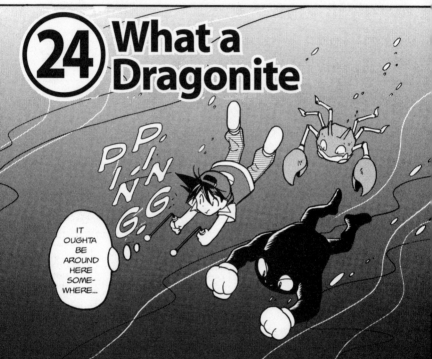

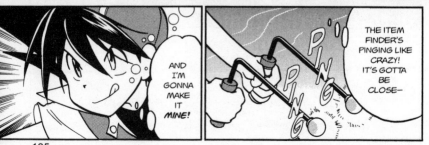

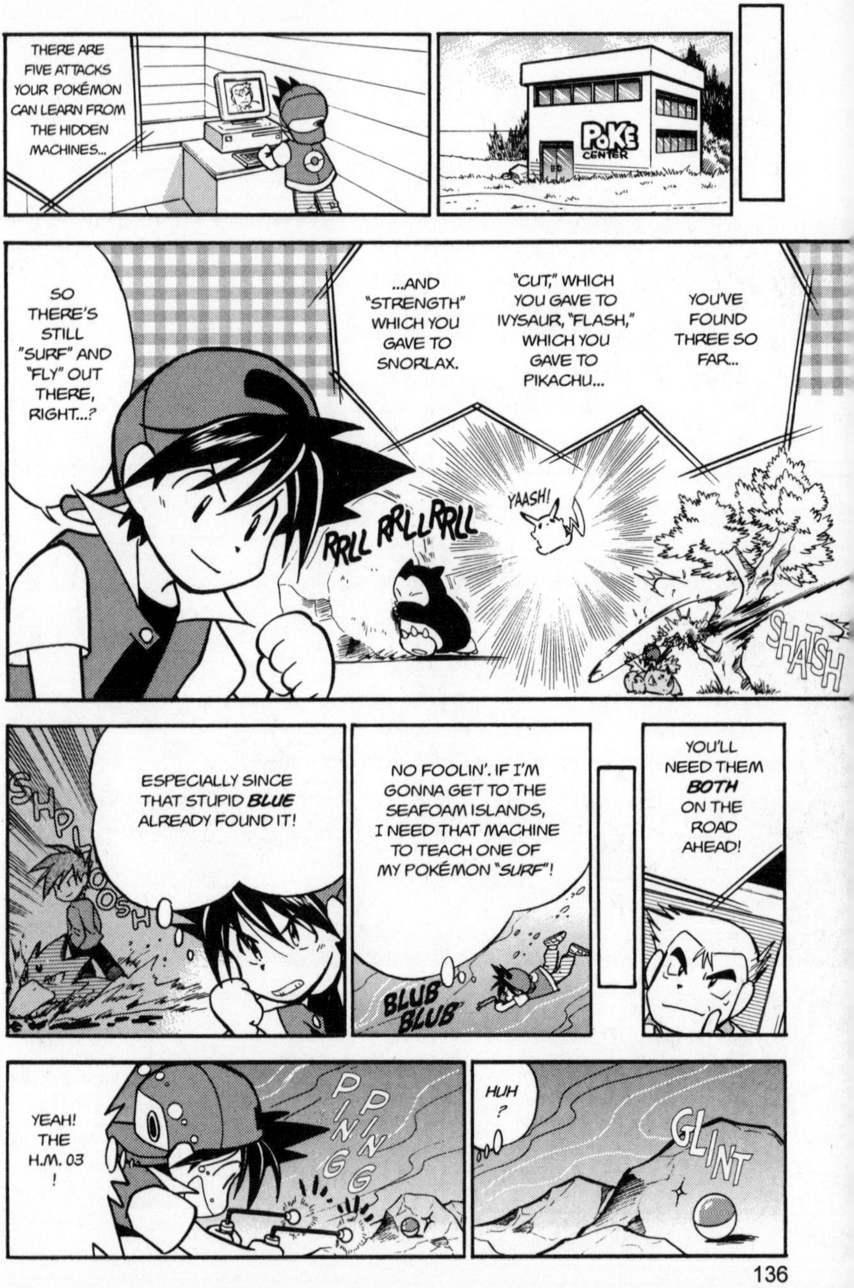
POKé CENTER
THERE ARE FIVE ATTACKS YOUR POKÉMON CAN LEARN FROM THE HIDDEN MACHINES...
YOU'VE FOUND THREE SO FAR...
"CUT," WHICH YOU GAVE TO IVYSAUR, "FLASH," WHICH YOU GAVE TO PIKACHU...
...AND "STRENGTH" WHICH YOU GAVE TO SNORLAX.
SHATSH
YAASH!
RRLL RRLLRRLL
SO THERE'S STILL "SURF" AND "FLY" OUT THERE, RIGHT...?
YOU'LL NEED THEM **BOTH** ON THE ROAD AHEAD!
NO FOOLIN'. IF I'M GONNA GET TO THE SEAFOAM ISLANDS, I NEED THAT MACHINE TO TEACH ONE OF MY POKÉMON "*SURF*"!
BLUB BLUB
ESPECIALLY SINCE THAT STUPID ***BLUE*** ALREADY FOUND IT!
GLINT
HUH ?
PING PING
YEAH! THE H.M. 03 !

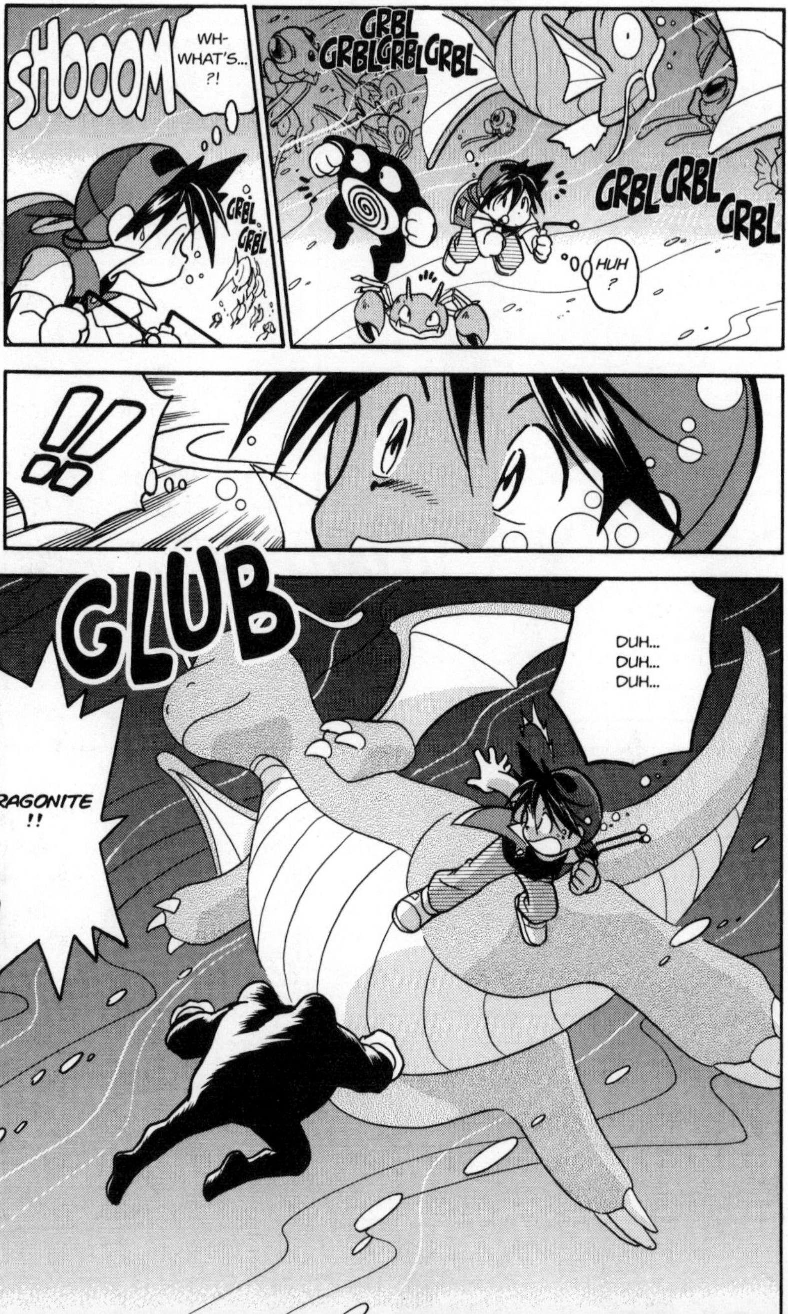
GRBL GRBLGRBLGRBL
GRBL GRBL GRBL
HUH ?
SHOOOM
WH- WHAT'S... ?!
GRBL GRBL
!!
DUH... DUH... DUH...
GLUB
DRAGONITE !!

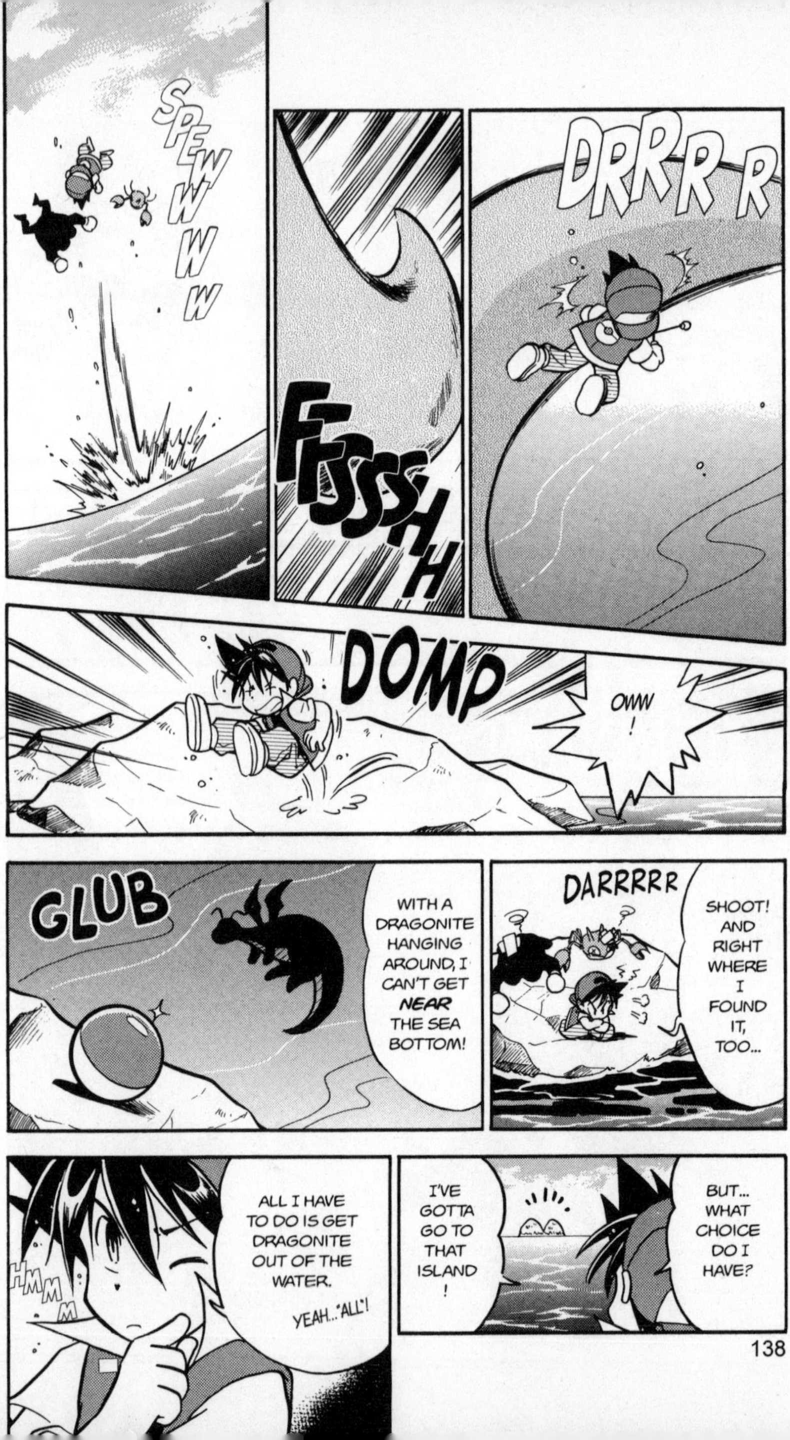
SPEWWWWWW
FSSSHH
DRRRR R
DOMP
OWW!
GLUB
WITH A DRAGONITE HANGING AROUND, I CAN'T GET *NEAR* THE SEA BOTTOM!
DARRRRR
SHOOT! AND RIGHT WHERE I FOUND IT, TOO...
HMMM
ALL I HAVE TO DO IS GET DRAGONITE OUT OF THE WATER.
YEAH... "ALL"!
I'VE GOTTA GO TO THAT ISLAND!
BUT... WHAT CHOICE DO I HAVE?

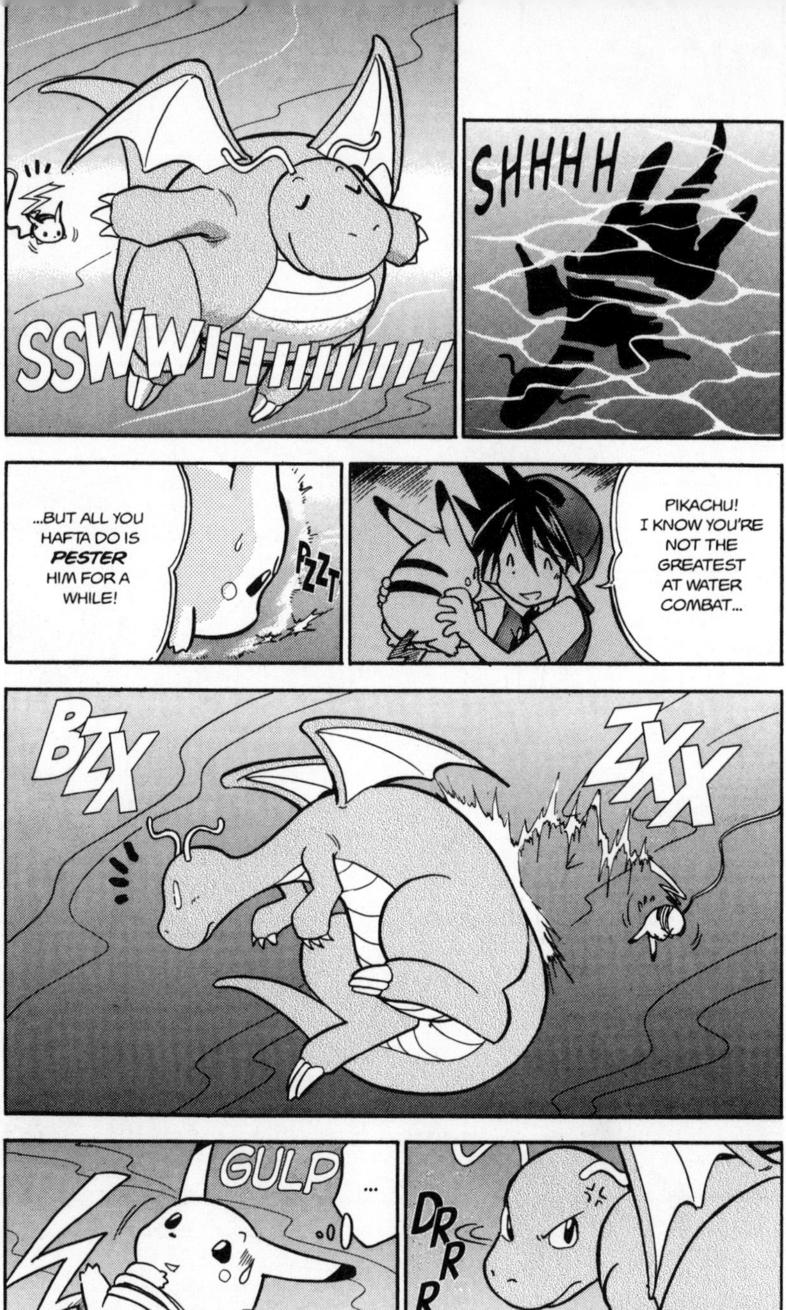
SHHHH
SSWWIIIIIIIIIII
PIKACHU! I KNOW YOU'RE NOT THE GREATEST AT WATER COMBAT...
...BUT ALL YOU HAFTA DO IS *PESTER* HIM FOR A WHILE!
PZZT
ZXX
BZX
DRRRRR
...
GULP

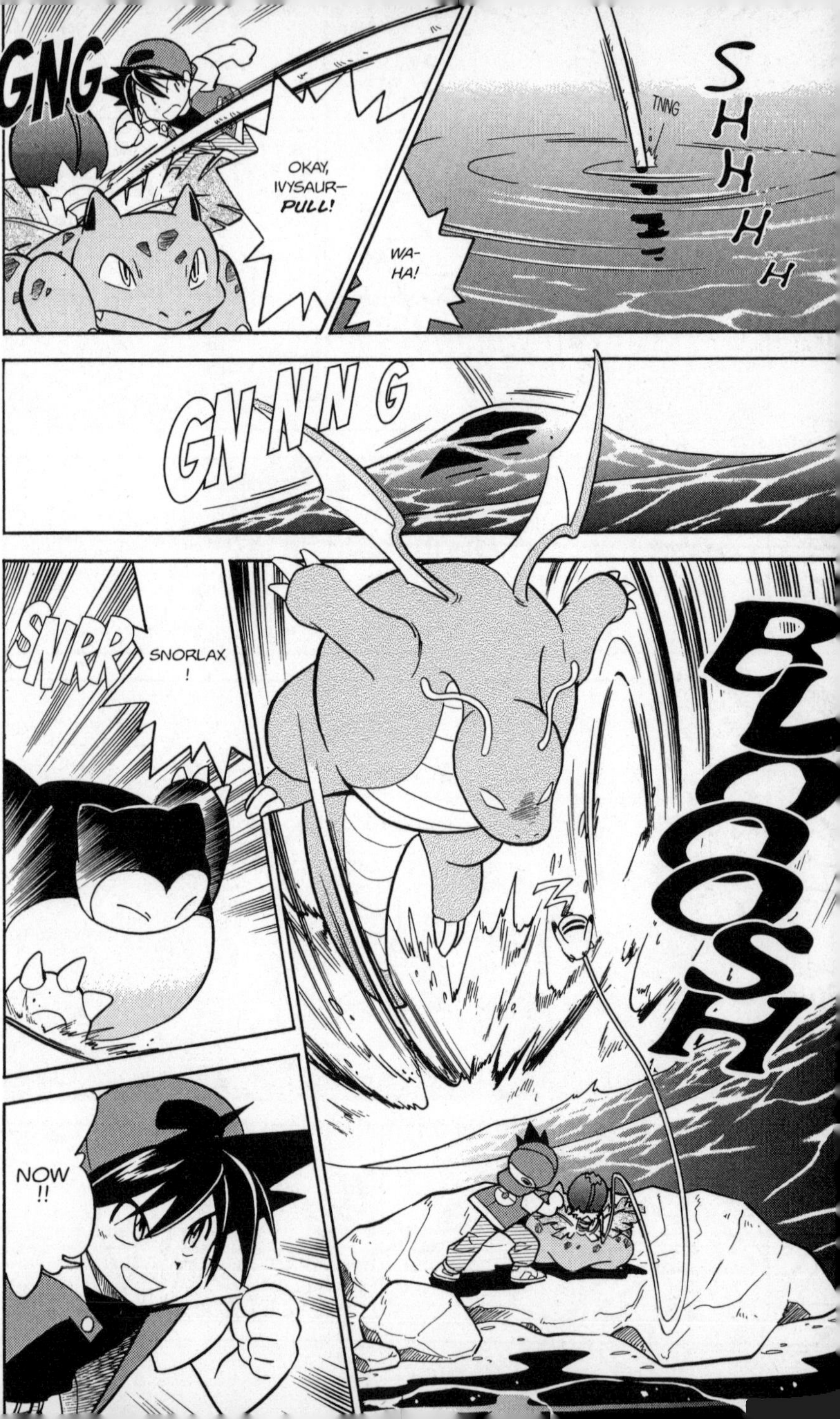
SHHHHH
TNNG
WA-HA!
GNG
OKAY, IVYSAUR—PULL!
GNNNG
BLOOOSH
SNRR
SNORLAX!
NOW!!

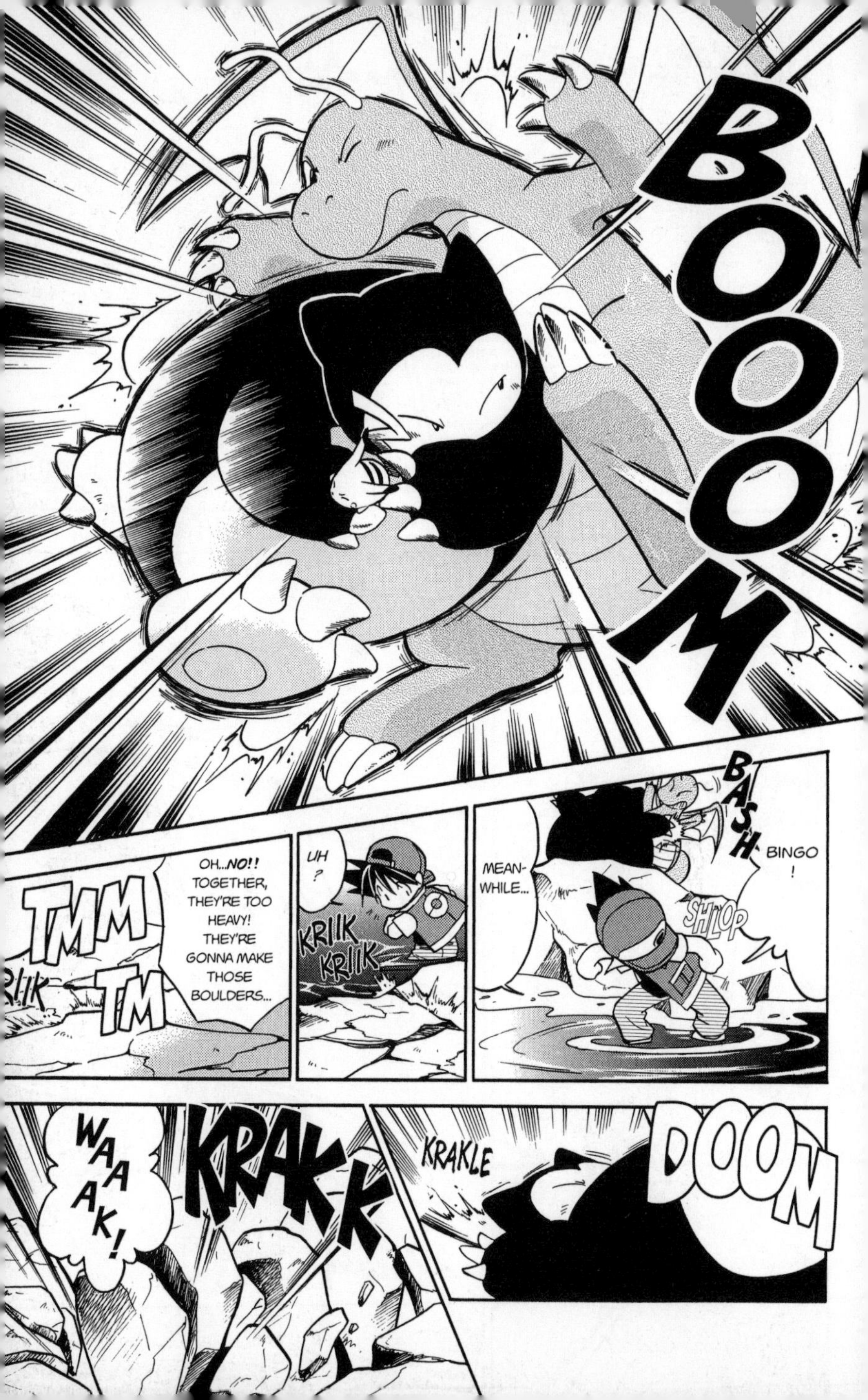
BOOOM
BASH
BINGO!
MEAN-WHILE...
SHLOP
UH?
KRIIK KRIIK
OH...NO!! TOGETHER, THEY'RE TOO HEAVY! THEY'RE GONNA MAKE THOSE BOULDERS...
TMM
TM
RIIK
DOOM
KRAKLE
KRAKK
WAAAAK!

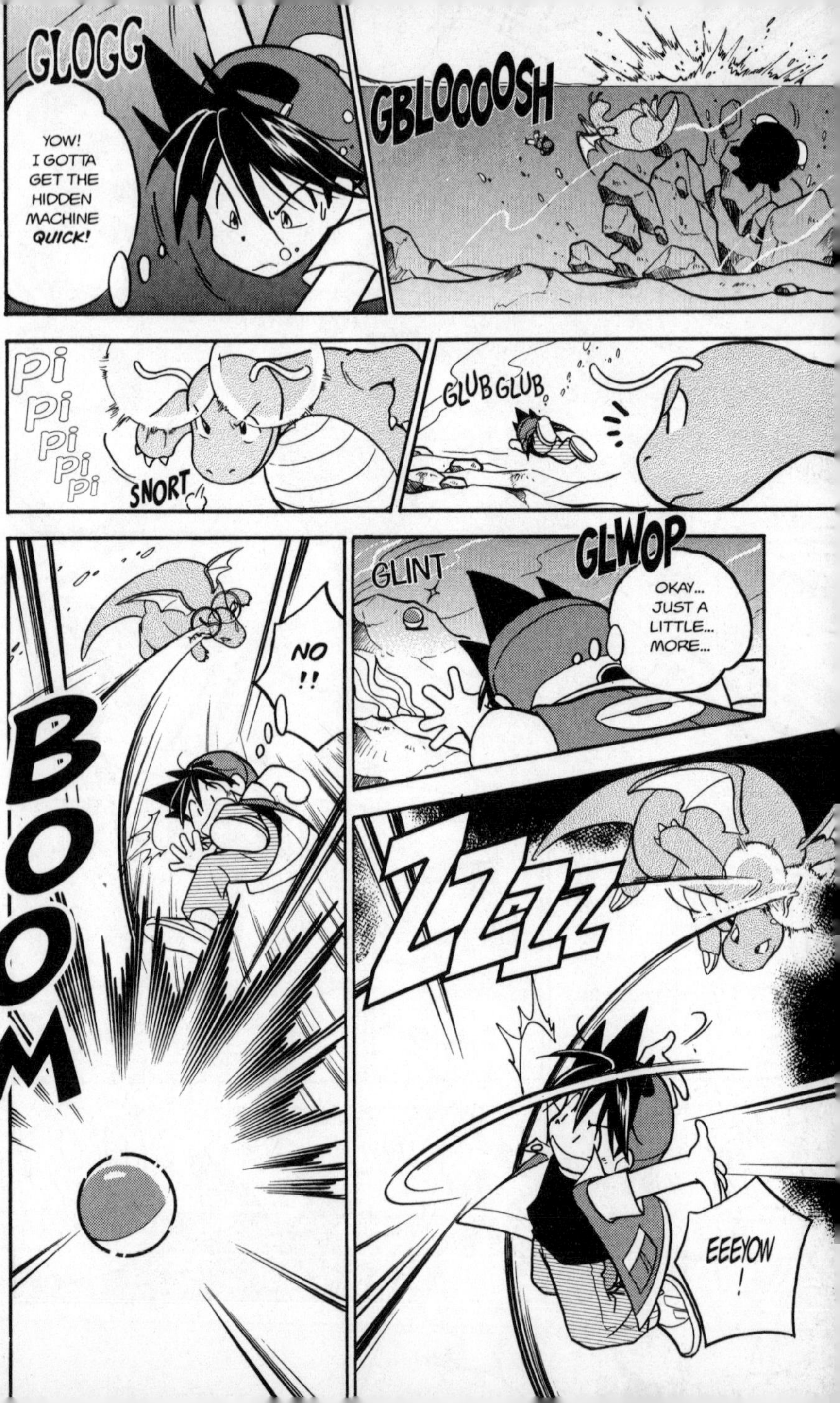
GBLOOOOSH
GLOGG
YOW! I GOTTA GET THE HIDDEN MACHINE **QUICK!**
GLUB GLUB
pi pi pi pi pi
SNORT
GLWOP
GLINT
OKAY... JUST A LITTLE... MORE...
ZZZZ
EEEYOW!
NO!!
BOOM

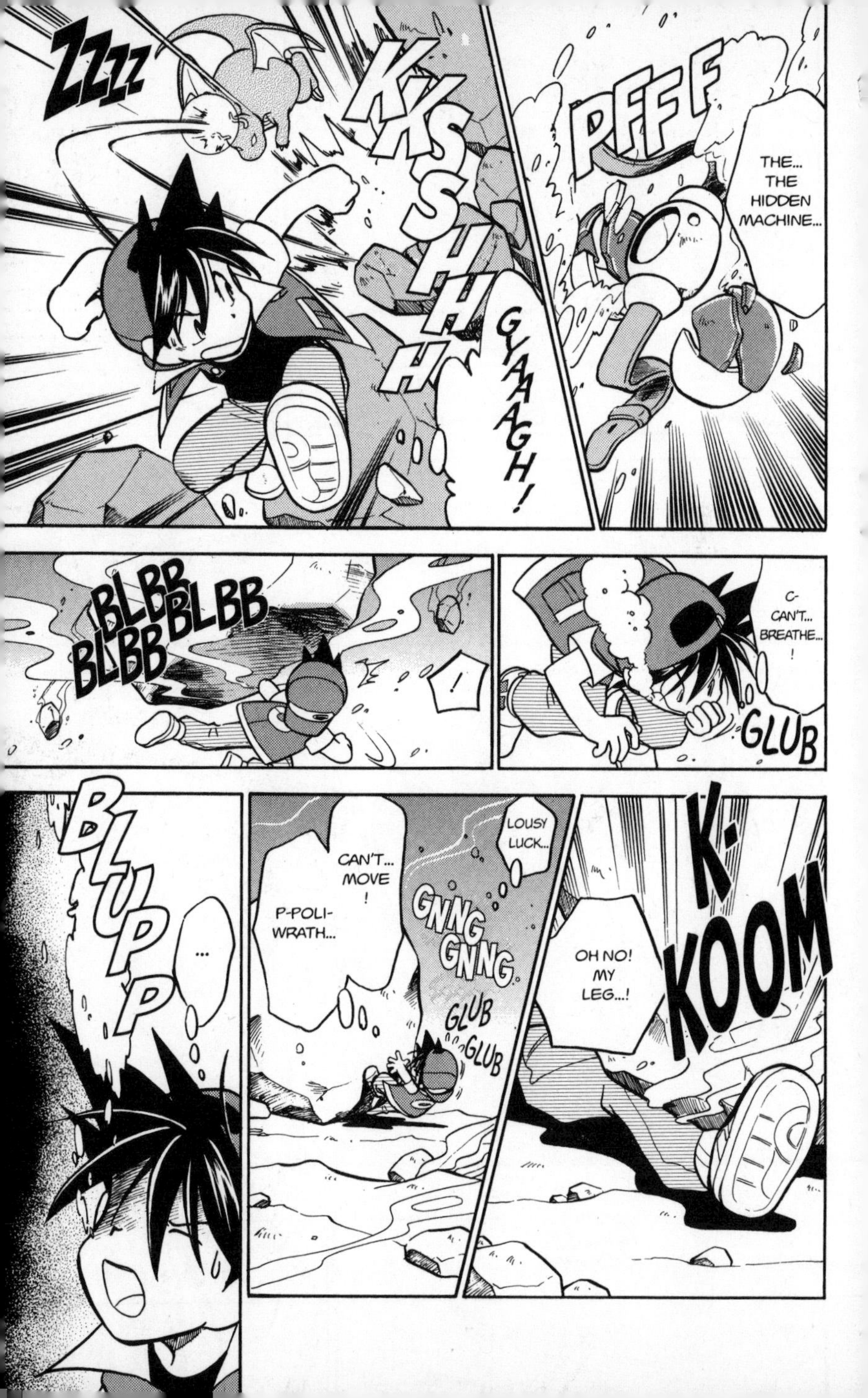
PFFF
THE... THE HIDDEN MACHINE...
ZZZZ
KKSSHHH
GYAAAGH!
C-CAN'T... BREATHE... !
GLUB
!
BLBB BLBB BLBB BLBB
K-KOOM
OH NO! MY LEG...!
LOUSY LUCK...
CAN'T... MOVE !
P-POLI-WRATH...
GNNG GNNG
GLUB GLUB
BLUPP
...

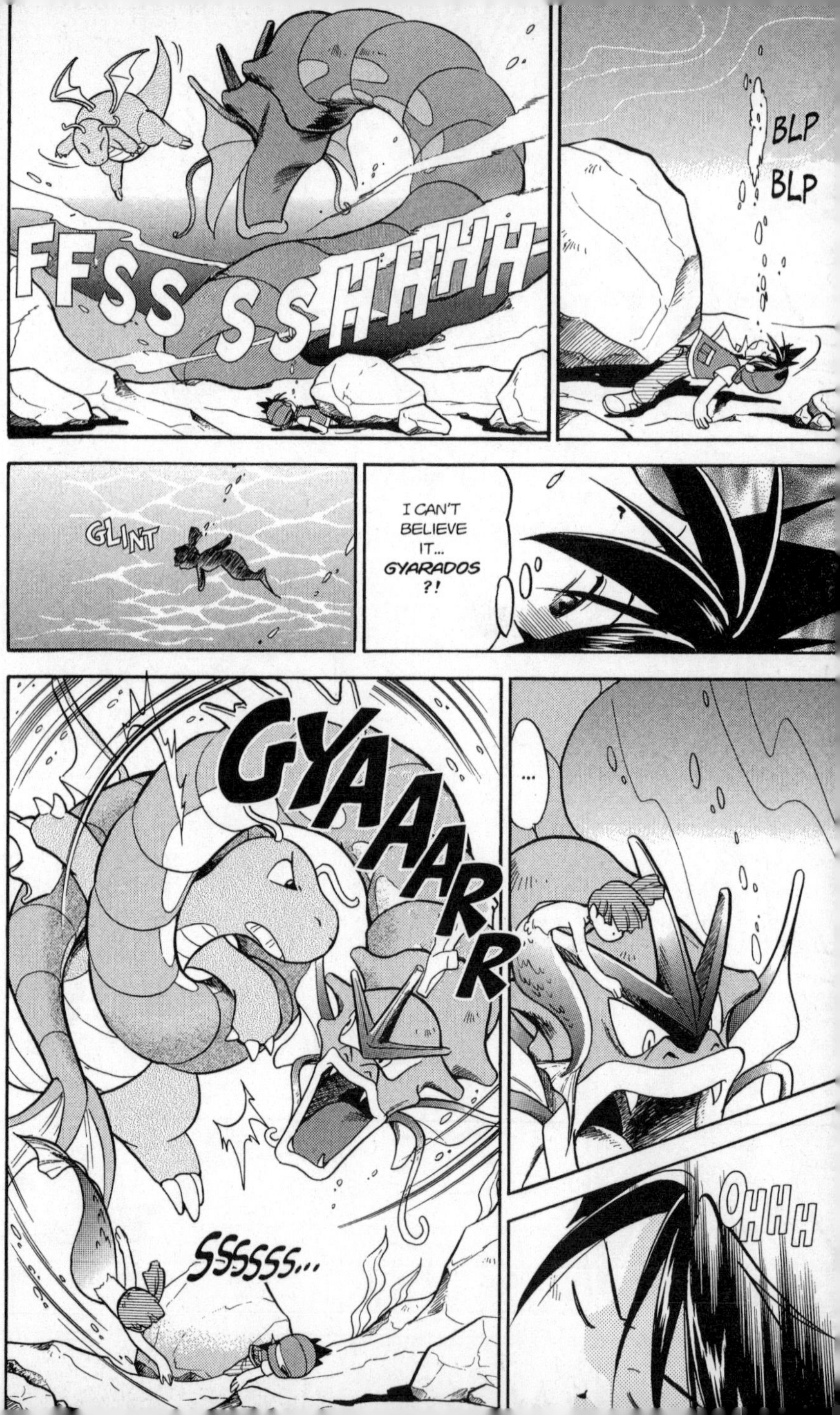
BLP
BLP
FFSS SSHHHH
I CAN'T BELIEVE IT... GYARADOS ?!
GLINT
...
OHHH
GYAAARRR
SSSSSS...

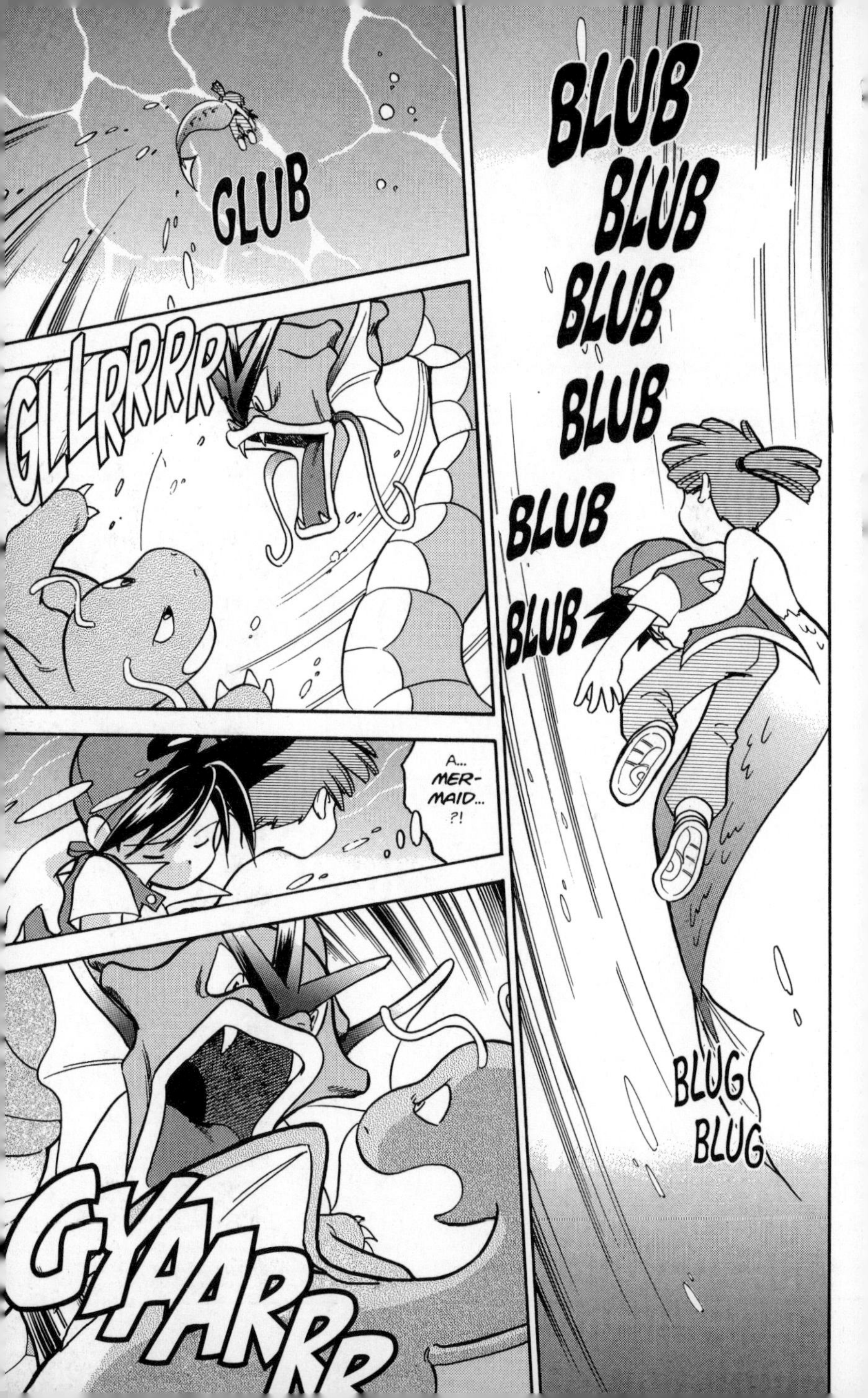
BLUB
BLUB
BLUB
BLUB
BLUB
BLUB
BLUG
BLUG
GLUB
GLLRRRRR
A... MERMAID... ?!
GYARRR

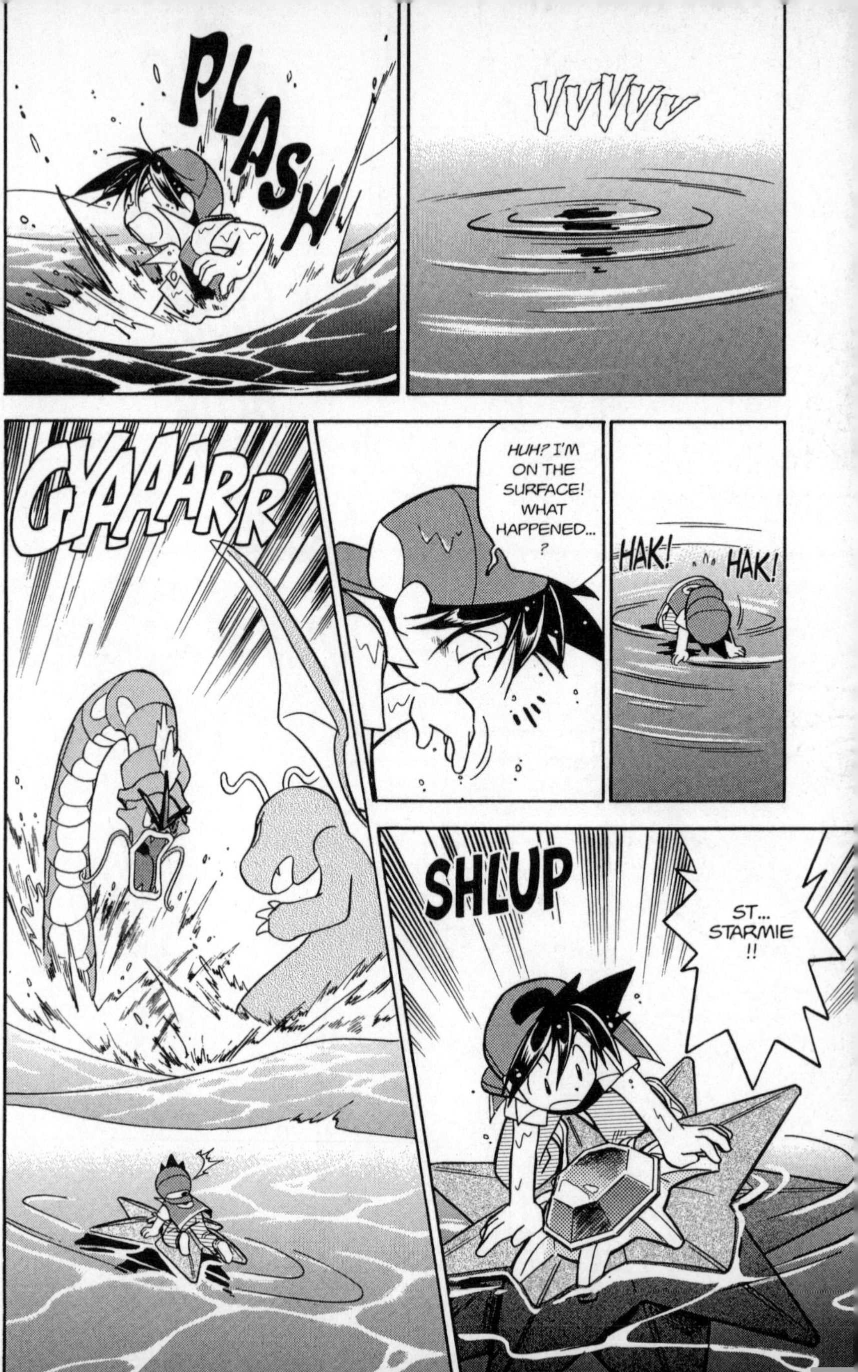
VVVVVV
PLASH
HAK! HAK!
HUH? I'M ON THE SURFACE! WHAT HAPPENED...?
SHLUP
ST... STARMIE!!
GYAAARR

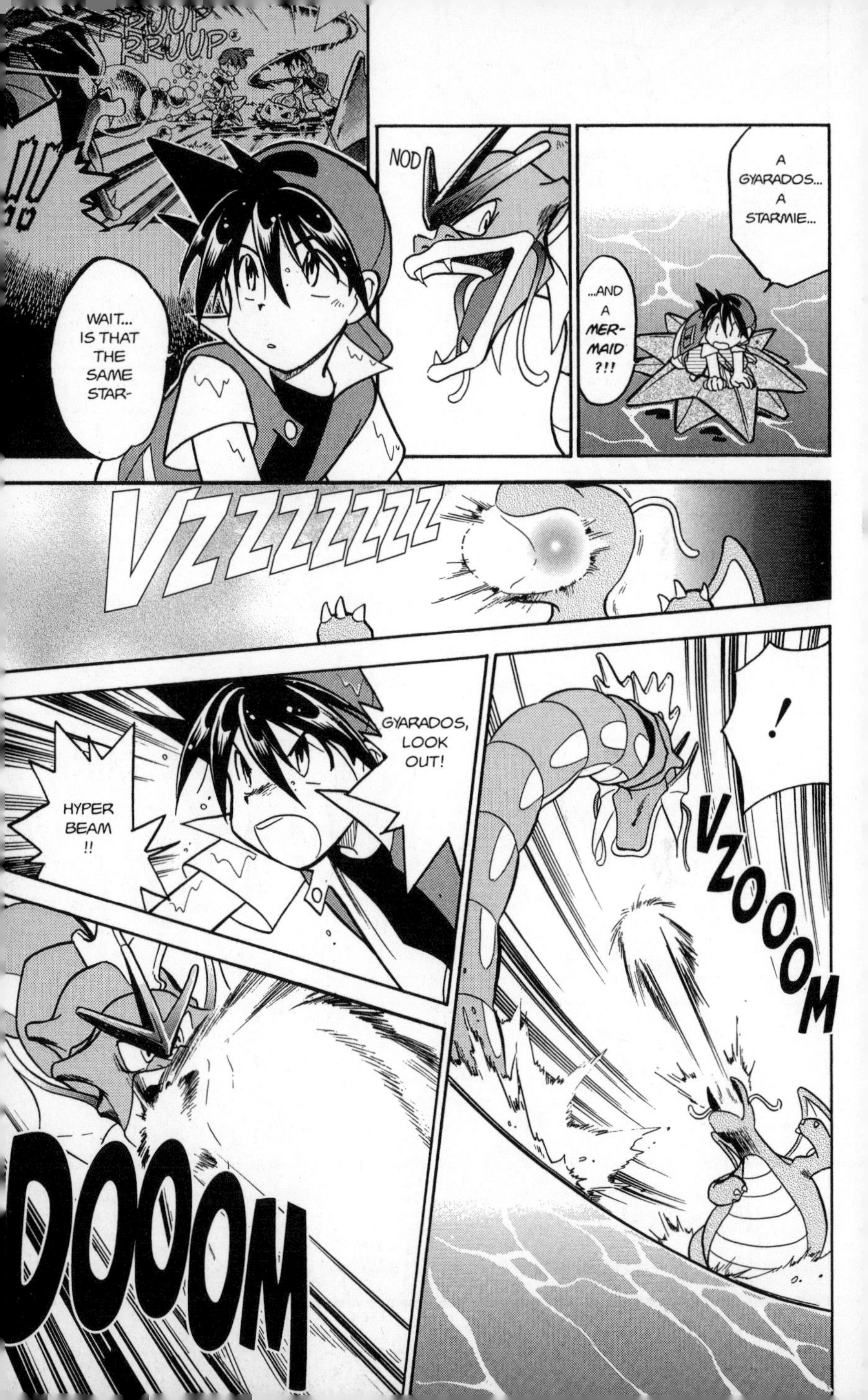
A GYARADOS... A STARMIE...
...AND A MER-MAID?!!
NOD
RRUUP RRUUP
!!
WAIT... IS THAT THE SAME STAR-
VZZZZZZZ
!
VZOOOM
GYARADOS, LOOK OUT!
HYPER BEAM!!
DOOOM

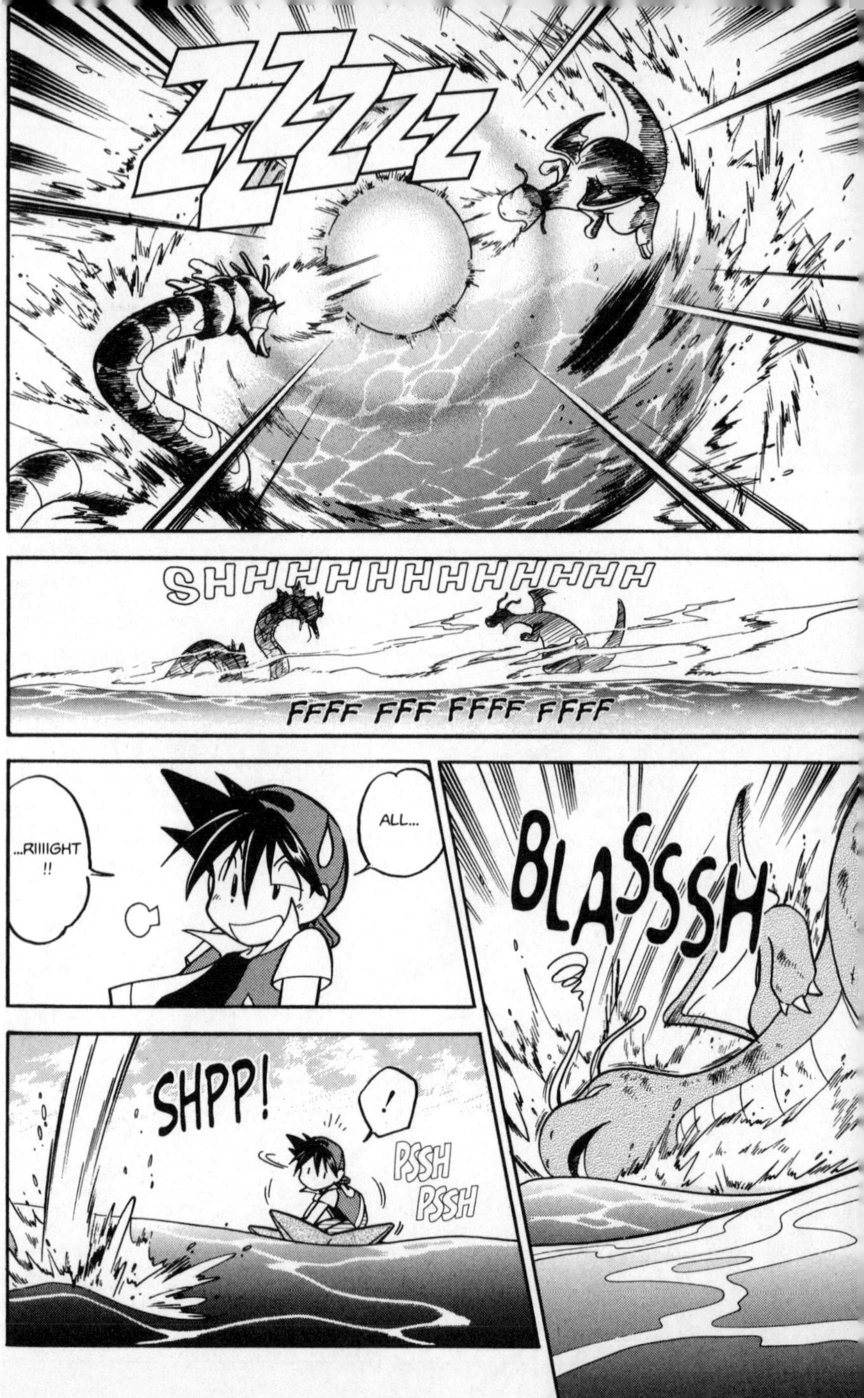
ZZZZZ
SHHHHHHHHHHHHH
FFFF FFF FFFF FFFF
BLASSSH
ALL...
...RIIIIGHT !!
SHPP!
!
PSSH PSSH

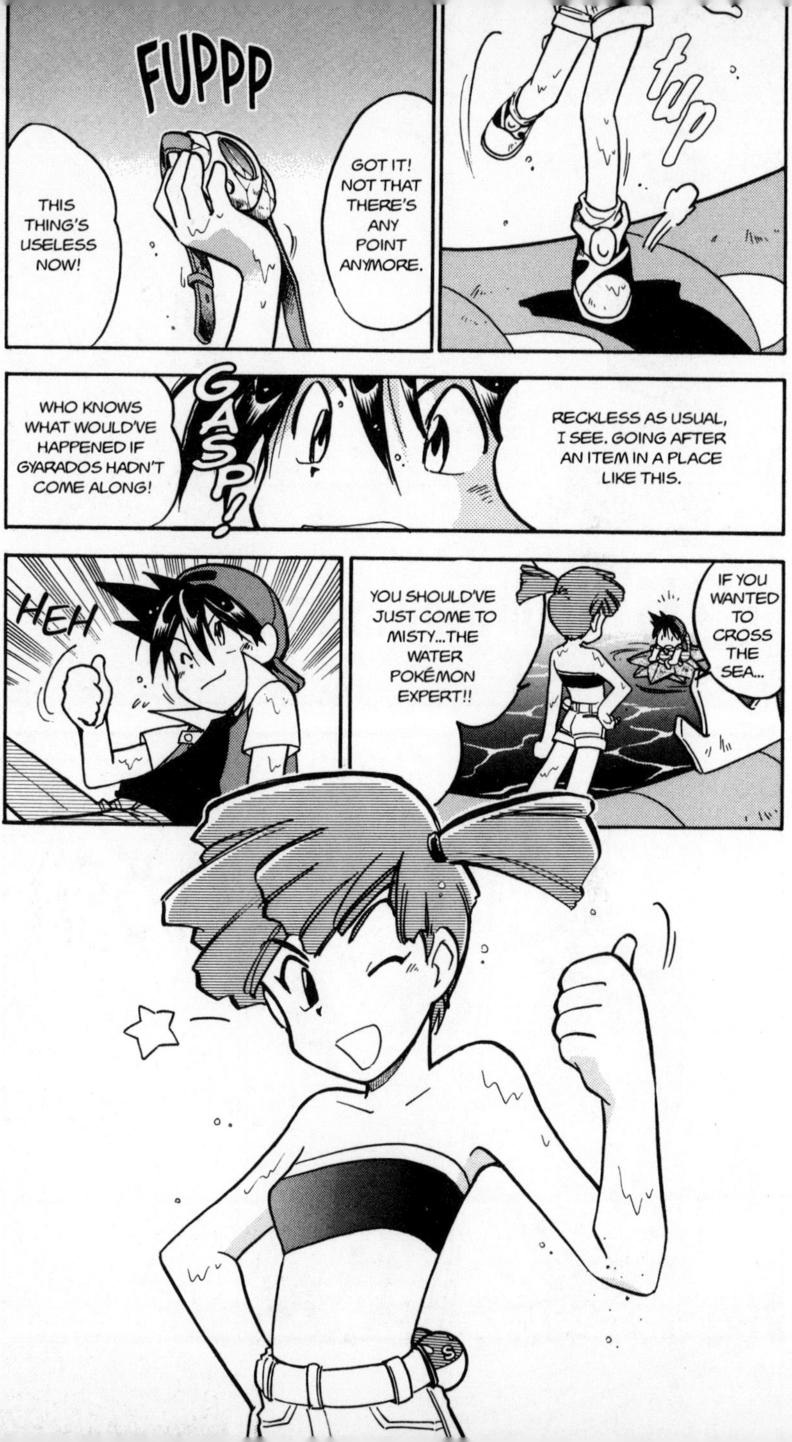
tup
FUPPP
GOT IT! NOT THAT THERE'S ANY POINT ANYMORE.
THIS THING'S USELESS NOW!
RECKLESS AS USUAL, I SEE. GOING AFTER AN ITEM IN A PLACE LIKE THIS.
GASP!
WHO KNOWS WHAT WOULD'VE HAPPENED IF GYARADOS HADN'T COME ALONG!
IF YOU WANTED TO CROSS THE SEA...
YOU SHOULD'VE JUST COME TO MISTY...THE WATER POKÉMON EXPERT!!
HEH

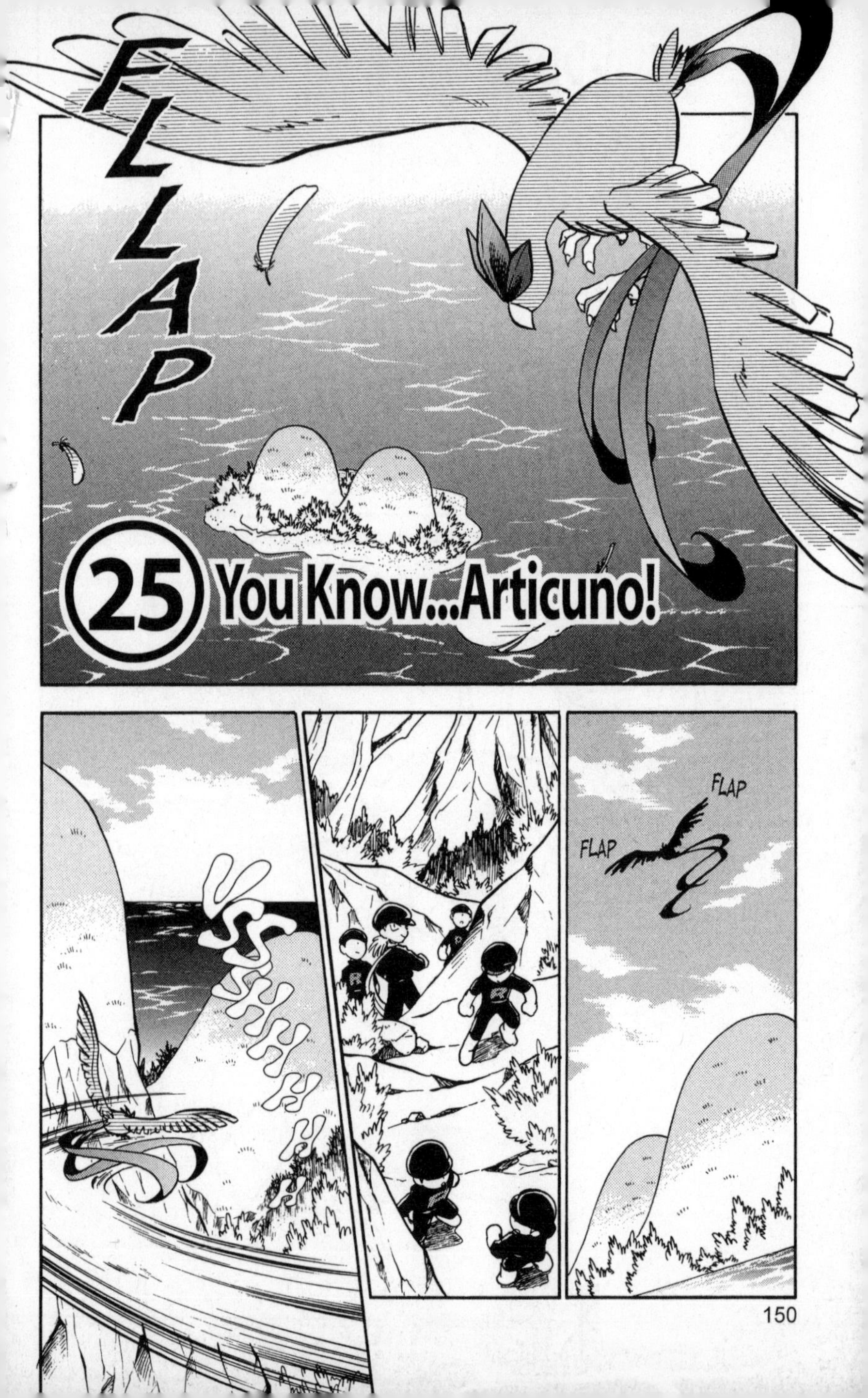
FLLAP
25 You Know...Articuno!
FLAP
FLAP

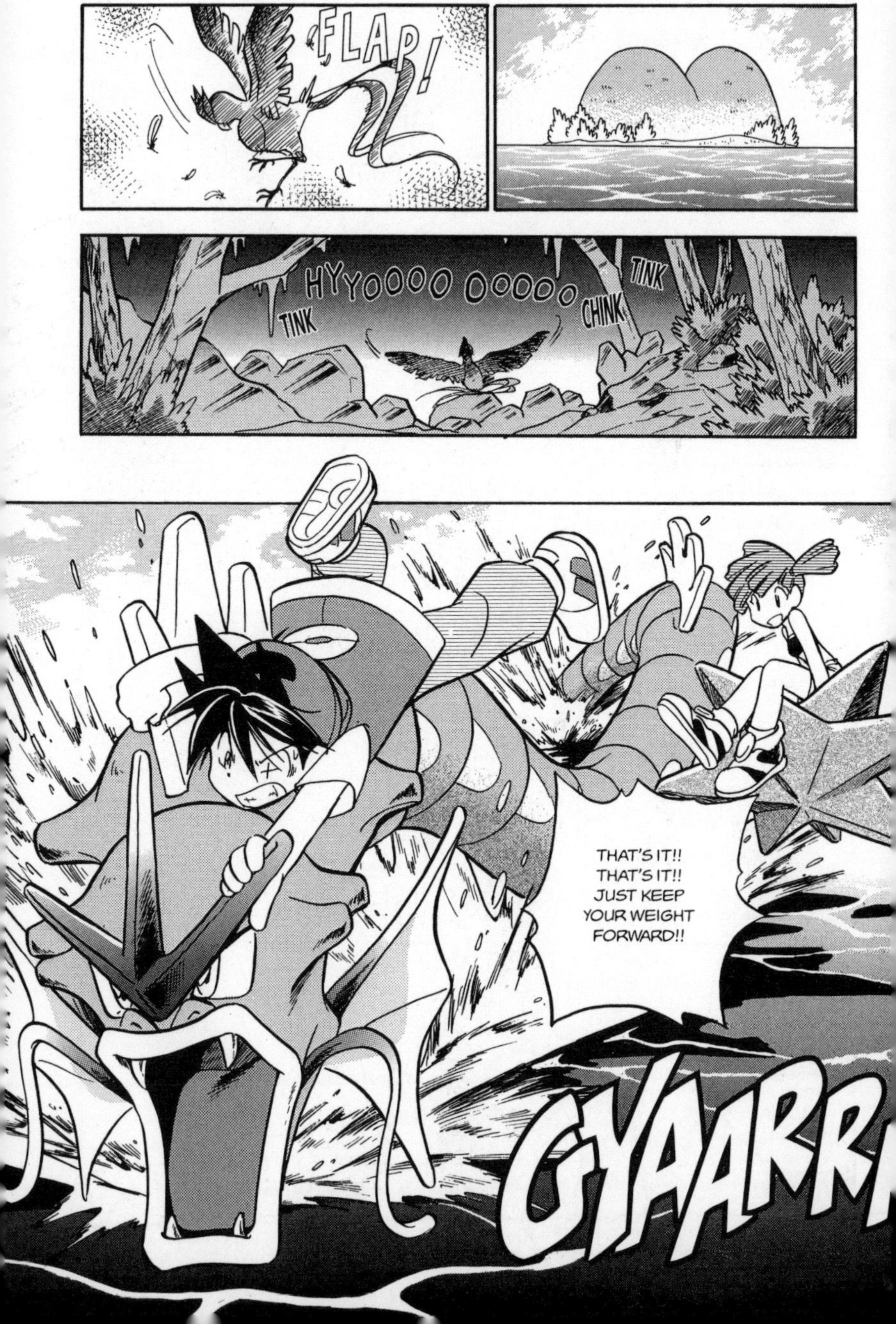
FLAP!
TINK
CHINK
HYYOOOO OOOOO
TINK
THAT'S IT!!
THAT'S IT!!
JUST KEEP
YOUR WEIGHT
FORWARD!!
GYAARR

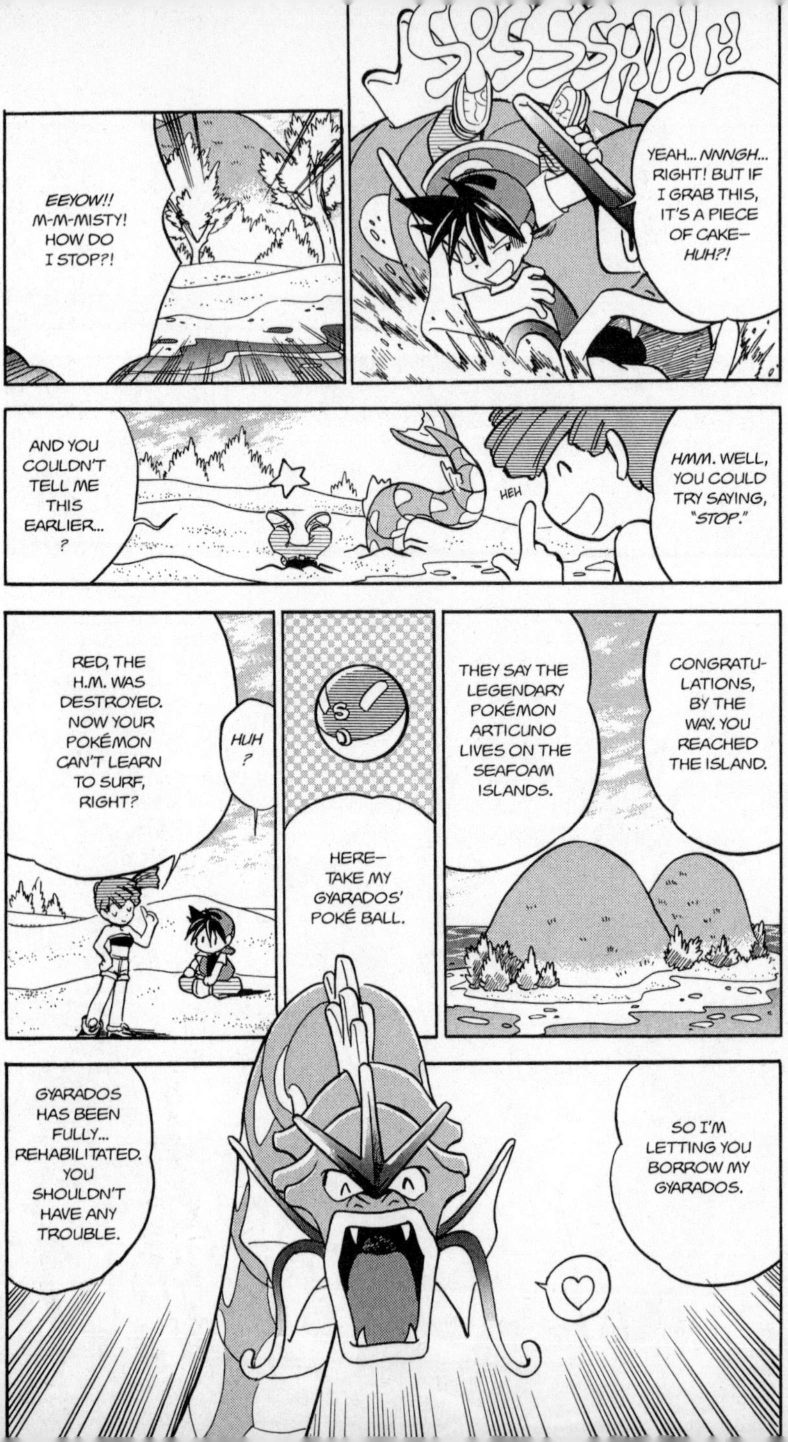
SPSSSHHH
YEAH... NNNGH... RIGHT! BUT IF I GRAB THIS, IT'S A PIECE OF CAKE— HUH?!
EEYOW!! M-M-MISTY! HOW DO I STOP?!
HMM. WELL, YOU COULD TRY SAYING, "STOP."
HEH
AND YOU COULDN'T TELL ME THIS EARLIER... ?
CONGRATU-LATIONS, BY THE WAY. YOU REACHED THE ISLAND.
THEY SAY THE LEGENDARY POKéMON ARTICUNO LIVES ON THE SEAFOAM ISLANDS.
HERE— TAKE MY GYARADOS' POKé BALL.
RED, THE H.M. WAS DESTROYED. NOW YOUR POKéMON CAN'T LEARN TO SURF, RIGHT?
HUH ?
SO I'M LETTING YOU BORROW MY GYARADOS.
GYARADOS HAS BEEN FULLY... REHABILITATED. YOU SHOULDN'T HAVE ANY TROUBLE.

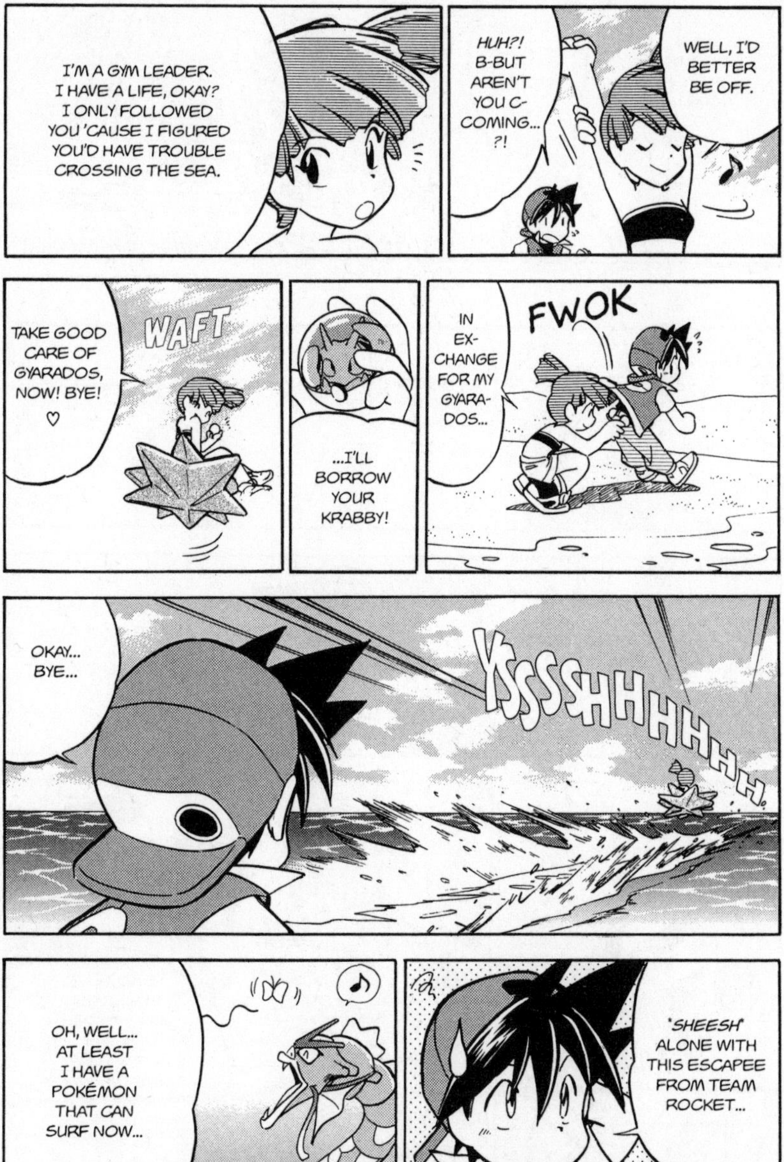
WELL, I'D BETTER BE OFF.
HUH?! B-BUT AREN'T YOU C-COMING...?!
I'M A GYM LEADER. I HAVE A LIFE, OKAY? I ONLY FOLLOWED YOU 'CAUSE I FIGURED YOU'D HAVE TROUBLE CROSSING THE SEA.
FWOK
IN EXCHANGE FOR MY GYARADOS...
...I'LL BORROW YOUR KRABBY!
WAFT
TAKE GOOD CARE OF GYARADOS, NOW! BYE! ♡
YSSSHHHHHHHHH
OKAY... BYE...
SHEESH ALONE WITH THIS ESCAPEE FROM TEAM ROCKET...
OH, WELL... AT LEAST I HAVE A POKÉMON THAT CAN SURF NOW...

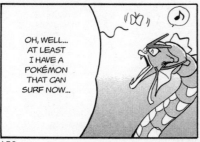

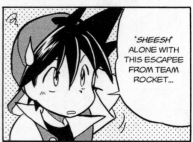

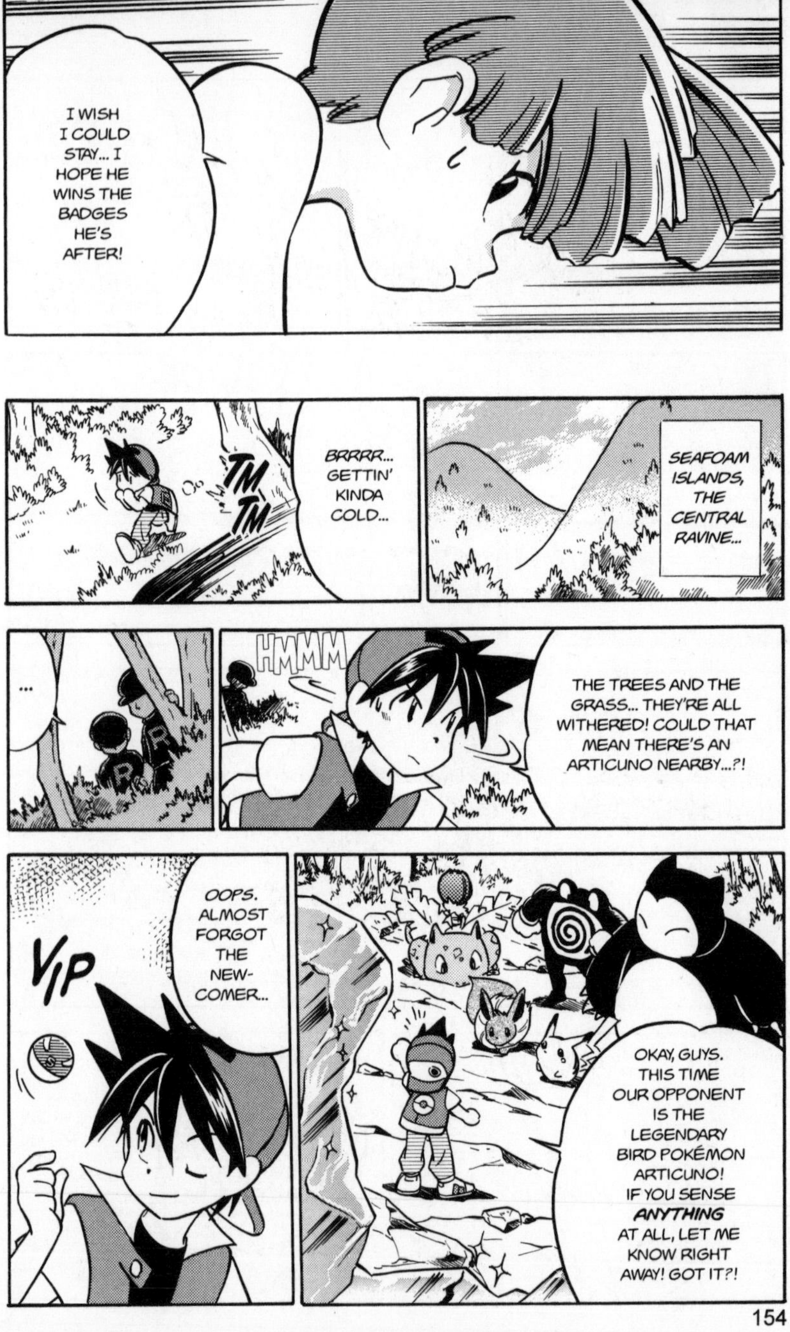
I WISH I COULD STAY... I HOPE HE WINS THE BADGES HE'S AFTER!
SEAFOAM ISLANDS, THE CENTRAL RAVINE...
BRRRR... GETTIN' KINDA COLD...
TM TM
THE TREES AND THE GRASS... THEY'RE ALL WITHERED! COULD THAT MEAN THERE'S AN ARTICUNO NEARBY...?!
HMMM
...
OKAY, GUYS. THIS TIME OUR OPPONENT IS THE LEGENDARY BIRD POKÉMON ARTICUNO! IF YOU SENSE ***ANYTHING*** AT ALL, LET ME KNOW RIGHT AWAY! GOT IT?!
OOPS. ALMOST FORGOT THE NEW-COMER..
VIP

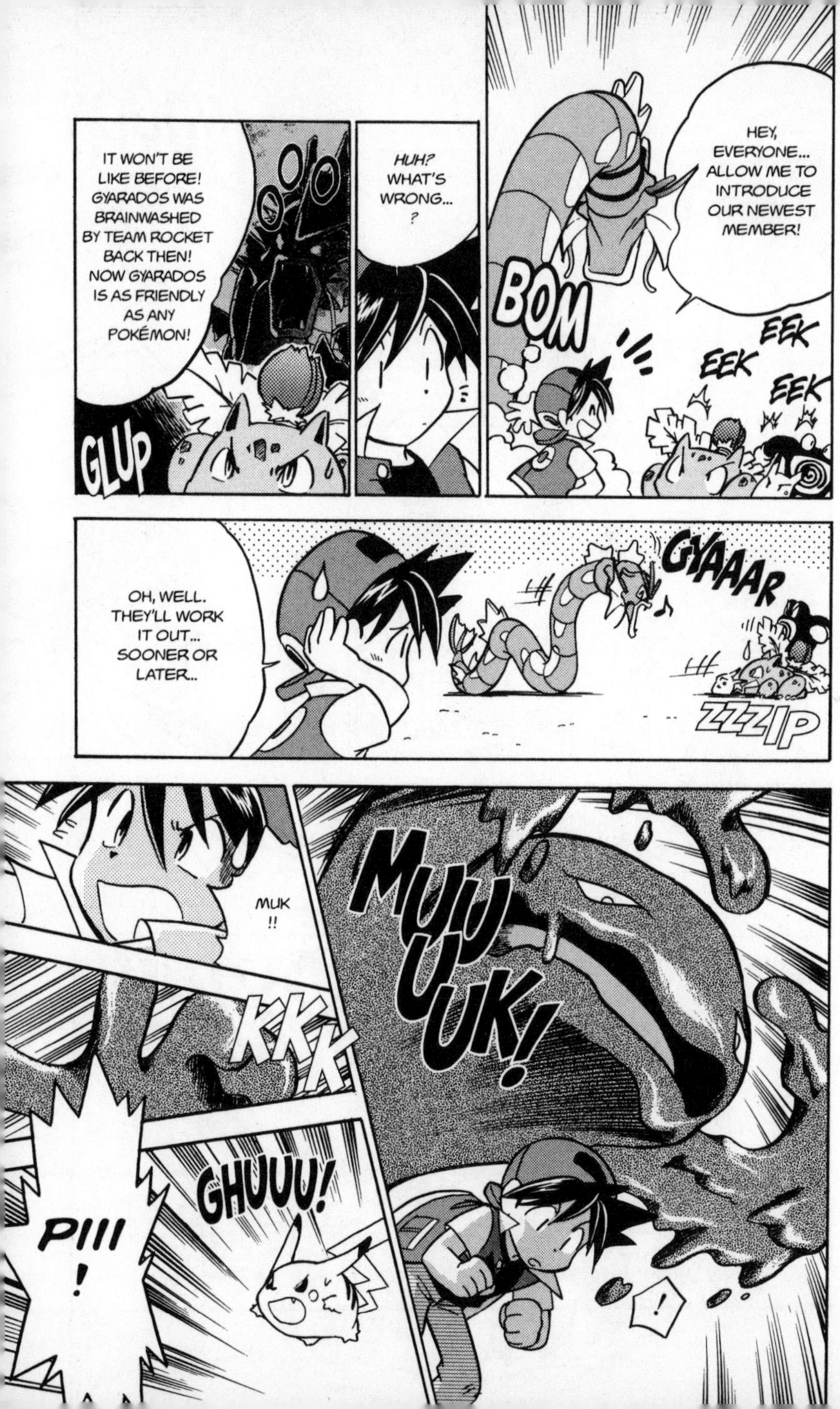
HEY, EVERYONE... ALLOW ME TO INTRODUCE OUR NEWEST MEMBER!
BOM
EEK
EEK
EEK
HUH? WHAT'S WRONG... ?
IT WON'T BE LIKE BEFORE! GYARADOS WAS BRAINWASHED BY TEAM ROCKET BACK THEN! NOW GYARADOS IS AS FRIENDLY AS ANY POKÉMON!
GLUP
GYAAAR
ZZZIP
OH, WELL. THEY'LL WORK IT OUT... SOONER OR LATER...
MUUUUK!
!
MUK !!
KKK
GHUUU!
PIII !

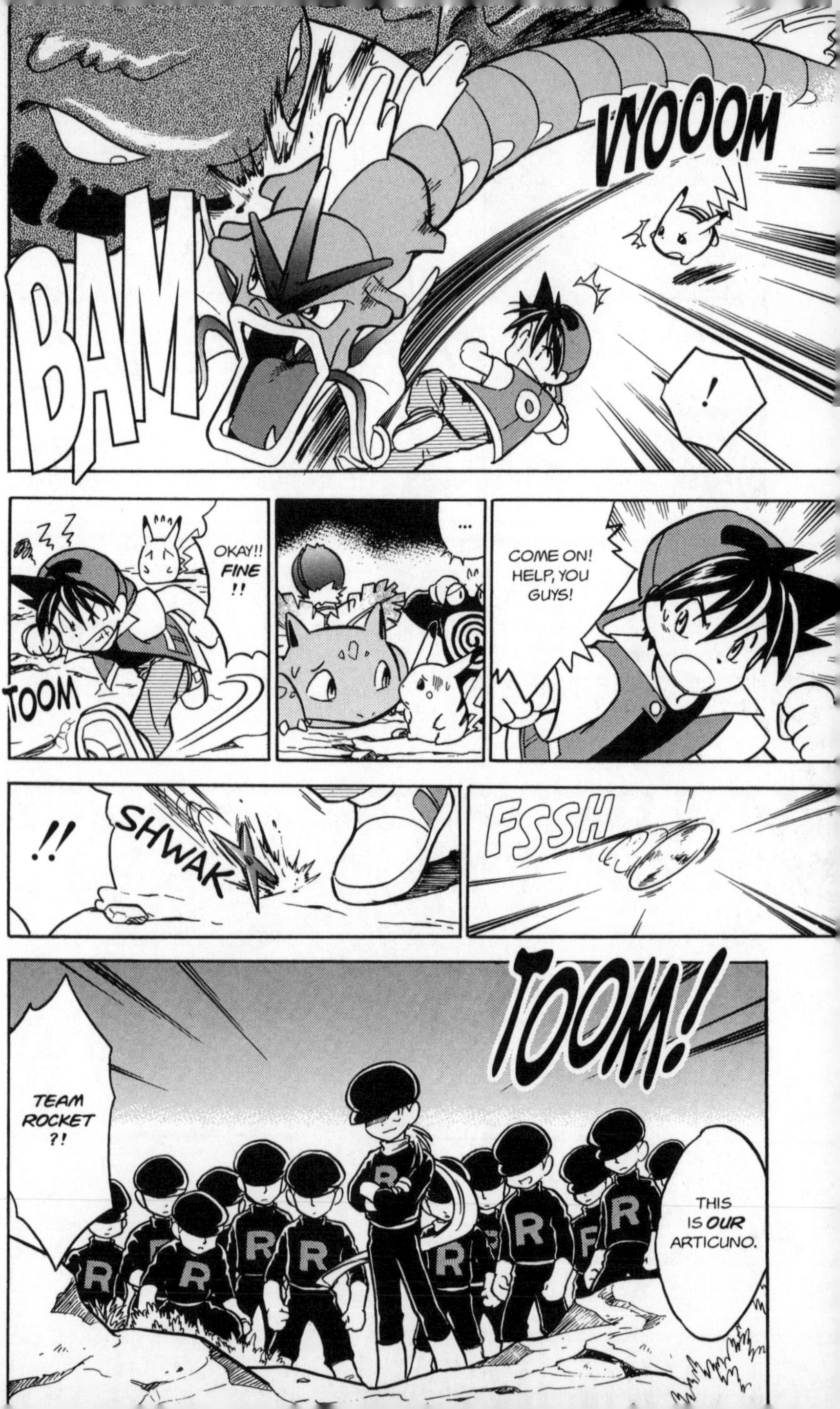
VYOOOM
!
BAM
COME ON! HELP, YOU GUYS!
...
OKAY!! FINE !!
TOOM
FSSH
SHWAK
!!
TOOM!
TEAM ROCKET ?!
THIS IS OUR ARTICUNO.

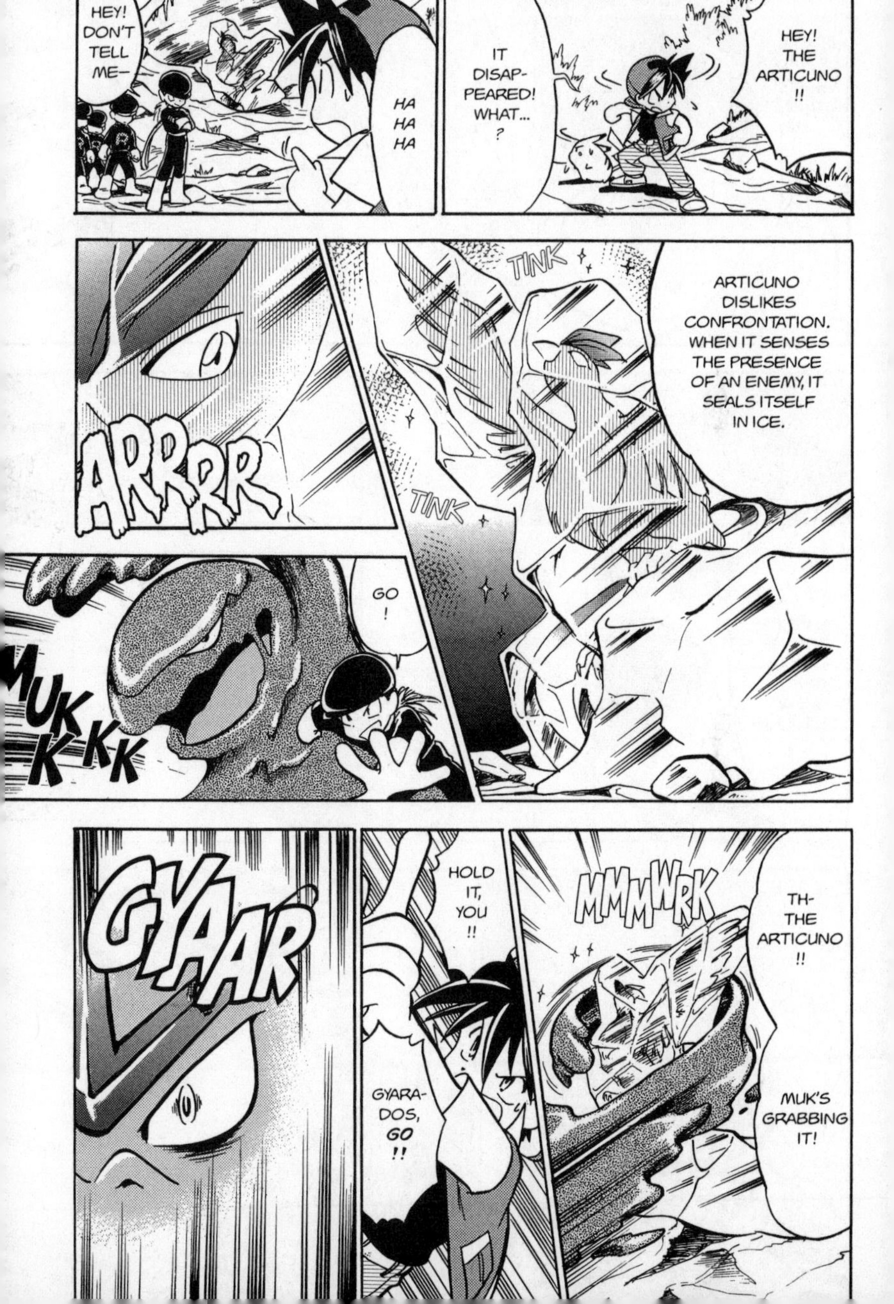
HEY! THE ARTICUNO !!
IT DISAP-PEARED! WHAT... ?
HA HA HA
HEY! DON'T TELL ME—
ARTICUNO DISLIKES CONFRONTATION. WHEN IT SENSES THE PRESENCE OF AN ENEMY, IT SEALS ITSELF IN ICE.
TINK
TINK
ARRRR
GO !
MUKKKK
TH- THE ARTICUNO !!
MMMWRK
MUK'S GRABBING IT!
HOLD IT, YOU !!
GYARA-DOS, GO !!
GYAAR

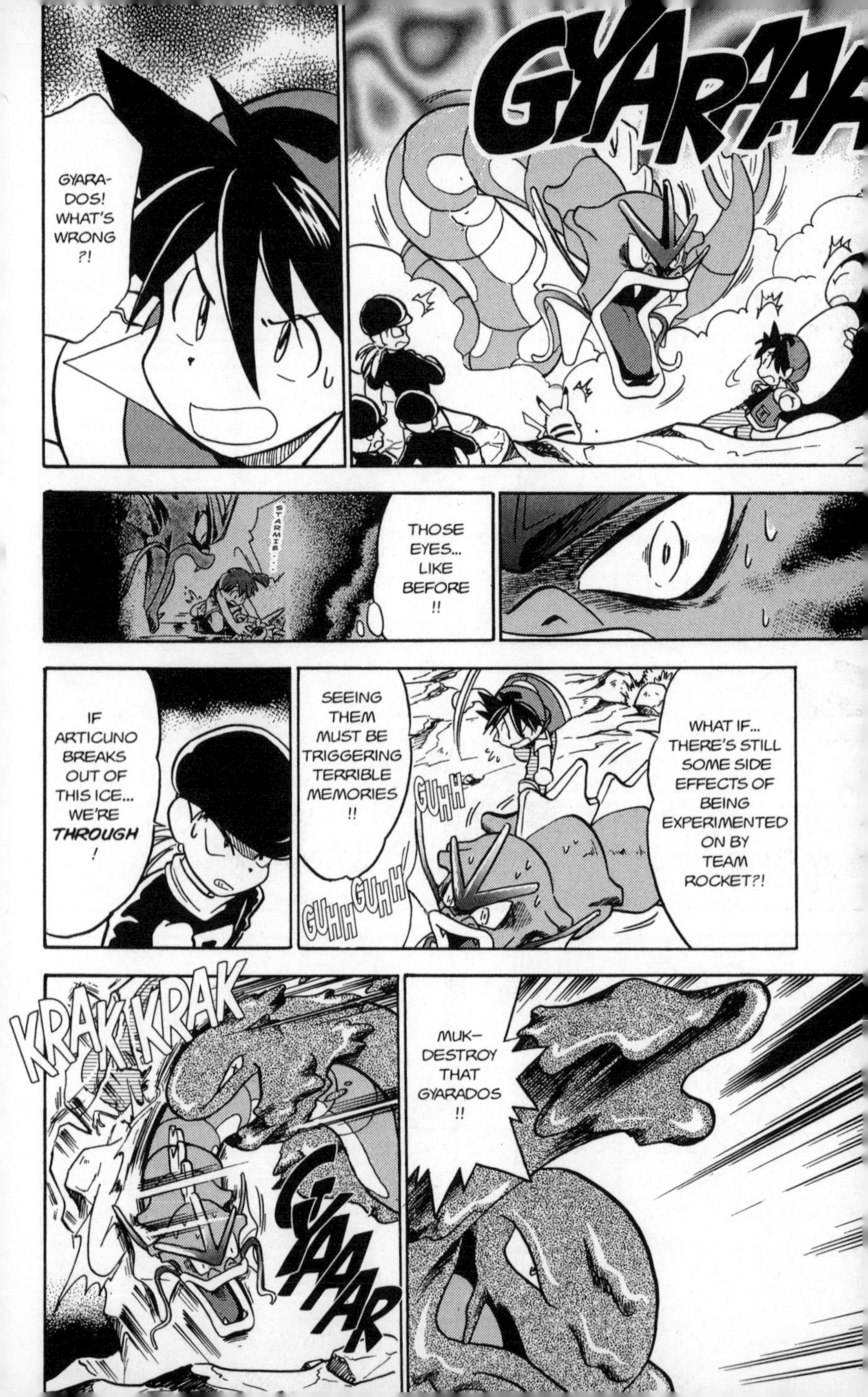
GYAR-AA
GYARA-DOS! WHAT'S WRONG?!
THOSE EYES... LIKE BEFORE!!
STARMIE...
WHAT IF... THERE'S STILL SOME SIDE EFFECTS OF BEING EXPERIMENTED ON BY TEAM ROCKET?!
SEEING THEM MUST BE TRIGGERING TERRIBLE MEMORIES!!
GUHH
GUHH GUHH
IF ARTICUNO BREAKS OUT OF THIS ICE... WE'RE **THROUGH**!
MUK—DESTROY THAT GYARADOS!!
KRAK KRAK
GYAAAR

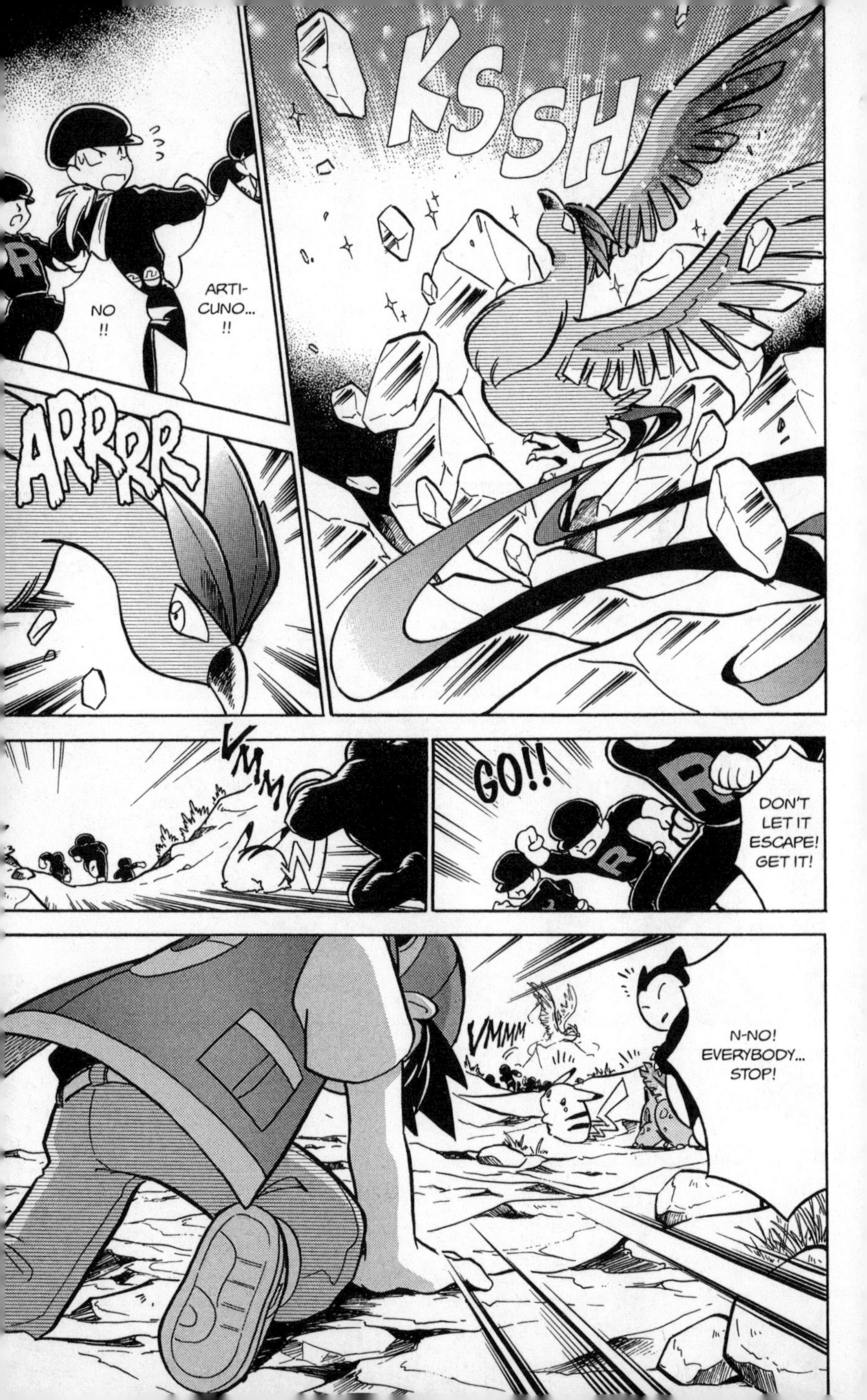
KSSH
ARTI-CUNO... !!
NO !!
ARRRR
GO!!
DON'T LET IT ESCAPE! GET IT!
VMM
N-NO! EVERYBODY... STOP!
VMMM

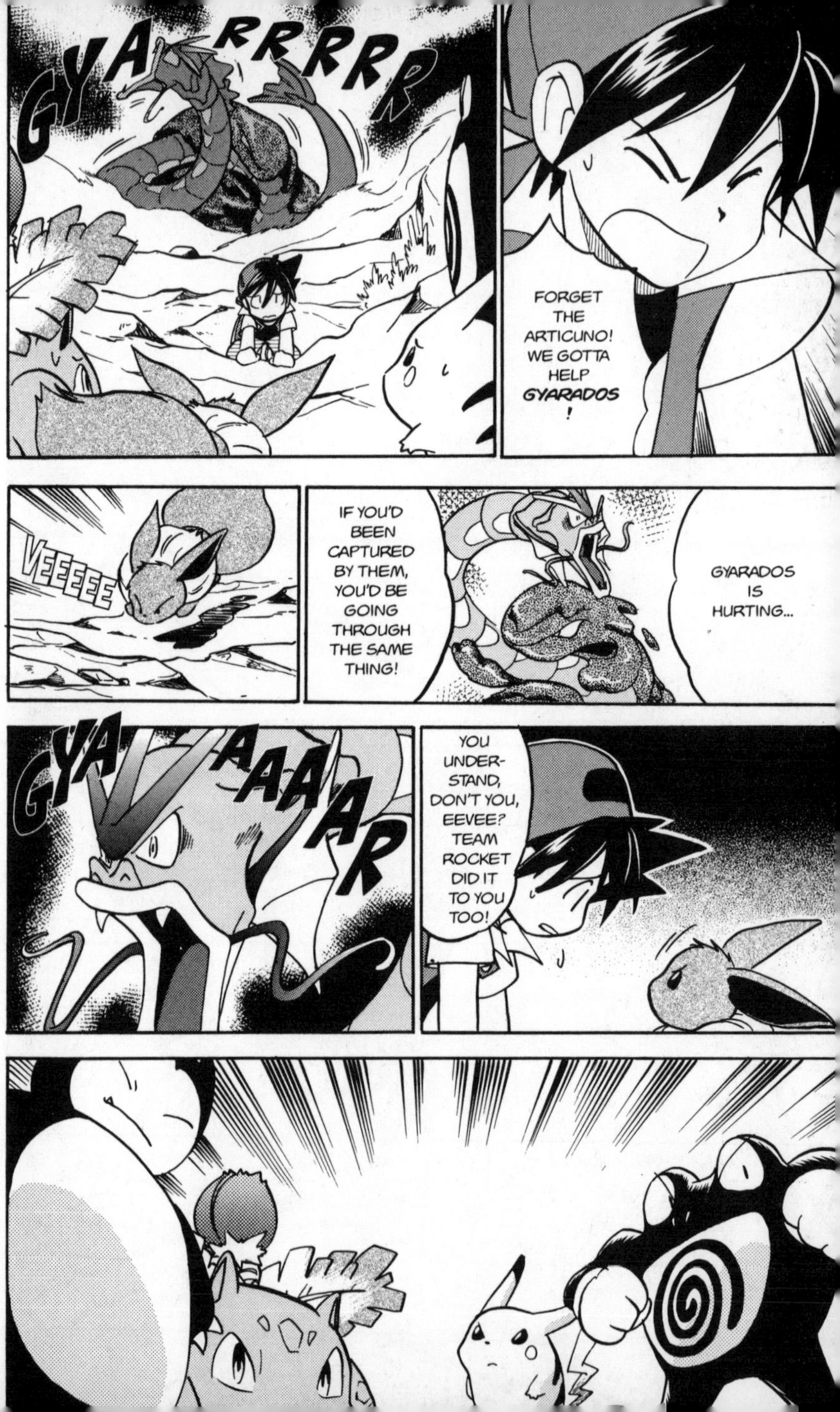
FORGET THE ARTICUNO! WE GOTTA HELP GYARADOS!
GYARRRRRR
GYARADOS IS HURTING...
IF YOU'D BEEN CAPTURED BY THEM, YOU'D BE GOING THROUGH THE SAME THING!
VEEEEE
YOU UNDER-STAND, DON'T YOU, EEVEE? TEAM ROCKET DID IT TO YOU TOO!
GYAAAAAR

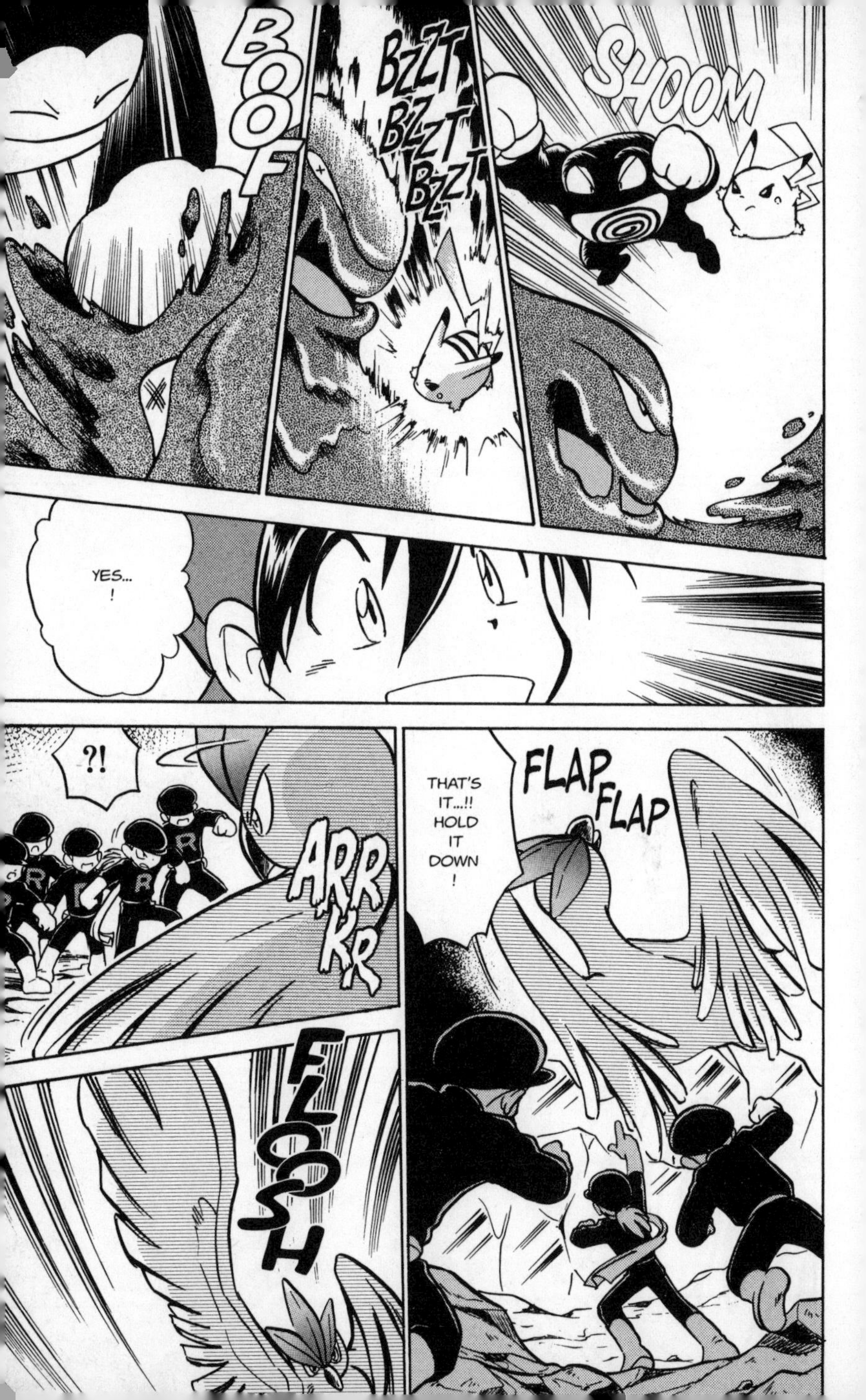
SHOOM
BZZT
BZZT
BZZT
BOOF
YES... !
FLAP
FLAP
THAT'S IT...!! HOLD IT DOWN !
?!
ARR KR
FLOOSH

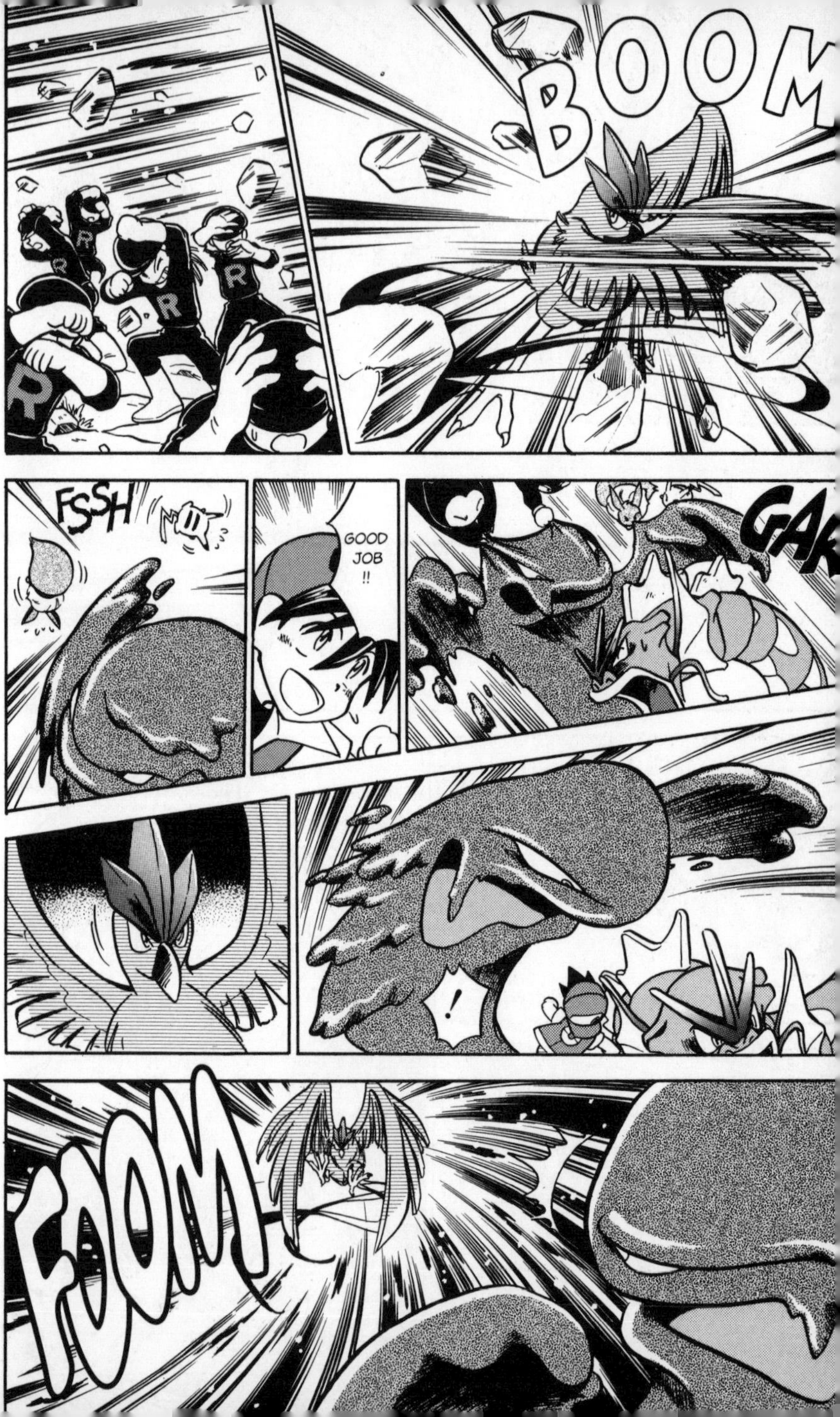
BOOM
GAR
GOOD JOB !!
FSSH
!!
!
FOOM

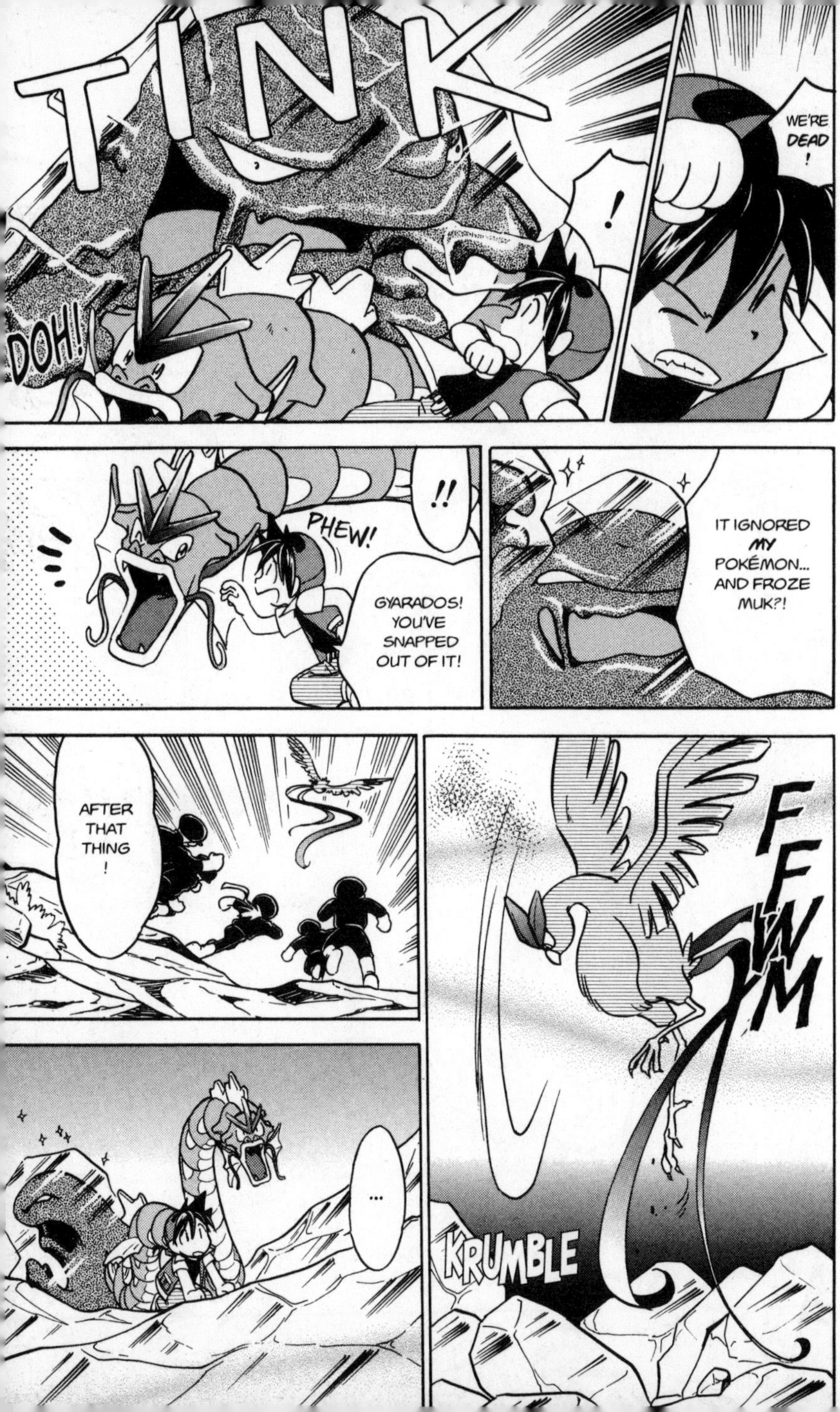
TINK
WE'RE DEAD!
!
DOH!
IT IGNORED MY POKÉMON... AND FROZE MUK?!
!!
PHEW!
GYARADOS! YOU'VE SNAPPED OUT OF IT!
FFWM
KRUMBLE
AFTER THAT THING!
...

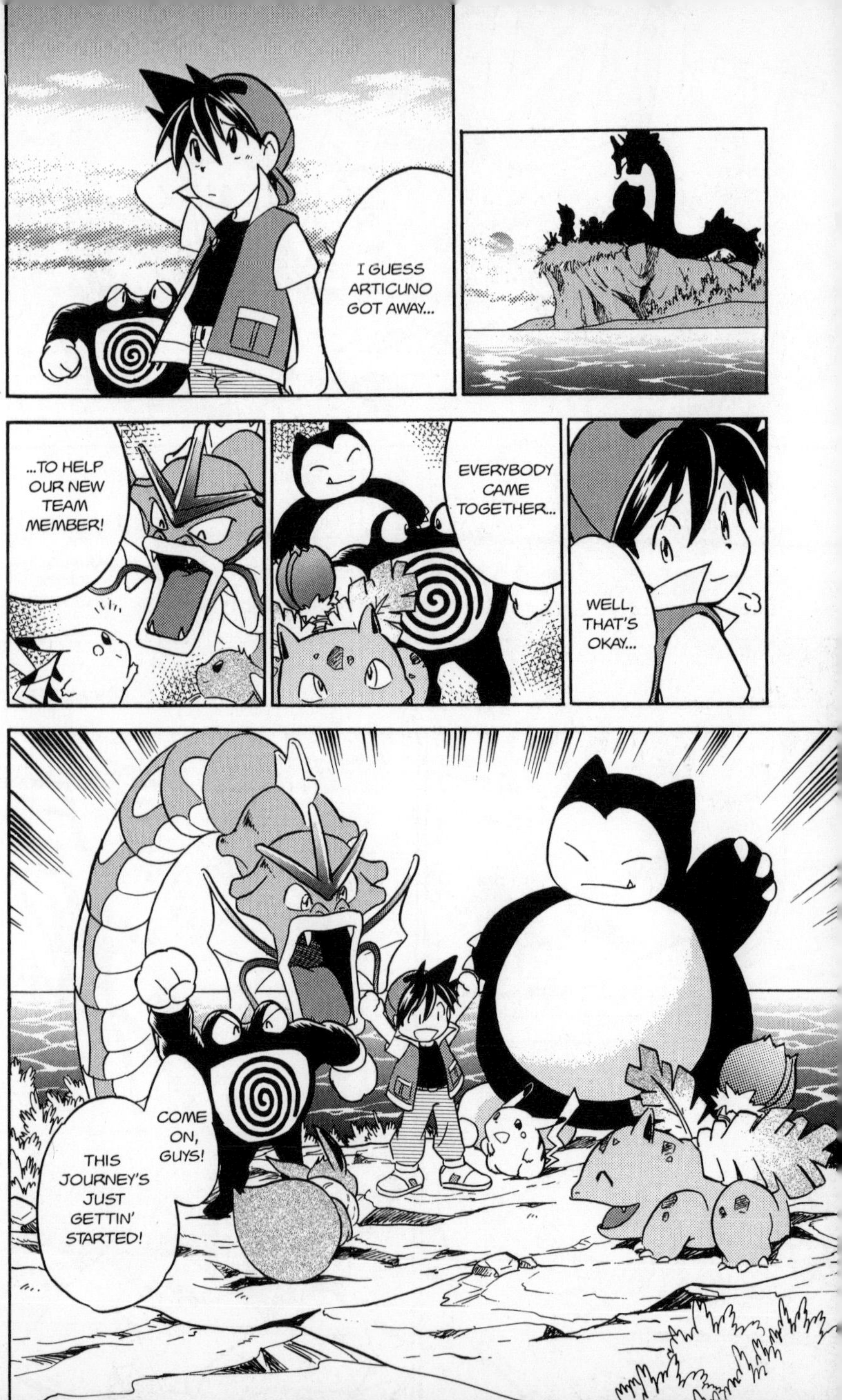
I GUESS ARTICUNO GOT AWAY...
WELL, THAT'S OKAY...
EVERYBODY CAME TOGETHER...
...TO HELP OUR NEW TEAM MEMBER!
COME ON, GUYS!
THIS JOURNEY'S JUST GETTIN' STARTED!

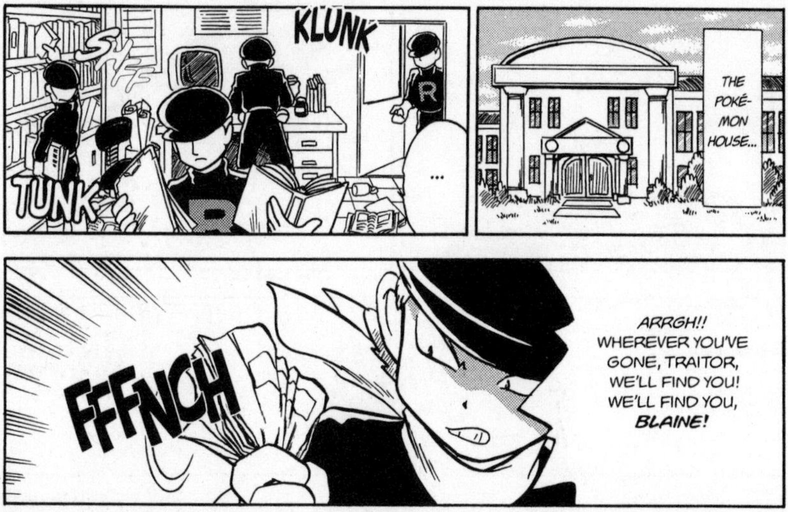
THE POKÉ-MON HOUSE...
KLUNK
SHFF
TUNK
...
ARRGH!! WHEREVER YOU'VE GONE, TRAITOR, WE'LL FIND YOU! WE'LL FIND YOU, BLAINE!
FFFNCH

26 Holy Moltres

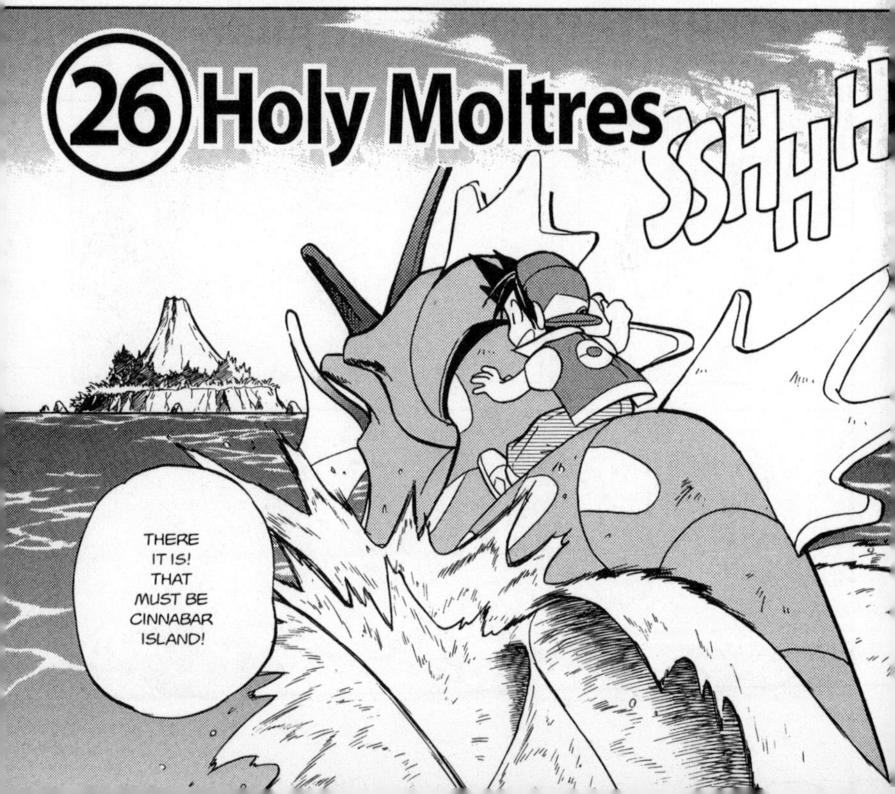
SSHHH
THERE IT IS! THAT MUST BE CINNABAR ISLAND!

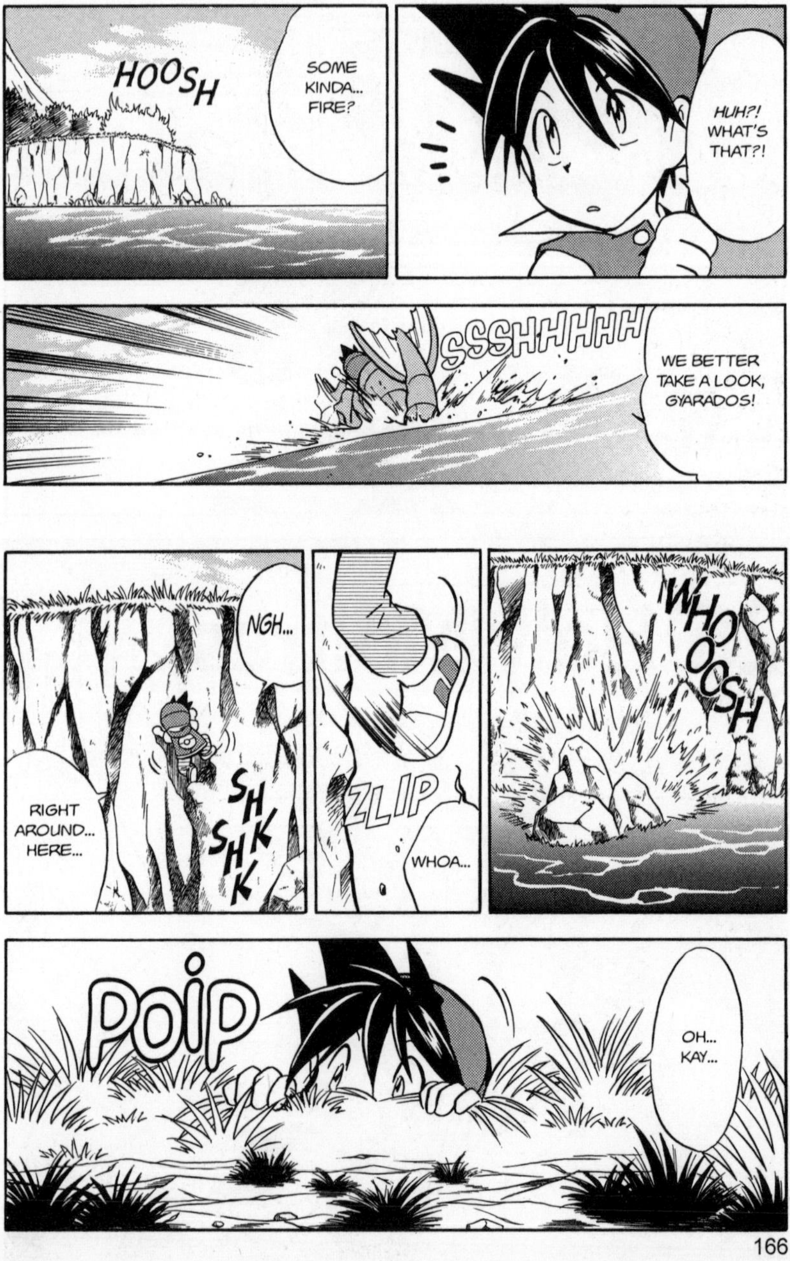
HUH?! WHAT'S THAT?!
SOME KINDA... FIRE?
HOOSH
WE BETTER TAKE A LOOK, GYARADOS!
SSSHHHHHH
WHOOOSH
ZLIP
WHOA...
NGH...
RIGHT AROUND... HERE...
SHK SHK
OH... KAY...
POIP

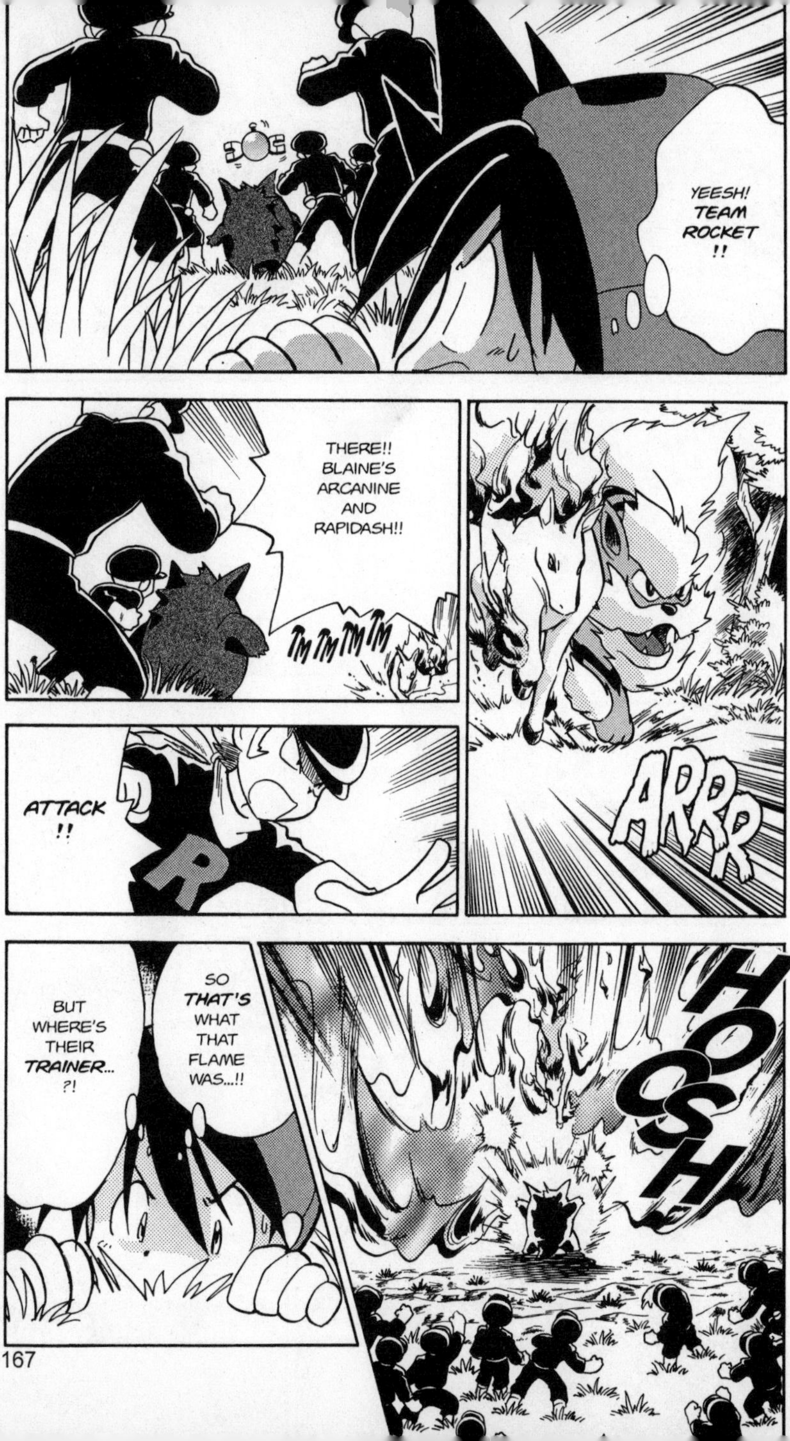
YEESH! TEAM ROCKET!!
ARRR
THERE!! BLAINE'S ARCANINE AND RAPIDASH!!
TM TM TM TM
ATTACK!!
HOOSH
SO THAT'S WHAT THAT FLAME WAS...!!
BUT WHERE'S THEIR TRAINER...?!

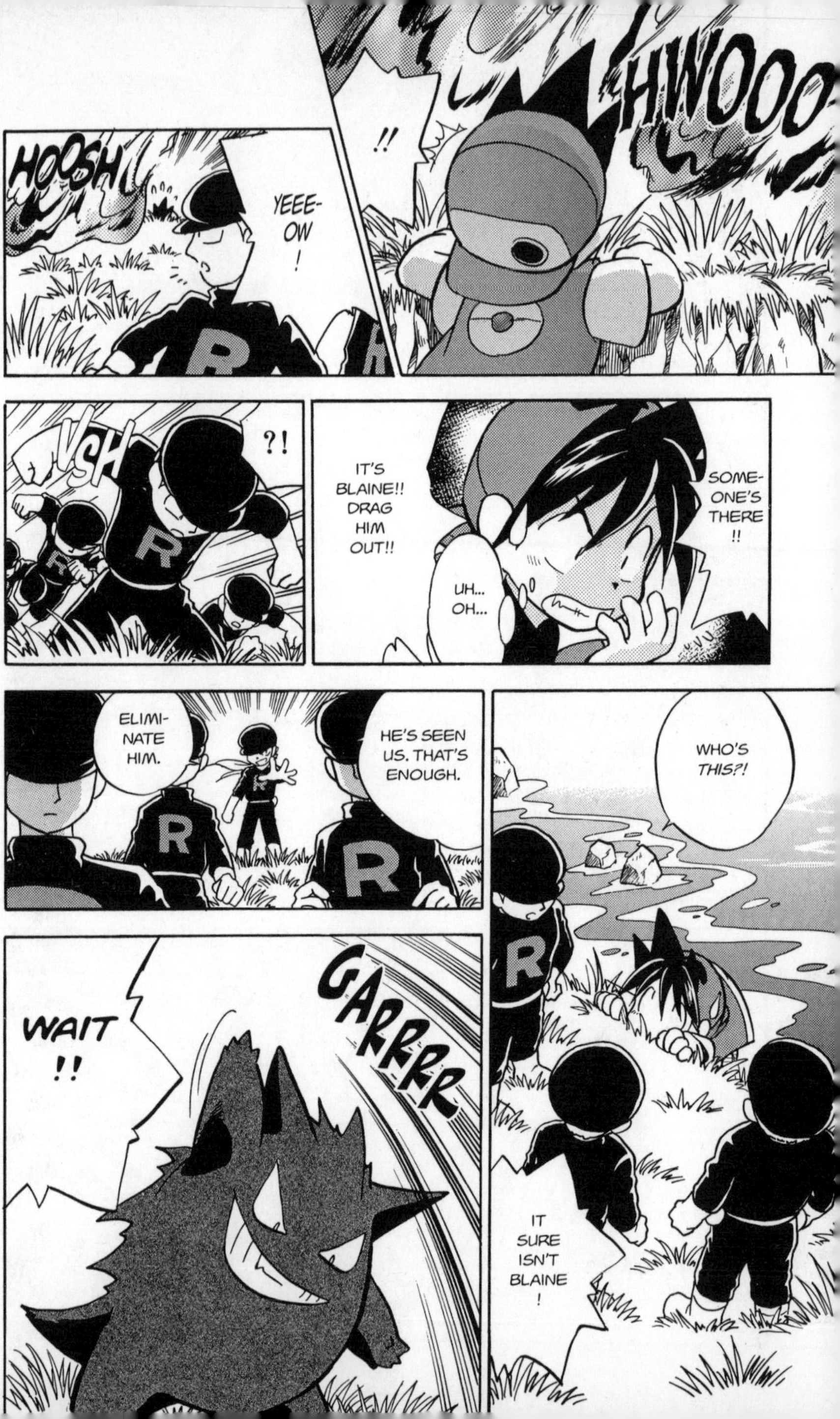
HWOOO
!!
HOOSH
YEEE-OW!
SOME-ONE'S THERE!!
IT'S BLAINE!! DRAG HIM OUT!!
UH... OH...
VSH
?!
WHO'S THIS?!
IT SURE ISN'T BLAINE!
HE'S SEEN US. THAT'S ENOUGH.
ELIMI-NATE HIM.
GARRRR
WAIT!!

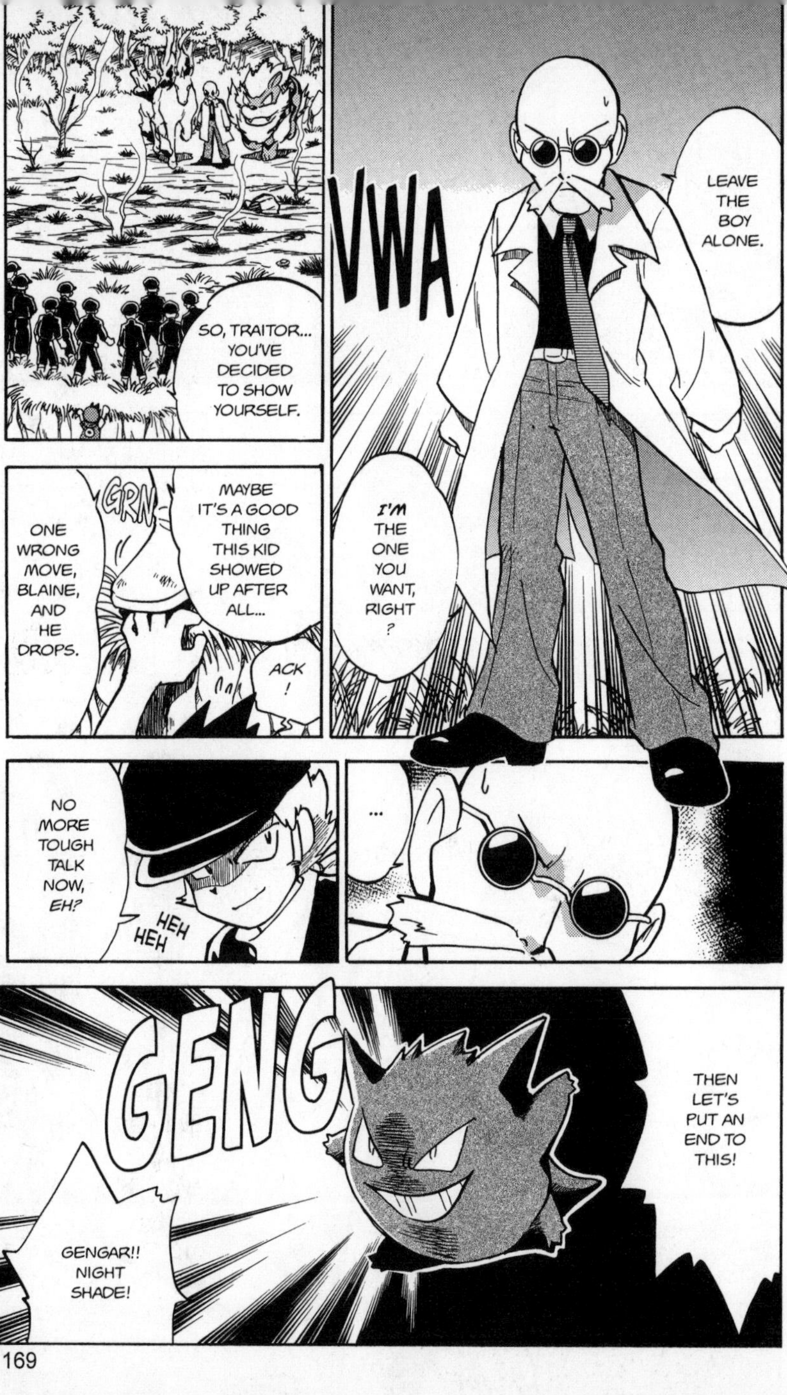
LEAVE THE BOY ALONE.
VWA
I'M THE ONE YOU WANT, RIGHT?
SO, TRAITOR... YOU'VE DECIDED TO SHOW YOURSELF.
MAYBE IT'S A GOOD THING THIS KID SHOWED UP AFTER ALL...
GRN
ONE WRONG MOVE, BLAINE, AND HE DROPS.
ACK!
...
NO MORE TOUGH TALK NOW, EH?
HEH HEH
THEN LET'S PUT AN END TO THIS!
GENG
GENGAR!! NIGHT SHADE!

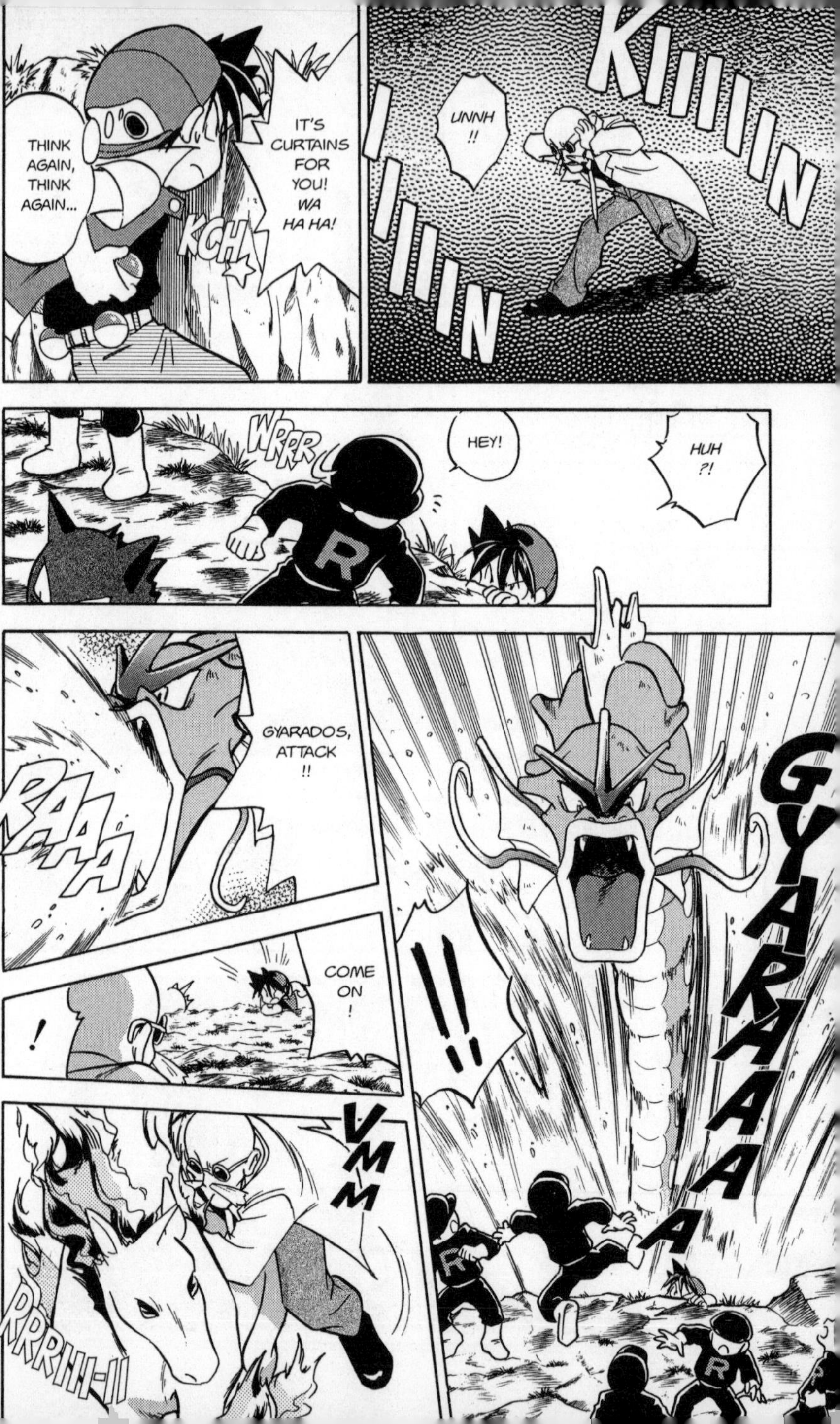
KIIIIIIN IIIIIIN
UNNH !!
IT'S CURTAINS FOR YOU! WA HA HA!
THINK AGAIN, THINK AGAIN...
KCH
HUH ?!
HEY!
WRRR
GYARAAAAAA
!!
GYARADOS, ATTACK !!
RAAAA
COME ON !
!
VMM
RRRIH-II

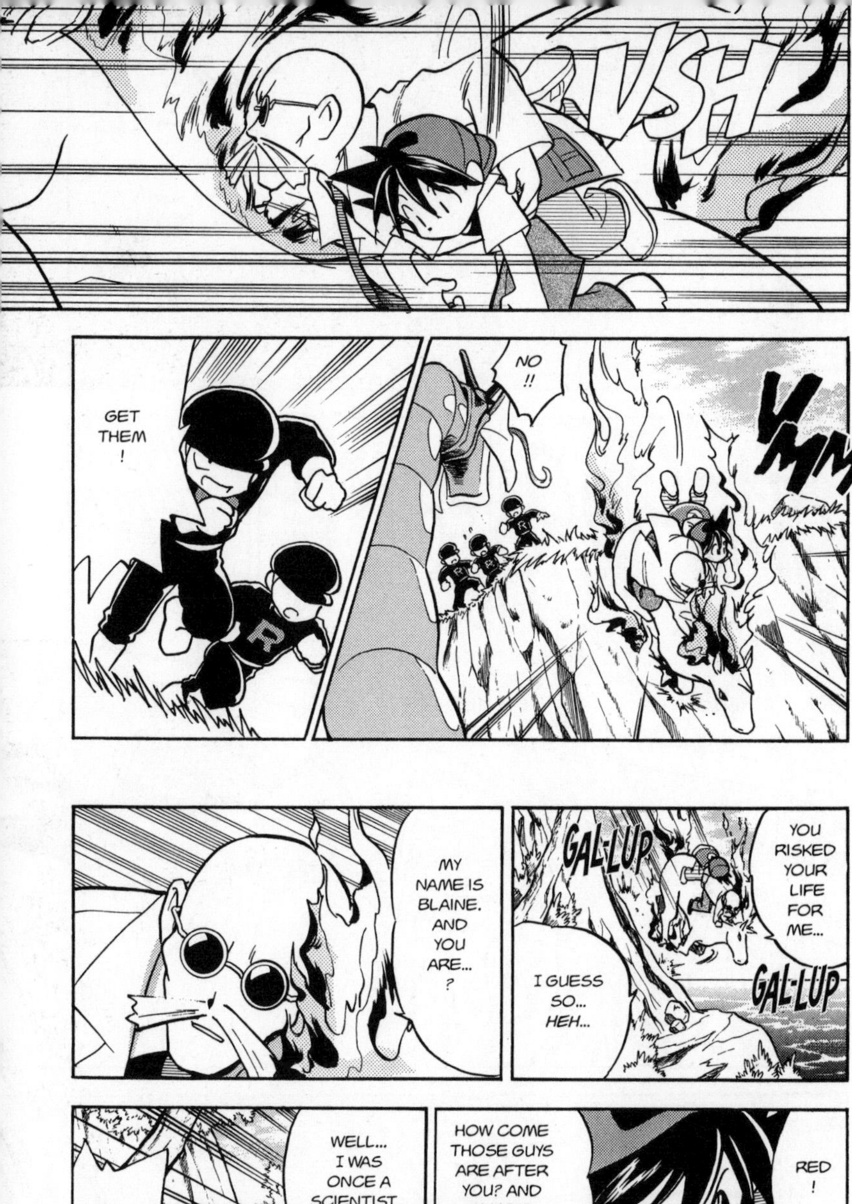
USH
NO !!
VMM
GET THEM !
YOU RISKED YOUR LIFE FOR ME...
GAL-LUP
I GUESS SO... HEH...
GAL-LUP
MY NAME IS BLAINE. AND YOU ARE... ?
RED !
HOW COME THOSE GUYS ARE AFTER YOU? AND WHY DID THEY CALL YOU A *TRAITOR?*
WELL... I WAS ONCE A SCIENTIST... FOR TEAM ROCKET...
WHAT?! FOR TEAM ROCKET ?!

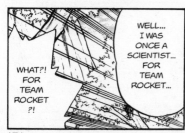

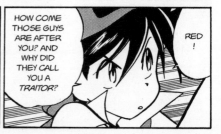

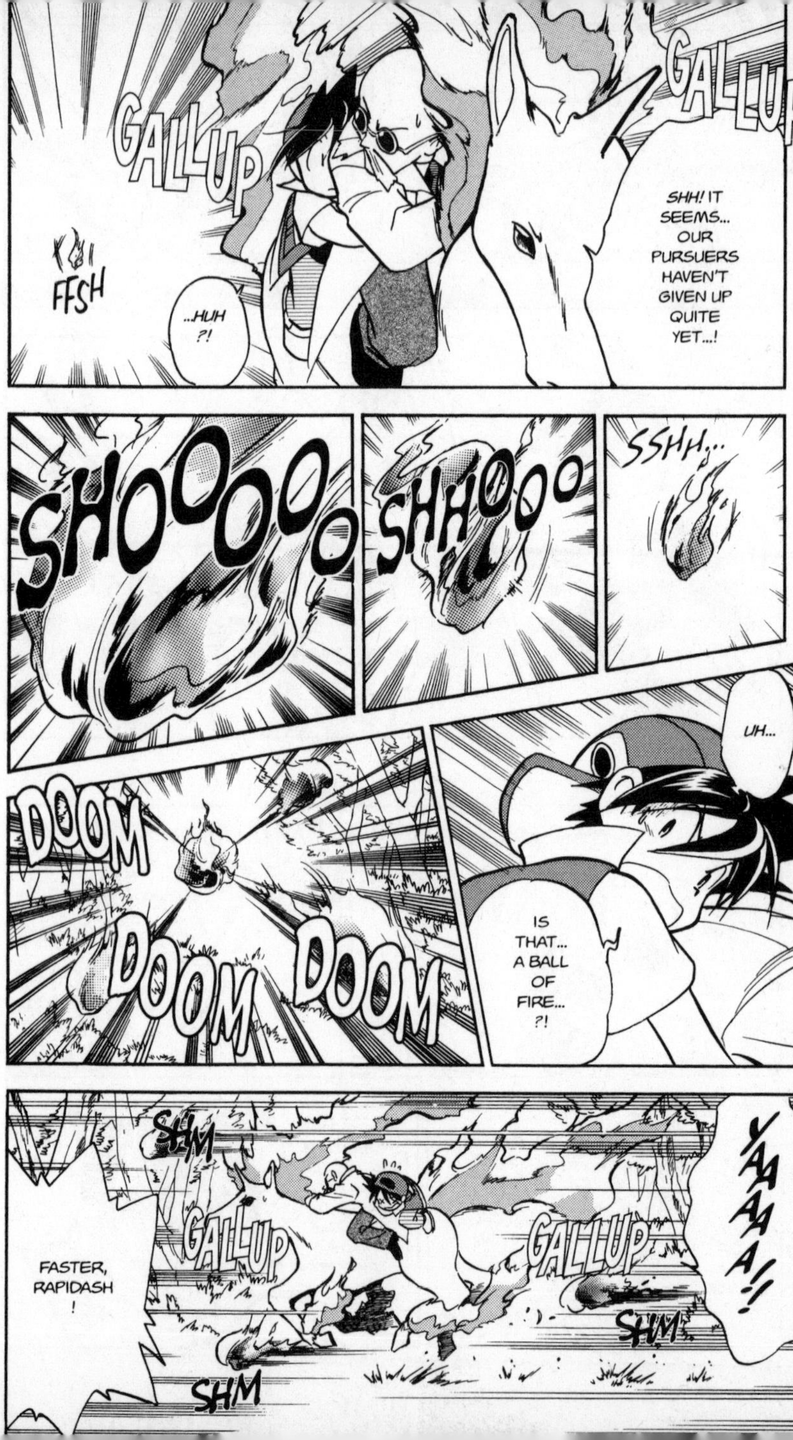
GALLUP
SHH! IT SEEMS... OUR PURSUERS HAVEN'T GIVEN UP QUITE YET...!
GALLUP
...HUH ?!
FFSH
SSHH...
SHHOOO
SHOOOOOO
UH...
IS THAT... A BALL OF FIRE... ?!
DOOM
DOOM
DOOM
YAAAAA!!
GALLUP
SHM
GALLUP
SHM
FASTER, RAPIDASH!
SHM

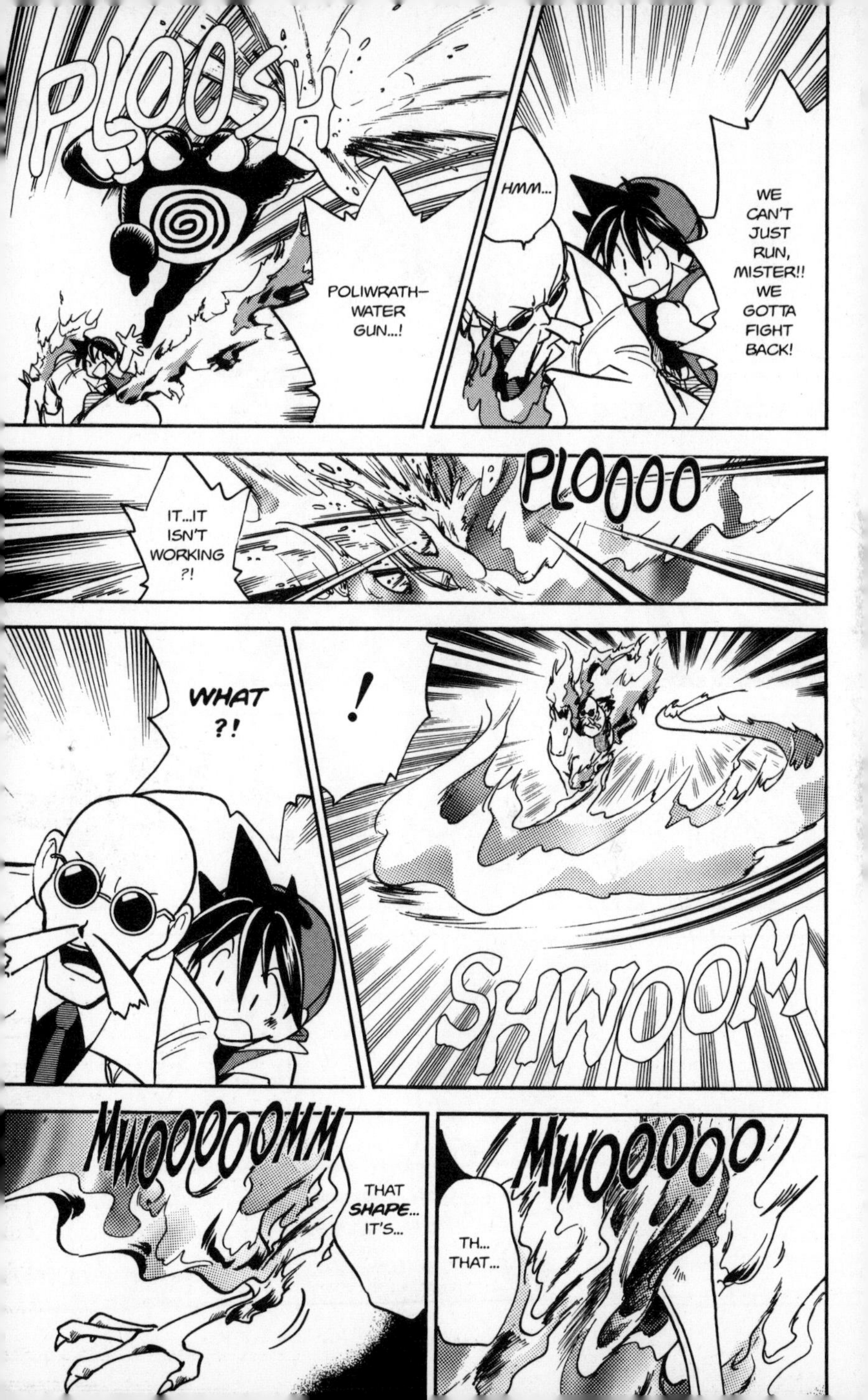
WE CAN'T JUST RUN, MISTER!! WE GOTTA FIGHT BACK!
HMM...
POLIWRATH—WATER GUN...!
PLOOSH
PLOOOO
IT...IT ISN'T WORKING?!
!
SHWOOM
WHAT?!
MWOOOOO
TH... THAT...
MWOOOOOMM
THAT *SHAPE*... IT'S...

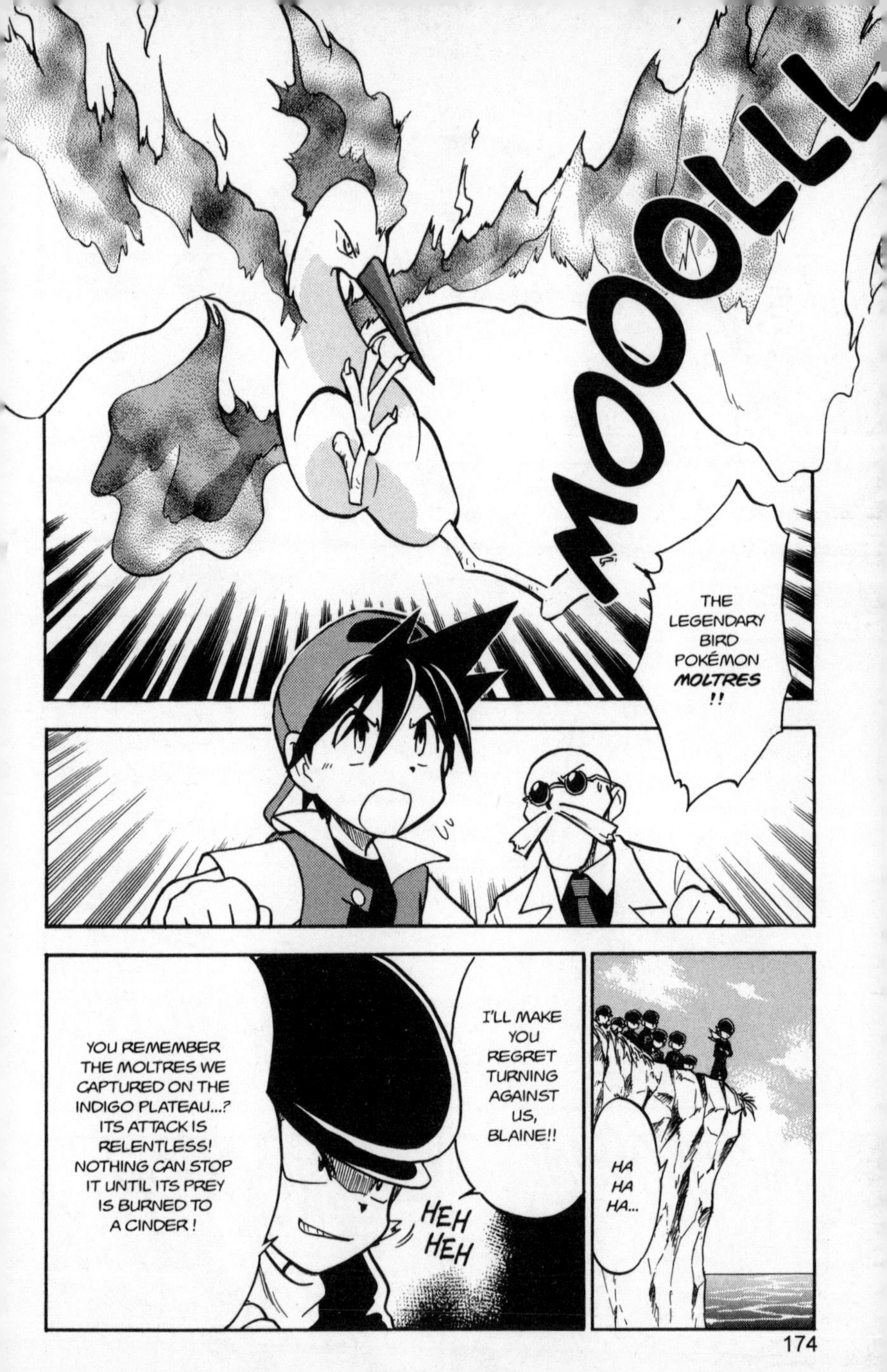
MOOOLLL
THE LEGENDARY BIRD POKÉMON MOLTRES !!
HA HA HA...
I'LL MAKE YOU REGRET TURNING AGAINST US, BLAINE!!
YOU REMEMBER THE MOLTRES WE CAPTURED ON THE INDIGO PLATEAU...? ITS ATTACK IS RELENTLESS! NOTHING CAN STOP IT UNTIL ITS PREY IS BURNED TO A CINDER !
HEH HEH

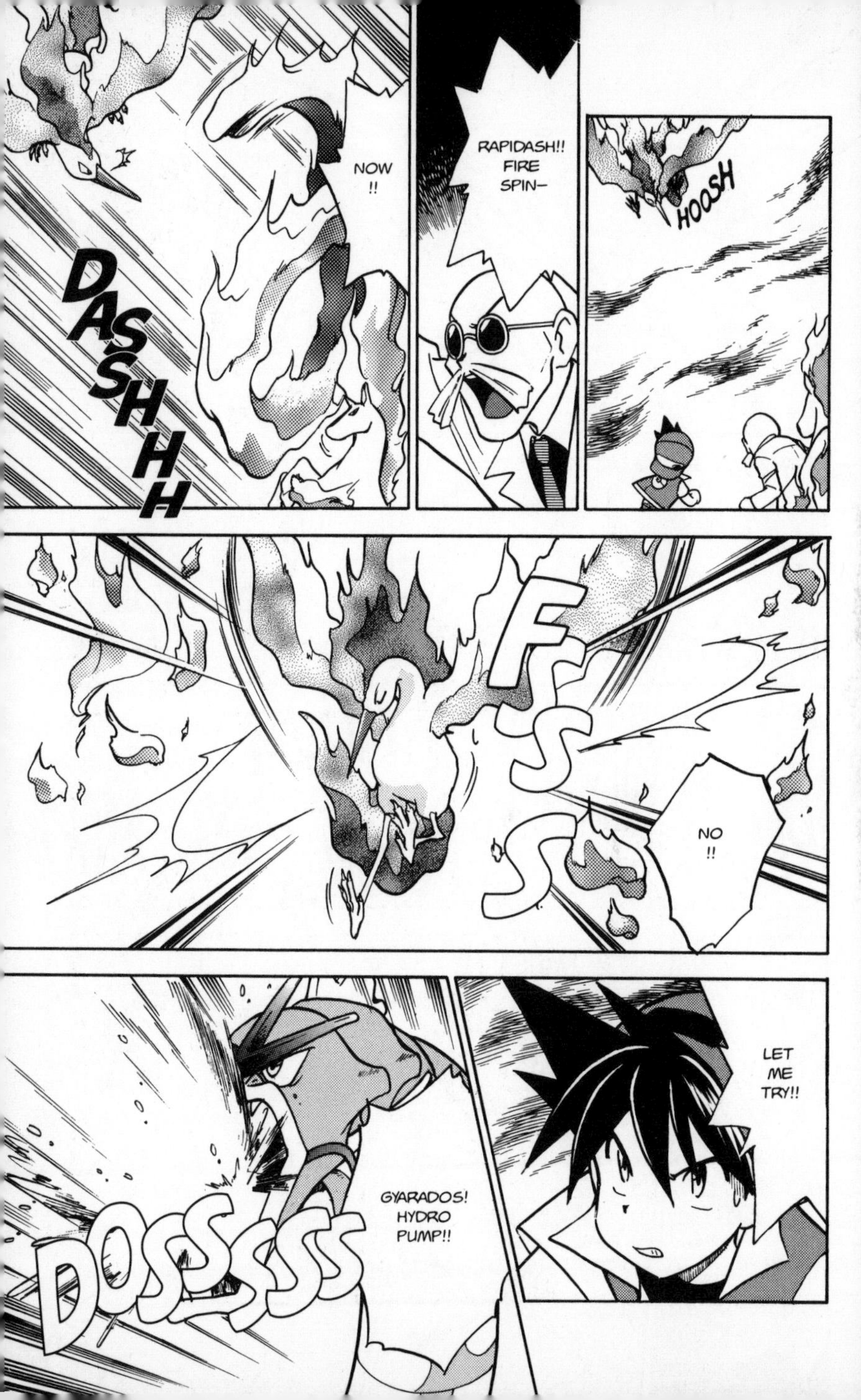
HOOSH
RAPIDASH!! FIRE SPIN–
NOW !!
DASHHHH
NO !!
FSS
LET ME TRY!!
GYARADOS! HYDRO PUMP!!
DOSSSSS

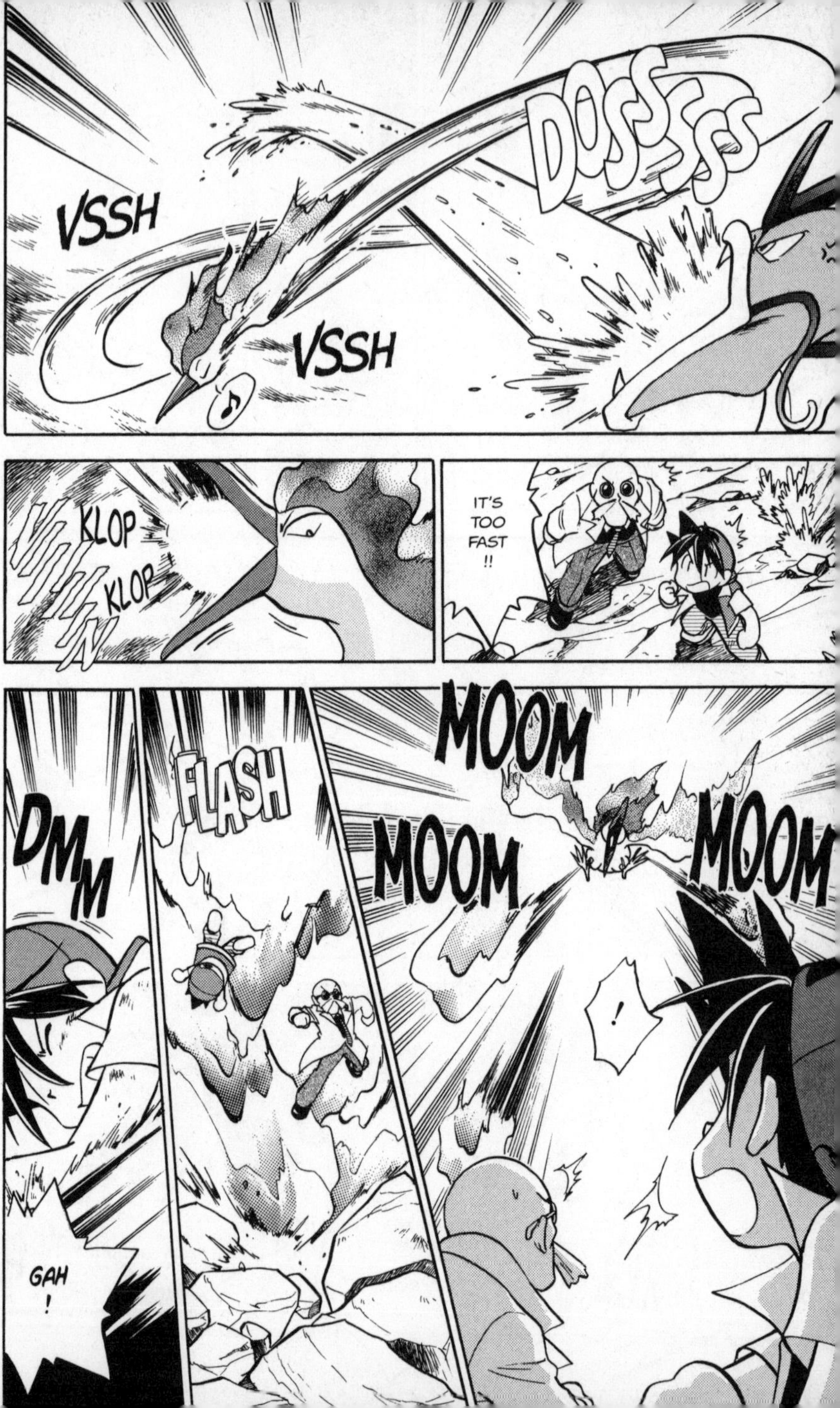
DOSSSSS
VSSH
VSSH
♪
IT'S TOO FAST !!
KLOP
KLOP
MOOM
MOOM
MOOM
!
FLASH
DMM
GAH !

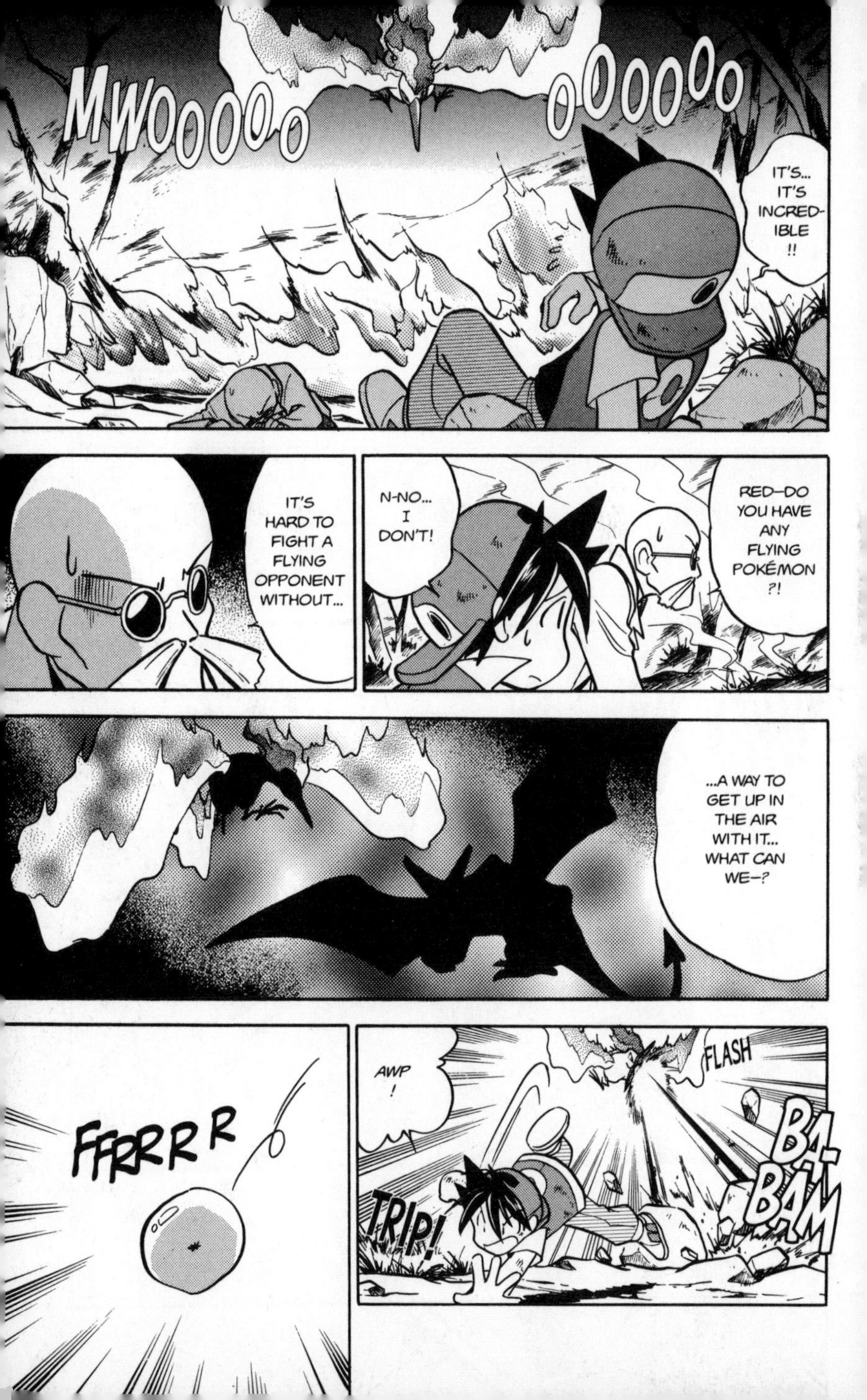
MWOOOOOO
OOOOOO
IT'S... IT'S INCREDIBLE!!
RED—DO YOU HAVE ANY FLYING POKÉMON?!
N-NO... I DON'T!
IT'S HARD TO FIGHT A FLYING OPPONENT WITHOUT...
...A WAY TO GET UP IN THE AIR WITH IT... WHAT CAN WE–?
FLASH
BA-BAM
AWP!
TRIP!
FFRRRR

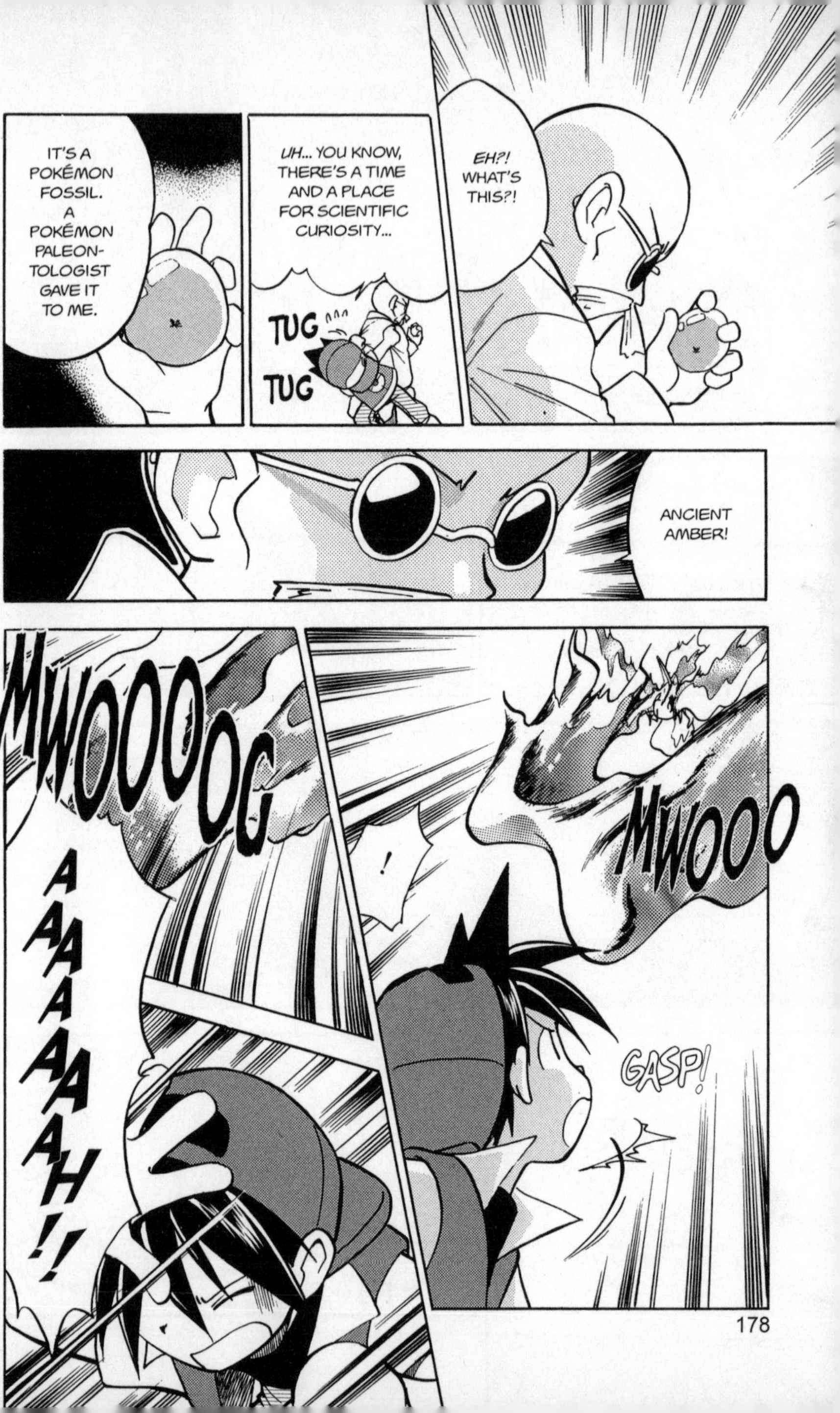
EH?! WHAT'S THIS?!
UH... YOU KNOW, THERE'S A TIME AND A PLACE FOR SCIENTIFIC CURIOSITY...
TUG
TUG
IT'S A POKÉMON FOSSIL. A POKÉMON PALEON-TOLOGIST GAVE IT TO ME.
ANCIENT AMBER!
MWOOO
!
GASP!
MWOOOOG
AAAAAAAH!!

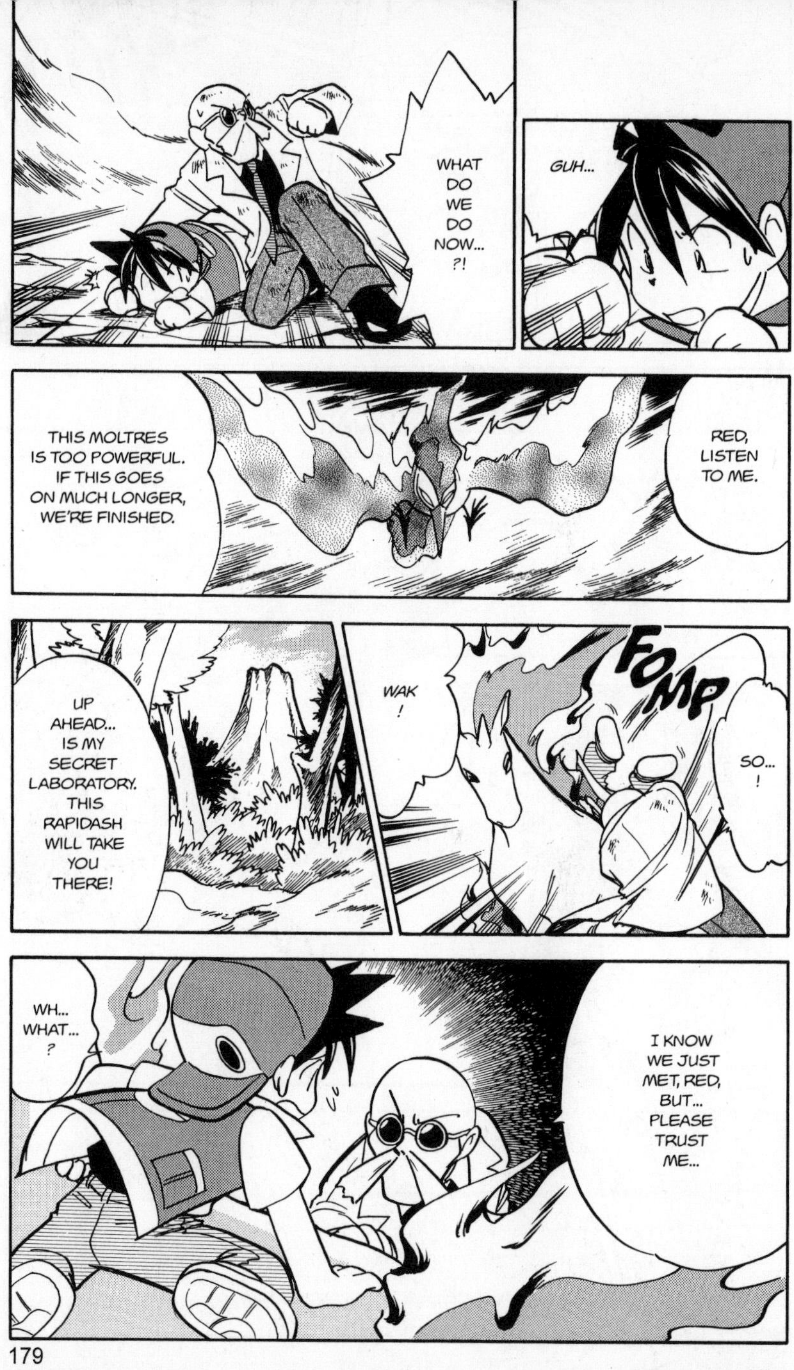
GUH...
WHAT DO WE DO NOW...?!
RED, LISTEN TO ME.
THIS MOLTRES IS TOO POWERFUL. IF THIS GOES ON MUCH LONGER, WE'RE FINISHED.
SO...!
FOMP
WAK!
UP AHEAD... IS MY SECRET LABORATORY. THIS RAPIDASH WILL TAKE YOU THERE!
I KNOW WE JUST MET, RED, BUT... PLEASE TRUST ME...
WH... WHAT...?

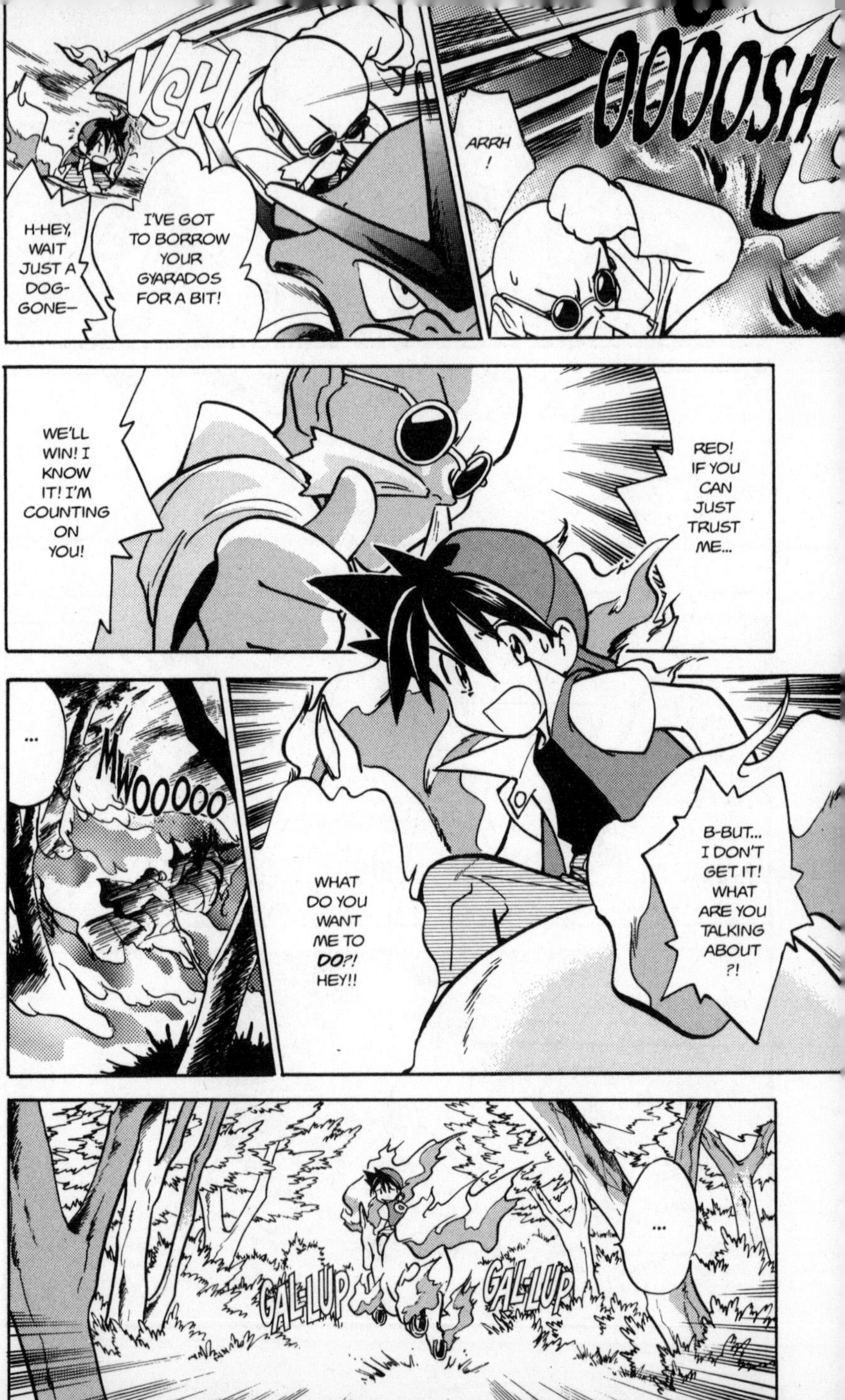
OOOOSH
ARRH!
VSH!
I'VE GOT TO BORROW YOUR GYARADOS FOR A BIT!
H-HEY, WAIT JUST A DOG-GONE–
RED! IF YOU CAN JUST TRUST ME...
WE'LL WIN! I KNOW IT! I'M COUNTING ON YOU!
B-BUT... I DON'T GET IT! WHAT ARE YOU TALKING ABOUT?!
WHAT DO YOU WANT ME TO DO?! HEY!!
...
MWOOOOO
...
GAL-LUP
GAL-LUP

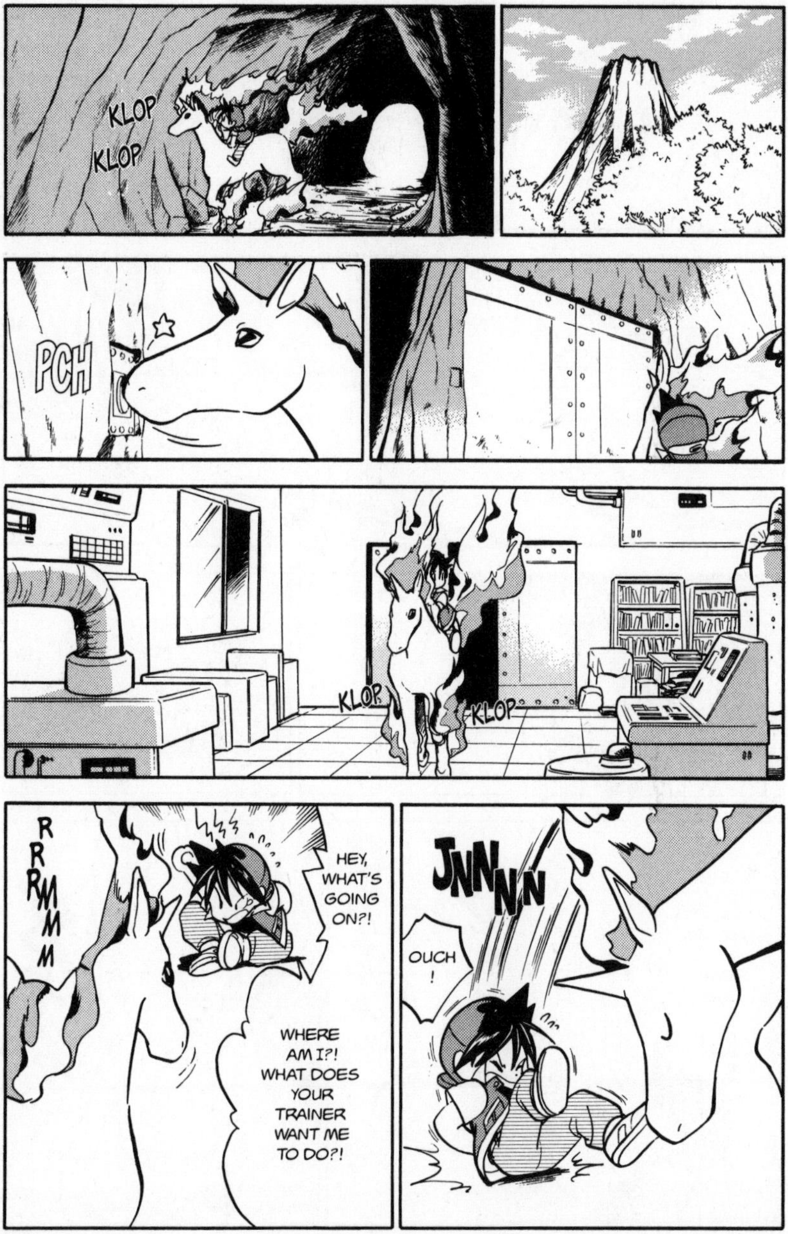
KLOP
KLOP
PCH
KLOP
KLOP
JNNNN
OUCH!
RRRMMMM
HEY, WHAT'S GOING ON?!
WHERE AM I?! WHAT DOES YOUR TRAINER WANT ME TO DO?!

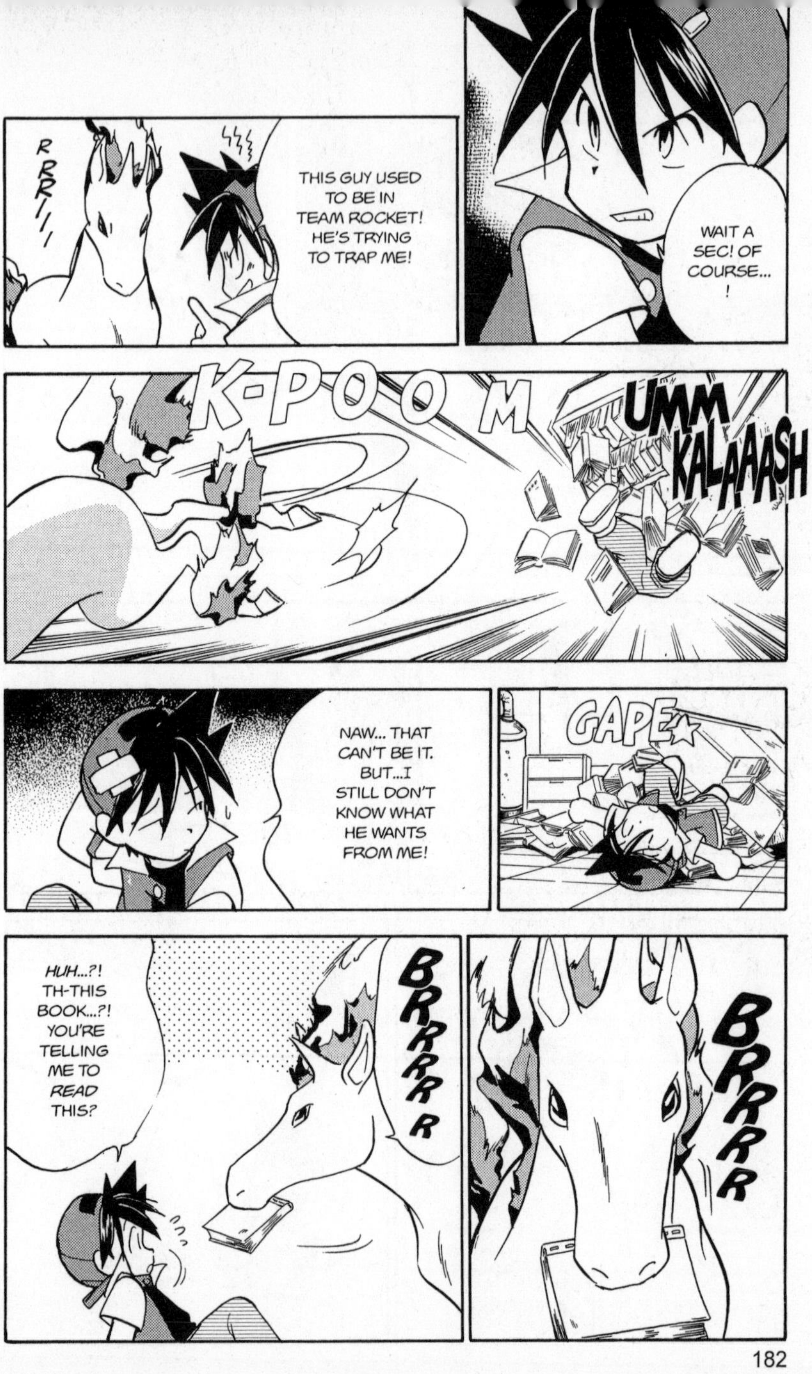
WAIT A SEC! OF COURSE... !
THIS GUY USED TO BE IN TEAM ROCKET! HE'S TRYING TO TRAP ME!
RRR///
UMM KALAAASH
K-POOM
GAPE★
NAW... THAT CAN'T BE IT. BUT...I STILL DON'T KNOW WHAT HE WANTS FROM ME!
BRRRRR
BRRRRR
HUH...?! TH-THIS BOOK...?! YOU'RE TELLING ME TO READ THIS?

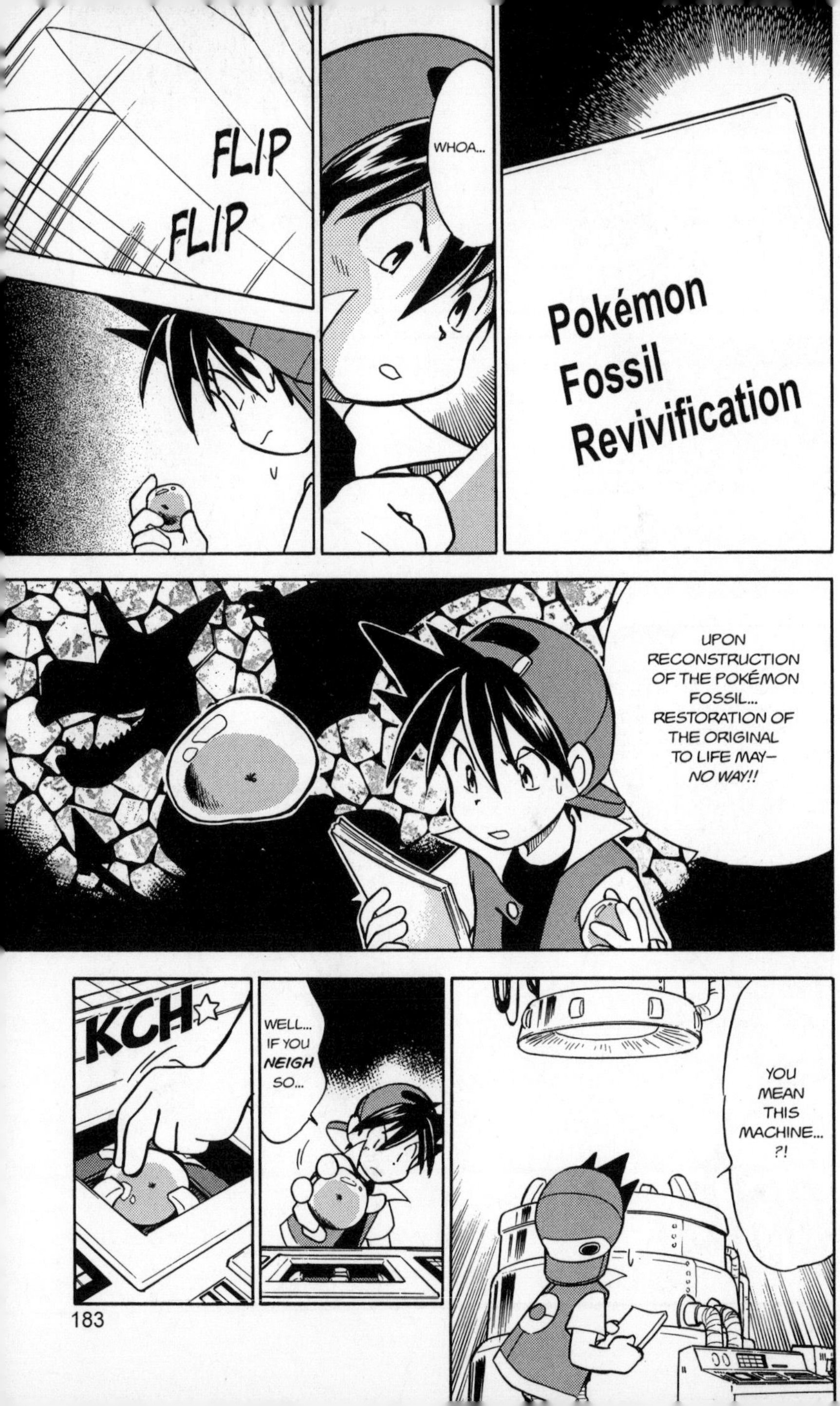
Pokémon
Fossil
Revivification
WHOA...
FLIP
FLIP
UPON RECONSTRUCTION OF THE POKÉMON FOSSIL... RESTORATION OF THE ORIGINAL TO LIFE MAY— *NO WAY!!*
YOU MEAN THIS MACHINE...?!
WELL... IF YOU ***NEIGH*** SO...
KCH☆

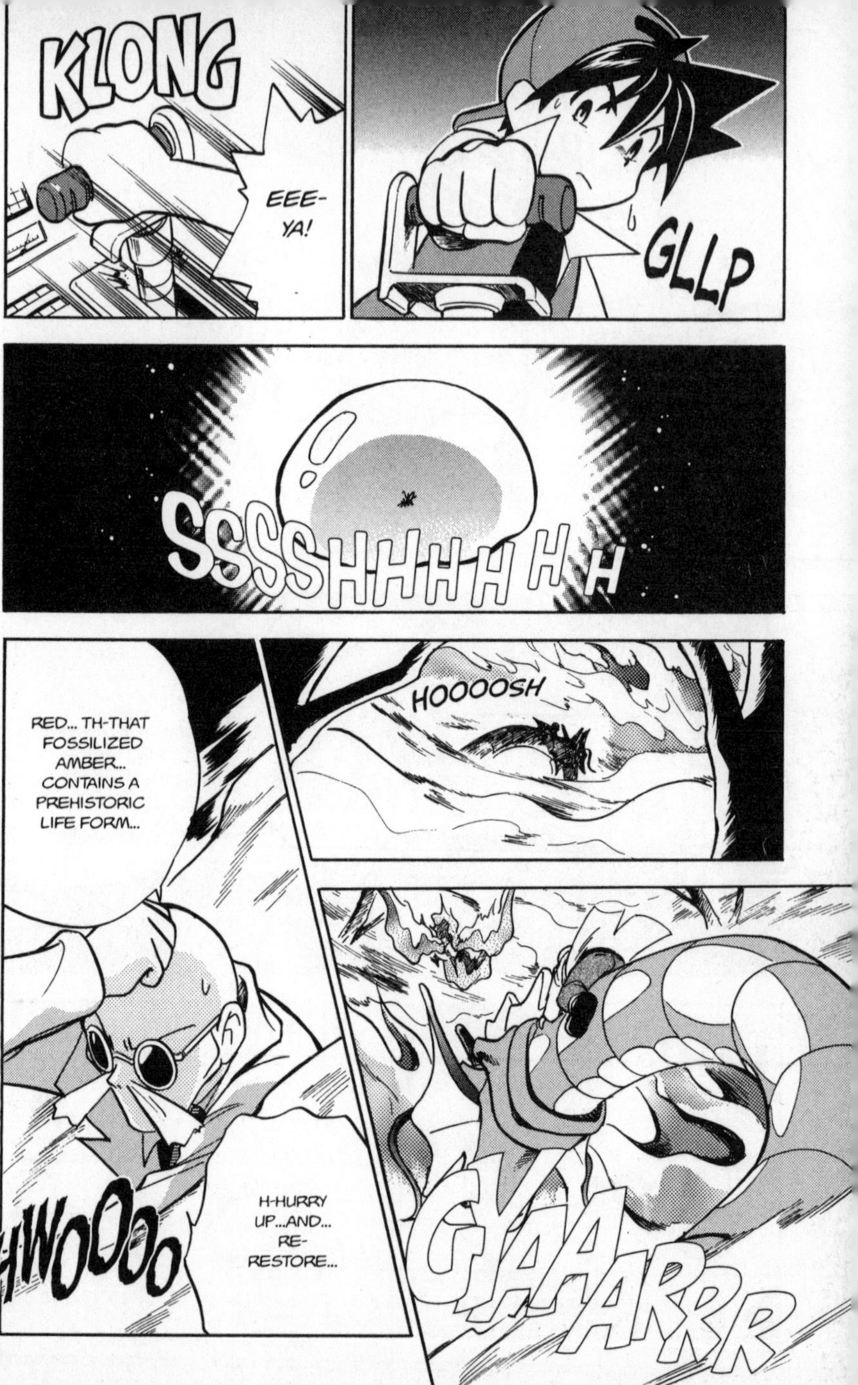
GLLP
KLONG
EEE-YA!
SSSSHHHHHHH
HOOOOSH
GYAARRR
RED... TH-THAT FOSSILIZED AMBER... CONTAINS A PREHISTORIC LIFE FORM...
H-HURRY UP...AND... RE-RESTORE...
HWOOOO

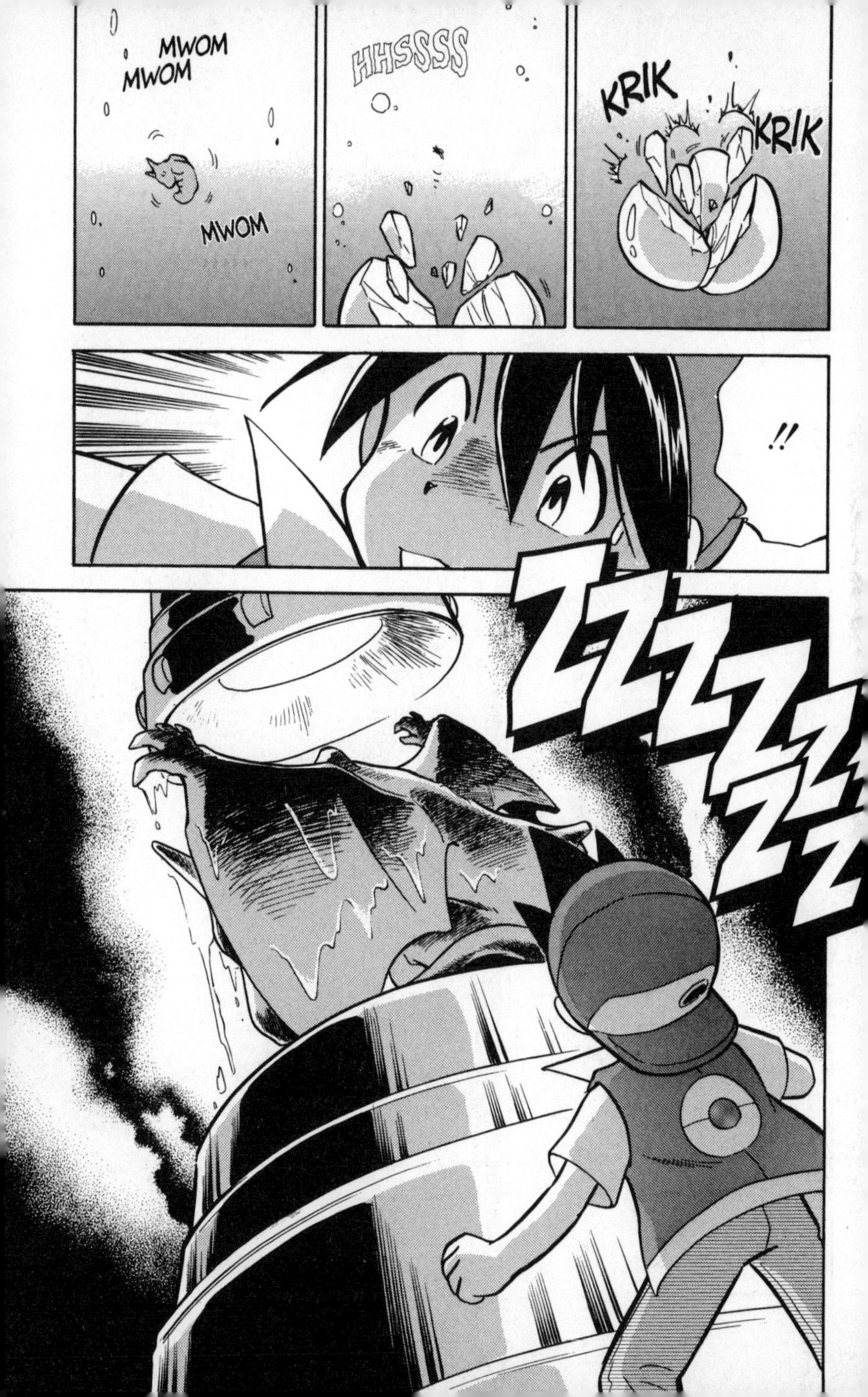
KRIK
KRIK
HHSSSS
MWOM
MWOM
MWOM
!!
ZZZZZZZ

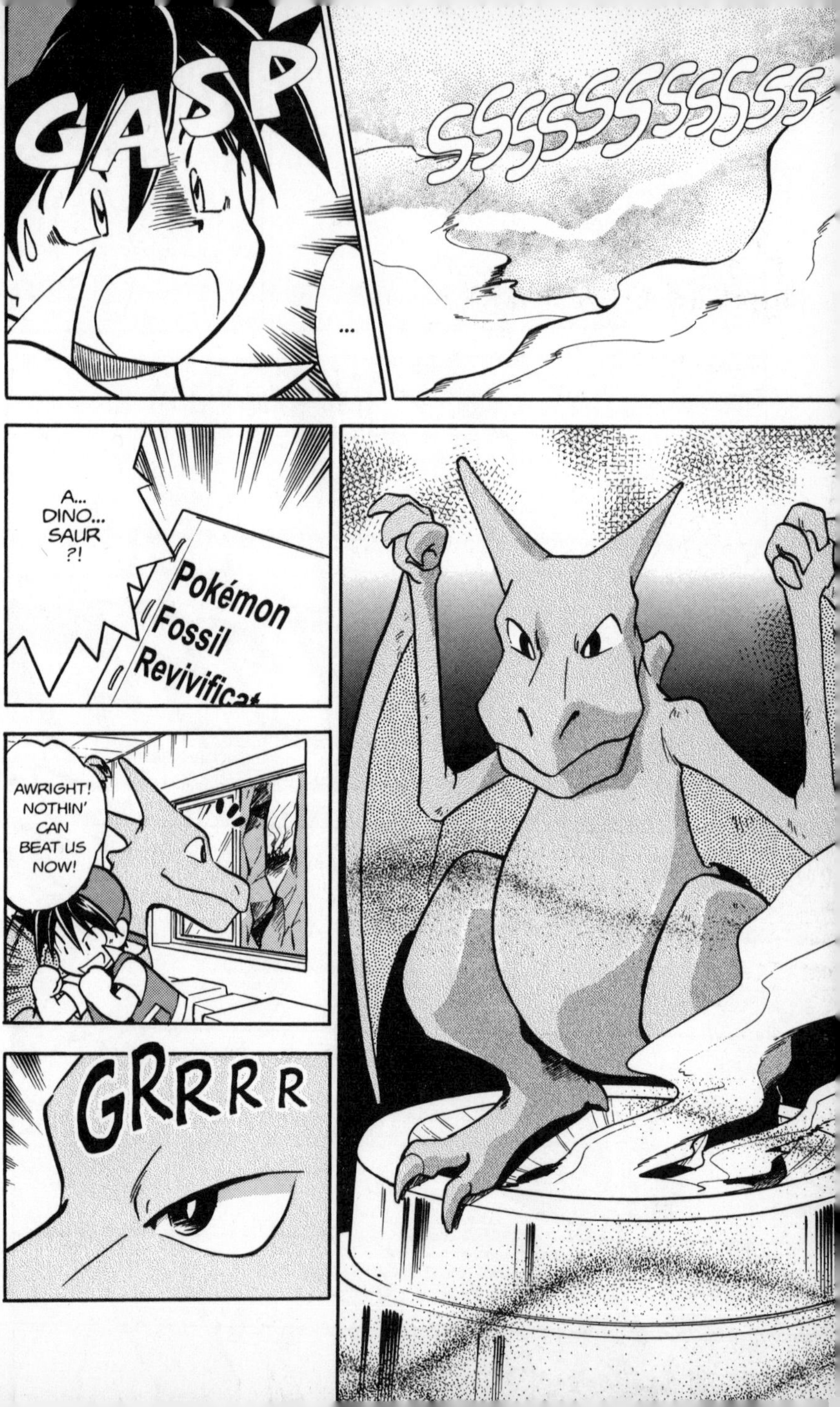
SSSSSSSSSSSSS
GASP
...
A... DINO... SAUR ?!
Pokémon Fossil Revivificat
AWRIGHT! NOTHIN' CAN BEAT US NOW!
GRRRR

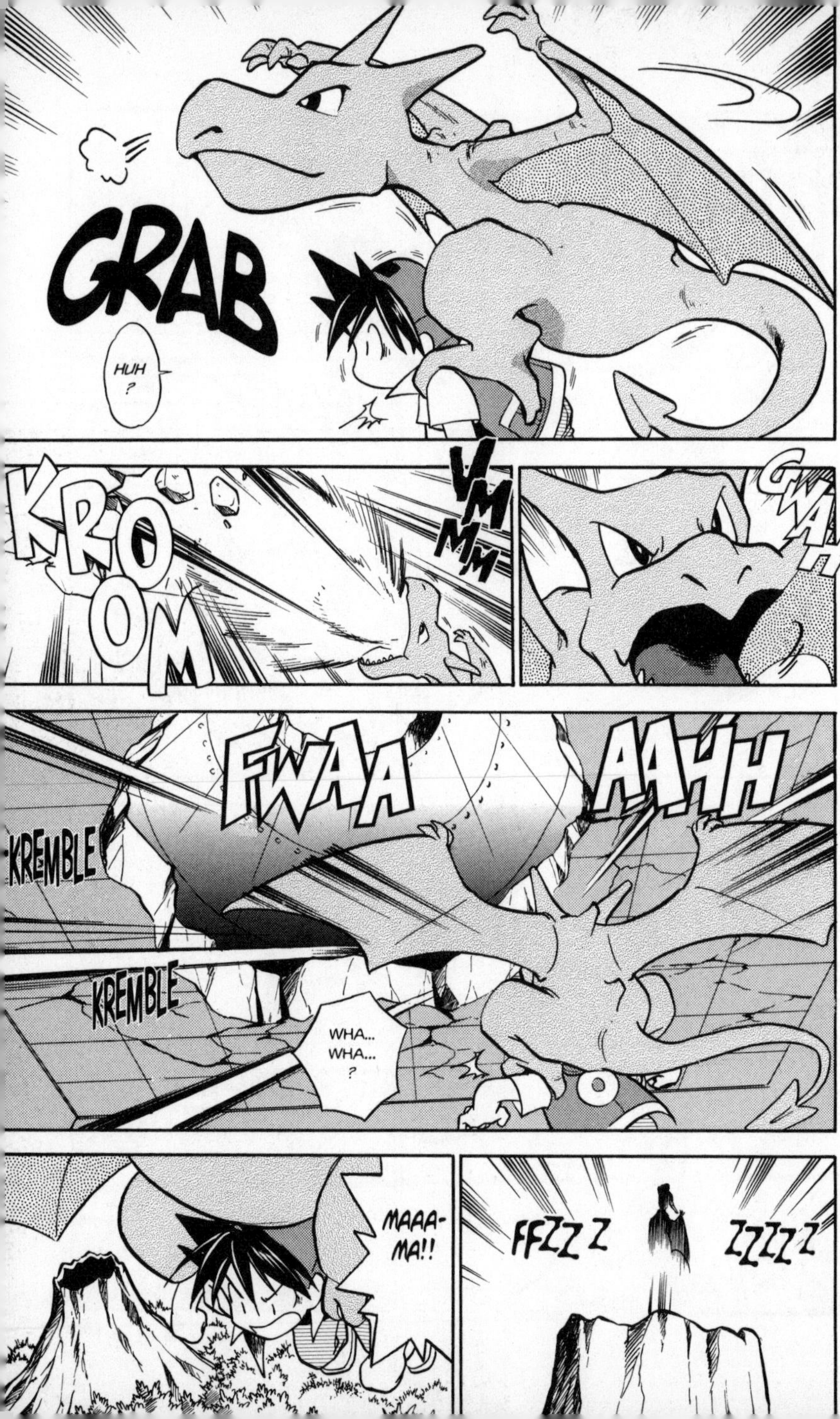
GRAB
HUH?
GWAH
VMMM
KROOM
FWAA AAHH
WHA... WHA...?
KREMBLE
KREMBLE
FFZZZ Z ZZZZZ
MAAAA-MA!!

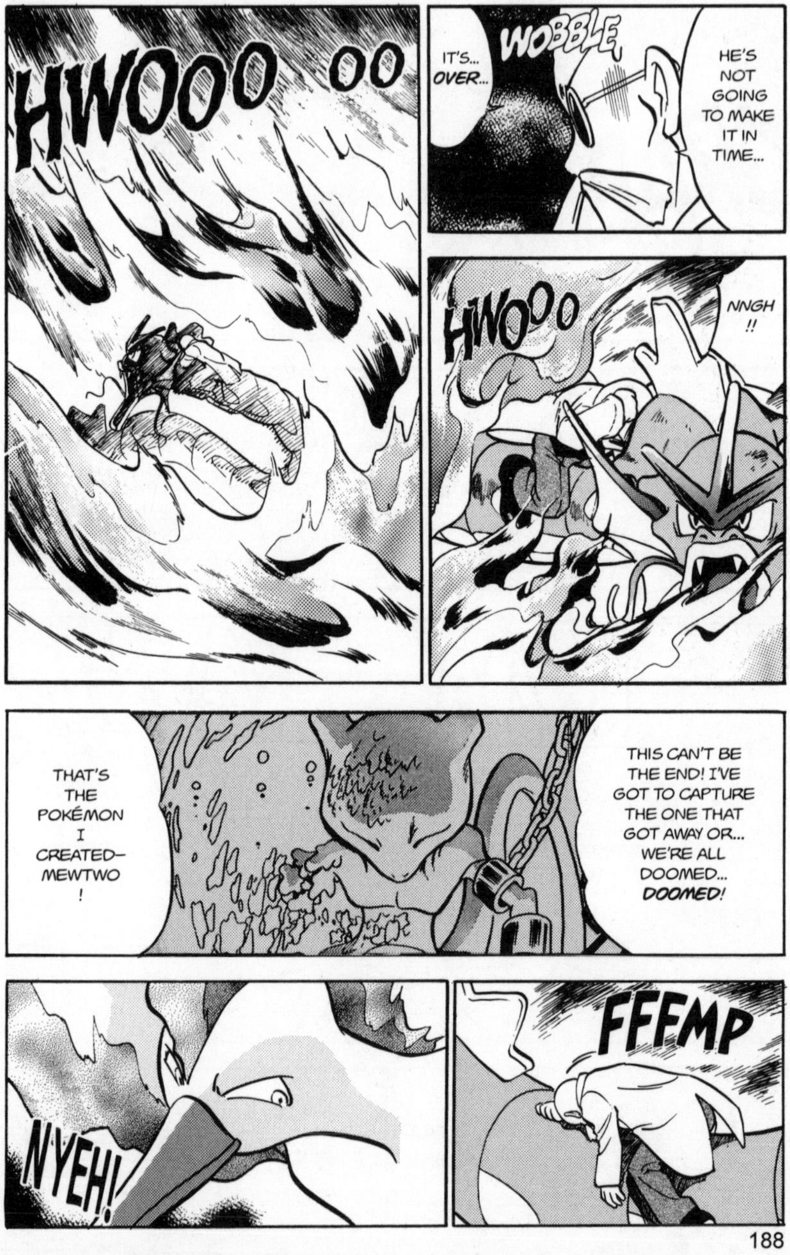
HE'S NOT GOING TO MAKE IT IN TIME...
WOBBLE
IT'S... OVER...
NNGH !!
HWOOO
HWOOO OO
THIS CAN'T BE THE END! I'VE GOT TO CAPTURE THE ONE THAT GOT AWAY OR... WE'RE ALL DOOMED... **DOOMED!**
THAT'S THE POKÉMON I CREATED— MEWTWO !
FFFMP
NYEH!

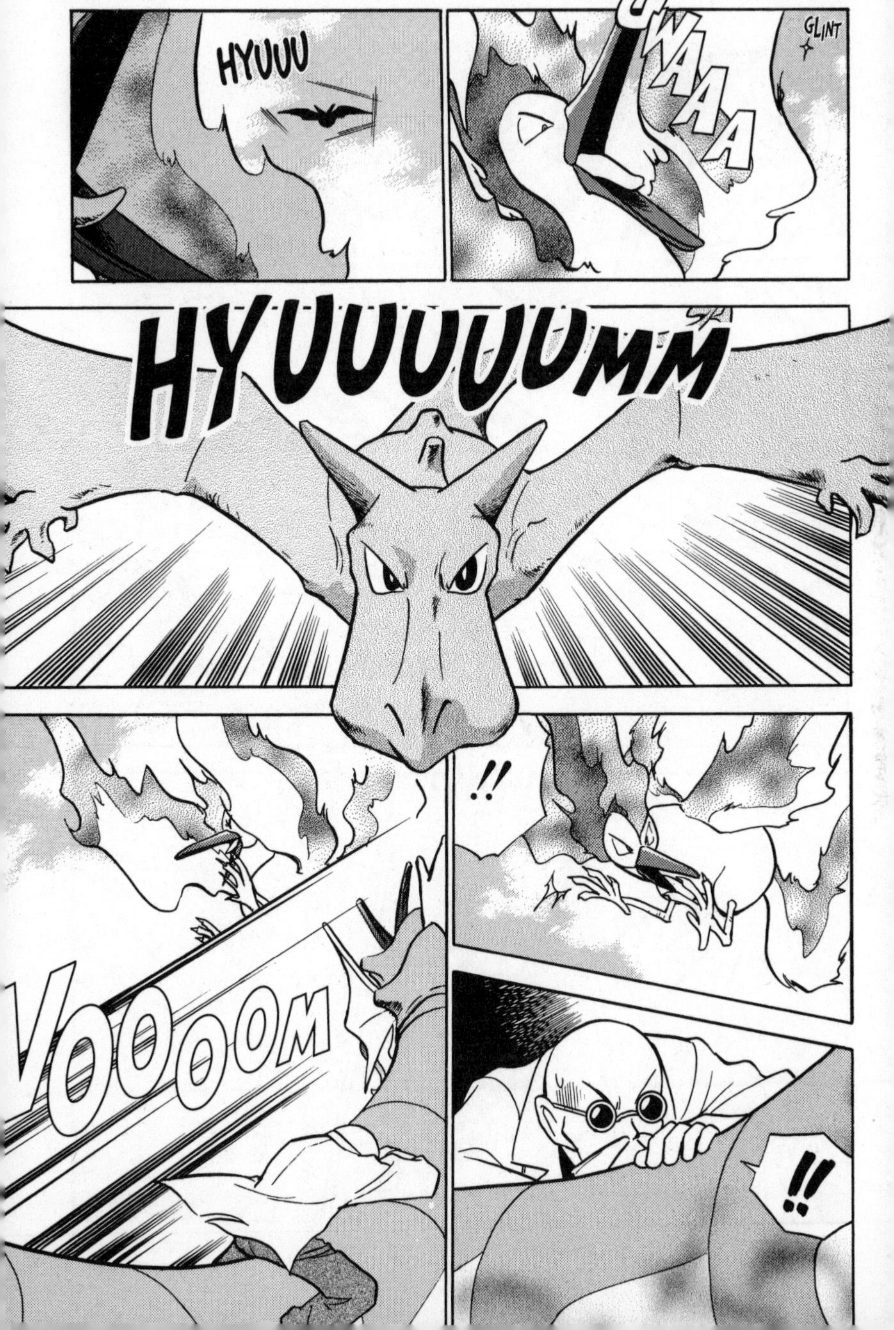
GWAAAA
GLINT
HYUUU
HYUUUUUUMM
!!
!!
VOOOOM

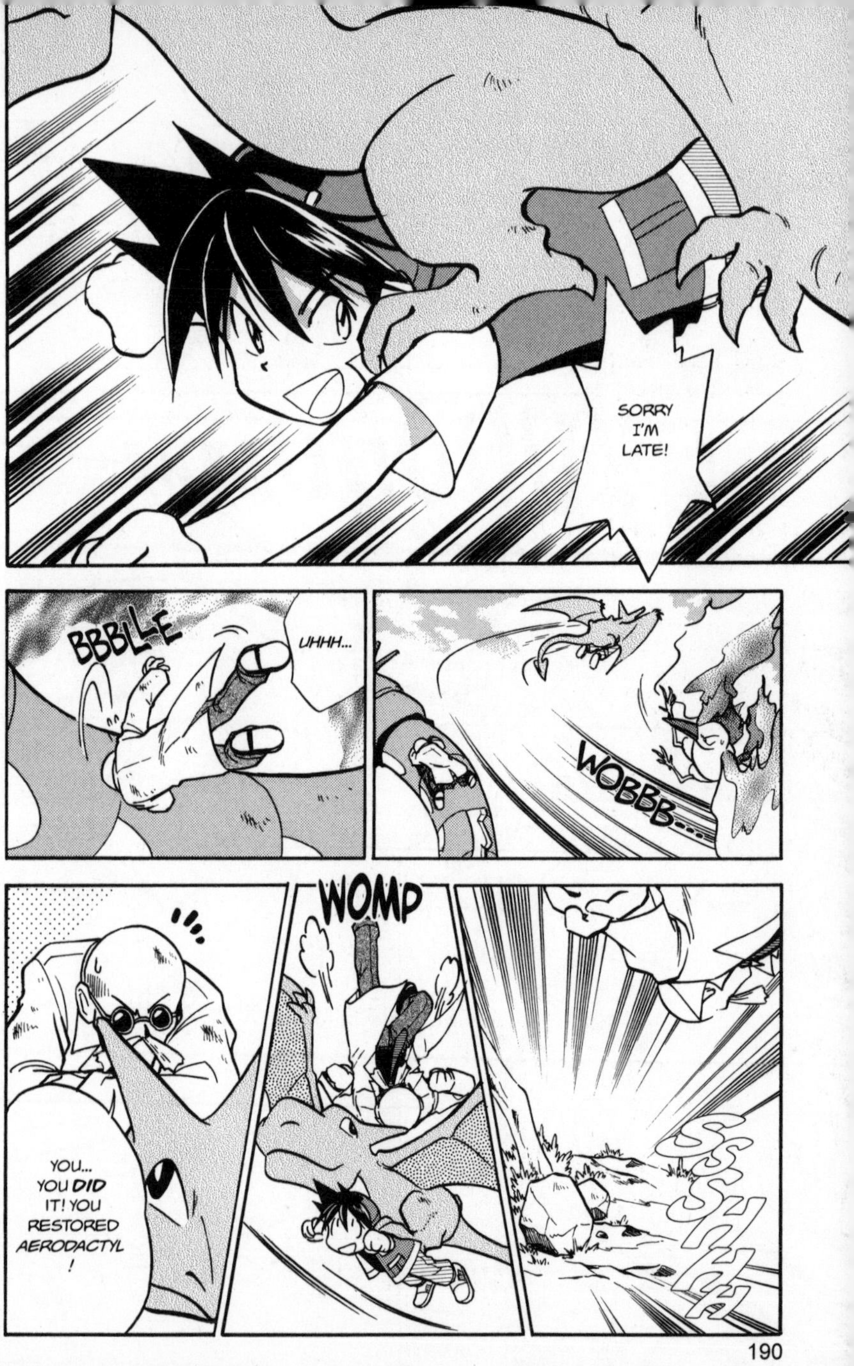
SORRY I'M LATE!
WOBBBB...
UHHH...
BBBLLE
SSSHHHH
WOMP
YOU... YOU **DID** IT! YOU RESTORED AERODACTYL!

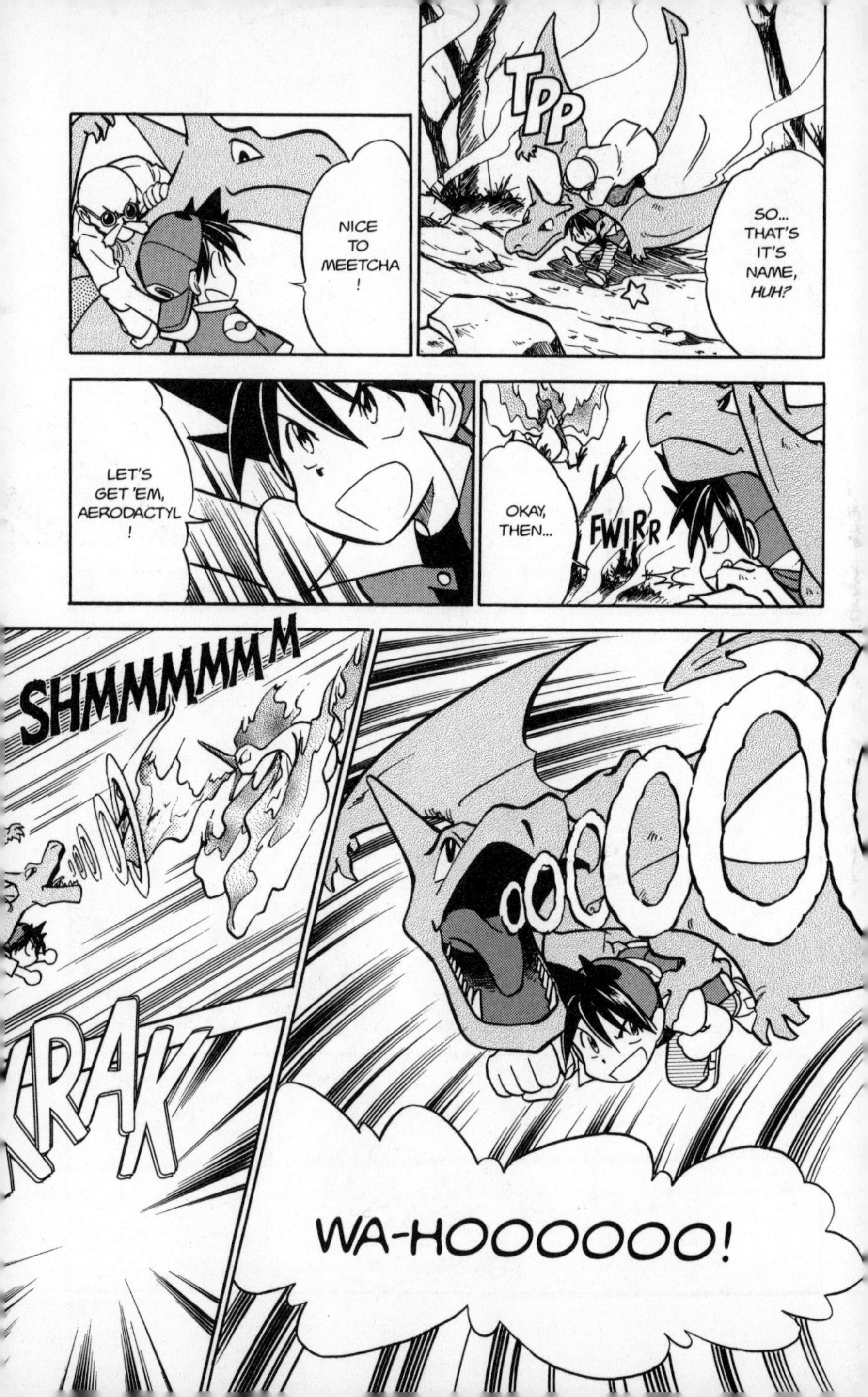
TPP
SO... THAT'S IT'S NAME, HUH?
NICE TO MEETCHA!
FWIRR
OKAY, THEN...
LET'S GET 'EM, AERODACTYL!
WA-HOOOOOO!
SHMMMMMMM
KRAK

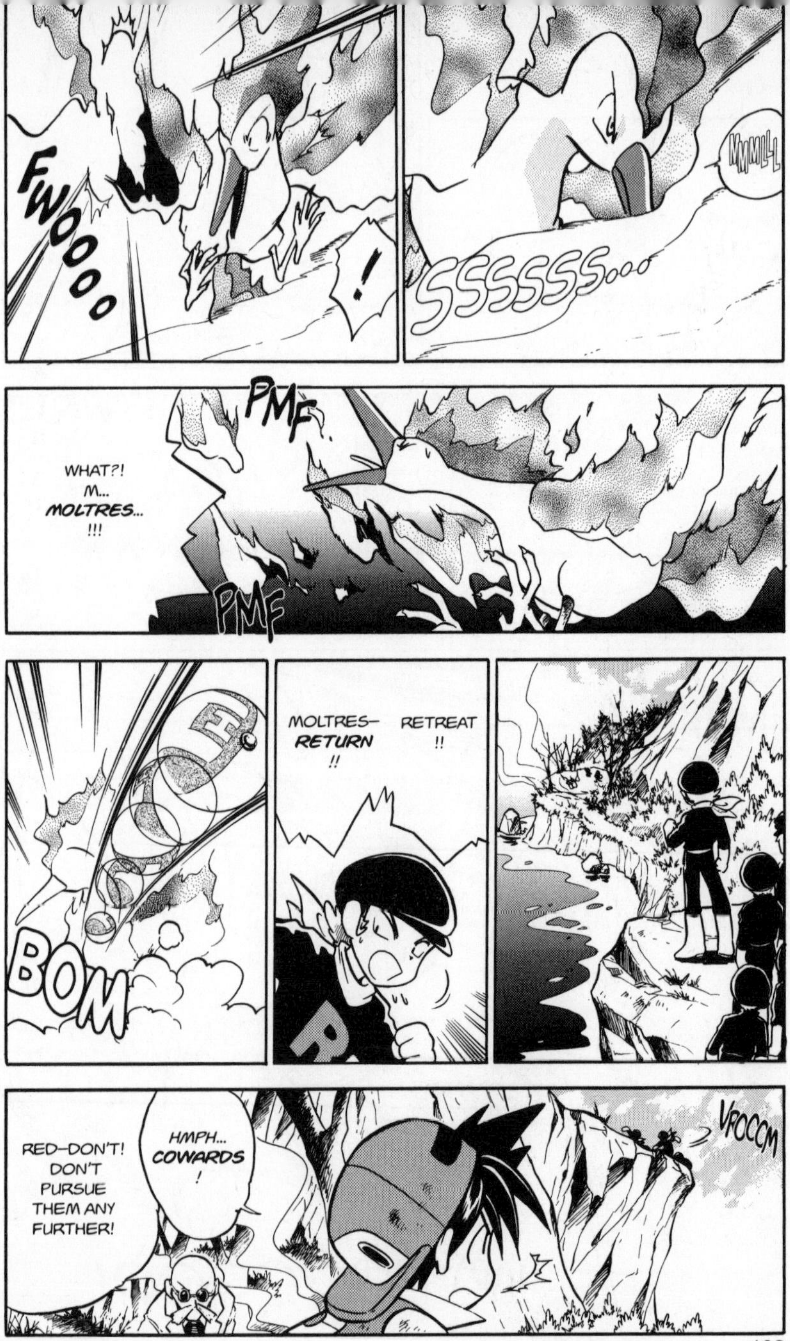
MMMLLL
SSSSSS...
FWOOOOO
!
PMF
WHAT?! M... MOLTRES... !!!
PMF
RETREAT !!
MOLTRES— RETURN !!
BOM
VROCCM
HMPH... COWARDS !
RED—DON'T! DON'T PURSUE THEM ANY FURTHER!

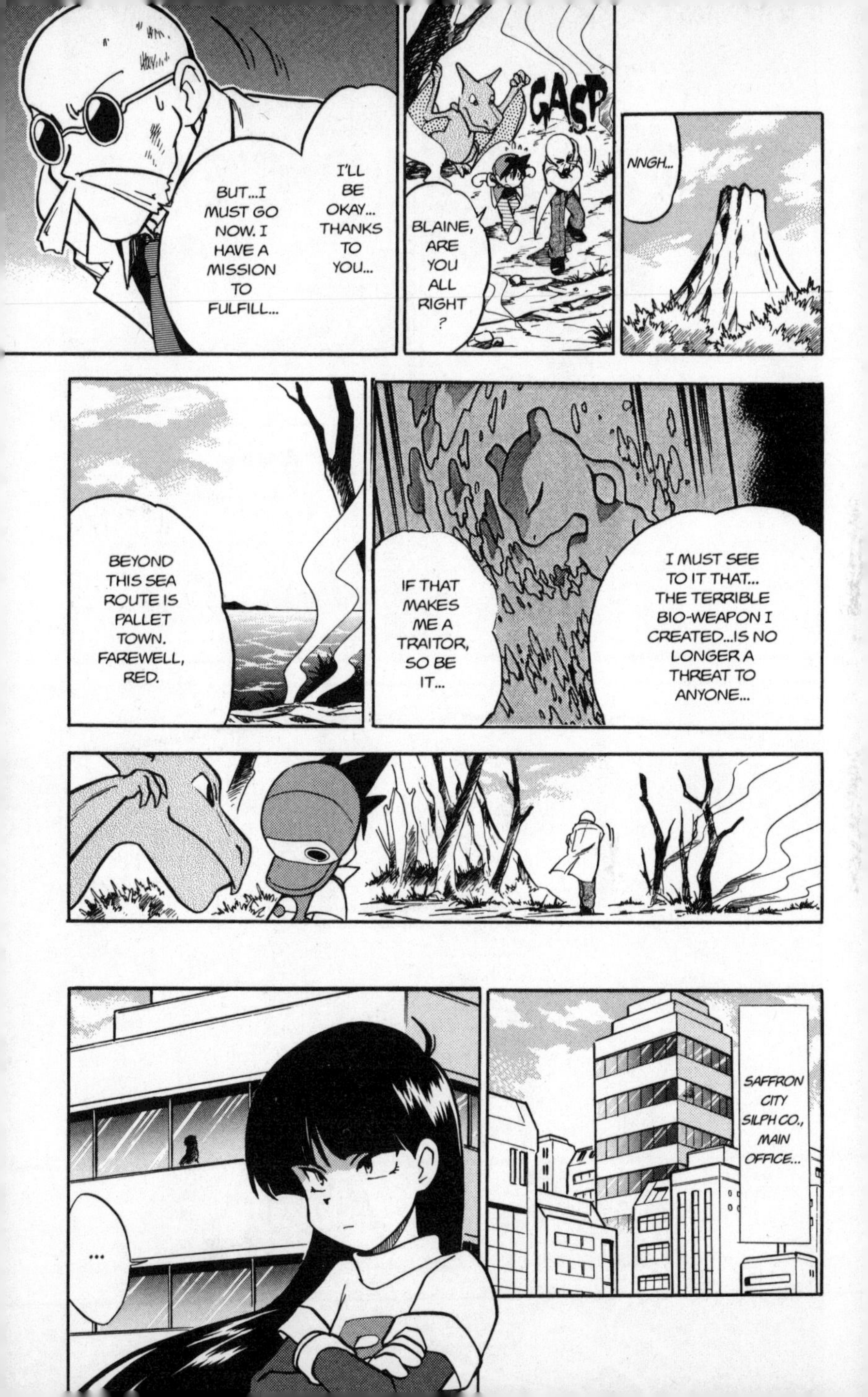
NNGH...
GASP
BLAINE, ARE YOU ALL RIGHT?
I'LL BE OKAY... THANKS TO YOU...
BUT...I MUST GO NOW. I HAVE A MISSION TO FULFILL...
I MUST SEE TO IT THAT... THE TERRIBLE BIO-WEAPON I CREATED...IS NO LONGER A THREAT TO ANYONE...
IF THAT MAKES ME A TRAITOR, SO BE IT...
BEYOND THIS SEA ROUTE IS PALLET TOWN. FAREWELL, RED.
SAFFRON CITY SILPH CO., MAIN OFFICE...
...

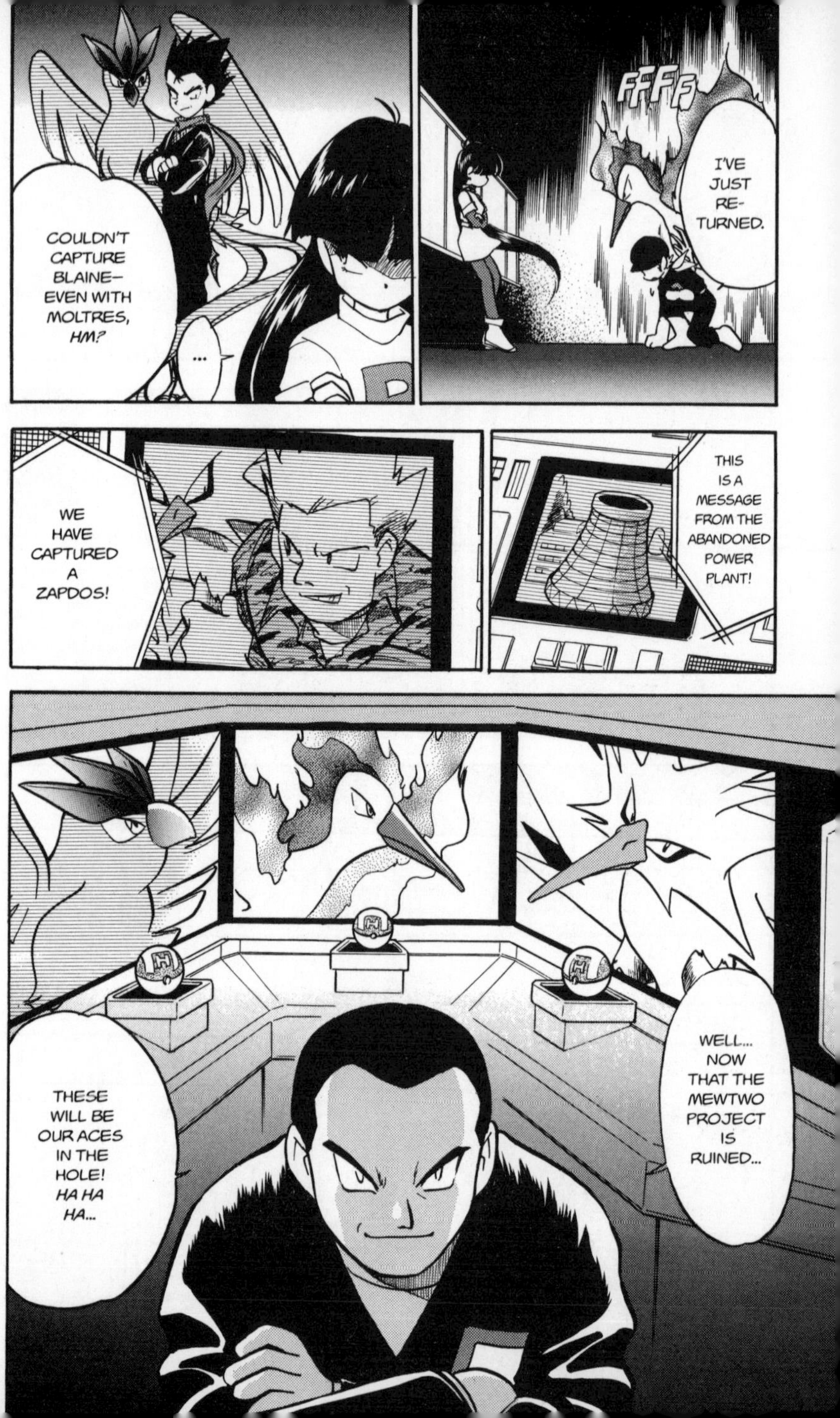
FFFF
I'VE JUST RE-TURNED.
COULDN'T CAPTURE BLAINE—EVEN WITH MOLTRES, HM?
...
THIS IS A MESSAGE FROM THE ABANDONED POWER PLANT!
WE HAVE CAPTURED A ZAPDOS!
WELL... NOW THAT THE MEWTWO PROJECT IS RUINED...
THESE WILL BE OUR ACES IN THE HOLE! HA HA HA...

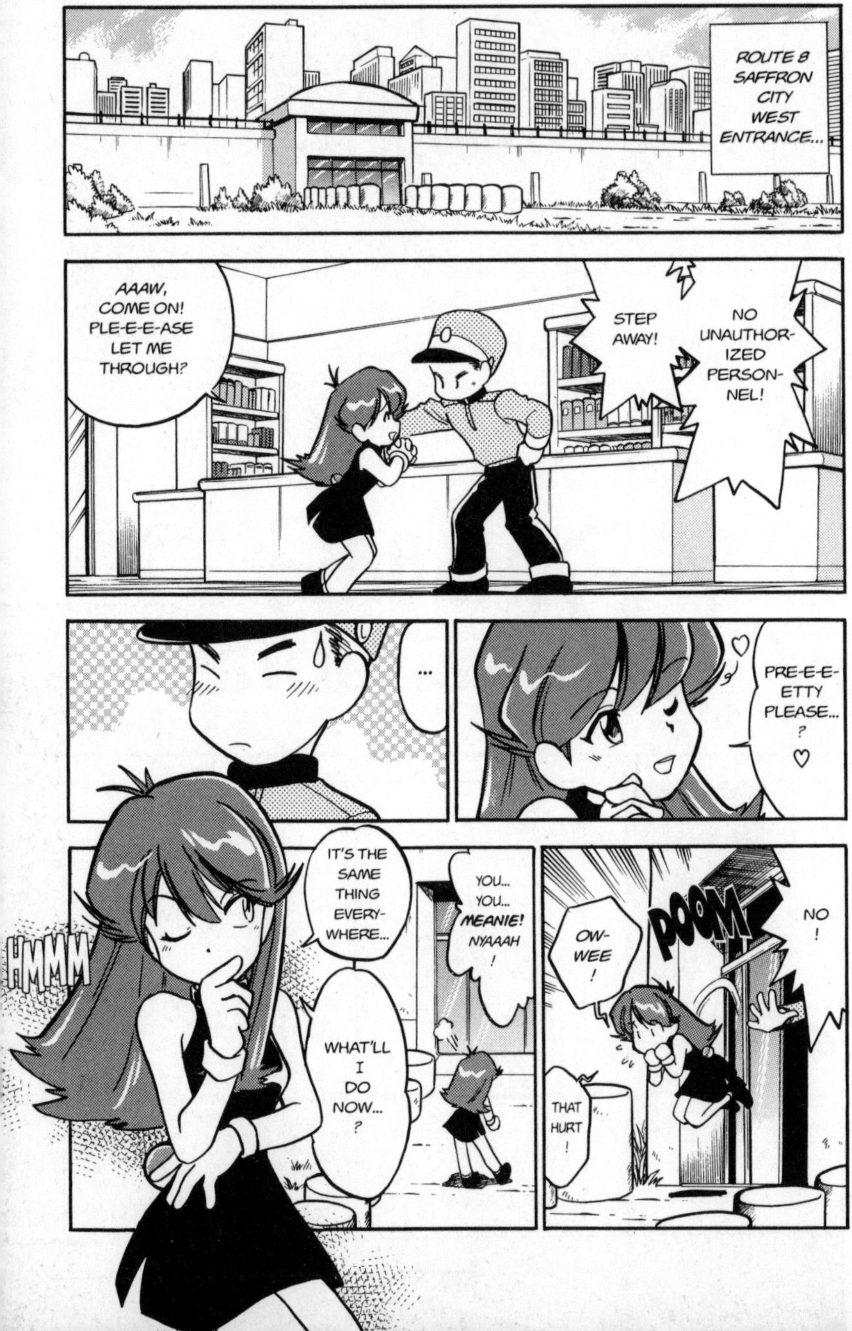
ROUTE 8 SAFFRON CITY WEST ENTRANCE...
NO UNAUTHORIZED PERSONNEL!
STEP AWAY!
AAAW, COME ON! PLE-E-E-ASE LET ME THROUGH?
PRE-E-E-ETTY PLEASE...?
...
NO!
POOM
OW-WEE!
THAT HURT!
YOU... YOU... MEANIE! NYAAAH!
IT'S THE SAME THING EVERYWHERE...
HMMM
WHAT'LL I DO NOW...?

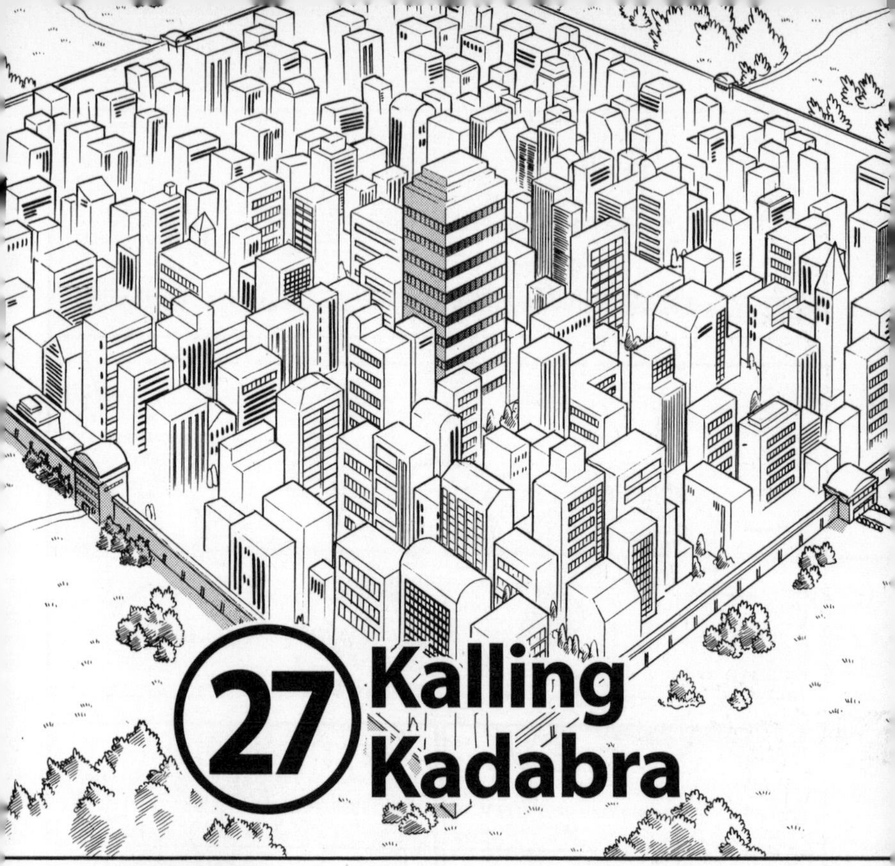
27 Kalling Kadabra

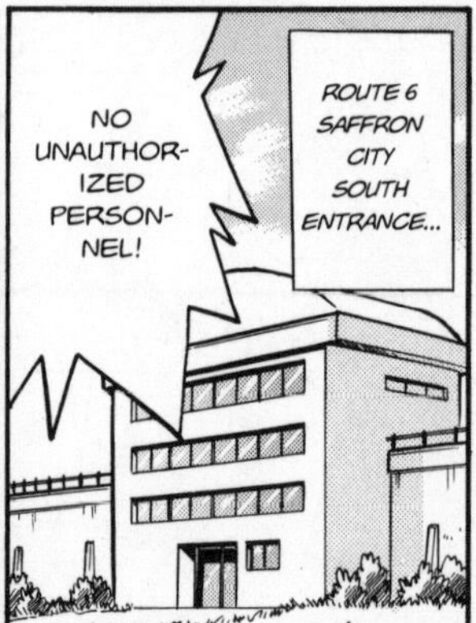
ROUTE 6 SAFFRON CITY SOUTH ENTRANCE...
NO UNAUTHORIZED PERSONNEL!

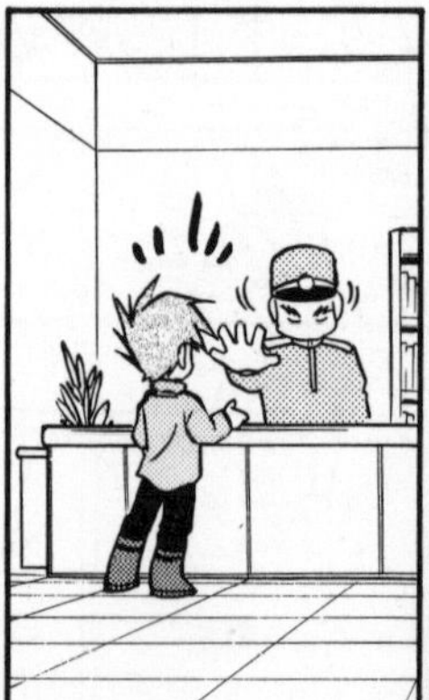

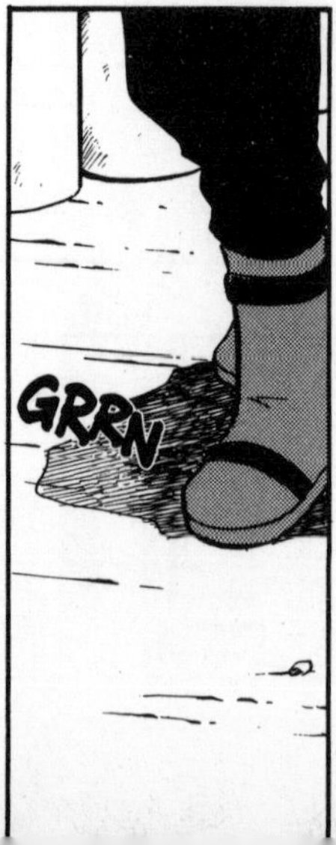
GRRN

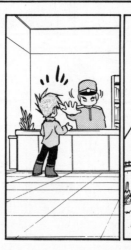

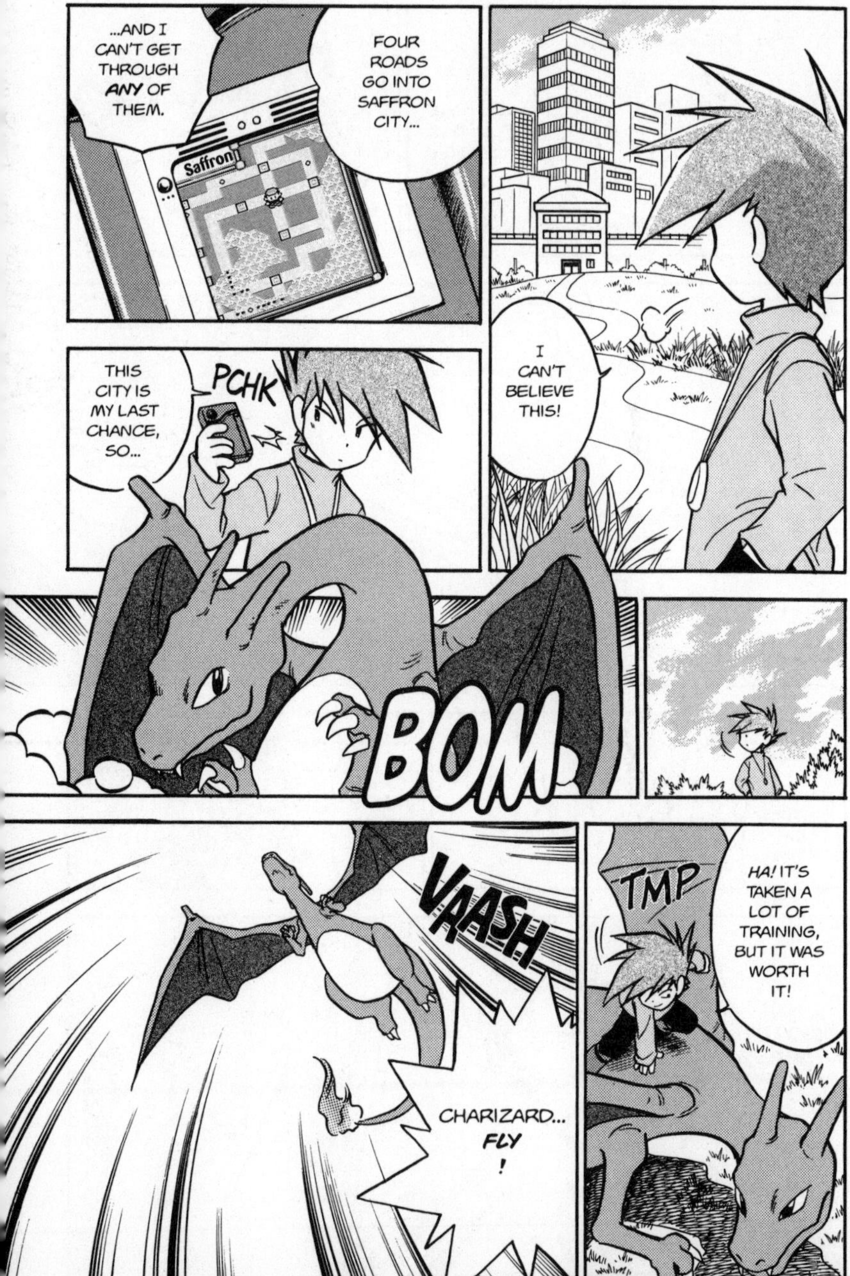
I CAN'T BELIEVE THIS!
FOUR ROADS GO INTO SAFFRON CITY...
Saffron
...AND I CAN'T GET THROUGH **ANY** OF THEM.
PCHK
THIS CITY IS MY LAST CHANCE, SO...
BOM
TMP
HA! IT'S TAKEN A LOT OF TRAINING, BUT IT WAS WORTH IT!
VAASH
CHARIZARD... **FLY** !

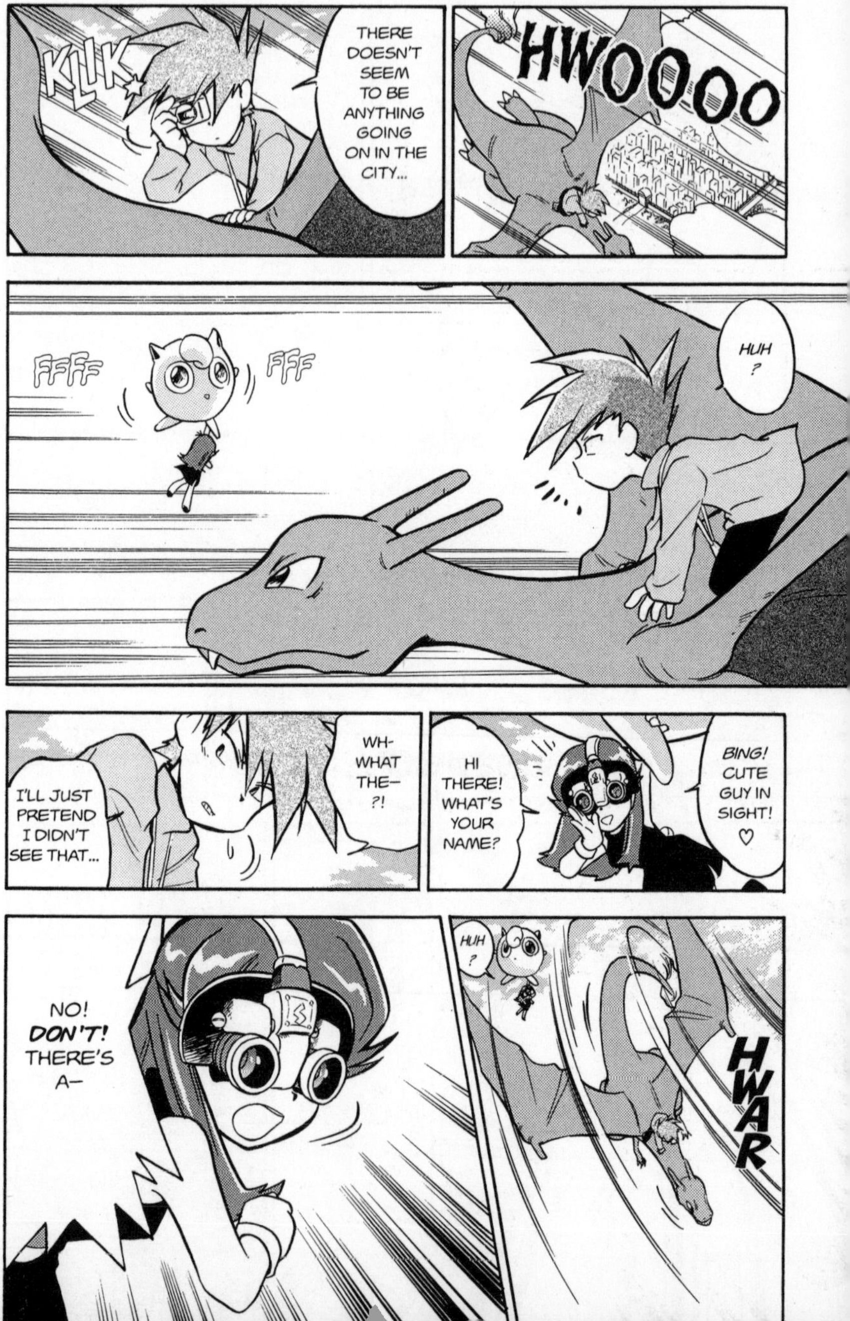
HWOOOO
KLIK
THERE DOESN'T SEEM TO BE ANYTHING GOING ON IN THE CITY...
HUH?
FFF
FFFF
BING! CUTE GUY IN SIGHT! ♡
HI THERE! WHAT'S YOUR NAME?
WH- WHAT THE–?!
I'LL JUST PRETEND I DIDN'T SEE THAT...
HUH?
HWAR
NO! DON'T! THERE'S A–

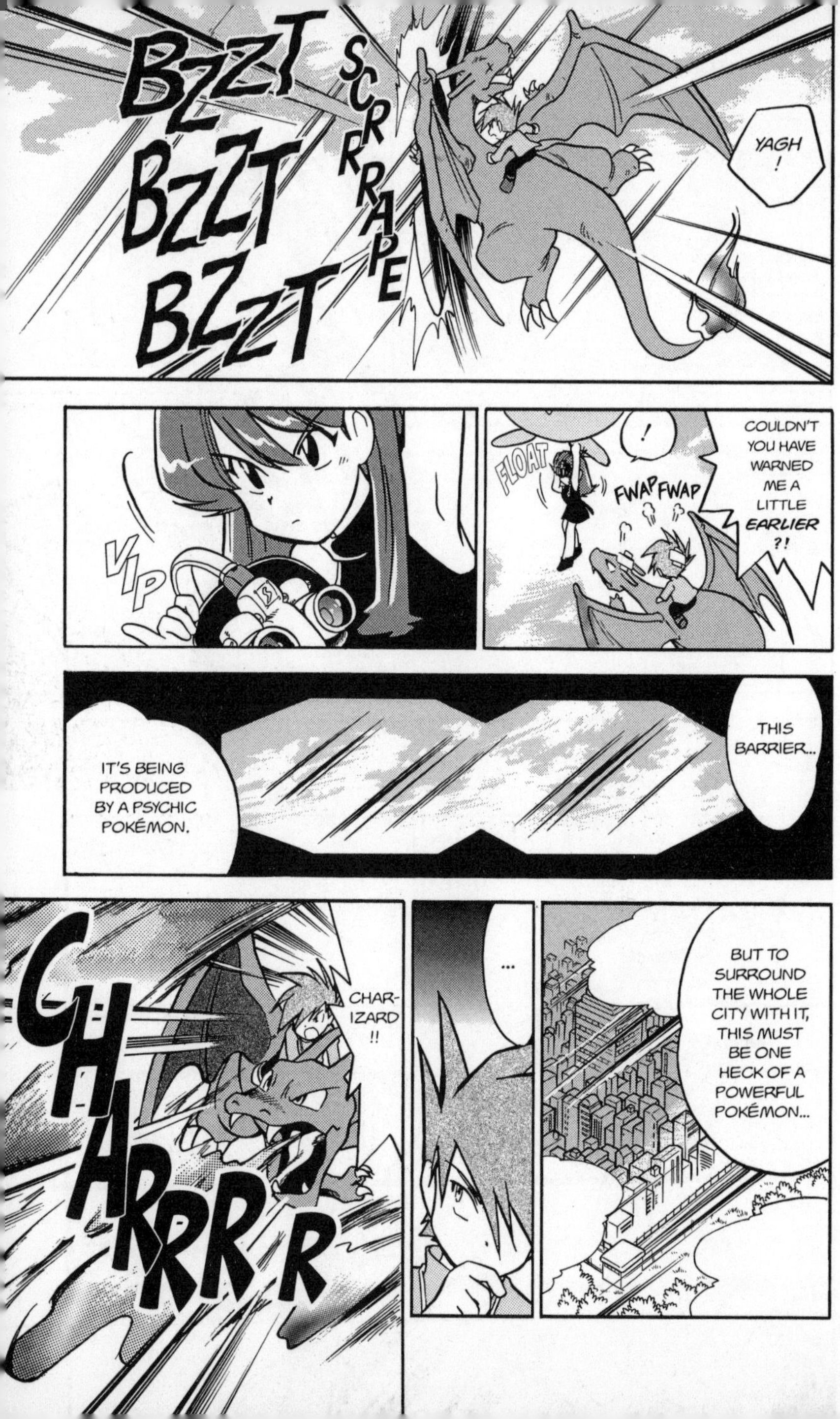
YAGH!
SCRRRAPE
BZZT BZZT BZZT
COULDN'T YOU HAVE WARNED ME A LITTLE EARLIER?!
!
FWAP FWAP
FLOAT
VIP
THIS BARRIER...
IT'S BEING PRODUCED BY A PSYCHIC POKÉMON.
BUT TO SURROUND THE WHOLE CITY WITH IT, THIS MUST BE ONE HECK OF A POWERFUL POKÉMON...
...
CHARIZARD!!
CHARRRRR

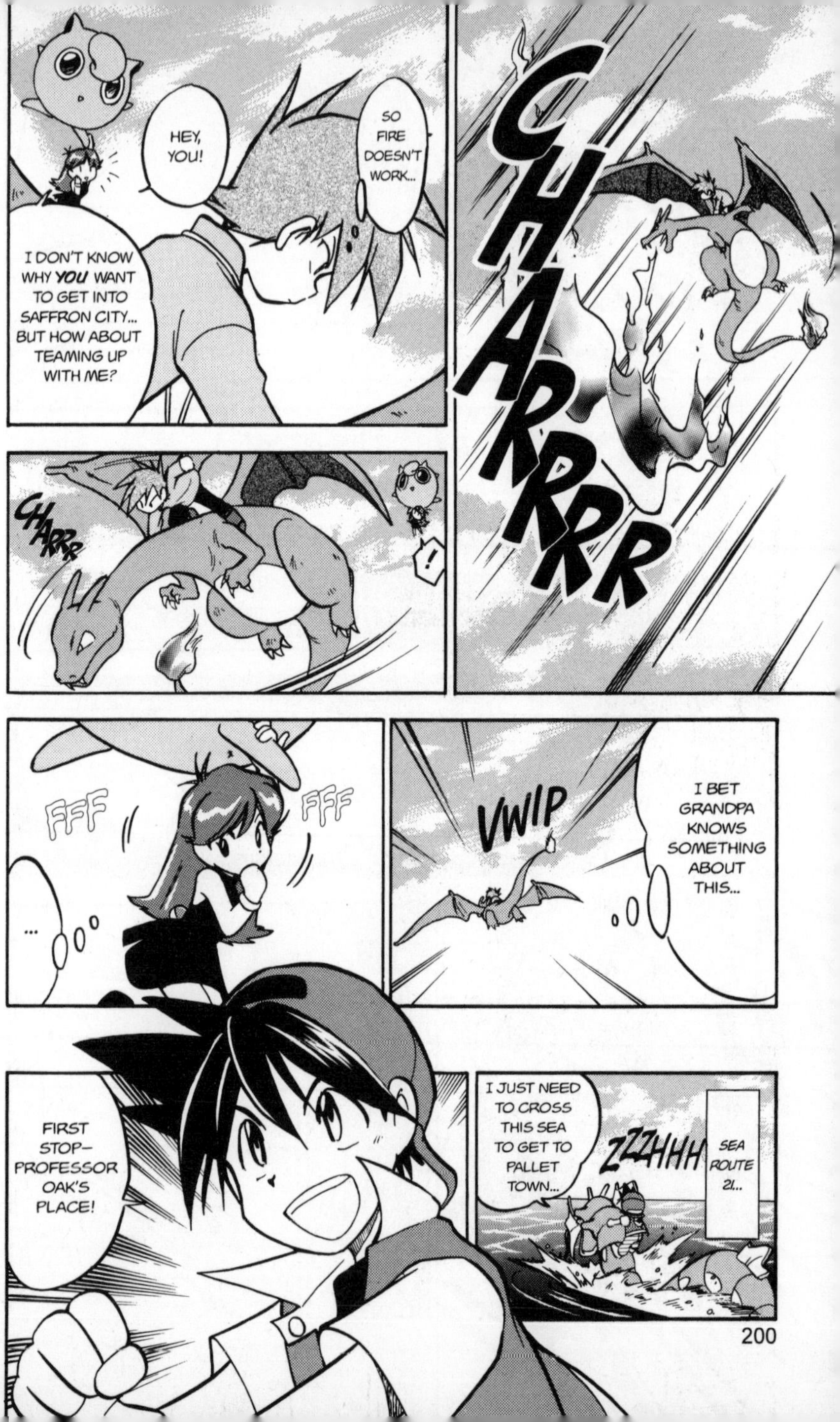

CHARRRRRR
SO FIRE DOESN'T WORK...
HEY, YOU!
I DON'T KNOW WHY **YOU** WANT TO GET INTO SAFFRON CITY... BUT HOW ABOUT TEAMING UP WITH ME?
!
CHARRR
I BET GRANDPA KNOWS SOMETHING ABOUT THIS...
VWIP
FFF
FFF
...
SEA ROUTE 21...
ZZZHHH
I JUST NEED TO CROSS THIS SEA TO GET TO PALLET TOWN...
FIRST STOP—PROFESSOR OAK'S PLACE!

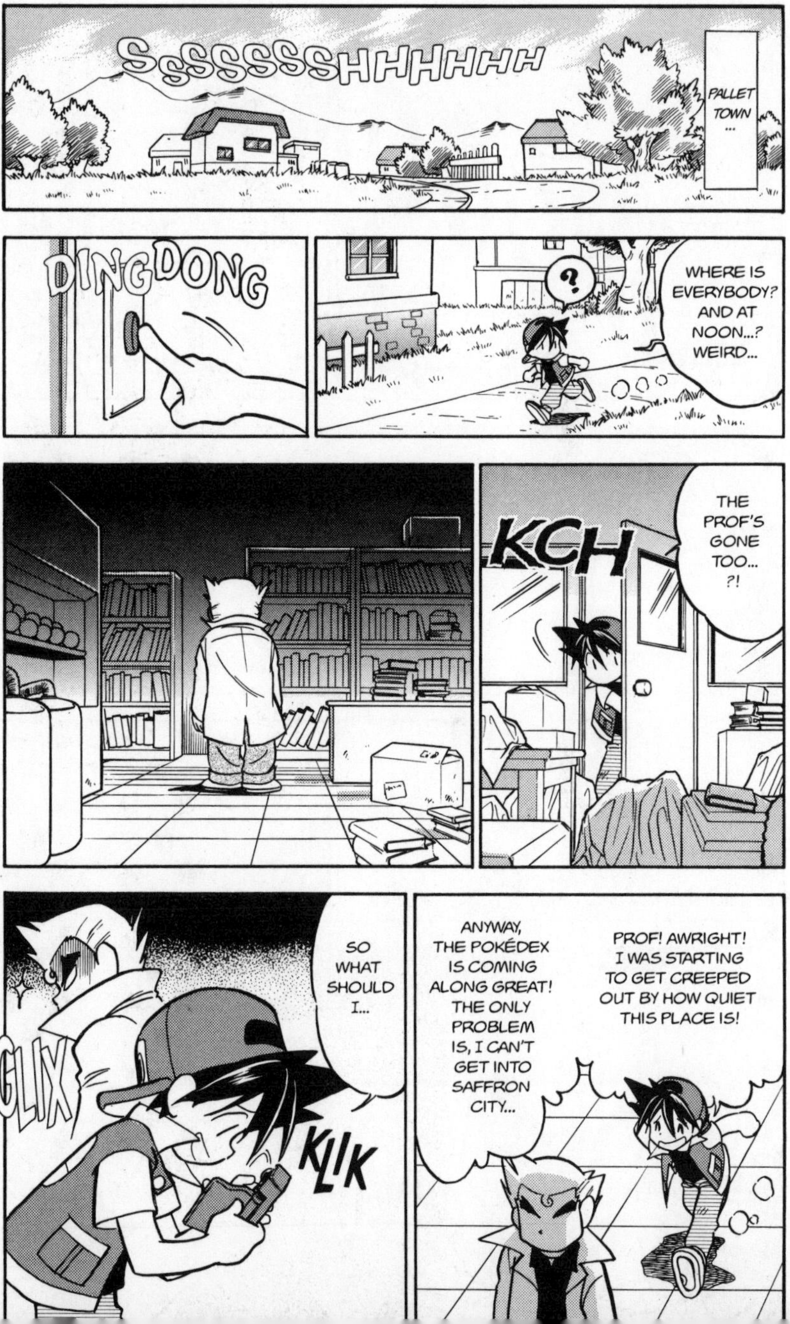
PALLET TOWN ...
SSSSSSSHHHHHH
?
WHERE IS EVERYBODY? AND AT NOON...? WEIRD...
DINGDONG
THE PROF'S GONE TOO... ?!
KCH
PROF! AWRIGHT! I WAS STARTING TO GET CREEPED OUT BY HOW QUIET THIS PLACE IS!
ANYWAY, THE POKÉDEX IS COMING ALONG GREAT! THE ONLY PROBLEM IS, I CAN'T GET INTO SAFFRON CITY...
SO WHAT SHOULD I...
GLIX
KLIK

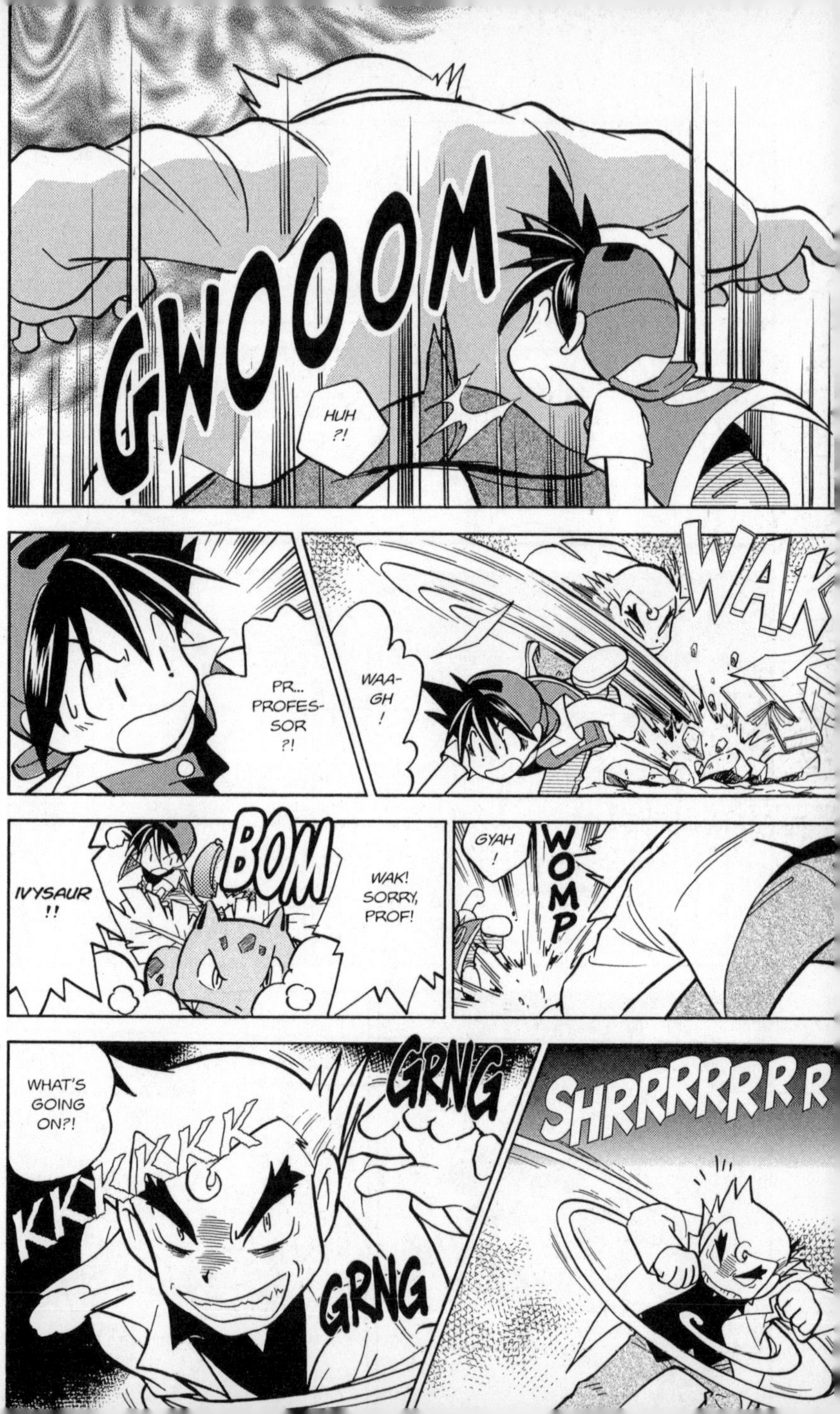
GWOOOM
HUH ?!
WAK
WAAGH !
PR... PROFESSOR ?!
GYAH !
WOMP
BOM
WAK! SORRY, PROF!
IVYSAUR !!
SHRRRRRRR
GRNG
WHAT'S GOING ON?!
KKKKKK
GRNG

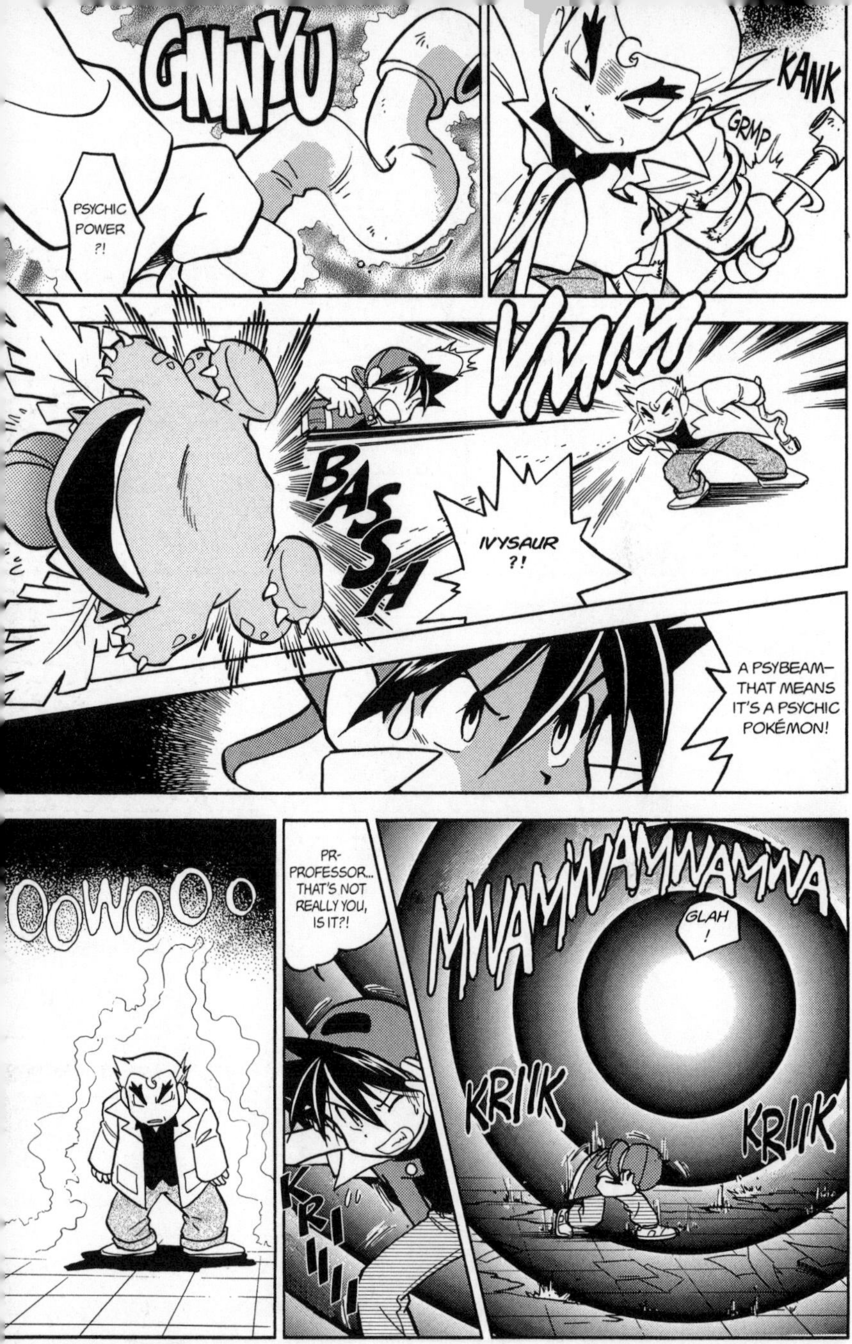
KANK
GRMP
GNNYU
PSYCHIC POWER ?!
VMM
BASSH
IVYSAUR ?!
A PSYBEAM— THAT MEANS IT'S A PSYCHIC POKÉMON!
MWAMWAMWAMWA
GLAH !
PR- PROFESSOR... THAT'S NOT REALLY YOU, IS IT?!
KRIIK
KRIIK
KRIIIII
OOWOOO

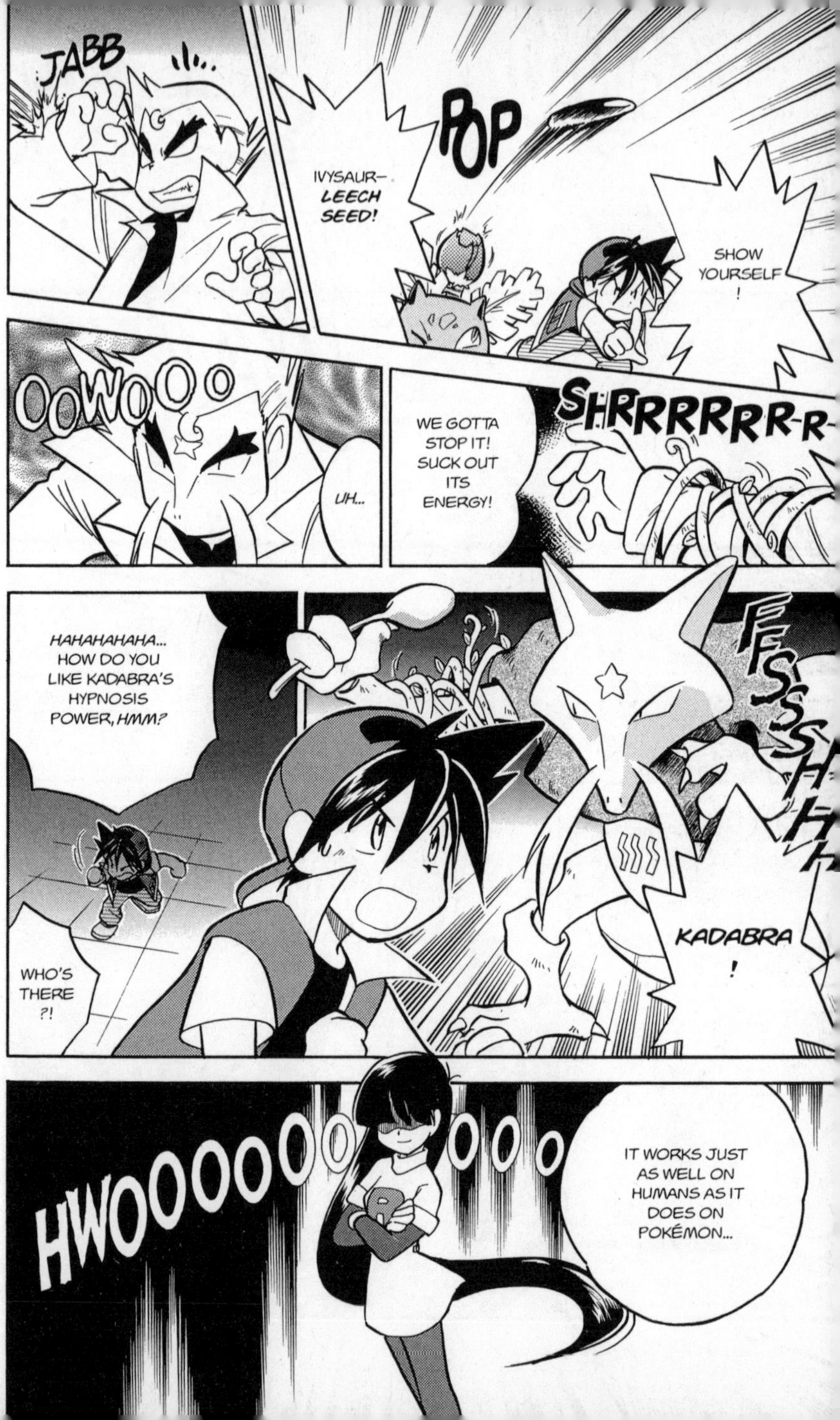
SHOW YOURSELF!
IVYSAUR— LEECH SEED!
POP
JABB
SHRRRRRRR-R-
WE GOTTA STOP IT! SUCK OUT ITS ENERGY!
UH...
OOWOOO
FFSSSHHH
KADABRA!
HAHAHAHAHA... HOW DO YOU LIKE KADABRA'S HYPNOSIS POWER, HMM?
WHO'S THERE?!
IT WORKS JUST AS WELL ON HUMANS AS IT DOES ON POKÉMON...
HWOOOOOOOOOO

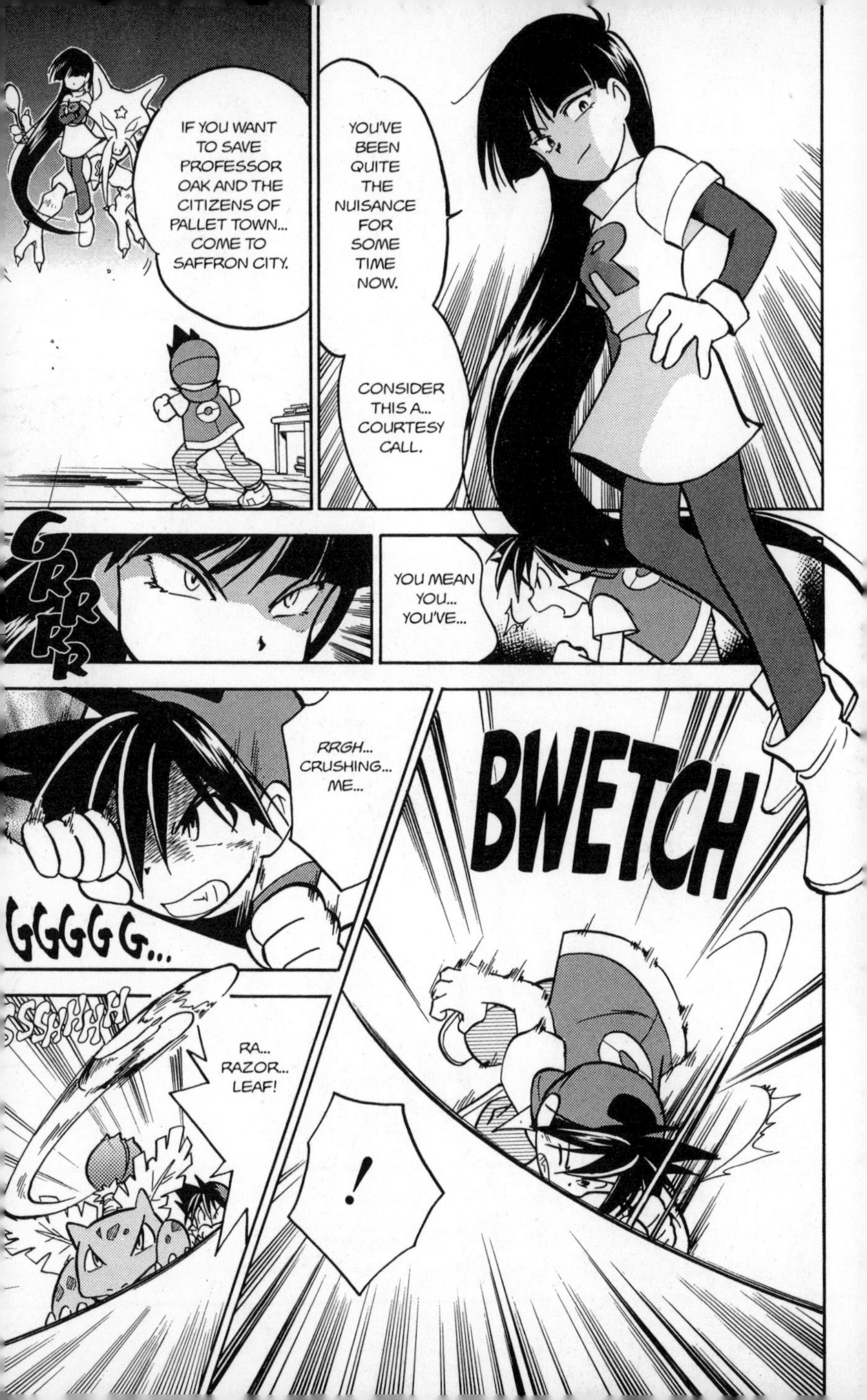
YOU'VE BEEN QUITE THE NUISANCE FOR SOME TIME NOW.
CONSIDER THIS A... COURTESY CALL.
IF YOU WANT TO SAVE PROFESSOR OAK AND THE CITIZENS OF PALLET TOWN... COME TO SAFFRON CITY.
YOU MEAN YOU... YOU'VE...
GRRRR
BWETCH
RRGH... CRUSHING... ME...
GGGGG...
RA... RAZOR... LEAF!
!

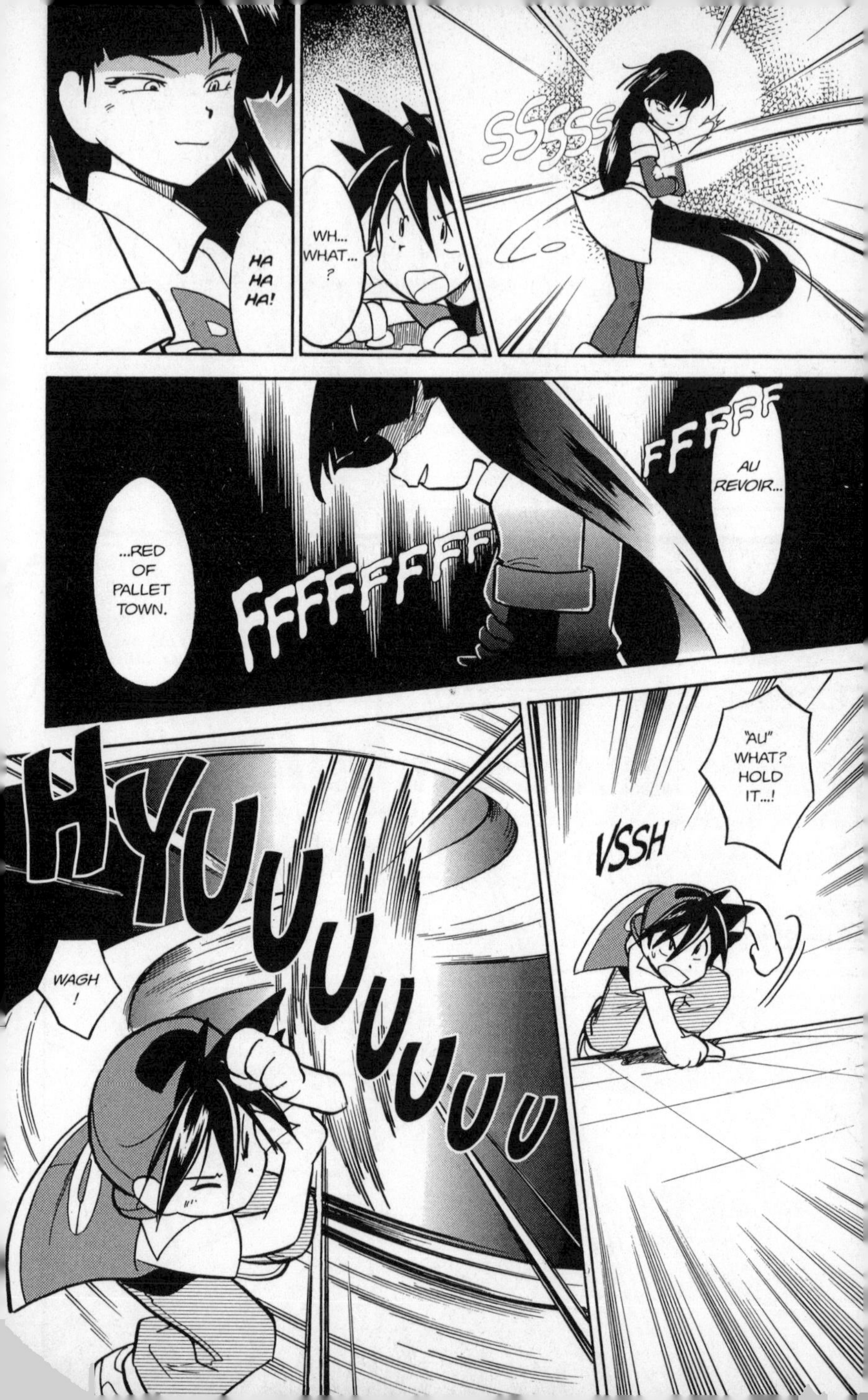
SSSSSS
WH... WHAT... ?
HA HA HA!
FFFFF
AU REVOIR...
FFFFFFF
...RED OF PALLET TOWN.
"AU" WHAT? HOLD IT...!
VSSH
HYUUUUUUUUUU
WAGH!

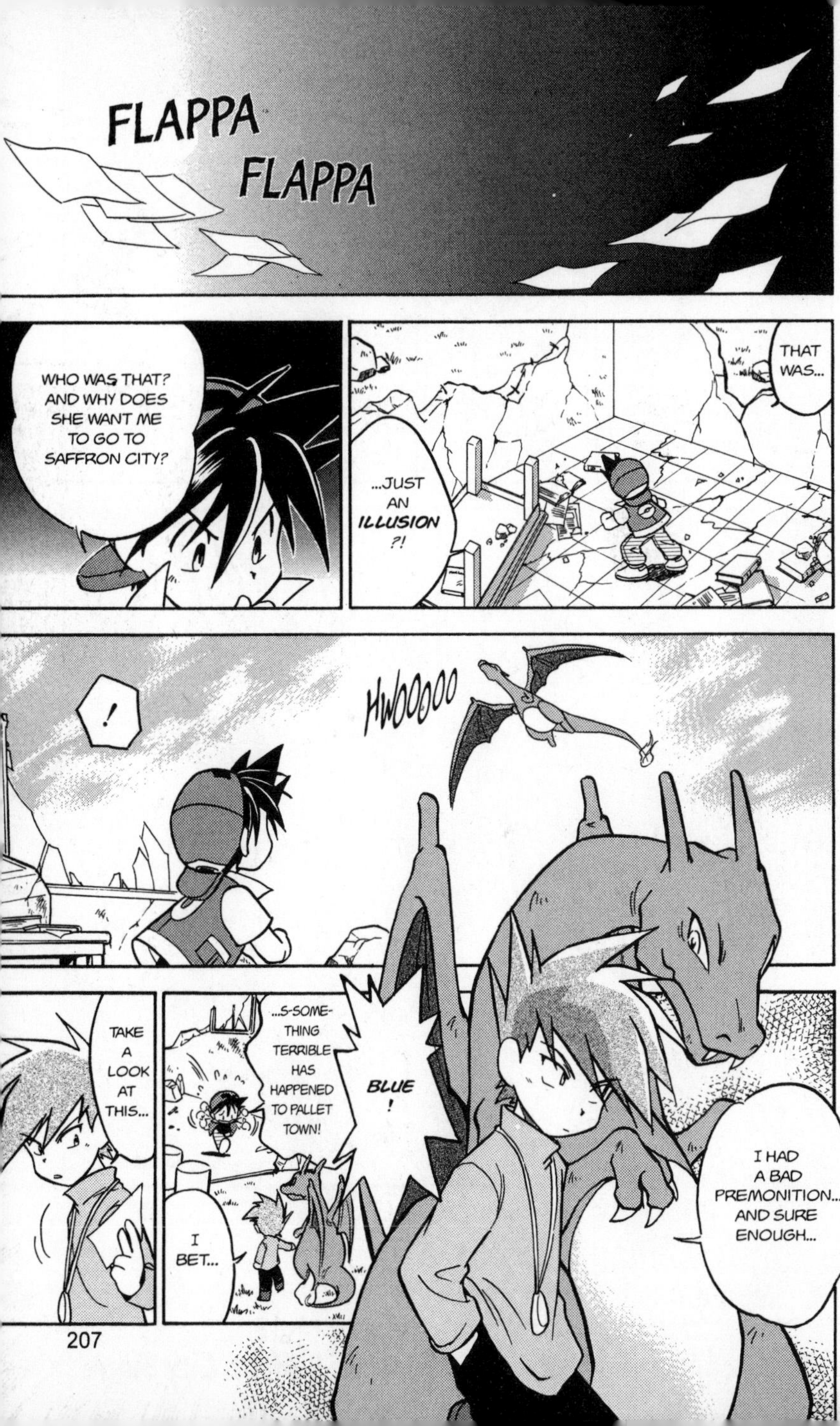
FLAPPA
FLAPPA
THAT WAS...
...JUST AN ILLUSION ?!
WHO WAS THAT? AND WHY DOES SHE WANT ME TO GO TO SAFFRON CITY?
HWOOOOO
!
I HAD A BAD PREMONITION... AND SURE ENOUGH...
BLUE!
...S-SOMETHING TERRIBLE HAS HAPPENED TO PALLET TOWN!
I BET...
TAKE A LOOK AT THIS...

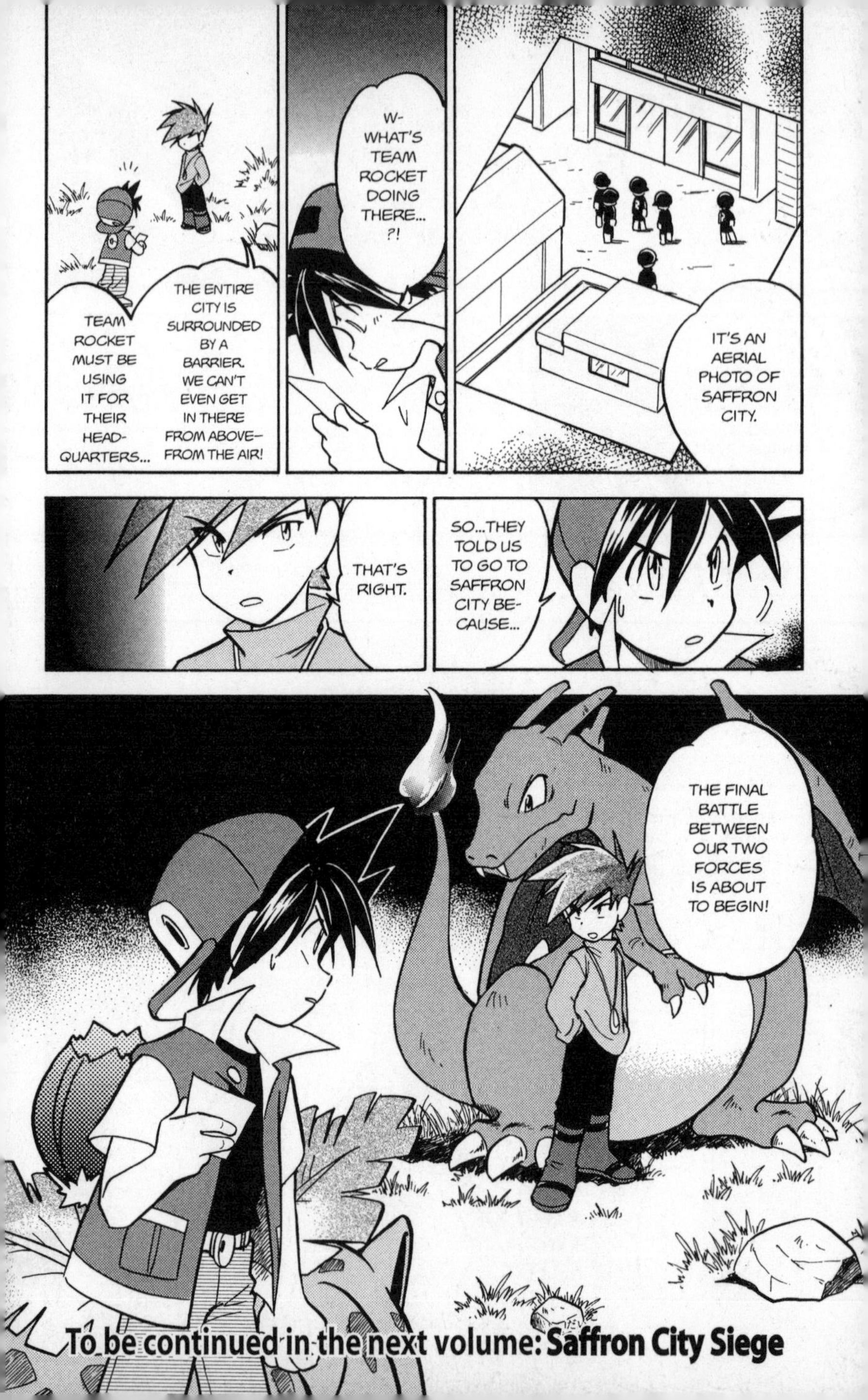
IT'S AN AERIAL PHOTO OF SAFFRON CITY.
W- WHAT'S TEAM ROCKET DOING THERE... ?!
THE ENTIRE CITY IS SURROUNDED BY A BARRIER. WE CAN'T EVEN GET IN THERE FROM ABOVE—FROM THE AIR!
TEAM ROCKET MUST BE USING IT FOR THEIR HEAD-QUARTERS...
SO...THEY TOLD US TO GO TO SAFFRON CITY BE-CAUSE...
THAT'S RIGHT.
THE FINAL BATTLE BETWEEN OUR TWO FORCES IS ABOUT TO BEGIN!
To be continued in the next volume: **Saffron City Siege**

COMING SOON IN VOLUME 3!

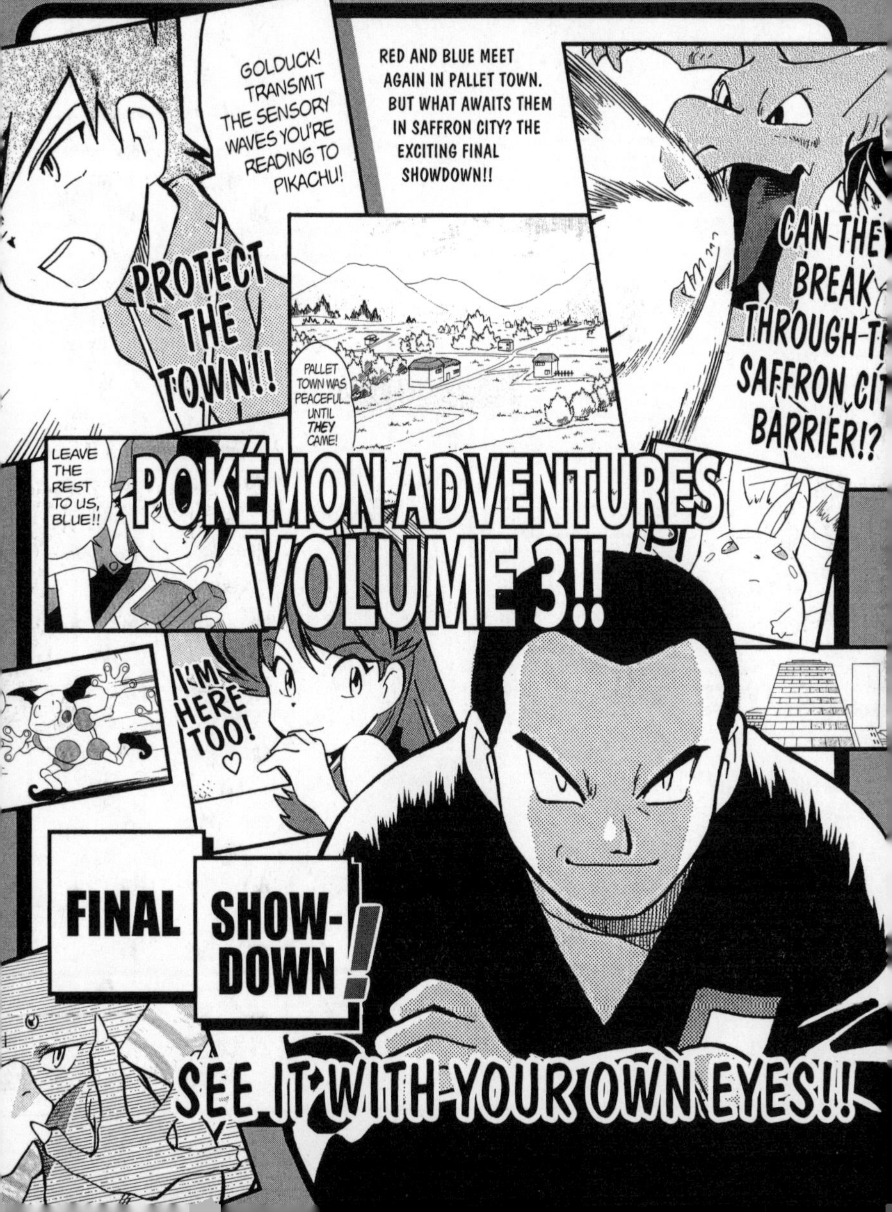

CAN THE BREAK THROUGH T SAFFRON CIT BARRIER!?
RED AND BLUE MEET AGAIN IN PALLET TOWN. BUT WHAT AWAITS THEM IN SAFFRON CITY? THE EXCITING FINAL SHOWDOWN!!
GOLDUCK! TRANSMIT THE SENSORY WAVES YOU'RE READING TO PIKACHU!
PALLET TOWN WAS PEACEFUL... UNTIL *THEY* CAME!
PROTECT THE TOWN!!
POKÉMON ADVENTURES VOLUME 3!!
LEAVE THE REST TO US, BLUE!!
I'M HERE TOO!
FINAL SHOW-DOWN!
SEE IT WITH YOUR OWN EYES!!

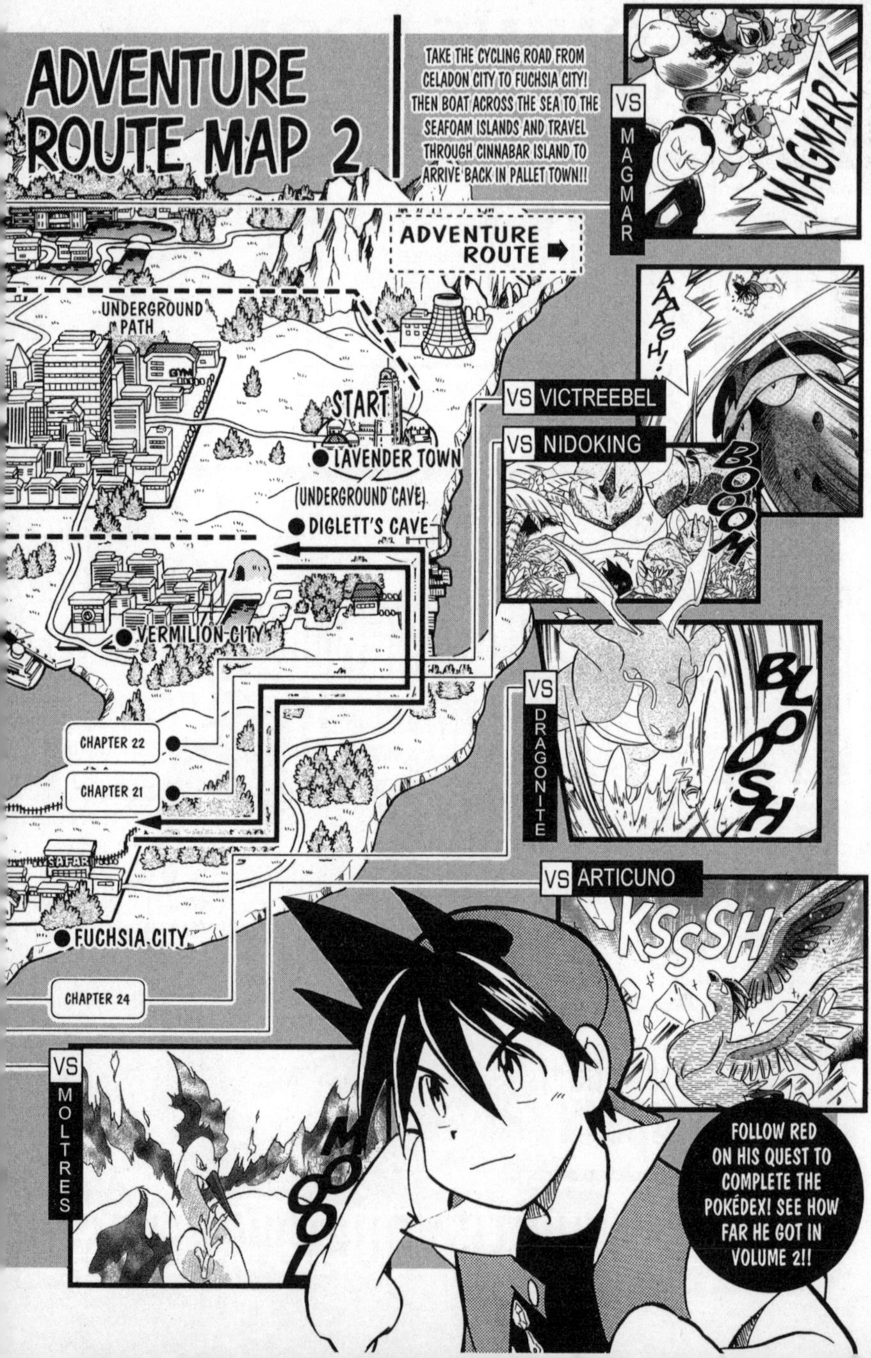
ADVENTURE ROUTE MAP 2
TAKE THE CYCLING ROAD FROM CELADON CITY TO FUCHSIA CITY! THEN BOAT ACROSS THE SEA TO THE SEAFOAM ISLANDS AND TRAVEL THROUGH CINNABAR ISLAND TO ARRIVE BACK IN PALLET TOWN!!
VS MAGMAR
MAGMAR!
ADVENTURE ROUTE
UNDERGROUND PATH
GYM
START
LAVENDER TOWN
(UNDERGROUND CAVE)
DIGLETT'S CAVE
VERMILION CITY
CHAPTER 22
CHAPTER 21
SAFARI
FUCHSIA CITY
CHAPTER 24
VS VICTREEBEL
AAAAGH!!
VS NIDOKING
BOOOOM
VS DRAGONITE
BLOOSH
VS ARTICUNO
KSSSH
VS MOLTRES
MOOOL
FOLLOW RED ON HIS QUEST TO COMPLETE THE POKÉDEX! SEE HOW FAR HE GOT IN VOLUME 2!!

GOTTA CATCH 'EM ALL!! ADVENTURE ROUTE MAP 2

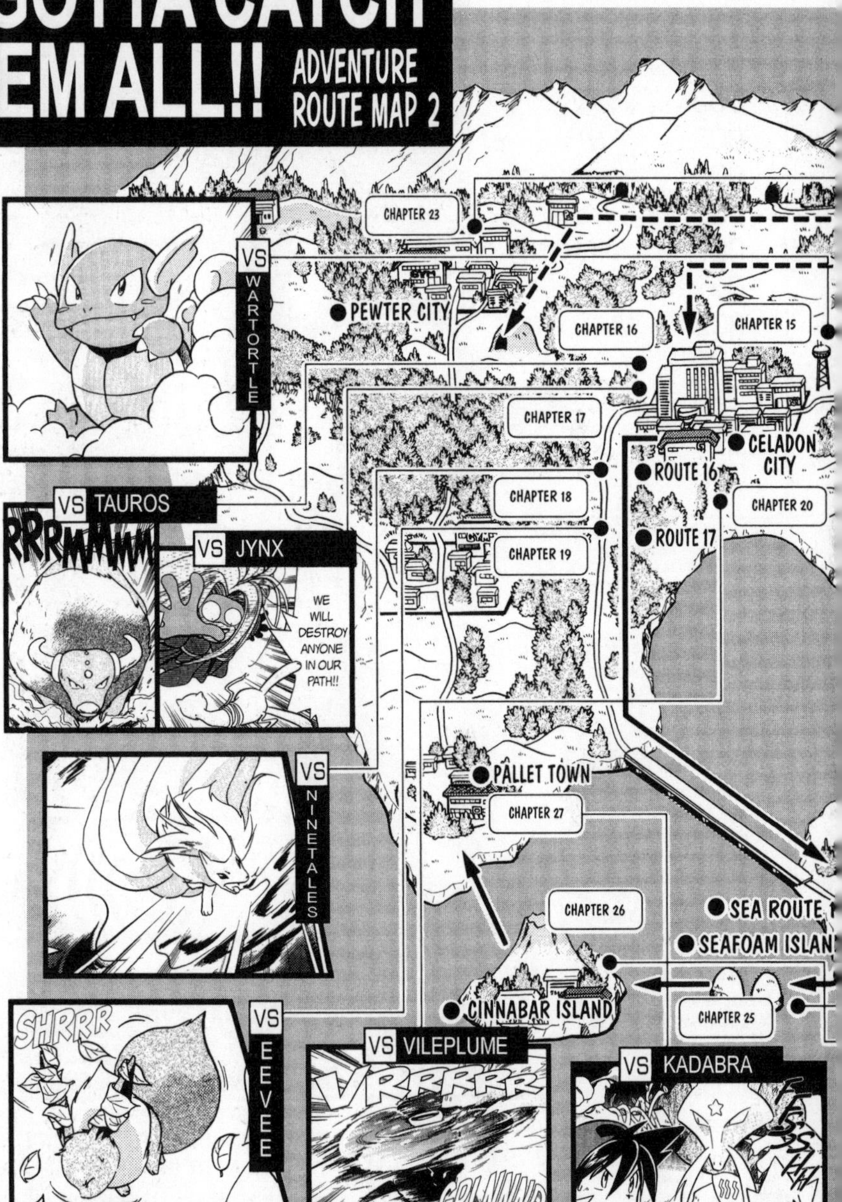

CHAPTER 23
VS WARTORTLE
PEWTER CITY
CHAPTER 16
CHAPTER 15
CHAPTER 17
CELADON CITY
ROUTE 16
CHAPTER 18
CHAPTER 20
ROUTE 17
CHAPTER 19
VS TAUROS
RRRMMMMM
VS JYNX
WE WILL DESTROY ANYONE IN OUR PATH!!
VS NINETALES
PALLET TOWN
CHAPTER 27
CHAPTER 26
SEA ROUTE
SEAFOAM ISLAN
CINNABAR ISLAND
CHAPTER 25
VS EEVEE
SHRRR
WOBBLE
VS VILEPLUME
VRRRRRR
GRLNNND
VS KADABRA
FSSSHH
KADABRA!

RED'S POKÉDEX!

TRAINER: RED
BADGES: 4
POKÉMON: 46

ENCYCLOPEDIA

▶001	◓ BULBASAUR
002	◓ IVYSAUR
003	------------------
004	CHARMANDER
005	◓ CHARMELEON
006	CHARIZARD
007	------------------
008	WARTORTLE
009	------------------
010	
011	
012	

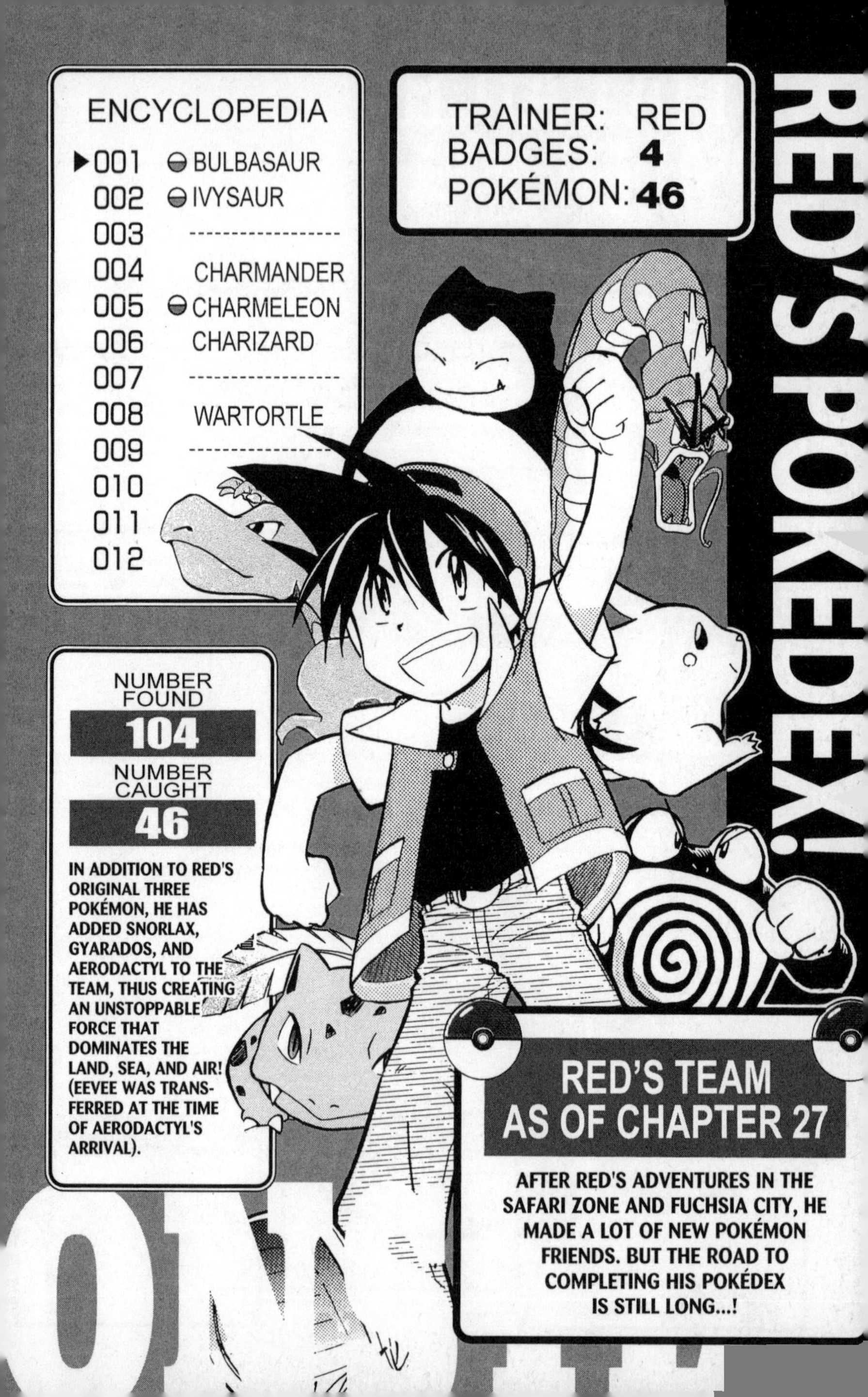

NUMBER FOUND
104

NUMBER CAUGHT
46

IN ADDITION TO RED'S ORIGINAL THREE POKÉMON, HE HAS ADDED SNORLAX, GYARADOS, AND AERODACTYL TO THE TEAM, THUS CREATING AN UNSTOPPABLE FORCE THAT DOMINATES THE LAND, SEA, AND AIR! (EEVEE WAS TRANSFERRED AT THE TIME OF AERODACTYL'S ARRIVAL).

RED'S TEAM AS OF CHAPTER 27

AFTER RED'S ADVENTURES IN THE SAFARI ZONE AND FUCHSIA CITY, HE MADE A LOT OF NEW POKÉMON FRIENDS. BUT THE ROAD TO COMPLETING HIS POKÉDEX IS STILL LONG...!

POCKET

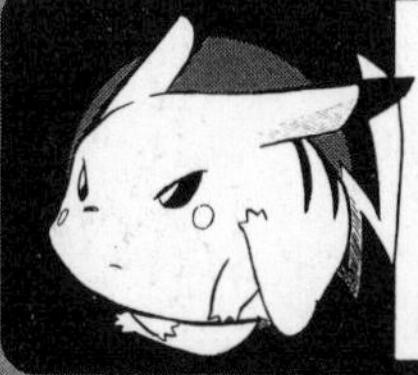

PIKACHU: L21
HP
NO.025

THE DYNAMIC LEADER OF RED'S TEAM HAS POWERFUL ELECTRIC ATTACKS!
NICKNAME: "PIKA."

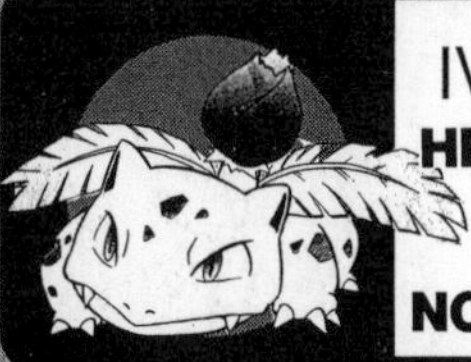

IVYSAUR: L38
HP
NO.002

BULBASAUR EVOLVED INTO IVYSAUR RIGHT BEFORE ARRIVING IN CELADON CITY. WHEN WILL IT TURN INTO ITS FINAL FORM...?!
NICKNAME: "SAUR."

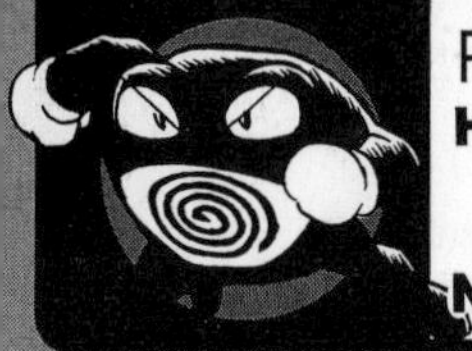

POLIWRATH: L40
HP
NO.062

RED'S OLDEST POKÉMON FRIEND HAS A VERSATILE SKILL SET AND IS VERY DEPENDABLE.
NICKNAME: "POLI."

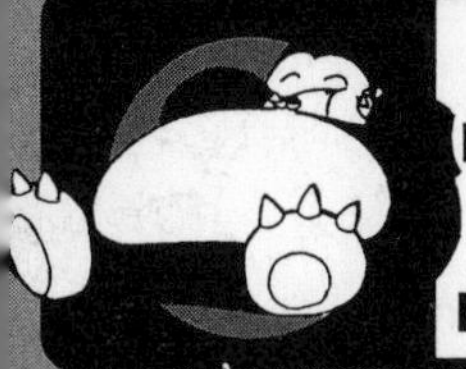

SNORLAX: L31
HP
NO.143

THANKS TO SNORLAX, RED ISN'T INTIMIDATED BY GIGANTIC FOES... BUT THE HUGE FOOD EXPENSES ARE A BIG LIABILITY.
NICKNAME: "LAX."

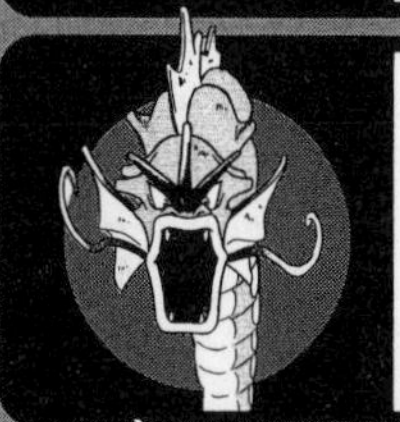

GYARADOS: L29
HP
NO.130

MISTY GAVE RED THIS NEW TEAM MEMBER. CAN TRAVERSE THE SEA WITH "SURF."
NICKNAME: "GYARA."

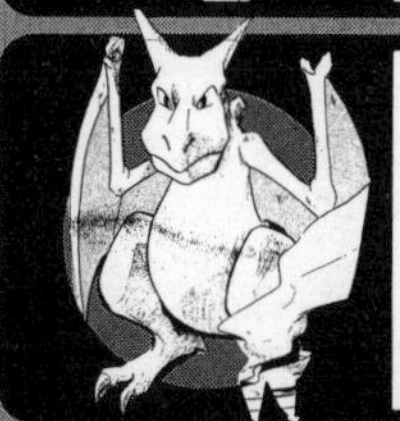

AERODACTYL: L25
HP
NO.142

RESURRECTED FROM PRE-HISTORIC AMBER ON CINNABAR ISLAND. NOW AERODACTYL IS A MASTER OF THE AIRWAYS!
NICKNAME: "AERO."

Message from
MATO

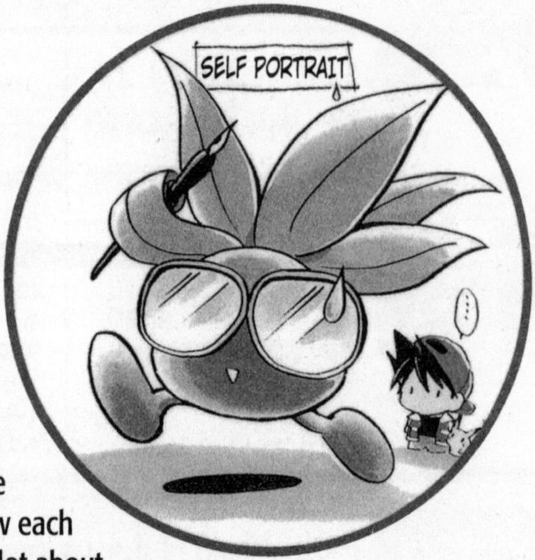
SELF PORTRAIT

Pokémon don't move in the video games, but in my manga, they run around all over the place. What's the most interesting way to show each Pokémon in action? I care a lot about that. I would be very happy if after reading this manga people who have never even heard of Pokémon before become fans and if Pokémon fans grow to love Pokémon even more than before!

About the Author...

MATO was born in Aichi Prefecture on November 27. Her astrological sign is Sagittarius. Her first manga story, "New Year X-mas," appeared in 1993 in the magazine *Shonen Sunday*. Her best-known works include the title *Nightingale*.

More Adventures Coming Soon...

Red is improving rapidly as a Pokémon trainer—and so is his competition. But now Red must team up with his biggest rival Blue and thief Green to defeat a common enemy!

And watch out for Team Rocket, Red... They won't let you into Saffron City!

AVAILABLE NOW!

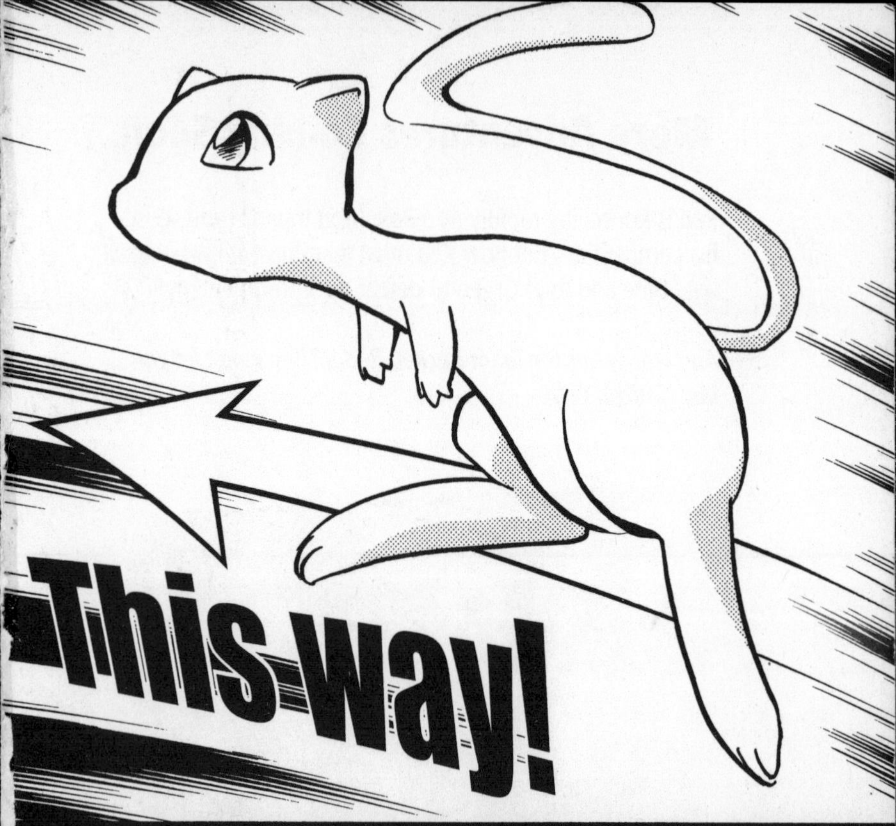
This way!

THIS IS THE END OF THIS GRAPHIC NOVEL!

To properly enjoy this VIZ Media graphic novel, please turn it around and begin reading from right to left.

This book has been printed in the original Japanese format in order to preserve the orientation of the original artwork. Have fun with it!

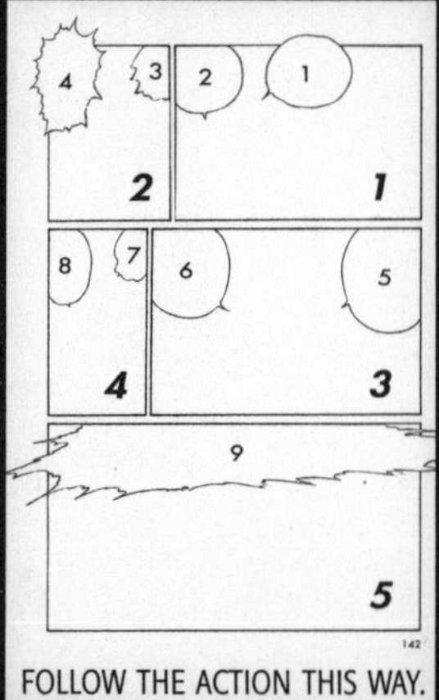

FOLLOW THE ACTION THIS WAY.